LOVE OR HATE

LOVE OR HATE

RITA POTTER

SAPPHIRE BOOKS

SALINAS, CALIFORNIA

Editor - Tara Young
Book Design - LJ Reynolds
Cover Design - Fineline Cover Design

Sapphire Books Publishing, LLC
P.O. Box 8142
Salinas, CA 93912
www.sapphirebooks.com

Printed in the United States of America
First Edition – July 2023

you for respecting the hard work of this author.

This and other Sapphire Books titles can be found at

Rita's other books

As We Know it Series
Upheaval
Survival
Betrayal

Stand Alone
Broken Not Shattered
Thundering Pines
Whitewater Awakening
Out of The Ashes

Dedication

For Terra: Our love story remains my favorite.

Acknowledgment

I'd like to thank Sapphire Books and Chris, who gives me the freedom to write the books I want. It meant more than you may know when I got the email that said you "LOVE, LOVE, LOVE" this book.

I want to thank my editor, Tara, who with each book teaches me something new. A special thanks for encouraging me to be brave and bold. It was the encouragement I needed.

There are so many friends and supporters I've made in the Sapphic writing community, I can never name you all, so I won't try. A special shoutout to my partner in crime Lori. Opposites truly do attract in this case.

As always, thanks to my work family. We've been together forever, and I couldn't imagine being on this journey without you.

Thanks to my mentor Jae. Your talent and graciousness will always be the standard I strive for.

Much gratitude to my beta readers Nan, Michele, and Cade. No other manuscript have I needed you more. Your comments and insights stretched me further than I wanted at times, but I am grateful for your willingness to always tell me the truth.

To Terra and Chumley, my little family. I love you both, even when you walk on my keyboard. Oh, that part only applies to Chumley. I can honestly say Terra has never done that.

And thank you to my readers, who allow me to write across genres and continue to read. You are why I continue to do what I do.

Chapter One

*O*ne thirty?
That couldn't be possible.

Rain Hargrove stared at the glowing green light of the alarm clock. She blinked several times, thinking her eyes must be playing tricks on her.

It had been ten when she'd tumbled into bed with Sasha, again. It hadn't taken more than fifteen minutes for both to get what they needed. She twisted her pelvis and squeezed her legs together. *Yep.* Still numb and satiated, so it hadn't been a dream.

Maybe the clock was wrong. She slid farther away from Sasha and edged toward the side of the bed. Her eyes had begun to adjust, so she was able to find her cellphone by the glow from the clock. Surely, she'd find that the time was off.

She snatched her phone, pressed her finger against the sensor, and plunged it under the covers. The last thing she wanted was for the light to awaken Sasha. Notifications blew up her screen. Had she gone viral? Fifteen missed texts. Twenty-seven emails. Forty-five Twitter alerts. *Wow.* Six hundred eighty TikTok notifications. Her video about gender identification had gotten traction.

Her gaze shifted from the notifications to the time. *Damn it!* One thirty-three. She'd been asleep for over three hours. Although she knew the week had exhausted her, she didn't realize she'd been this tired.

Now things could get awkward. She'd vowed never to spend the night with Sasha. It could send the wrong message. Rain glanced over at the sleeping woman. Her long red hair cascaded over her pillow. In this lighting, it looked almost crimson and could be mistaken for blood flowing against the white pillowcase. *Wow.* She needed to stop watching so many thrillers.

Rain couldn't make out Sasha's freckles, but she knew they were there. No doubt, Sasha was beautiful and damned good in bed, but they'd vowed to keep it casual until the right woman came along for both. Lately, Sasha had been more demanding of Rain's time, so being here now was not a good idea.

As if sensing Rain's gaze, Sasha muttered in her sleep and threw off the sheet covering her torso. Her perfect breasts were as tan as the rest of her body. Sasha wouldn't be caught dead with tan lines. Good thing Sasha's parents owned a secluded beach house in Florida, which allowed her to maintain a bronze glow year-round.

Rain contemplated checking her messages before she made her escape but thought better of it. The longer she stayed, the greater the odds that Sasha would wake up, and knowing Sasha's insatiable appetite, it would be hard to get away.

When Rain pushed the covers off, goose bumps covered her body. *Damn.* Late April in Illinois still made for chilly nights. She glanced at Sasha, her chest rhythmically rose and fell, unaffected by the cold.

Rain squinted, hoping it would help her find her clothes that Sasha had strewn across the floor a few hours ago. Of course, she had to wear black underwear, which made it harder to find in the dim glow of the clock. She made a mental note to wear tighty whities on the next encounter. *Ugh.* She needed to stop thinking about the next time. No wonder Sasha seemed to be getting more possessive. They were doing this far too often. Her libido needed to come down a notch or two or three.

She'd once heard the best way to curb sexual tension before a date was to masturbate. Maybe she should try it next time. Not that they dated. It was more meet up for a beer and then end up in bed. If she relieved herself before having a beer, would she even want to meet up with Sasha?

Rain shook her head. Now was the *wrong* time to be thinking about it. She needed to find her clothes and get the hell out of here. She located her blue jeans and T-shirt easily and lucked out when she stepped on her underwear. Thankfully, she'd decided against wearing a bra today. One less piece of clothing to find. Her socks proved to be a little more elusive. She'd found her first sock without difficulty, but she feared the other had rolled under the bed.

Rain sighed and dropped to her knees. It wouldn't be the end of the world if she didn't wear socks home, but the thought of a lone sock without its counterpart made her cringe. Stupid, she knew, but it would gnaw at her brain. Maybe if she left both it would be okay, but what message would that send to Sasha?

She pushed her face against the carpet and reached under the bed. She swept her hand first one way and then the other, hoping to contact something cloth. Instead, her arm ran through a spiderweb. *Gross.* The heebie-jeebies coursed through her body, and she yanked her hand back.

"Is that ass an offering to the moon gods or me?"

Rain flinched and banged her head against the bed rail. "Shit, you scared me." She rubbed the top of her head and searched for a lump.

"Come back to bed, and I'll kiss it and make it all better." Sasha chuckled. "I wouldn't mind kissing that creamy white ass, either."

Rain's face warmed. Her ass cheeks, in all their glory, rose toward the ceiling. With a twist, she flipped onto her backside and plopped onto the carpet. She crossed her legs as if it would somehow cover her buttocks, only to realize her mistake as she glanced down at her exposed crotch.

Sasha turned on the bedside lamp. "Oh, I like that even better." She licked her lips. "I love that you don't wax or shave."

Without thinking, Rain grabbed her T-shirt and covered her pubic hairs. She struggled with a comeback.

"*Au naturel*," Sasha said. "The bushier the better."

"Stop!" Rain practically shouted. She knew Sasha was teasing her, but she had never been comfortable talking about her own body. "I was just looking for my sock."

Sasha stuck out her bottom lip. "Where are you going at one thirty in the morning?"

"Home." Rain probably should have said more, or at least not said it so harshly, but the conversation about her ass and her privates made her uncomfortable. *Really? Privates?* Was she a grade schooler?

Sasha patted the empty side of the bed. "Come on. I promise I won't bite." A mischievous grin played on her lips. "Unless you want me to."

Rain felt a stirring under the T-shirt she held in her lap but pushed it aside. She wanted to get out of here. Fast. This needed to be the last time she slept with Sasha. It was going nowhere. Other than great sex, she wasn't even sure she particularly liked Sasha. "No. I need to go, and we..." Rain stood and quickly slid her underwear on before she pulled her jeans up to her hips. Feeling less exposed, she could think straight again. Her bare chest didn't make her feel self-conscious since her A-cup boobs didn't exactly draw attention.

"And we what?" Sasha's voice hardened, and her face matched the color of her hair.

Shit. She'd obviously figured out where Rain planned to go with this conversation. "We can't—"

"No." Sasha pointed at her. "You aren't going to tell me we can't do this anymore. It's the middle of the fucking night. And I wake up to your ass in the air. This is not how you're going to end it."

Rain sighed as she pulled on her T-shirt. "We're not dating, so what is it that I'm going to end?" As soon as she saw the fury cross Sasha's face, she knew she'd said the wrong thing, again.

"No, we're not dating. You're just fucking my brains out whenever you get the chance."

Rain cringed at Sasha's crass words. Was that what they were doing? It certainly wasn't making love. She'd not promised Sasha anything, so why was she feeling guilty? "Do you have to say it like that?"

"Oh, how would you like me to say it?" A cruel glint flashed in Sasha's eyes.

Rain stared down at the socks in her hand. She wanted to put them on and run, but she knew better than to sit on the bed. It would put her way too close to the angry Sasha. "What do you want from me?" Rain motioned her hand between the two of them. "This is what you agreed to."

"What if I changed my mind, and I want more?" Sasha flashed her perfect white teeth at Rain. "Or what if I just want another go at you tonight?"

Rain's pulse quickened. That smile always made her body tingle. *No.* She couldn't do this again tonight. "I have to be to work on time tomorrow." The words even sounded lame to Rain, so she continued. "My parents are overseas, so the foundation is completely in my hands."

Sasha tilted her head, but the angry look had subsided. "Europe? What's their cause this time?"

"Climate change." Rain hoped they were moving toward safer ground.

"I see." Sasha nodded. "So A Bridge to the Future can't function without you?"

Rain scowled. "It probably could, but you know how important the causes are to me. I can't leave it in just anyone's hands." When Sasha continued to stare, Rain said, "You know how my parents are." What a loaded statement that was. Sasha's father's company had been the target of Rain's parents and A Bridge to the Future on more than one occasion.

"Point taken." Sasha's shoulders had relaxed, and she leaned back against the headboard. She'd still not bothered to slip into a T-shirt, so her large firm breasts remained a distraction for Rain. With the chill in the air, her nipples protruded, but Rain suspected she knew that, too.

With the crisis seemingly averted, Rain sat on the corner of the bed, careful to stay as far from Sasha as she could. "Plus, I have to prepare for the rally on

Saturday." She shook out her socks and slid one onto her foot and then the other.

"What is it this time?" Sasha rolled her eyes. "Immigration? Gun control? Cake bakers?"

Rain ignored the sarcasm in Sasha's voice. "School vouchers."

Sasha's lip curled, and she scrunched up her nose. "Sounds kinda boring. Not your usual issue of the day. You getting soft?"

Rain bristled but held it in check. They were back on solid ground, so no sense shattering the tentative peace. "It has more implications than you think. The crazy right-wingers are trying to get taxpayer dollars to run their hate-filled schools." Rain slammed her fist onto the bed, the gesture not nearly as satisfying had she had a table to pound on. "They'll ban any talk or teaching of sexuality, gender identity, or even race."

Sasha grinned. "You're so sexy when you get all passionate about one of your little causes."

Little causes, seriously? Rain took a deep breath. Sasha would never share her passion for social activism. "Nothing good can come from a political conversation at two a.m. I need to get home."

"Stop pouting." Sasha frowned. "You get so self-righteous sometimes. There is more than one way to look at the world, or have you forgotten?"

Sasha sounded just like her environmentally destroying capitalist father. Rain measured her words. "History will show that there was only one right side."

Sasha snorted. "No shades of gray, are there?"

Rain knew she shouldn't take the bait, but she couldn't help herself. "Shades of gray are for those with privilege."

Sasha laughed. "For someone who's into diversity, you seem to only want to look at the world from one viewpoint."

Rain bit her lip. "I really need to get going."

Sasha slid over and ran her hands over the shaved sides of Rain's head. "I love your stubble."

Rain's head tingled as Sasha moved her hand against the grain of the tiny hairs. She shuddered. "Stop. You know that tickles."

"I could tickle some other hairs instead, if you'd like." Sasha's hand trailed toward Rain's lap.

Rain jumped from the bed. "I gotta get an Uber."

"Fine." Sasha pulled out her phone. "I'll get you one."

"I can get my own." *Right.* Like that would happen.

Sasha winked. "I have to ensure you come back." Her hand glided over the screen. "It'll be here in ten minutes."

"Thanks," Rain muttered. She shouldn't let Sasha pay for everything, but she wasn't going to argue with her tonight.

"Do you want me to go with you to the rally on Saturday?"

Rain shook her head. "It's not your thing."

"I'd go if you promise to put out afterward." Sasha licked her lips.

"Uh, I'm not sure how long it will last, so don't count on it."

Sasha's face dropped. "I'll be at Augie's if you decide you want to see me."

"Augie's?"

"Yeah, some of the gang from the Merc are getting together on Saturday night."

"I'll see. Don't wait for me." Rain hoped the

distaste didn't show on her face. She had nothing in common with Sasha's colleagues from The Chicago Mercantile Exchange. They were all heavy hitters in global derivatives or something like that. She zoned out when Sasha went on about her big financial deals. Sasha and her friends were the same greedy capitalists she protested.

Sasha wiggled her fingers at Rain as she exited the room.

Chapter Two

Ivy Nash pulled her coat tighter around herself. The day had started out warmer, but the cold wind blowing in from the north took her breath away. Even though it was officially spring, at least on the calendar, it sure didn't feel like it.

Spring was her favorite season, so she wished it would just start and stay springy. There was something about the buds on the trees and the smell of fresh dirt in the fields that made her feel alive after a long winter. She'd threatened to move south from her home in northern Illinois, but she knew she'd never leave her family. But it was still nice to dream of weather that was warm year-round.

She pulled open the door of her twenty-year-old Chevy, and the rusty hinges creaked. Eventually, she'd get a new car, but her brother Max was a wizard with all things mechanical, so for now, he kept it running.

"Red, you're stuck with me, old girl." Ivy patted the roof of the car before she climbed in.

When she'd bought her car, it had surprised everyone that she wanted such a flashy car. They'd tried to steer her to a practical blue or gray, but she'd stubbornly insisted on red. She half smiled to herself. *Probably the only time I'd ever done anything remotely rebellious.*

Ivy shook off the thought and put the key in the ignition but didn't turn it. She dropped her head against the steering wheel. Her bones were tired, if that was possible. It had been a long week, and she was thankful it was finally over. The kids had been especially rambunctious today. It happened every spring, but this year seemed worse. She swore the COVID years had robbed the children of socialization and left them permanently behind.

She shook her head. Mr. Haskins, the substitute teacher who had replaced Mrs. Jennings, wasn't helping the situation, either. Being an aide was hard enough, but with Mr. Haskins more interested in flirting with her than teaching, it meant she'd spent most of the week chasing around a bunch of hyper first-graders. Thankfully, there was only a month left in the year. Mrs. Jennings better come back from maternity leave, or Ivy might have to look for another job.

She pushed the thoughts from her mind and lifted her head. *Darn.* Mr. Haskins strode across the school parking lot with a large grin on his face. Could she pretend not to see him and speed away? She could try. She cranked the engine. *Thank you, Red.* The car started right away. She rammed Red into gear and hit the gas. She smiled and waved at Mr. Haskins as she blew past him.

Whew. Crisis averted for now. How much longer could she hide from him? At least, she'd made it through another week. She turned onto the highway that led to her home in Mullins Creek. It was only a twenty-minute drive, but she wished it were longer. Most days, it was the only time she had to be alone until late into the evening.

She cracked her window slightly to let in the fresh air, and for a split second, she considered opening it farther and turning up the heat, but she couldn't do it. Her papa would tell her it wasted gas. She'd always wondered if that was true but never thought to Google it when she wasn't driving.

Ivy straightened and pushed back her shoulders. The loud cracks seemed to have gotten worse the last couple of years. *Age?* That seemed to be her answer for anything anymore, but she doubted she was washed up at thirty-four. So why lately, at the end of the day, did she always feel so drained and as if she were just going through the motions?

At least it was the weekend. She groaned. *Shoot.* With the crazy week, she'd forgotten she'd been signed up for the rally tomorrow. She wondered what it would take to get out of going. Maybe one of her siblings would be willing to take her place. Possibly, she could barter with them.

Her shoulders sagged. No, Pastor Devlin wouldn't stand for it. Besides, she'd been lucky to get this assignment. It shouldn't be as bad as some of the others he'd forced the congregation to attend. Most of the rallies had been against something: abortion, gun control, gay rights. At least this one, they'd be marching *for* something.

Heaviness descended on her. It wasn't like her to be so drained. Everyone always commented on her boundless energy. Maybe she needed to find a good multivitamin or something.

She yawned as she turned off the highway toward Mullins Creek. What she'd give for a trashy novel and a bubble bath. Maybe later. She'd help Mama with dinner, but then hopefully, she could slip away early if nobody needed her help.

She slowed and flipped on her turn signal, even

though there was no one else on the road. It was a habit and a good one. If she got lazy out here, she might forget to use her blinker in town. *Nope.* She'd keep herself honest even when no one was looking.

She pulled into the lane that led to her parents' old farmhouse. With little thought, she weaved around the potholes that seemed to get worse each season, but gravel was expensive, so they'd made do with the obstacle course they'd become accustomed to.

The fields surrounding the house would soon be planted. Her chest tightened at the thought. She loved seeing the tiny plants peeking out of the soil, but she wondered how much longer her father could hold out. All the farms in the area, except for theirs and the Feldman's farm, had been sold. A corporation had swooped in and gobbled up all the farmland. The megafarms had such an advantage. It had become harder and harder for a small farmer to make a living.

She pulled her car into her grandma's driveway. The tiny cottage sat next to the big house where her parents and younger siblings lived. After she killed the engine, she sat and stared at nothing. Her bag on the passenger seat vibrated, but she made no move to search for her phone. What was the matter with her? She closed her eyes. Just tired.

The vibration started again, so she yanked her purse onto her lap and foraged for her cellphone. When she finally found it, the phone had stopped ringing. Two missed calls. Both her mom. Her heart raced. Mama knew she would be home soon, so why would she be calling?

Ivy's fingers danced over her phone, and she hit the call icon.

"Ivy," her mother said on the first ring. "Where

are you?"

"In the driveway."

"Thank god." Her mother's voice sounded harried. "Jimmy, um, I mean James, forgot his baseball cleats."

Ivy smiled. Last month, her brother Jimmy had announced to the family that at eighteen he was too old for such a childish nickname and henceforth would be known as James. It had taken awhile for them to get it right, but now, there were only rare slips. "Do you need me to take them to him?" Ivy tried to put pep in her voice, so Mama wouldn't sense her mood. At least, she'd get another drive all to herself. Her mood perked up a touch.

"You're such a darling. Hold on." Ivy heard movement on the other end of the phone as if her mother was moving around. "Violet," she called, "run your brother's cleats out to your sister."

Unintelligible muttering sliced through the air, but all Ivy could clearly make out was her mother's exasperated breathing.

"Now! She's waiting. And his game starts in half an hour," Mama yelled. After a pause, she said, "I'm sure your sister would love to have you ride along."

Ivy inwardly groaned. So much for her quiet drive. Violet would surely talk her ear off. Weren't teenagers supposed to be sullen? At fourteen, Violet still loved to give Ivy a complete rundown of all the happenings in the eighth grade at Mullins Creek Junior High.

Chapter Three

Rain bounced on one foot as she tried to straighten her sock. "Shit." She tipped to the side and bumped against the wall, so at least she didn't fall to the floor. Maybe if she weren't trying to do three things at once, she could manage a simple task like putting on her socks.

"Why are you swearing at us?" Her mother's irritated voice came across the speaker on her cellphone.

Shit! She'd only been half listening to what they'd been telling her for the past ten minutes as she scurried around the house trying to get ready for the rally. "Uh, sorry. I was just trying to get my sock on."

"And that requires swearing?" her father asked; his deep voice held a note of scolding.

Rain sighed and sat on the couch. She'd take the extra couple of minutes to get her clothing on properly. If she were late, so be it. "Sorry. So what were you saying about the climate conference?"

Seemingly satisfied with her apology, her father launched into another monologue about the keynote speaker at the event. Rain was careful to grunt in all the right places, and she even sprinkled in a few choice words—*interesting, fascinating,* and *amazing.* It seemed to appease them as they continued to talk.

Once she got her sock fixed and shoe on, she took her cellphone to the bathroom to have one final look. *Damn!* Her hair looked a bit flat this morning. *Almost time for a haircut.* She ran her fingers through it, trying to give it more lift. As soon as she took her hand away, it flopped back to its original position.

"You should have seen your father," her mother said. "He stood right up and blasted the idiot with a question he couldn't answer."

"Go, Dad," Rain added, not sure what she was cheering him on for but sensed it was the right response.

Her father laughed. "Yep, go, Dad."

Rain grabbed the bottle of mousse off the counter. *Pssst. Pssst.* She squirted a generous amount into her hand.

"Was that aerosol?" her mother asked.

Damn. Bat ears. "Aerosol? No. Must be a bad connection. After all, you are halfway across the globe." Rain was careful to gently rub the product into her hair, so they didn't hear the sound.

"Probably," her mother said. "You know we don't approve of the use of aerosols."

"Of course." Rain scowled and put conviction into her voice. "Aerosol is the anti-Christ." *Overkill? Maybe.* But her parents never seemed to notice when she went for over the top.

"So where were we?" her mother said.

Shit. Rain hoped she wasn't expected to answer.

"You were talking about the moment I put that loudmouth in his place," her father said.

Whew. She dodged a bullet on that one.

"Oh, yes, so...." her mother continued.

Satisfied that her hair on top was sufficiently lifted, Rain examined the shaved sides. They could use a trim, but they'd have to do since she didn't have time.

She scowled at her plain black T-shirt. While it hugged her in all the right places to show off her muscular physique, she was still disappointed in herself. Normally when she attended a rally, she had a T-shirt to match the occasion. Granted, there wasn't a large demand for school voucher T-shirts, like some of the big-name issues, but she still should have put more effort into the cause.

"Your mother wasn't a slouch herself. She schooled the lady sitting in front of us—"

"Go get 'em, tiger," Rain said.

Her dad chuckled.

Deciding that the shirt would have to do, she unbuckled her belt and unzipped her blue jeans so she could tuck the shirt into her pants. She ran her hand across her flat stomach and pulled her shirt up so she could admire her abs. Maybe not quite a six-pack but at least a four.

"Did you hear what I just said?" her mother asked.

Shit. "Sorry. I'm just so much in awe of the things you do sometimes. It leaves me speechless."

"Oh, honey," her mom gushed. "It's not like we're heroes."

Perfect. "You are to me," Rain delivered the line she knew would make them forget whether she was listening to them.

With her shirt tucked in and her chunky belt fastened, she flipped off the bathroom light and made her way into the living room. She glanced at the clock and realized she'd be cutting it close. It all depended on the traffic.

A light coat should be enough, so she plucked

the olive green cargo jacket out of the closet. She'd bought it a month ago but hadn't had occasion to wear it. Maybe she wouldn't completely be dressed the part, but she'd look smashing. If she were lucky, she might meet a lonely lady. As she grabbed her keys off the side table by the door, she grinned to herself at the thought of hooking up with someone new.

"I hate to cut you short," Rain said, "but I have to get going."

"Oh, where are you off to?" her father asked.

Seriously? She'd just told them about the rally less than half an hour ago. They'd probably forget that she'd been asked to join the board of SWAN, Stand with the Alphabet Nation. No matter how many causes she championed or honors she received, it never seemed to get their attention other than the obligatory *we're so proud of you*. And then they'd promptly forget. "The rally. The one for school vouchers."

"Oh, that's right," her mom said. "Such an important cause. We're so proud of you, aren't we, Jeffrey?"

"Of course we are, Joyce," her father responded. The line he used so often that it almost seemed rehearsed.

"Thanks," Rain delivered her line. "Well, enjoy yourselves. Are you still planning on coming home next week?"

"Um, well, we meant to mention that to you," her mother said.

Here it comes. She knew that two weeks would likely turn into much longer, but she let them keep their illusions every time they jetted off. "Something come up?"

Her mother let out a sigh. "We met a couple

from the Netherlands who've invited us to join a group of like-minded people for a planning session. It's a progressive think tank."

"How exciting." Rain glanced at the clock. She needed to get moving. Every minute she stayed on the phone was a minute later she'd be.

"And the best part," her mother continued. "They're picking up all our expenses."

And there it was. For founders of a foundation, her parents always seemed to be able to afford to travel, mostly at someone else's expense. "Well deserved," Rain said. "I should really be going, though. Send me an email with all the details."

"Of course," her father said. "We don't want to keep you."

Rain closed the door behind her and checked that it was locked. She hurried toward her car parked on the street. "Thanks. It was great talking to you. Same time next week?"

"Certainly," her mother said. "You're taking the train, aren't you?"

Rain's finger stopped before she hit the button to unlock her car door. "Of course, it's much better for the environment."

"That's good," her father said. "I'm glad you've finally learned to leave a little earlier to do the right thing."

"I learned from the best." Rain held her finger over the button, waiting for the call to end, so she could open the door. "Talk to you later."

"Goodbye," her parents said in unison.

Chapter Four

Ivy sprinted across the church parking lot. By the smell of diesel in the air, the bus was already running. And just like her, a couple of stragglers were rushing toward it.

Pastor Devlin stood outside the open doors. His brow was creased, and his lips formed a frown. He'd perfected the disapproving look, but it normally wasn't directed at her. Her goal was to stay under the radar with him.

Being late was something rare for her. She glanced at her watch. Actually, she had two minutes to spare, but normally, she'd show up half an hour early for something like this. She scolded herself again. All she'd wanted to do was find the perfect seat. Maybe with Mrs. Pruitt, who fell asleep as soon as she sat down anywhere, or Mrs. French, who normally had her head in a book.

Then Ivy could put on her headphones and listen to the new Jenna Blake album she'd downloaded last week. It had been her big splurge from her tax refund. The rest she'd put into her savings account for a rainy day.

As she approached the bus and Pastor Devlin, she couldn't help but smile to herself. He'd be livid if he realized she listened to Jenna Blake. He probably wouldn't be happy with her other favorites—Black Sabbath, Metallica, and Megadeth—either. Although, he'd more likely approve of her love for heavy metal music over a lesbian pop star.

"Miss Nash," Pastor Devlin said with a sneer. "I'm glad you could make it."

"Um, sorry. I fell asleep on the couch last night after I helped Papa and never got up to bed." Ivy knew she should leave it at that, but his piercing, nearly black eyes made her want to continue. To make him understand she wasn't being irresponsible. "Papa's been trying to fix his plow. We were up until midnight fighting with it. No luck. Hopefully, Max will come by today and help him. Then this morning, Granny's vertigo was acting up, so I had to make her breakfast because Mama had to sew up James's baseball pants. He ripped a hole in them when he scored the winning run last night, but he had a double header this morning, so I had to package up the cookies." She finally took a breath and shoved the bag toward the pastor. "Here. Mama's famous cookies. For the trip."

Pastor Devlin stared at the package for a couple of beats before he reached for it. He finally smiled when he opened the sack. She wished he hadn't. His oversized eyeteeth made him look sinister. Although most of the other ladies from the church found him handsome and charismatic, she found him creepy.

"Thank you, Miss Nash." He patted her hand. "Tell your mother thank you from me and the others who'll enjoy her offering."

Ivy nodded.

"Go ahead and find a seat. There's only a couple spaces left." He smiled again as he placed his hand on the small of her back.

She tried not to flinch. Instead, she shot up the bus stairs to get away from his touch. "Thanks," she called over her shoulder.

Her heart sank when she reached the top of the stairs. After a quick scan of the bus, she realized she only had three choices of seats. Mr. Haskins sat by himself near the back of the bus and waved frantically. She averted her gaze. No way would she sit with him. That left Mrs. Newburg or Mrs. Capri. Both loved to gossip, but Mrs. Capri was kinder, so she slid into the seat next to her.

"I hope you don't mind having a seatmate," Ivy said as she sat.

"Of course not, dear." Mrs. Capri patted her arm. She was only a couple of years older than Mama, who was in her mid-fifties, but she came off much older. Papa always said that was what getting in other people's business could do to someone.

❧❧❧❧

They'd been traveling for nearly forty-five minutes, and Ivy had given up all hope of listening to Jenna Blake's new album. Mrs. Capri had done most of the talking, so Ivy only needed to nod in all the right places. She had learned several things she didn't know about her neighbors, including some things she didn't want to know.

"Oh, my goodness." Mrs. Capri grabbed Ivy's arm. "I almost forgot to ask if you've heard the big news."

Ivy raised her eyebrow. Something seemed calculated in the way Mrs. Capri had delivered her line. It would be just like her to save a juicy piece of gossip for the middle of the trip. Mrs. Capri always had a flair for the dramatic. "I'm afraid I don't hear much nowadays." It seemed like a safe response.

Mrs. Capri leaned toward Ivy and pursed her lips. "Well, I don't want to be a bearer of bad news." A hint of sadness crossed her eyes before an excited spark filled them.

Ivy weighed how to respond. Part of her wanted to tell Mrs. Capri that maybe she shouldn't share it then, but she suspected her insolence would get back to Mama before she returned home. "I hope everyone is okay." Another safe response.

Mrs. Capri smiled. "More than okay."

Ivy's thoughts churned as she contemplated her next move. It was like a chess match when she talked to Mrs. Capri. "I'm afraid you've lost me. How could it be considered bad news if everything is better than okay?"

Mrs. Capri squeezed her arm. "I'm afraid the bad news will only be bad for you."

And there it was. What petty gossip was going around town now? She couldn't think of a proper response, so she nodded. A gesture to encourage Mrs. Capri to go on.

"I'm afraid your beau is getting married." Mrs. Capri shook her head and looked down at her hands. She wrung them for good measure.

Beau? Since when did she have a beau? She hadn't dated in years. "I'm afraid I don't understand."

"John." Mrs. Capri raised her gaze with a look of triumph.

"John?" Ivy stared at Mrs. Capri, knowing she was missing something. Then realization hit her. She smiled. "You mean John Mercer?"

"What other John is there?" Mrs. Capri raised her voice, obviously irritated by Ivy's reaction. "Your ex-husband. Have you forgotten?"

Ivy smiled and patted Mrs. Capri's hand. The tension she felt earlier, awaiting the news, drained from her body. "John and I have been divorced for nearly seven years. I'm glad he found someone."

"Oh, sweetie. You can tell me the truth. I know it has to hurt."

"I moved on with my life." And divorcing John was the best decision she'd ever made, but she wouldn't tell Mrs. Capri that.

"But he's such a handsome man. A catch for any woman." Mrs. Capri smiled. "I figured you've been pining for him all these years."

Pining? Where had she gotten such an absurd idea? "Um, nope. No pining going on here. I'm happy for him."

Mrs. Capri frowned. "We all know you've never gotten over him. Why else would a pretty girl like you not have dated anyone in all these years?" Mrs. Capri took her hand. "Come on, dear. You can tell me. He broke your heart, didn't he?"

Ivy bit her tongue so as not to laugh. Broke her heart? Not even close. The marriage had been a mistake from the beginning. He was a nice man, although a bit boring. She certainly wouldn't tell Mrs. Capri that it was her who asked for the divorce. In a small town like Mullins Creek, everyone assumed it must have been the man who left. She'd done nothing to correct the rumors nor had he. It kept his ego intact.

Ivy knew she needed to choose her words carefully. "He's a great guy. I wish him nothing but the best, but I hate to disappoint you." *Crap.* By the set of Mrs. Capri's jaw, that had been the wrong thing for her to say. "I mean, no, I'm not suffering from a broken heart."

"Then why haven't you dated anyone?" Mrs. Capri's voice held a note of contempt.

"Afraid I don't have much time, and nobody interesting has come along."

Mrs. Capri wriggled her eyebrows. "I hear that handsome Mr. Haskins has taken a shine to you."

Her stomach dropped at the mention of Haskins. He made her skin crawl. "I'm afraid I have no interest." Hopefully, that would get back to him. "Besides, I'm too busy for a relationship."

Mrs. Capri shook her head. "You know you can't live for that family of yours forever. You need to have your own life. It's not natural. Why your parents decided to have more kids is still a mystery."

Ivy's jaw clenched. Violet, her youngest sister, was fourteen, so it wasn't like this was breaking news. "I guess they just loved the first batch so much, they decided to have a second." Ivy used the line from their ongoing family joke.

Mrs. Capri snorted. "Batch is fitting. You're the oldest, right?"

Ivy nodded. She had no doubt that a busybody like Mrs. Capri already knew the answer. Not having any patience for this cat-and-mouse game, she said, "Yes. I was born the year after Mama and Papa graduated. Then two years later came Max, and Rose two years after him."

"Just like clockwork." Mrs. Capri leaned over, put her hand on Ivy's arm, and whispered. "We thought Jimmy was an accident, and then they go and pop out Frank and Violet."

Ivy wasn't about to admit she'd thought the same thing. She'd been shocked when they'd announced

they were having a baby when she was sixteen, and
then Frank when she was eighteen, and finally Violet
shortly after she turned twenty. "He goes by James
now." Ivy thought a change of topic would be for the
best.

"James?" Mrs. Capri squinted.

"Yes. Jimmy wants to be called James."

"Hmph." Mrs. Capri rolled her eyes. "I hear
your mama doesn't care for his name change."

Really? Name change. She hardly thought going
from Jimmy to James was a huge leap, although Mrs.
Capri was right. For some reason, it had gotten under
Mama's skin. "It's taken her a while to adjust. She's
been calling him Jimmy since the first time she held
him in her arms." It was what Mama always said
whenever she forgot and called him Jimmy. "He's
eighteen, so he wants to be seen as a man. He says
Jimmy is a boy's name."

"That sister of yours is growing up fast, too. She
looks more and more like you every day." Mrs. Capri
let out a mirthful laugh.

Ivy wasn't sure what the laugh was for but
decided to ignore it. "Yep, we're the only two with
Papa's sandy blond hair."

"And the curls." Mrs. Capri grabbed a handful
of Ivy's hair.

Ivy resisted pulling away. "Yes, and the curls."

"Are you still being mistaken for Violet's mother?"

Ah. That must have been the reason for the
earlier laugh. Mrs. Capri wanted to draw attention to
their twenty-year age gap. "Not much anymore. Now
that she's wearing her hair swept to the side like mine,
she's looking older."

"A fourteen-year-old girl has no business looking like that. It'll only lead to problems." Mrs. Capri's gaze darted around the bus before she said, "Could lead to pregnancy."

Ivy clenched her fists. Maybe she should have sat next to Mrs. Newburg. Over the last couple of years, Mrs. Capri had become increasingly bitter and nasty, and now it seemed she rivaled Mrs. Newburg. Nothing good could come from responding directly, so she said, "I love them all so much. My family's amazing."

Mrs. Capri pointed toward Ivy. "By the bags under your eyes, they're running you ragged."

Ivy glanced out the bus window. They were still on Interstate 55, so she was trapped for at least another half an hour, so she might as well see if she could put an end to her misery. Besides, how could she defend the fatigue she'd felt the last couple of months?

Mrs. Capri took her silence as an opportunity to forge on. "Hildy, I mean Mrs. Newburg, said you've looked tired lately. I see what she means."

Wow. Confirmation that she was a target of their gossip. A single woman in their small community seemed to raise suspicion. "Let me assure you that I'm perfectly happy." Was she? Maybe not perfectly, but she wasn't going to have that conversation with Mrs. Capri. "My family is my biggest blessing."

"I'm sure they are." Mrs. Capri gave her a smug smile. "But a pretty girl like you needs to start her *own* family."

So ugly girls shouldn't, she wanted to say. What had gotten into her lately? "I'm sure God will bring me a family if that's what he wants me to have." *Let's see if Mrs. Capri can argue with God.*

"Well, dear. God brings the things we need to us, but we still need to do something to grab his blessings."

Yep. Mrs. Capri found a way to skirt God. "So you think I should grab a handful of Mr. Haskins?" *Dang.* She needed to stop being so sassy. Would Mrs. Capri pick up on her double entendre?

Mrs. Capri studied her for several seconds, while Ivy tried hard to maintain a look of innocence. Mrs. Capri must have been satisfied when she said, "I think you should."

Ivy stifled a giggle. Mrs. Capri just told her to grab a handful of Mr. Haskins. God, she wished she had someone to tell. But she doubted her family would find it amusing. She needed to move this conversation on to a safer topic. "So I've never been to a rally before. Maybe you can tell me what to expect."

"Never?" Mrs. Capri's eyes widened. "How'd you manage that?"

Ivy shrugged. "We've not been with Autumn Harvest Church very long."

"Of course." Mrs. Capri slapped her leg. "Your family stuck it out with that old rinky-dink church until the end."

Rinky dink! Ivy missed their old church, although she'd never say it to Mrs. Capri. "We did. I remember the last day when we shut off the lights for the final time."

"It was a blessing in disguise when that old church closed." Mrs. Capri must have seen the look of horror on Ivy's face. "Um…I mean, Pastor Armstrong's passing was sad, of course."

It had been the saddest day of Ivy's life. "It's a shame we couldn't find another minister."

"Pshaw." Mrs. Capri waved her hand. "Autumn Harvest Church is so much better. Does so much more."

"I suppose." Ivy knew not to argue directly with Mrs. Capri. Pastor Devlin had circled the congregation at her old church like a vulture and swooped in before Pastor Armstrong's body was even cold. He recruited so many of the parishioners even before Pastor Armstrong's death that it had been impossible to keep the church going. "But it was nice to have the church right in our backyard so to speak. And we knew everyone there, too." She needed to be careful how much she criticized the megachurch, or it would get back to Pastor Devlin.

"More people to spread the word of God." Mrs. Capri sat up straighter. "Just like today. We're doing something to make our country great again."

Ivy was glad she wore a jacket, so Mrs. Capri couldn't see the goose bumps that rose on her arms. "I just wish everyone could get along."

"Get along!" Mrs. Capri's voice rose two octaves, and some of the other passengers on the bus looked in their direction.

Heat rose in Ivy's cheeks. She certainly didn't want any of the other congregants to get involved. As she glanced around, she realized she only knew around ten percent of the people on the bus. Which wasn't surprising since the congregation numbered in the thousands.

Ivy fumbled with the bottom of her jacket, realizing it could use a good washing. "Um, I just meant that Jesus taught love and all."

"Well, we can't love the godless."

Ivy decided now wasn't the time to discuss the

teachings of Jesus. The irony wasn't lost on her. "But how do we decide who's godless?"

"Don't you listen to Pastor Devlin's sermons?" Mrs. Capri asked. "The evil is here, and we must fight it. The liberals are trying to take Jesus away from us. Shoving abortion, homosexuality, men becoming women, immigrants, critical, um, critical racism, and privilege down our throats."

Ivy bit her tongue. She was pretty sure that critical racism wasn't right, but it wasn't a discussion she wanted to have. Ivy decided redirection was the best defense. "Um, since I've never been to a rally, is there anything I should know?"

Mrs. Capri patted her leg. "Well, let me tell you..."

Whew. Crisis averted. Ivy pretended to listen but stared past Mrs. Capri out the bus window. Soon, they'd cross into Chicago where 55 turned into Lake Shore Drive. One of her fondest memories of the city had been the time her parents had taken them to the Field Museum and Shedd Aquarium right on Lake Michigan. Even though they'd only spent the day, she'd felt like they'd been on vacation.

She sighed. It had been too long since she'd been to the city or anywhere else for that matter. She returned her focus to Mrs. Capri. No sense longing for something she'd never have.

Chapter Five

Rain weaved through the crowd. They needed a fast lane on the sidewalk in the city, so those serious about getting somewhere didn't have to be bothered by the gapers. Nina was going to be pissed. At the thought, Rain picked up the pace and was practically sprinting by the time she reached Daley Plaza.

As she neared, the amplified voice from an angry protester filled the air. *Shit.* If she missed Nina's speech, she'd never live it down. When she skidded around the corner, she was surprised by the throngs of people lining the streets.

Passengers streamed from three buses pulled up along Randolph Street. She squinted, trying to get a better look as the people descended. *Crap.* It looked like the opposition was out in force. *Bunch of holy rollers.* Lately, it seemed that a few of the megachurches were busing people in from all over Illinois and Wisconsin to show a larger force.

Not only had the local media picked up on it, but some of the national news media were also starting to send crews to the city. It would only encourage more crazy evangelicals to overrun Chicago. Just what they needed.

Rain scanned the throng, looking for Nina's signature pink hair. Unfortunately, in this crowd, it wasn't as helpful as one might think, so she made a beeline for the stage. The speaker continued to yell into the microphone with one fist raised above his head. A good sign she'd have a little more time to find Nina.

Holy shit. There must be at least five thousand people here. She hadn't expected more than a thousand. By the loud chants from the opposition trying to drown out the speaker, Rain suspected her side was outnumbered. Another thing she wasn't used to in the city. What was wrong with people, and where did all the crazies come from?

She was glad she wasn't wearing a T-shirt that identified what side of the issue she was on as she slid through a large group all wearing bright blue T-shirts that said, *Religious Fight! Give us Our Schools!* For a brief moment, she thought of making a crude comment but then thought better of it. Besides, she needed to find Nina.

As she jostled through, she took a couple of elbows to the ribs, not sure if they were intentional or not. Likely the former since no one would mistake her for straight. After the fourth blow that nearly took her breath away, she tucked her elbows against her sides and formed her hands into loose fists to stave off any more errant elbows.

Finally, she found Nina about twenty yards away, waving both arms over her head. Rain thought of returning the wave, but it would require her leaving her ribs exposed, so instead, she put her head down and walked faster.

"Where the hell have you been?" Nina yelled over the noisy crowd. She held up her watch. "Fifteen minutes late." Nina shook her head and leaned in closer to Rain, so her mouth nearly touched Rain's ear. "Actually, forty-five. You were supposed to be here early to help us set up."

Rain turned her head into position near Nina's ear. "Accident on 290," she lied. There were always accidents, so Nina would be none the wiser.

"You drove? Would your parents approve?"

"No." Rain glowered but doubted Nina could see in the position they stood. "But they aren't here, so what they don't know won't hurt them."

"Unless someone tells them."

"What's the game plan?" Rain asked, ignoring Nina's threat.

"The gang's behind the stage. I was sent to wait for your ass. Let's go, so I don't have to keep feeling your breath on my neck."

"You love it." Rain made sure to breathe harder as she spoke into Nina's ear.

"Gross." Nina scowled and wiped her hand down the side of neck.

Rain laughed and followed Nina around to the back.

※※※※

Ivy clutched her blue jean jacket closed as she exited the bus. Never in a million years would she have expected to see so many people here. *There must be ten thousand.* She'd expected a couple hundred at most.

And boy were they loud. The screechy man on the stage raised his fist over his head and said something incomprehensible, while half the crowd cheered as the others booed.

Ivy rubbed her temples. Pressure built behind

her eyes, and she'd likely end up with a headache before the day was over. She glanced at her watch. At least they'd arrived late since the bus driver had gotten lost, which meant only an hour and forty-five minutes before they'd get to leave.

Another positive, Mrs. Capri had run off to find Mrs. Newburg. She wondered why they hadn't sat together on the bus. Probably so they could collect more gossip from their seatmates. *Intel.* More than likely, everything Ivy had said was already being repeated.

The crowd let out a loud roar. *Maybe not.* Who could talk over this noise? Suddenly, she realized she'd been gaping at the crowd and hadn't paid attention to where the others had gone. *Great.* Lost in the city. Just what she wanted to do on her day off. Maybe she could sneak away, get back on the bus, and wait for it to be over.

When she felt a hand on her back, she jumped and spun around. *Haskins. Great.*

"I didn't mean to startle you," he said as he brought his face closer to hers.

She flinched and stepped back. "Where are the others?" she yelled over the crowd but didn't move any closer to him.

He studied her for a moment before he pointed off to his right. He began to lean in but must have thought better of it and straightened. "They wanted to get closer to the stage," he shouted.

She nodded and marched off toward the group without looking back, although she sensed he followed behind. Her march was soon halted. The crowd grew heavier, and throngs of angry people waved signs and shouted. This was not what she signed up for.

Why did she have to be so naïve? She'd not expected this level of tension and anger. Sure, she knew there would be people from opposing sides, but she'd not expected anything like this. She'd been on the debate team in high school, so she'd thought each side would present their viewpoint as the crowd listened in, clapping at all the appropriate times. But shouting one another down seemed so barbaric.

Her forward progress was stopped by a group who'd locked arms and made a human fence. They were chanting. *A hymn?* Her eyes widened. Had they just said what she thought they did? *No!* She must have misunderstood. Nobody would use the F-word in the same sentence with Jesus.

One of the chanters met her gaze and smiled. He looked her up and down until she suddenly felt exposed. Maybe she shouldn't have worn her Sunday dress here. The flowing white dress, covered with beautiful blue flowers, stood out in the sea of blue jeans and T-shirts.

Dumb. Why hadn't she asked anyone what attire was suited for a rally? She pulled her jean jacket tighter around herself and kept her arms crossed over her chest. Mr. Haskins stepped up beside her, and for once, she was almost glad to see him.

Ivy's gaze darted around, looking for an exit. She made eye contact with an older woman whose arms were locked with a man on each side. Her long gray hair fluttered in the light breeze, but it was her intense gray eyes, which nearly matched her hair, that mesmerized Ivy. They were searching, almost as if they were looking into Ivy's soul. The woman's gaze flickered to Mr. Haskins but then returned to her.

The woman nodded, almost imperceptibly, and

beckoned Ivy toward her. Ivy stepped forward. The woman released her arm from her companion and tilted her head toward the opening. Ivy smiled and mouthed a *thank you* as she passed.

She'd taken a couple of steps and turned to say something to Mr. Haskins and saw him standing, still detained on the other side of the line. *Odd.* Why hadn't they let him through? Right now, she wasn't going to think too hard about it. She just wanted to get with the group and stick as close as possible to them until it was time to leave.

❧ ❧ ❧ ❧

Rain puffed out her breath. "It's been a wild one," she said to Nina.

"No doubt." Nina wiped the sweat from her brow. "Who'd have guessed so many would be this passionate about school vouchers?"

"Damned zealots." Rain glanced around at the thinning crowd, happy they could talk without shouting. There were still several groups milling around, but at least half had left. "They won't stop until they can use taxpayer money to dole out their hatred."

"Insane, isn't it?" Nina tilted her head toward the loudest groups that remained. "Apparently, they're going to have a sing-off."

Rain laughed. "*Pitch Perfect*? Didn't they call it a riff-off?" Rain cocked her head, trying to hear the words the opposing groups were singing but couldn't make them out.

"Stop! You know I'm visual. I don't want to imagine a bunch of nuns trying to riff."

"There aren't any nuns out there." Rain scowled. "Stop being so melodramatic."

Nina nodded in the direction of the singing. "Tell me that you can't tell the difference between the two groups, even if they aren't wearing habits."

Rain smirked. "You have a point. Look at them. I've not seen that many women in dresses since the Easter parade."

Nina slugged her in the arm. "Since when have you gone to an Easter parade?"

"Geez. It was an analogy."

"A dumb one." Nina rolled her eyes.

One of the organizers of the event waved to Nina and called, "Nina. We wanted to get a picture of everyone that spoke on stage before Clarence leaves."

"Coming," Nina called back.

"Hey, I forgot to tell you. Your speech killed."

Nina smiled. "Thanks, man."

"Hurry up," the organizer called.

"Shit." Nina pointed. "We left a pile of our signs over there. Mind getting them while I smile for the camera?" She tossed her long pink hair a couple of times for emphasis.

"I'm on it."

≈≈≈≈≈

Ivy's head pounded, and blood throbbed in her ears. She turned and slipped through the crowd. She'd rather lick the toilet at a gas station than do this again. The angry singing would be stuck in her brain for weeks. She just wanted to go home, but it might be a while since Pastor Devlin seemed to be right in the thick of the warring groups.

While trying to stay as far from the fray as possible, she'd uncovered the reason for Pastor Devlin's passion. Mrs. Newburg had let slip, or maybe it was purposeful, that Autumn Harvest wanted to start its own school. Hopefully, it didn't happen until Violet graduated. She'd hate for her to be taught by the likes of Devlin. That was an odd reaction, she thought, but didn't have time to dwell on it.

As she pushed past the last of the singers, she emerged into a more open area and took a deep breath. She hadn't realized how stifling it had been in the crowd until she'd emerged. Maybe she'd find a bench to sit on until this hell was finally over.

She started toward the bus, but a loud male voice caused her to turn. What in the world was Mr. Haskins up to?

About forty yards away, Mr. Haskins stood with his arms across his chest, facing off with another smaller man. She glanced toward the inviting benches, but Mr. Haskins's voice caused her to turn.

"Don't you fucking mess with me." Mr. Haskins thrust his finger toward the man's face. Even from this distance, Ivy could see that his face was bright red. She imagined spittle was flying from his mouth, too.

The idiot was about to get into a fight in the middle of Chicago. *Good way to get himself shot.* She sighed. As much as she'd love to ignore it, maybe she could calm things down. Begrudgingly, she took her first step toward the two men.

"Fuck you. These are our signs," the other man shouted.

Man? If that was a man, his voice was awfully high pitched. Ivy stared at the man. Woman. Whoever. Her gaze locked on the other person, trying to figure it out.

Their head was shaved on each side, but their nearly black hair stood at least two inches on top. Ivy shifted her gaze to their body. They wore a tight black T-shirt that showed off their wide shoulders that tapered into a narrower waist. *Nice muscles.* He had to be a man, especially looking at his slender hips and tight buttocks.

Ivy shook her head. She shouldn't be staring at the man's tush.

Mr. Haskins took a step forward and stepped on the signs the man looked like he was trying to collect.

"What is your problem?" the man yelled and shoved Haskins to get him off the pile.

That voice sure didn't sound like a man's. She glanced at the person's chest and thought she detected a hint of breasts. Ivy picked up her pace when she noticed Mr. Haskins's balled fists. He didn't need to be hitting the man and certainly shouldn't punch a woman.

☙☙☙☙☙

"What's going on here?" a woman's voice called out, just as Rain was about to make her move on the idiot who stood on her pile of signs.

Rain turned toward the voice. A slender, yet shapely, woman hurried toward them. Her long blond hair was swept to one side and flowed freely in the breeze.

Rain stared as if she'd never seen a woman before. Maybe it was the white dress with the blue flowers or the jean jacket that somehow made the woman appear even softer.

"Ivy, you need to go back to the rest of the group. It's not safe for you here," the man said as he stepped off her pile of signs.

His wife? An idiot like him shouldn't have such a beautiful wife. *Jesus.* She needed to put it back in her pants. The woman was obviously one of the enemies.

The woman, Ivy, fixed him with a glare. "It looks like this...um...this individual isn't safe with you." She pointed at his clenched fists. "I think you need to cool down." Before he could respond, the woman put her hand over her mouth, and a look of shock registered on her face. "Sorry. I shouldn't have said that."

Apparently, she wasn't used to talking to him that way. *Abuser?* Rain edged closer. Her gaze never left Ivy's face. Ivy's light brown eyes had an amber tint to them, which made her already soft features appear even softer somehow.

"But she..." The man pointed at Rain. "She started it."

If Rain wasn't so angry, she'd probably laugh at his juvenile response. "I was simply trying to collect our signs when this moron decided to harass me."

"Who are you calling a moron?" The man stepped toward her again.

Rain studied him. While he stood at least six inches taller than her and considerably outweighed her by fifty pounds, she could likely inflict some damage before she went down. Who knew, with her martial arts training, he might fall easier than she thought.

"Please, Mr. Haskins. Would you please go?" Ivy pleaded.

Mr. Haskins? Most likely not her husband. Although, some of those right-wingers called their wives Mother, so maybe they called their husbands

Mister. No, that was a stretch.

He paused and leered at Ivy. At least that was how Rain saw it. She wondered if Ivy saw it the same way. "Sit with me on the bus on the way back?" He gave her a cheesy smile.

Ivy closed her eyes and sighed. "Okay. If you go now."

The man, Rain couldn't bring herself to think of him as Mr. Haskins, said, "Come with me." He held out his hand to Ivy.

"No. You go first. I'm going to help this lady pick up her signs."

Haskins pointed his finger at Rain. "You're lucky Ivy saved your ass," he said before he turned away.

Rain laughed, knowing it would get under his skin. "How can you resist such a manly man who goes around threatening women?" Rain said in a stage whisper to ensure he'd hear.

He stopped, and his back stiffened. Before he could turn, Ivy said, "I'll see you on the bus."

Haskins continued walking away.

"I'm sorry about that," Ivy said.

"Why? You didn't do anything. The asshole you're with did. Why do women like you defend guys like him?"

"Women like me?" Ivy's amber eyes flashed anger. "And what kind of woman would that be?"

"Um...um...." Rain held out her hand and motioned from Ivy's head to her toes. "Women who dress like that." *Oh, god.* Why did she say that?

"I see." Ivy put her hand on her hip and drew her lips together. "I suppose I should dress like a man. Like you?"

Snap. This one at least had some spunk. "Never mind." Rain flicked her wrist with a dismissive wave. "Go follow your man."

"He's not my man. And I don't like your implications."

"Implications. Whoa. A little hoity-toity, aren't you?" *Damn it.* Since when was she someone who said *hoity-toity?* This woman was really getting under her skin. She needed to get her signs and get the hell out of here.

Ivy crinkled her nose. "You're calling me hoity-toity?" She smirked and pointed at Rain's Doc Martens. "Those boots probably cost more than all my shoes combined."

Without thinking, Rain glanced down at Ivy's feet. Big mistake. Her bright red toenails peeked out of her sandals. Who the hell wore sandals to a rally? This woman obviously wasn't a regular protester. But damn, painted toenails always drove Rain nuts.

"What?" Ivy said while Rain stared at her feet. "Something wrong with my discount shoes?"

Rain lifted her gaze. "Why are you so angry?" spilled out of Rain's mouth before she could edit herself.

"Because you're so full of judgment."

Rain bristled. Ivy was the second woman to tell her that this week. "Judgment? Are you serious? You and your lot think you've been anointed the morality police. Well, you've got another thing coming if you think you can use my tax dollars to spread your hate."

"Hate!" The vein in Ivy's neck throbbed. "Jesus is about love not hate."

"Seriously? You honestly believe that shit? You people are the most hateful people I've ever seen."

"You people. Who exactly is you people? You don't know a thing about me." Ivy's eyes flashed, and her nostrils flared.

"If I know one of you, I know you all." Rain's voice rose, even though she was trying to keep her cool. This woman was unbelievable.

"Really? Since you know so much about me, tell me, who do I hate?"

Rain stood taller and thrust out her chest. "Immigrants, blacks, gays." Rain ticked them off on her fingers as she spoke. "Transgender. Muslims. Anyone that's different than you."

Ivy's face fell, and her eyes glistened. For a moment, Rain felt sorry for her, until she bent and picked up one of the signs from the ground. "And what do you call this?"

Rain's eyes widened when she read the sign. *Jesus sucks! Harsh.* She hadn't paid any attention to the signs, and she'd certainly not written it. Rain snatched at it and grabbed the corner, but Ivy held on.

"No. Tell me," Ivy yelled. "Tell me if you think this is okay. Tell me that this isn't hateful."

Rain tugged harder on the sign, but Ivy seemed to have a death grip on it and wouldn't release it. "It's not my sign." It even sounded ridiculous to her ears.

"Seriously, that's the best you've got?" Ivy pulled harder.

An electric charge filled the atmosphere, and a strong smell of sulfur permeated the surroundings. It was as if all the air had been sucked out of the area, and Rain gasped for breath.

Something is wrong. Just as she thought it, she realized that the sounds of the rally were gone as if they were in a vacuum.

An older woman with long gray hair and eyes that nearly matched the color of her hair stepped toward them. She pointed her index finger at Rain, and then turned it on Ivy. "Love. Hate. Hate. Love."

When Rain glanced at Ivy, she stood with her mouth open, an expression Rain suspected matched her own.

The older woman grasped the sign, and Rain's hand involuntarily opened, releasing the sign. Ivy let go, as well, and the woman held it over her head. "Love or hate. Hate or love," she chanted over and over.

A loud thunderclap reverberated between the buildings as she ripped the sign in half and threw it to the ground.

The older woman locked gazes with Rain. "Will you choose love or hate?" Then she turned to Ivy and repeated the words.

Rain gasped for breath as a light misty smoke filled the air around them. She blinked once and then a second time.

The gray-haired woman was gone.

Rain and Ivy stared at each other for a beat. "What the fuck was that?" Rain asked.

Ivy's eyes widened, and then she turned and ran off.

Chapter Six

Ivy's sandals slapped against the wet pavement as the water sloshed onto her bare toes. *Brr.* It was cold. All she wanted was to get home and take a hot shower.

What a horrible day. As if the rally wasn't bad enough, they'd gotten caught in a deluge. Pastor Devlin was in the middle of debriefing them when the clouds rolled in, seemingly from nowhere. The blue skies turned gray in a matter of minutes, right after the strange encounter with the gray-haired, gray-eyed woman.

There'd been no forecast for rain, so no one had carried an umbrella. She'd scrambled to the bus, but by the time she was able to board, she was soaked through. Luckily, she had on a jacket, or her white dress would have shown more of herself than she'd want Mr. Haskins to see.

Now, running through the parking lot, she feared her coat wasn't long enough to cover her backside, which Mr. Haskins likely watched from outside the bus. He'd asked to walk her to her car, but she'd said no and ran. What had gotten into her?

Ever since the weird encounter, she'd felt unsettled. It was as if the electric charge had permeated her skin and coursed through her body. Nearly two hours later, her arms felt as if worms were crawling just under the surface.

As Ivy fumbled with her keys, she muttered at the driving rain. Her key fob had stopped working years ago, so now she had to open the door the old-fashioned way. After three attempts, she was finally successful in shoving the key into the keyhole.

She ripped open the door and practically dove into her car. The rain, which had turned to sleet, bounced off Red's hood. Her keys fell to the floor and bounced under the seat.

Damn it. As much as she loved Red, it was times like these that made her wish for a car with a push-button starter. Maybe someday. She fumbled around under her seat and came up with three French fries, several straw wrappers, an old grocery list, and fifteen cents, before her fingers brushed against her keys that were much farther under the seat than she expected.

Once she got Red started, she cranked up the heater. The cold air blasted her in the face and nearly took her breath away. She dialed the heater to defrost, relieved to have the gust hitting the windshield instead of her.

The events of the day played over in her mind as she pulled from the parking lot. The bus ride home was a blur. All she could remember was Mr. Haskins' droning voice. That and how he kept patting her on the leg as he talked. It creeped her out.

It likely would have bothered her worse if her mind wasn't fixated on the infuriating dark-haired woman with the piercing blue eyes and extra-long eyelashes. *Odd.* It was as if the woman's face was embossed in her brain. Whatever the old woman had done, it left Ivy unnerved. She forced the images from her mind, replacing them with thoughts of the steaming shower she'd soon enjoy.

The rain tapered to a light drizzle as she got closer to home. When she turned into the driveway, the rapidly moving clouds parted and allowed the sun to peek through. It was probably her imagination, but it already seemed warmer.

Her mother stood on the front porch, holding an oversized pot. Mama lifted her hand to wave but pulled her hand back and clutched the pot to her chest. Ivy stopped in Granny's driveway.

"Whatcha got?" Ivy asked when she stepped from the car.

"I'm so glad you're home." Mama smiled and held up the pot with two hands. "I was just about to take this to your brother. Max Jr. is sick, and Didi had to work a double, so Max is in charge of taking care of him."

"Homemade chicken soup?" Ivy asked.

"Cures everything." Mama smiled. "Oh, and Violet needs a ride to her friend's house. They're going to the movies tonight."

Ivy's shoulders sagged, and she glanced down at her still damp dress. "Where's Papa?"

"That's right." Mama snapped her fingers. "Since Max can't come out with the little one sick, Papa was hoping you could help him in the barn."

Ivy held back a sigh. She didn't want Mama to pick up her agitation. "Um, okay. I need to change out of these wet clothes, though."

Mama's eyes narrowed, and she studied Ivy. "Sweetie, what happened to you? Your pretty hair looks like you got caught in a tornado."

"Close." Ivy put on a smile. "It downpoured at the rally. I'm still not dried out."

"Oh, dear, you need to get out of those wet

clothes." She held up the pot. "I can take this back inside until you've changed."

"Thanks, Mama." Ivy turned toward Granny's house.

"Funny, but we didn't get a lick of rain here," Mama said.

❧ ❧ ❧ ❧

The throbbing bass filled Rain's car as she sped down Interstate 290. Maybe with enough speed and music she could erase the afternoon from her mind. *Not working.* She cranked the stereo dial farther. The sound so intense that her hair vibrated.

Even though she knew it wasn't good for her hearing, she didn't care. She just wanted to stop thinking about those amber eyes and that crazy old lady. Since the *incident,* as she'd decided to call it, her insides were jumbled. Her hand gripping the steering wheel had a visible tremor. If she could crawl out of her skin, she would.

Ivy. That had been the woman's name. Why had she become so angry at Rain? At first, Ivy had defended Rain from her Cro-Magnon boyfriend, or whoever the guy was, but then she'd turned on Rain.

If that wasn't enough, one of Nina's friends, an organizer of the event, had given Rain a dressing-down for not being well versed on the issue. *Fuck her.* Rain had at least shown up, hadn't she? Arrogant was the only word Rain could use to describe Nina's friend. What kind of moron chases away an ally? Rain would likely think long and hard before she attended another rally for the cause.

She shot around a semi-truck to pass just as

another car came from the outer lane into the center. The car forced her to slam on her brakes and skid back in behind the truck. Rain swiped at the stereo volume. The music was making it hard for her to concentrate on her driving, but it still hadn't erased the blonde from her thoughts. Her headache pounded worse than the bass, so she turned the music off. The exit for Oak Brook was next, so she'd be home soon. She'd thought about going out tonight, but all she wanted to do was take a shower, climb into bed, and binge-watch Netflix.

❧❧❧❧

After Rain had showered and unsuccessfully browsed through hundreds of movies that weren't calling to her, she grabbed her cellphone. The events of the day still played in her mind, and she swore she could feel the electric pulse surging up her arm. She needed to talk to someone. But who?

She scrolled through her contacts. *Pathetic.* Hundreds of names, but only one person she knew would shoot straight with her. *Tracie Bennett.* When Rain was in college, they'd met at a LGBTQ+ event. Tracie was the keynote speaker, and Rain had approached her after her presentation. They'd spent nearly two hours talking until the building manager kicked them out so he could lock up. Even though Tracie was nearly thirty years Rain's senior, they'd hit it off, and Tracie became her mentor. The one person she knew she could count on.

Rain poked the call button.

"Hello." Rain had expected to hear Tracie's

raspy voice, but instead, a pleasant voice had greeted her. *Jeannie Bennett*, Tracie's wife.

"Jeannie. How are you?"

"Rain. I wanted to congratulate you again."

"Congratulate me?"

"Being asked to be on the board of SWAN. What a prestigious honor. We are so proud of you."

"Thanks." Rain's face warmed. Jeannie was right that being a member of Stand with the Alphabet Nation was the biggest honor she'd ever received, and it still hadn't entirely sunk in. "But I think the text, the card, and the flowers were congratulations enough."

Jeannie chuckled. "We wanted to make sure you knew how proud we were."

A loud bang sounded followed by a string of curse words. "Rain...um...hold on."

Rain smiled as she heard a commotion in the background. What was Tracie up to?

"Rain. Hi. Sorry," Jeannie said. "Grumpy is under the sink, trying to fix a leak."

"By the sounds of it, you might need to call a plumber."

Jeannie chuckled. Rain loved her laugh. It was easy and contagious. While Tracie was gruff and rough around the edges, Jeannie was the kindest and most gracious woman she'd ever met. "I mentioned that over half an hour ago, but someone is rather stubborn."

"Goddamn it. Did that little twerp say I needed a plumber?" Tracie's loud voice carried through the phone line.

"Hmm," Rain said. "She sounds subdued today. Only called me a twerp instead of an asshole. She's going soft."

Jeannie laughed again.

"What did that little asshole say now?" Tracie called out.

"Better?" Jeannie asked.

Rain laughed, already feeling more settled hearing their banter. It had been a while since she'd seen them. They'd moved just outside of Madison, Wisconsin, several years ago when Tracie had been offered her dream job. Rain hated that she couldn't just drop in on them like she once did. "Good to know she's not going soft."

"You know she's a marshmallow," Jeannie pretended to whisper, but Rain was sure it was loud enough for Tracie to hear. Her suspicions were confirmed when Tracie mumbled in the background.

"Tell the little shit I'll be with her in a minute. I need to wash up," Tracie called.

"Did you hear that?" Jeannie asked.

"Loud and clear. She's giving up?"

"Are you calling it quits?" Jeannie asked.

"Hell no. Just taking a break to talk to Rain. Then I'll tame that bastard. That pipe will never defeat me. Just you wait and see."

"Is it possible she's getting grumpier?" Rain asked.

"Um..." Rain heard a door close before Jeannie continued. "She's been having a little bit of a rough patch. Something at the conference she went to last week, but she keeps telling me she's still processing it."

"Any clue what happened?" Rain tried to keep the surprise from her voice. Tracie was one of the strongest women she'd ever known. She'd gallantly fought so many battles for equality that Rain didn't think anything could derail her.

"I think some of her...oh, honey, are you ready to talk to Rain now?" Jeannie said. Obviously, Tracie had returned, and Rain wouldn't get the rest of Jeannie's story. "She's all cleaned up. Here she is. Love you."

"You too," Rain said.

"Aww, how sweet, you love me," Tracie said, her raspy voice a complete contrast to Jeannie's melodic tone. "So whatcha need, kid?"

Rain smiled. Leave it to Tracie to cut right to the chase. "I wanted to talk to you about a weird experience I had earlier."

"How many times do I have to tell you that I don't want to hear about your sex life?"

Rain chuckled. "Well then, I guess I'll have to let you go. I thought you could give me advice on the best way to maximize the use of my nipple ring during sex."

Tracie's deep laugh was music to Rain's ears. "Ya take it out. Nipples aren't supposed to have extra holes in them."

"What in god's name are you two talking about?" Jeannie said.

"Just giving Rain a little sex ed."

"A conversation I don't want to hear," Jeannie said. "I'm going to go back to reading *Backwards to Oregon*. I was hoping to finish it before you decided to play plumber."

"Don't get too comfortable," Tracie said. "Round two after I'm done talking with Rain."

"Rain," Jeannie called out. "Please, for me, keep her on the phone for a while."

Tracie chuckled. "God, I love that woman."

Rain's heart filled. One day, she wanted what they had. They'd been together since they were twenty-two, forty-two years. Ten years longer than Rain had been alive. "You're lucky she puts up with you."

"She's one lucky woman." Tracie chuckled. "So what's the matter?"

"I dunno."

"Glad you cleared that up. Like me to guess? Woman or should I say women?"

"I guess there was a woman involved. Two actually."

"Whoa. I told you. None of your kinky stuff."

"Very funny." Rain smiled. "I was at a rally today, and the weirdest thing happened. I haven't felt right since."

"Hold on. Let me grab a beer. Something tells me this is going to be interesting."

After nearly fifteen minutes of relaying her story, Rain said, "And that's what happened. I still feel the electric charge under my skin. It's like caterpillars are crawling through my veins."

"Stop. You're making my arms itch," Tracie said. "Sounds like the little hottie got to you."

"Now you stop." Rain wrinkled her nose. "She's the enemy." Rain refrained from mentioning her amber eyes or how sexy that damned flower print dress was. She shook her head. Country bumpkin. A right-wing hayseed wasn't her thing.

"You talked about electricity. Sounds like attraction to me."

"No." Rain shook her head violently, even though Tracie couldn't see her. "It was different than that. Literally, there was a sulfur smell, and shortly afterward, the sky opened up."

"Lightning strike nearby?"

"Hmm, maybe. I hadn't thought of that. Could a

weather event make me feel so disoriented?"

"Possibly, but I ain't a scientist. Stranger things have happened, though. What was this rally for, again?"

"School vouchers."

"And what side were you on?"

"Seriously?"

Tracie chuckled. "Just screwing with you. How many causes are you involved in?"

"A few." Rain grabbed her calendar off the end table. One of the things she was still old school about. Even though she kept an electronic calendar, she always had her paper backup. Irrational fear of an apocalypse, she supposed. Which made it more irrational since she wouldn't need her schedule then.

"A few? Meaning five or fifty?"

Shit. Tracie knew her too well. Rain scanned the page that showed at least one event most days; some had two or three. "There are so many important causes. People need to be more committed."

"You can't be committed to everything, but God knows you try."

"I do." This was a conversation they'd had often. Rain championed every cause she could, while Tracie focused her passion on a couple. "Somebody has to save us from the devils on the right."

Tracie sighed.

"Can we skip the lecture?" Rain said. "And get to the part where you tell me to pull my head out of my ass?"

Tracie laughed. "At least you're listening."

"Somebody needs to fight the enemy."

"The enemy isn't always who you think it is."

"What the hell is that supposed to mean?" Rain

tried to keep the bite out of her voice but feared she'd failed.

"You're so sure that everything you believe is right, and everything the other side believes is wrong."

"Damned right. What happened to the woman I met fifteen years ago, fighting the good fight?"

"Fuck you, Rain."

Shit. She'd hit a nerve. Tracie never talked to her like that. Jeannie's earlier words rattled in her head. "Whoa. I thought we were having a friendly debate. Who pissed in your Cheerios?" Rain hoped that using one of Tracie's favorite sayings would lessen the tension.

Tracie let out a half-hearted chuckle. "Been doing lots of thinking lately. We're losing the battle. I see people like you marching for all these causes. Yelling loud and proud. Can you tell me what you're marching for? Or more accurately, can you tell me what the other side's position is? Really tell me, not some convoluted sound bites?"

Rain bristled. *Sure.* She knew what she was marching for, didn't she? She didn't want to think about it, so she switched her focus back on Tracie. "Why so angry?"

"I'm sick of seeing all the progress we've made go up in smoke because the radicals on both sides are having a pissing match. Have you been watching the news?"

"Of course I have." Now Tracie was just trying to bait her. "Why do you think I attend so many rallies?"

"No!" Tracie's loud voice caused Rain to flinch. "Not just the news that supports your side of things. Do you read about the entire issue?"

"Why do I want to know what those idiots are

saying? They're trying to destroy our country."

"And that's exactly what they say about us."
Tracie sighed. "And in the meantime, we backslide
and lose more and more rights. It makes me sick."

"Come on. You can't agree with the things those
morons say."

"And that's what political discourse has come
to. Half-informed people calling each other names,
and taking a stand, whether they know what the fuck
they're talking about or not."

"Now I'm an uninformed halfwit?"

"You said it. I didn't." There was no denying
the defensiveness in Tracie's tone. "All the progress
we've made is being eroded. We're pushing away good
people in droves when we should be changing hearts
and minds one person at a time."

"And how do you propose I do that?" Rain
wanted to hang up the phone. This shit day just kept
getting shittier.

"Stop yelling down anyone that has a different
opinion than you. Did you ever think that's what
the lesson of the day was? Maybe instead of fighting
with the cutie in the flower dress, sit down and have
a conversation with her. Find out why she feels the
way she does. Maybe then you can bring about real
change."

"Are you for real?" Rain hated fighting with
Tracie and hated even more that she was losing
respect for her. "What's happened to you? Ever since
you moved to Wisconsin, you've been different."

There was silence on the other end of the phone
for several seconds before Tracie said, "Maybe I am."
She let out a snort. "Maybe I've been exposed to a
different kind of diversity."

Now Rain knew she should have stayed in bed this morning. Nothing good could come from answering, but Rain couldn't let it go. "Really?" She didn't even try to hide the sarcasm. "So you're in a bastion of diversity with all the racist, homophobic, rednecks you run with?"

"Listen to yourself. You preach tolerance and acceptance, but here you are making assumptions about people you don't know. How is that any different than the way lesbians have been judged all these years?"

When had Tracie become so ignorant? "Us queer folx have been putting up with their judgment forever, so don't even try and compare the two."

"That's right. Your generation has had it the *worst*. You came of age, what, early 2000? Try being a lesbian in the seventies, and then come back and tell me how hard you had it."

The venom in Tracie's voice caused Rain to flinch. Where was all the anger coming from? *Damn it.* Tracie had always been the constant in her life. Truth be told, she relied on Tracie more than she ever did her parents, and the thought of alienating Tracie left her cold. "We've just both had a bad day," Rain said, trying to save the situation.

"I'm not letting you off that easy. You just called some of my friends racists and homophobes. They've welcomed us with open arms, and they watch out for us. Only a couple assholes have ever made us feel unwelcome, but the others put them in their place. Word in the neighborhood is not to mess with the girls."

"The girls. Really?" Rain's stomach roiled. "Do you know how condescending that is? You're in your sixties. Don't let them talk to you like that."

"And that's the crux of our problem. I'm not shaming good people because they might not have the *right* language. Best way to have them turn against us, which is what I see happening now. Treated right, they become our allies, but treated wrong, they become our foes. Think about that, Rain. Everyone doesn't have to be *woke* to be a good person."

Ugh. Tracie did not just say the word *woke* in a condescending manner, did she? "Maybe you need to turn off the news...um, I mean...the entertainment channel I won't name." Rain knew she was being snarky, but Tracie's woke comment had pushed all her buttons.

"I can see this conversation is going nowhere." Tracie's voice came out low, almost sad. "I have a pipe to fix."

"Yeah. I should let you go." A vise grip squeezed her chest. Rain loved Tracie, but lately, they were drifting apart ideologically, and she hated it. "Tell Jeannie goodbye for me."

"Will do."

No! Rain wanted to scream. Tracie was her anchor. Her north star. Without her influence, Rain wasn't sure where she'd be. The room around her suddenly seemed darker. "Tracie?"

"Yeah, kid?"

Good sign. Tracie called her kid, obviously trying to lighten the moment. "You know I rely on you more than anyone in my life, but sometimes, I worry when you talk like this."

"And sometimes, I worry when you talk like you do. The world isn't just black and white. Good and bad. There's positive and negative in each of us. We can't just throw out people because they don't think like we do. Hive mind isn't a good thing."

"But what about all the divisiveness? Now more than ever, we need to stick together."

Tracie snorted. "Hate's coming from both sides. I lived through more hate than I hope you'll ever experience in your lifetime. But I can't stomach it from our side, either. Sometimes, I worry you're willing to give a pass to the people you agree with, even when they're being hateful. I can't abide that."

An image of Ivy flashed in Rain's mind. The tug-of-war over the *Jesus sucks* sign played in a loop. She needed to end the conversation. "Points to ponder."

"That it is." Tracie sounded tired. "Duty calls. It was nice hearing from you. Let me know if you have any other weird repercussions from the lightning strike or whatever the hell it was."

Rain smiled. Maybe that was it. Whatever happened today had put her so on edge that she was missing Tracie's point. Her chest loosened. That was what she'd choose to believe. What she had to believe. "Don't be too stubborn to call a plumber."

Tracie grunted.

Feeling on safer ground, Rain smiled. "You better not bust a pipe, or Jeannie will have your ass."

"Hmm, maybe I should go ahead and bust one then."

"Eww, stop it. I will have that image in my head for the rest of the evening." Rain laughed. Her spirits rose when Tracie joined in.

"I'm glad I could leave you on a high note," Tracie said.

"I'd call it a low note," Rain said with a chuckle.

Chapter Seven

Rain groaned. So much for staying away from Sasha. She glanced over at the sleeping woman in the bed next to her and then glanced toward the window where light streamed in.

Fuck. It was daylight. Not only had she slept with Sasha, but she'd spent the night. Just great. So much for not sending the wrong message. Could she sneak away now?

She stared at the ceiling. She wasn't to blame. After the weird experience at the rally and then the conversation with Tracie, she'd had to get out of her house before she went stir crazy. It wasn't like she'd sought out Sasha. Sure, Sasha had said she'd be at the bar, but still there was a chance she might have already left.

Rain hadn't arrived until nearly midnight. She'd tried to ride out her anxiety but finally gave in after starting her fifth movie, only to decide after less than ten minutes that she hated it, just like the others.

To her credit, she'd held out until nearly closing before she'd agreed to go home with Sasha. Now here she was, trying to figure out how to escape her bed, again. Would she ever learn?

"Hey, baby." Sasha trailed her finger up Rain's stomach toward her breasts. "Up for a little morning fun?"

"I shouldn't have stayed." Rain's gaze darted

around the room as if she'd find an escape hatch.

"Well, since you're here." Sasha's finger circled Rain's breast. With each pass, she got closer to the center.

Rain involuntarily shuddered when Sasha's thumb brushed her nipple.

"Um," Sasha purred. "I think someone's awake." Before Rain could respond, Sasha's mouth replaced her finger and engulfed Rain's nipple.

Shit. The sensation went all the way through her. There was no denying that Sasha knew how to use her mouth. Rain should make her escape, but then Sasha flicked her tongue, and she lost all sense of what she should do.

"You were so tense last night," Sasha said.

Rain wanted to press her breast back into Sasha's mouth but resisted. "Uh-huh?" Rain subtly adjusted her body so Sasha could continue to pleasure her.

Sasha ran her hand down Rain's body until she found her wetness. "Apparently, you need a little more help in the relaxation department."

Rain nodded and put her hand on the back of Sasha's head. She refrained from begging her, despite the throbbing between her legs.

"I think I can help you with that." Sasha's fingers lightly stroked Rain.

Rain lay back and closed her eyes. This was exactly what she needed. She'd end it with Sasha next week.

❧❧❧

Ivy opened the oven to check on the breakfast casserole as her mother sliced the fresh bread. Ivy's mouth watered. The last Sunday of the month was her favorite. The entire family would be there for brunch. Of course, she saw her three youngest siblings often since they still lived at home, but it was a treat to see Max and Rose and their families.

She and Mama had gone to the early church service, so they could get everything ready for when the clan arrived. It would be a full house. As the family grew, sometimes everyone couldn't make it, but today, they'd all be here.

"We'll have sixteen," Mama said as she lined the breadbasket with a towel. "One of Violet's friends spent the night."

"Which one?"

Mama shrugged. "Casey? Macy? I can't remember. All their names sound the same."

Ivy laughed. "Don't you think we should know who Violet drags in?"

Mama shot Ivy a look. "I'd hardly call it dragging someone in. The family attends our church, so they have to be okay."

"Maybe if it were our old church," Ivy muttered under her breath.

"Ivy June," Mama snapped. "I heard that. What burr's gotten under your saddle this morning?"

Ivy shrugged. Ever since the rally yesterday, she'd been out of sorts. The weird argument with the handsome woman had left her unsettled. *Handsome.* Where had that come from? The woman's piercing blue eyes were etched in her mind. Probably because of the bizarre phenomenon or whatever it was.

Sewer gas. At least that was what she'd settled on. She'd read somewhere that sewer gas could escape through the manhole covers in the city. Maybe it was farfetched, but the stench and charge in the air had to have been caused by something. The hair on her arms tingled.

"Are you listening to me?" Mama asked.

"Uh, sorry, what?"

"I think I heard the others drive up. Do you want to pull out the casserole?"

Ivy slipped on an oven mitt and looked at the food displayed on the countertop. It was beautiful, but it would soon look like a pack of wolves had descended. She sighed. All their hard work would be undone in a matter of minutes.

"Something smells delicious," Papa said as he pushed into the kitchen. He wore his navy blue Sunday suit. In his early fifties, he could pass for a much younger man. The hair around his temples had just begun to gray in the past couple of years, but he still sported a thick mop of blond hair. If his hairline was receding, she sure couldn't tell.

"We made your favorite casserole, Papa."

He met Ivy's gaze. His eyes held the twinkle she loved, and the crow's feet at the corner of his eyes made him look even more mischievous. With a quick flip of his wrist, he scooped out a tiny piece of casserole and crammed it into his mouth.

"Benjamin James," Mama scolded, but the love dancing in her eyes gave her away. "Do not do that when the little ones are around. You'll teach them bad habits."

Papa hunkered down and rapidly turned his head from side to side. "Coast is clear. I don't see any of them here."

As if on cue, the door swung open, and several members of the Nash family poured into the kitchen.

"Shoo." Mama waved her towel. "All of you. Out." She turned to Ivy. "Except for you." She spun toward Papa, who'd taken a few steps toward the casserole she'd moved away from him. "Don't you think about it."

He lowered his gaze and smirked. "You heard the woman. Let's get washed up, so we can get a taste of this amazing food." He stopped and gave Mama a peck on the cheek.

Ivy smiled. After all these years, her parents still adored each other.

Mama glanced over her shoulder at the retreating clan before she pulled a piece of casserole out of the pan and held it out toward Papa's mouth. He grinned and ducked his head, taking the bite right out of her hand. As he chewed, he said, "I heart you, Joan Nash."

"And I heart you back, Benjamin Nash."

Ivy smiled. The entire family had picked up Violet's childhood obsession. She'd become fixated on the heart emoji and went around telling everyone she hearted them, until it had stuck. Now the entire Nash clan used the term exclusively.

Once Papa left, Mama turned to Ivy. "Thank you. I couldn't take care of this big rambunctious family without you."

Despite her exhaustion, Mama's words put a spring in Ivy's step.

Once they'd gotten the food on the table, they linked hands and bowed their heads. Mama always said the prayer during their Sunday gatherings. As Mama began, Ivy smiled to herself. Somehow, she didn't think Pastor Devlin would approve of a woman having the honor. She wasn't sure why it gave her so much satisfaction, but it did.

❧❧❧❧

Rain moaned and put her hands on the back of Sasha's head. Sasha took her time trailing her kisses down Rain's body. Rain fought the urge to hurry Sasha to the spot that craved her attention.

She should probably stop this. After all, she'd already given Sasha the wrong message by spending the night. Sasha flicked her tongue around Rain's navel and flicked her hardened nipple with her thumb. All rational thought left her mind. She arched her back and could no longer resist wrapping her hand in Sasha's hair.

Sasha stopped and smiled. "Looks like someone woke up horny." She slowly kissed down Rain's body.

"Uh-huh," Rain said between moans. She thrust out her hips toward Sasha's mouth.

"Patience." Sasha chuckled and ran her tongue along Rain's inner thigh.

Rain gripped the bedsheets. The way her body felt, she knew she was in for a toe curler. She closed her eyes and let the sensation of Sasha's warm and skillful tongue work its magic.

After a couple of minutes, Rain hovered on the edge. She wove her fingers in Sasha's hair and applied slightly more pressure, so Sasha would go deeper.

Sasha obliged, and Rain arched her back. "Oh, god, right there," Rain called out.

Sasha's tongue moved faster.

Rain moaned. "Don't stop. That feels so good. Right there. I love it—"

Electricity.

Sulfur.

Chapter Eight

What the hell was that? Ivy's eyes popped open, and she stared up at the ceiling. Where was she? And why was she lying down?

All of a sudden, an intense feeling gripped her, and she involuntarily thrust her hips. *Holy shit.* That felt amazing.

Ivy screamed.

"Jesus," a female voice called out.

Ivy's gaze shifted to the strange woman whose head was buried between her thighs. She screamed again. At the same time, her body continued to throb. No, it was only her clitoris and vagina that pulsated. The feeling of release was intense.

"What the fuck has gotten into you, Rain?" The woman glared at her.

Ivy pushed the woman away and slid to the other side of the bed. *Sulfur.* She breathed in deeply. Definitely sulfur. Where else had she smelled it recently?

She glanced down at her body and screamed again.

"Son of a bitch. The neighbors are going to call the cops," the woman said.

Ivy stared down at her body—her boobs. What happened to them? They'd shrunk. She grabbed them—hard.

"Kinky." The woman smiled. "Squeeze them for

me, babe."

At the woman's words, Ivy dropped her hands in horror. "No!" she shouted, finally getting out something other than a scream.

"Come on." The woman slipped her hand between her own legs. "I'm dripping wet. I need you to finish me off." The naked woman rolled over, wiping her mouth. "That was a gusher. You were riding my tongue so hard."

Ivy leapt from the bed. She needed to get out of here, but where was here? And where were her clothes?

Holy shit. Where did all these muscles come from? She gazed at her stomach. *Six-pack?* She ran her hand over her hard stomach muscles.

"If you keep touching yourself like that, you're gonna make me come." The woman seductively ran her tongue over her lips.

Ivy ran from the room. *Shit!* Where should she go? She opened the first door on her left, and it opened into another bedroom. Next door, closet. She pushed open the last door in the hallway. Bathroom. *Perfect.* She pushed inside, slammed the door, and locked it.

"Rain? What in the fuck is wrong with you?" the woman called from outside the door.

Rain? Why did she keep talking about rain?

❧ ❧ ❧ ❧

Rain gaped at the faces staring back at her from the table. Where the hell was she and who were these people? She silently counted. Fifteen people shouldn't be crammed into a room this small, but they all seemed to be happy and smiling.

"Are you going to serve that pie or what?" an

attractive older gentleman said. He had a glint in his eyes as he winked at her.

Oh, god. She was having the waitressing night-mare again. The one where she couldn't remember anyone's orders. "Um, are you the one that ordered the pie?" she said to the man. She thought it was a good guess since she held a tray full.

"Very funny, Ivy," another man who looked a lot like the older gentlemen said. "Just serve the dessert. We have to leave in a few, and the kids aren't going to be happy if they don't get any pie."

Rain glanced around the table, trying to take it all in. *Family?* Several of them had a distinct resemblance to one another. Something pinged in her mind. She snapped her head around and stared at the man in the suit. His eyes—amber. She'd seen those eyes before. *Wait.* The other guy had called her Ivy.

Thoughts of the rally flooded her mind. The amber-eyed woman's name was Ivy. Did she just have such an intense orgasm that it scrambled her brain? Was that possible? *No.* This had to be a dream. She must have fallen back to sleep after her orgasm.

"Sweetie, are you okay?" An older woman, prob-ably in her early fifties, wearing a peach dress stood from the table and walked toward Rain. "Honey, you're pale. Why don't you sit down and let me serve the pie?"

"I told you she's been running herself ragged," the elderly woman at the head of the table said. "The girl needs a vacation, or she's gonna collapse one of these days."

"Can we just have some pie already?" a teenage boy said.

Chatter began in earnest around the table as

calls for pie grew louder. The sweet-faced woman in the peach dress put her hand on Rain's arm. Normally, Rain didn't like it when strangers touched her, but there was something comforting in the gesture. The woman took the tray. "It's okay, dear." She pointed to the seat next to the older gentleman. "Sit down next to Papa. I've got this."

Papa? She stared at the fair-haired man with slightly leathery skin, likely from time spent outdoors in the sun.

The man stood and put his arm around her shoulders. At first, she stiffened, but something in him exuded a genuine concern, so she let her shoulders relax.

"You're as tense as a cat in a room full of rocking chairs," the man said. "I think Granny's right. We've been leaning on you too much." He brushed a piece of hair from her face.

Hair? Why the hell did she have so much hair? Dreams could be so weird. She flicked at the offending hair, and her fingers entwined in a thick mass. *What the hell?* She grabbed the hair and pulled. *Ouch.* It was connected.

"Wow, she's losing it," one of the teens said. "Can't Ivy have a breakdown after we get our pie?"

"Violet!" The woman in the peach dress glared. "You won't get any pie if you talk about your sister like that."

"Fine." She crossed his arms over her chest. "Sorry, Ivy."

Ugh. She needed to wake up from this dream, but it felt eerily real.

The older gentleman reached out for the tray of pies. "Um, I think maybe you should handle this," he said to the woman. "You're better at these things. I'll make sure everyone gets their dessert."

The woman turned over the tray. She put her hand on Rain's arm. Rain looked down and jumped backward. What in the hell was she wearing? *Oh, my god.* She hadn't worn a dress since she was in the first grade, but here she stood in a sleeveless sundress. Her gaze traveled to the floor. Open-toed white sandals with painted toenails. *Eek.*

Her heart raced. This dream needed to end—*soon.*

"Honey, I think you need to lie down. You look like you've seen a ghost." The kind woman took a step toward her but stopped short from touching her. "You're acting like you want to jump out of your own skin."

Rain nodded several times, not caring that she likely looked like one of those dashboard bobbleheads.

"Why don't you go to your room and rest for a bit?" The woman turned to the man who had begun handing out slices of pie. "Can you scoop one up for Ivy, so she can take it to her room?"

"On it." He studied the last pie that he'd yet to dig into. "I've got the perfect piece." He slid the pie server into the pan.

"Man. I wanted that one. It's the biggest," the teenage boy said and turned up his nose.

"Give him the damned pie. I don't care," Rain snapped. She needed to get out of here.

The older woman's mouth dropped open. "What in the world has gotten into you?"

The man shot a disapproving look at the teenager. The young man sheepishly looked down at the table. "Sorry. Ivy should have that piece," he muttered.

The man held out the plate to her, and she took it. No sense causing any more of a scene.

"You've got your pie now, dear. Go ahead to your room," the woman said.

"My room?" What the hell was this woman talking about?

The elderly woman at the end of the table pushed herself to her feet. "Come on, dear." She took Rain's elbow and looked back over her shoulder. "I'll see you all later. I heart you."

A chorus of *I heart you* answered back.

Rain stared. *Weird.* Who said *I heart you*? She smiled. Now she was sure it was a dream.

᪣᪣᪣᪣

Ivy leaned against the bathroom door as if the lock wasn't enough to keep the woman out. Her sex dream had turned into a stalker dream. She closed her eyes and took a deep breath. Why wasn't she waking up?

"Come on, Rain. Open up." The woman rapped on the door. "So what, you farted when you came. It happens sometimes."

Farted? What was this crude woman talking about? "I did not fart," Ivy said, hoping her indignation came through in her voice.

"Sure you didn't. That's why the entire bedroom smells like sulfur."

Sulfur? That's right. It was the same pungent smell from the rally. "Leave me alone."

"What the fuck? Is this because you finally spent the night? Don't worry, I won't read too much into it. You keep telling me we're just fuck buddies. I got it."

Ivy cringed. *Fuck buddies?* She certainly didn't

do that, especially not with a woman. What kind of dream was this? "I want my clothes."

"Fine," the woman said through the door.

Silence. Good. She needed a few minutes to think.

She pushed herself away from the door and opened her eyes. There was a mirror above the sink, so she turned to it.

Ivy screamed and jumped back from the mirror.

She stared at the woman from the rally. She'd know the woman's face anywhere, but why was it staring back at her? The piercing blue eyes were made more pronounced by the nearly black hair. Ivy touched the square jaw. *Handsome.* Even though she'd never liked that word to describe a woman, it fit in this case.

She leaned in closer. *Nice skin.* It was smooth, without a blemish. She blinked her—their— eyes.

Her knees buckled, and she collapsed to the floor. The cold tiles felt good against her bare skin.

The woman knocked on the door. "I've got your clothes."

"Leave them outside the door." Ivy managed to get to her feet and went to the sink to splash water on her face. She stared at the soft hands. Not a single callous. The cuticles perfect as if they'd been manicured, and the nails were cut short.

"Come on, Rain." The woman's voice was full of irritation. "I'll get you an Uber."

Quietly, she unlocked the door and opened it a few inches. She glanced both ways down the hallway, but it was empty. The clothes lay in a neat pile on the hardwood floor. She snatched them up, slammed the door, and relocked it.

Maybe if she weren't naked, she'd feel less exposed. She began to dress.

Chapter Nine

The elderly woman led Rain from the house. When they stepped outside, Rain took in the area. They seemed to be on a farm. A large red barn with a green tractor out front was about fifty yards from the house. A pile of equipment, much of it covered with rust, sat around outside. The gravel pathway to the barn had numerous potholes. All full of water.

They'd made it halfway down the sidewalk when Rain turned back toward the farmhouse. It was white and two stories, and it had seen its better days. The large wraparound porch tilted a little on one side, and the entire place could use a coat of paint. Several large trees filled the yard providing shade.

"Did you forget something?" the elderly woman asked.

Rain shook her head. "No. Just looking." Rain pointed at a grove of trees not far from the barn. "What are those?"

"You mean the fruit trees?" The woman's eyes narrowed. "You're not feeling well, are you?"

Shit. That was a dumb question. "No. I meant those birds." She hadn't seen any birds, but she hoped the old woman's eyesight was bad enough that she wouldn't question her.

The woman thrust her head out and squinted. "I didn't see 'em."

"Uh, they must have flown off."

"Must have. Come on. Let's get you home."

There were several cars lined up around the property, probably belonging to some of the guests inside. At least, they didn't all live together. The woman turned on a path lined with large bushes. Rain glanced at the plants. She was no expert, but by the looks of them, they might be roses.

A tiny cottage sat on the other side of the shrubs, and an old bright red car sat in the driveway. Was that the car this old woman planned on driving her home in? The woman walked past the car toward the front door.

Rain stopped and stared between the car and the woman. Maybe she needed to get her car keys. When the woman pushed open the front door, she turned back to Rain. "Aren't you coming?"

"Um, I'll wait outside." Rain leaned against the car.

"Ivy June, I don't know what you're playing at, but you need to get your keister inside right this minute."

Keister? What in the hell was a keister? Rain glanced around the yard. The only thing in the yard that looked like something she could take inside was a colorful garden gnome holding a bouquet of sunflowers.

Rain marched over to the gnome and snatched it from the ground. Maybe if she stopped acting so hesitant, they'd stop looking at her like she was an alien that just landed on earth. She strode to the house with the gnome clutched in her arms.

The old woman stared. "Um...you're bringing Sven inside?"

"Yep." Rain nodded with more confidence than she felt.

"Okay." The old woman patted her arm. "If he makes you feel better."

~~~~~

Ivy stared at the driver's license as the Uber driver continued to chatter at her. She'd been wordlessly staring at it for the past ten minutes, willing herself to wake up.

This no longer seemed like a dream, but how could it not be? People couldn't change bodies in real life, could they?

Rain Anne Hargrove. Definitely the woman from the rally. Thirty-two years old, living in Oak Brook. Which meant Ivy was about forty-five minutes from her home in Mullins Creek. The thought brought her comfort. Not that she could show up on her parents' doorstep in this body.

Ivy smiled. Actually, she likely could. Her parents would take her in since they were never one to turn away a stranger in need. How many people had they housed over the years?

Her chest ached. They'd take her in, but would they ever believe she was really their daughter? *Possibly.* She held so many memories from her childhood that eventually they'd have to believe her.

Stop. Now wasn't the time to think like this. She needed to figure out how to find her own body, not concern herself with the prospect of being caught in this one forever.

She gasped and sat up straighter.

"Everything okay?" the driver asked.

"Um, yeah. Sorry." She tried to put on a smile. "Just thinking."

That much was true. Why hadn't she had this thought earlier? If she were in Rain's body, could Rain be in hers?

She didn't have much time to contemplate before the driver pulled up in front of a townhome.

On wobbly legs, she walked up the sidewalk toward the house. She glanced down at the license and then at the building, trying to find Rain's unit.

Did Rain live alone? Likely, since she was in bed with a woman earlier. Ivy shuddered. Not that she had anything against gay people, but it certainly wasn't anything she'd expected to be involved in today. Not that she was really involved.

Ivy's eyes widened. Maybe Rain was married to a man. She glanced down at the license she still held in her hand. *Doubtful.* Not that she wanted to stereotype, but Rain looked like many of the lesbians she'd seen on television.

She shook her head. Mama would yell at her for being so inconsiderate, and she'd deserve it. Guilt washed over Ivy. Rain was likely a lovely woman. The situation had just rattled Ivy so much that she was behaving badly.

Ivy searched Rain's jacket pocket and pulled out a set of keys. Hopefully, one of them would work. After trying three, the lock clicked. *Thank God.* She needed a place to think. Her stomach growled. And something to eat. A wave of sadness washed over her at the thought of food. She was missing Mama's apple pie. *Really?* That was what she was worried about at a time like this?

She entered the house, closed the door, and immediately locked it.

❧❧❧❧

Rain sat at the rickety wooden desk in the corner of the tiny bedroom. She'd pushed several books and notebooks aside to clear a spot for her plate. While she ate, the reality that this wasn't a dream set in.

People didn't switch bodies, though, but they did lose their minds. Was that what was happening to her? The thought terrified her, so she pushed it from her mind.

She considered browsing through the notebooks, but something held her back. She couldn't bring herself to invade Ivy's privacy. There was something about the room that held a presence—an essence of Ivy.

The room was painted a light green. A color Rain would never have picked, but somehow, it worked with the flower print curtains and comforter. The twin bed was pushed against the wall, giving the room a more open feel. As open as such a small space could have. What adult slept in a twin bed nowadays?

The room was sprinkled with framed photos, all the faces in them seemed to be of the people she'd met next door—Ivy's family. Rain stood and circled the room looking at each one. Most of the shots were candid, giving Rain a sense of a family full of joy and laughter.

A twinge of envy hit Rain. Then she scowled. Sure, like Ivy has it so good crammed into a room not much bigger than a closet while she slept on a puny bed. *No thanks.*

Despite not wanting to invade Ivy's privacy,

Rain found her purse and looked inside. She needed information, and that seemed the best way to find it. She discovered that Ivy June Nash was thirty-four and lived in Mullins Creek.

Then Rain found Ivy's phone. She pressed her finger against the sensor. Nothing happened. She tried every finger. Nothing. *Fuck.* Another indication she'd lost her mind. Who just had a passcode with no biometrics set up on their phone?

Rain returned to the desk. No sense letting the apple pie go to waste. She put the last bite of apple pie into her mouth and chewed slowly, savoring the flavors. It was possibly the best dessert she'd ever eaten. She glanced down at her—Ivy's—slender body. How did she stay so trim if she ate food like this?

She needed to come up with a solution, but her head pounded. *Crap.* Maybe she'd had an aneurysm and was in the hospital in a coma. That might explain it. They'd put her into a drug-induced coma, causing her to hallucinate.

She sighed and glanced down at her empty plate. A tiny piece of crust that looked to have a hint of apple filling on it sat in the middle. With her index and forefinger, she snagged the treasure and popped it into her mouth.

Her gaze landed on the full-length mirror on the back of the closed door. The mirror beckoned her. As she approached it, her gaze trailed up and down Ivy's body. Rain ran her hands along her sides and enjoyed the curve of Ivy's hips. No doubt, Ivy was an attractive woman.

Rain picked up a brush from the dresser and ran it through Ivy's hair. Grade school was the last time Rain had hair long enough to warrant a brush.

She marveled at how well Ivy's hair had been trained to flow all to one side. So casual yet sophisticated. Weren't farm girls supposed to be in ponytails?

Rain snorted. She'd watched too many movies with the stereotypical innocent farm girl. She looked into Ivy's amber eyes. There was something intimate about it. Was she seeing Ivy's eyes as they were, or did Rain being inside change Ivy's natural expression? The thought made her head pound worse. She couldn't be in Ivy's body.

She needed to lie down. Did someone lie down in a dress? Rain's eyes widened. If she changed clothes, it wouldn't be her fault if she got a glimpse of Ivy's naked body. It was settled. She tried a couple of drawers until she found a pair of shorts and a T-shirt. In one drawer, she'd found nightgowns, but that wouldn't be any better than sleeping in a dress.

Rain's heart raced as she pulled the dress over her head. *Wow.* Ivy's body didn't disappoint. Her breasts were much larger than Rain's. *C or D cup?* There was only one way to find out. Rain unhooked her bra and let it fall to the floor.

Rain swallowed hard. She put her hands under the firm breasts that didn't need any help to stay in place. *Wow.* She jumped up and down several times and watched them bouncing. Guiltily, she glanced around the room. It was wrong to be playing with Ivy's body, especially with all the pictures of Ivy's family staring at her.

She snatched the T-shirt off the dresser and slid it over her head. The shorts were next. She only peeked at Ivy's ass in the mirror for a split second; she counted it as a moral victory. Although, that split second caused her pulse to race.

Now that she had Ivy's body fully covered, maybe she could get some rest. A pleasant surprise greeted her when she lay down. The bed wasn't nearly as uncomfortable as she suspected it would be. Rain pulled the covers all the way over her head and closed her eyes.

Even though exploring Ivy's body felt all too real, it didn't make sense. Hopefully, she'd wake up from her nap and everything would be back to normal. She closed her eyes, willing the mind-numbing headache away.

☙☙❧❧

Ivy had wandered around the sparse house for the past fifteen minutes, trying to get a sense of the occupant. It appeared that Rain hadn't lived here long based on the décor. There were no decorations on the walls and only two framed pictures on the nightstand in the bedroom.

Everything was neat and tidy, but the lack of personal effects made it difficult for Ivy to get a clear picture of who Rain was.

Ivy had brought the two pictures with her to the kitchen. She studied the pictures for clues, while she sat at the island and picked at a peanut butter sandwich. When she'd entered the house, she'd been hungry, but she'd quickly lost her appetite.

It didn't take long to figure out that the people in the photos were the same, but it looked as if they'd been taken at least ten years apart. Ivy smiled at the young Rain.

In the picture, Rain looked like the woman Ivy had spent several minutes staring at in the mirror but with a hint of baby fat on her cheeks. Rain's eyes held a hint of childlike wonder as she stood in the hot air balloon with the two older women.

Did Rain have two moms? Maybe that was why she'd been in bed with that woman. *No.* Ivy was pretty sure that wasn't the way it worked, even though Pastor Devlin claimed it did.

Ivy pulled her gaze from Rain and focused on the two women. One of them was much more masculine. *Butch?* Wasn't that the word people used? Ivy clamped her hand over her mouth. Maybe that was considered rude, and she certainly didn't want to offend Rain.

Ivy slapped herself in the forehead. *Dummy.* It wasn't like Rain was here to know what she was thinking. Ivy jumped up from the barstool. *Oh, no.* What if Rain was still in this body, too? Did she know everything that Ivy thought?

"I'm sorry," Ivy said aloud. "I didn't mean any offense."

Ugh. She was cracking up, having a conversation with someone who wasn't there. Well, her body was, so... *No.* She couldn't wrap herself in that loop again.

Ivy took a calming breath like she'd learned in yoga. She'd loved that class, until Pastor Devlin had said yoga was the devil's exercise put forth by Muslims to indoctrinate Christians. Ivy found his arguments ludicrous but hadn't wanted to upset Mama and Papa, so she'd quit.

Ivy flinched at the sound of music. She cocked her head and listened. It seemed to be coming from the living room. Kelly Clarkson's familiar voice filled the air. *Because of You.* She loved that song, but where was it coming from?

In the living room, the sound came from Rain's

coat. Her cellphone. *Duh.* Why hadn't she thought to look for it sooner?

The song stopped. Should she check? Ivy bit her bottom lip as she thought. Maybe it was Rain. Maybe she'd figured out how to get a hold of her—of herself. *Brilliant.* She could call her own phone and see if Rain answered.

She rushed to the table and snatched the phone. As soon as it was in her hand, Kelly Clarkson's voice sang out again. *Mom* flashed on the screen. Ivy battled herself. What if Rain's mom needed something? She'd never ignore a call from her own mama. Rain's mom would likely be worried if Rain didn't answer.

With her decision made, Ivy answered. "Hello."

"Oh, thank god you answered," a woman's voice said on the other end of the phone. "I wasn't sure if you would since it isn't Saturday."

Why would it matter what day it was? Ivy couldn't ask, so instead she said, "Mom?" She was tentative, choosing to use the name Rain had put into her phone, even if it felt strange rolling off her tongue.

"Rain, I need you to do me a favor."

"Of course."

"Your father left his phone back in the room, and we need Taylor Sidwell's phone number. I don't seem to have it, but Dad said you would."

"Um, let me check." Ivy scrolled through Rain's phone, found the number, and recited it to Rain's mother.

"Thanks," a male voice said.

"Dad?"

He chuckled. "Who else would it be, your mom's lover?"

Ivy tried to laugh but feared it came out as a

nervous giggle. They were going to suspect something if she wasn't careful. She never should have answered the phone.

"Are you still there?" Rain's mom asked.

"Yeah. Sorry. I was just finishing the last bite of my peanut butter sandwich." Ivy didn't like to lie but thought in this case she'd be forgiven.

"Peanut butter?" Rain's dad said. "You hate peanut butter."

Great. Why in the world would Rain have peanut butter in her house if she hated it? Maybe the strange woman liked it. *Or worse.* Maybe someone else lived here and would show up soon. Blood pounded in Ivy's ears.

"Rain?" Rain's mom said.

Maybe she should just hang up the phone and act like it was a dropped call. No, that wouldn't be fair to Rain's parents. "I'm here. Um, there wasn't any other food in the house."

"You should go grocery shopping then," Rain's mom said.

Wow. Ivy's mom would have shown more concern that she didn't have food in the house. "I will. Is there anything else you need?"

"Oh, yeah," Rain's dad said. "Could you send your uncle Harry a birthday card from us? His birthday's next week."

"Sure."

"You're not even going to bitch and moan about it?" Rain's dad asked.

Harsh. Ivy's father would never swear at her like that. She wanted to answer with, *no, sir,* but deduced that would be the wrong thing to say. "Um, I'm just tired today."

"We need to go. Our friends are waiting," Rain's mother said.

Holy cow. That was abrupt, and Rain's parents didn't even ask why she was tired. It was for the best but still didn't seem right. "Okay."

"Talk to you next Saturday," Rain's father said.

"Sounds good. I hea—" Ivy bit her lip. She doubted they used *I heart you*. Thinking quickly, she coughed. "Sorry. Frog in my throat. I love—"

Electrical charge.

Sulfur.

Chapter Ten

U m...we love you, too," Rain's mother said.
"Are you feeling okay?"

Rain's gaze darted around the room. *Home!* She
caught a disgusting whiff of peanut butter mixed with
sulfur. *Yuck.* She pushed the sandwich away.

"Rain?" Her father's deep voice filled the air.

"Um, yeah." Rain needed to think. *Wait.* Had
her mom just said she loved her? What the fuck was
going on? They weren't an emotional family, so it
wasn't how they normally ended a call.

Had she just woken from her dream and fallen
into another, or was this still part of her emotional
breakdown?

"We really need to get back to the Janssens,
and..." Her mother paused and cleared her throat.
"And thanks for taking care of the card for Uncle
Harry."

Shit. What kind of card was she supposed to
send Uncle Harry? "No problem. Do you want to give
me a recap, so I get it right?"

Her father snorted. "Damn it. You need to listen
better. It's his birthday next week."

"Yeah, yeah, that's what I thought. Geesh, I was
just confirming."

She put her hand to her head, relieved to discover
her shaved scalp and not long blond hair. *Good sign.*

On autopilot, Rain ended the conversation and

hurried to her bedroom. She yanked open the door and entered. It was her room not the tiny closet-sized bedroom of Ivy's. She resisted the urge to run and jump on the king-sized bed.

Thank god she was home. She put her hand on the uncluttered surface of her dresser and frowned when she looked to her nightstand. Her pictures were missing. They'd been there since she'd moved in nearly eight years earlier, so where were they now?

With a deep breath, she turned her gaze to the full-length mirror. Relief flooded over her. No more long blond hair, flower dress, or curvy body. Rain stared into her own blue eyes and felt a pang. Was she missing Ivy's amber eyes?

What was happening to her? She let her gaze drop to the rest of her body. The same clothes she'd worn to go out last night. Had she gone to the club? *Shit.* Her last memory before all hell broke loose came flooding back. Sasha's bed. She'd been just about to have an enormous orgasm. Maybe she'd had an aneurysm when she came.

As if on cue, Sasha's ringtone came from Rain's phone. She snatched it off the dresser. *Should I answer?* It might be the only way to find out what happened, or it could make things worse.

"Hello," Rain said, knowing her voice came out hesitantly.

"I'm surprised you answered." Sasha's sarcasm wasn't lost on Rain.

"What's up?" Casual seemed to be the best way to play it.

"Why were you such an asshat? I know you said you didn't want to spend the night, but you sank to a new low even for you."

Shit. Shit. Shit. How could she respond when she didn't know what she'd done? *Silence.* Didn't psychiatrists and cops use that technique to get someone to talk? She clamped her teeth together, fighting the urge to speak.

"Of all the dick moves you've made, this has to be the worst," Sasha said.

It was working, so Rain chewed on her lip and waited for Sasha to say more.

After a couple of beats, Sasha continued. "You left me hanging. What kind of jerk gets off and then doesn't return the favor? You've never pulled that shit before. And screaming like you'd been bit in the ass. Who does that?"

Ah. Okay, she was getting closer to what happened. Silence was working.

"Aren't you going to say anything in your defense?" Sasha's voice rose a few octaves.

The silence stretched on. Sasha had given her enough information to formulate a response, but would an apology just make Sasha angrier?

"Come on, Rain. So you farted."

What? Rain peeled herself away from her thoughts and focused on Sasha.

"I mean, what, did you eat like a dozen hard-boiled eggs or something? There's still a hint of sulfur in my bedroom."

Sulfur? The same disgusting smell from the rally and her kitchen. Was this more evidence it was real? Her thoughts were a jumble. People didn't switch bodies. It was impossible.

Rain wanted to get off the phone, so she could think, but she needed to pacify Sasha first. "I was so embarrassed," Rain said. "It was humiliating," she added for effect.

"Oh, Rain." Sasha's voice softened. "You're not the first person to ever have it happen."

"I know. But you know I don't handle shame well." Hopefully, that would move the conversation along.

"Oh, baby, I'm not trying to shame you. But you might want to go see a doctor if...well, if your farts always smell like that."

"I had an egg salad sandwich for dinner," Rain lied.

❧ ❧ ❧ ❧

Ivy blinked and gazed around the room. *Her room.* She touched her stomach. A little squishy, certainly not fat, but not the rock-hard abs she'd felt earlier.

Pushing back the covers, she swung her legs over the side of the bed. The sun dress she wore earlier had been replaced by a ratty pair of shorts and a T-shirt. Her gaze fell on her dress that lay in a heap on her floor. She never treated her clothes that way. She sprang from the bed and grabbed the dress.

It was wrinkled, so she ran her hand down its length several times to smooth it. With a flick of her wrist, she shook it out. *What time was it?* She glanced back at her tussled bed. *How long had she been asleep?* The last thing she remembered was getting ready to serve pie and then that crazy dream.

She'd almost thought it was real, but apparently, her exhaustion had caught up with her. Obviously, she'd lain down for a nap and had one heck of a dream.

The empty plate on her desk caught her eye.

Only a few crumbs remained, but it was enough for her to conclude it had held a slice. Why had she eaten it in her room?

And why in the hell was Sven sitting on her desk? She walked over to the gnome and picked it up. This kept getting weirder.

Her dream of the woman from the rally Rain had been so vivid. Had it caused her to block out part of her day? She lifted the phone from her desk. *Yep, still Sunday.* It was just a little past one, so she'd not been asleep for too long.

She pushed open her bedroom door and quietly walked down the stairs. Granny usually liked to take a nap on Sunday afternoons, so she didn't want to wake her. The television blared in the living room. Granny needed to get her hearing aids checked.

Ivy peeked her head into the room. A fully reclined Granny slept with her mouth open. Her snore could be heard over the TV. *Impressive.* Ivy tiptoed into the room, snatched the remote from Granny's stomach, and turned down the volume.

Granny bolted to a sitting position. "What's that?"

Oops. She'd not wanted to wake her. Maybe if she turned the volume up, Granny would fall back to sleep. Ivy hit the up arrow.

"What in tarnation are you doing?" Granny yelled over the sound.

"Um, just adjusting the volume." Ivy held up the controller for emphasis.

"Well, turn it down. Can't an old lady sleep around here?"

"Sorry." Arguing would do her no good. Granny would never believe she'd had the television so loud. As Ivy lowered the volume, her ears thanked her.

"What's gotten into you?" Granny said.

Ivy didn't know how to respond. With a sigh, she sat on the couch across from Granny. She had no idea what she'd done or what had happened after she carried the pies into the dining room. "I've just been tired lately." It was the truth.

"That's what I told your mama." Granny slapped her palm against her leg. "I told her we all rely on you too much. You're thirty...um...thirty—"

"Four."

"Yeah, thirty-four. You shouldn't be here taking care of your old granny. You should be out having fun with your friends."

Friends? Did she actually have friends? There were a few aides she worked with at the school she enjoyed and one or two from church who were okay. "They all have young kids, so they don't have much time for get-togethers unless it's a play date for their children."

"If you're always doing for this family, then you'll never have the chance to have your own and fit in with the others."

She waved her hand. "I have everything I need right here. Besides, who'd take care of you if I left?"

Granny scowled. "I'm doing better now. I can take care of myself. Besides, your ma and pa are right next door."

Ivy knew it was true. When she'd divorced nearly seven years ago, the family had made a big deal out of needing her to return to help with Granny. Ivy hadn't been fooled. They were just giving her an out, a reason to come home. "Well then, who would take care of me?"

Granny laughed. "Some handsome young man,

maybe?"

"Stop." Ivy's cheeks warmed. A change of subject was in order, and since Granny loved gossip, she had the perfect topic. "Guess what Mrs. Capri told me yesterday."

"That she's got herpes." Granny gave Ivy an angelic smile.

"Granny! Why would you say something like that?"

"Don't let her holier-than-thou act fool you. Her legs have been opened more times than the doors at Walmart."

"Granny!" Ivy couldn't help but giggle. "You're terrible."

"What did the old biddy tell you?"

Ivy decided not to point out that Granny was old enough to be Mrs. Capri's mother. "John's getting married."

"Your John?"

Ivy scowled. "He's not my John."

Granny nodded and pursed her lips. "I never liked him anyway. He's a putz."

Ivy stifled a giggle. Granny hadn't exactly been subtle about her dislike of John. The rest of the family had hidden it better but not Granny. She claimed that an old lady was allowed to say things that others couldn't. Papa assured Ivy that Granny had been outspoken even when he was a boy, but Ivy would allow Granny her illusion.

"Oh." Granny clapped her hands together. "Speaking of the past, I heard that Nadine Forester is coming back to town. Her mama's got cancer. Real bad, I hear."

Ivy's stomach lurched. She'd not talked to

Rita Potter

Nadine in years. Literally the day they'd graduated from high school, Nadine lit out of Mullins Creek. She'd wanted Ivy to leave with her, but Ivy couldn't possibly leave her family. They'd emailed for a time, but like it happens, their correspondence lessened, until it fell away entirely.

"Are you sure she's coming back?" Ivy asked. "She never liked it here."

"That's what Millie said, and she's rarely wrong when it comes to gossip."

Ivy nodded. "When is she going to be here?"

"Sounds like soon. Word has it she sold her business in New Jersey for an obscene amount of money, so she can stick around as long as she needs."

Ivy's chest tightened. *Ridiculous.* Was she really hurt that Nadine hadn't contacted her, considering what happened the last time she'd seen Nadine. "That's nice that she'll be here for her mother." The sentiment felt odd even to her own ears, but she hoped Granny wouldn't pick it up.

"Want to try again?" Granny narrowed her eyes. "Judy Forester was...is a horrible woman. A beast. Why else would Nadine have rushed out of here no sooner than she'd taken off her cap and gown?"

Ivy picked at her cuticle and averted her gaze from Granny. "She wasn't the nicest woman I've ever known, but we shouldn't speak ill of the sick. Besides, maybe Nadine's decision to return is an indication that her mother's softened some over the years."

Granny snorted. "Sure, honey. Familial guilt is a strong pull. But I think it'll be good for you."

"Me?" Ivy's eyebrows shot up. "What will be good for me?"

"Nadine." A large smile lit Granny's wrinkled

face, making her look years younger. "Don't give me that surprised look. She was always good for you."

Had Granny gone senile? "She always got me in trouble."

"Exactly."

"That's a good thing?"

"Absolutely."

Ivy stared at Granny, who sat with a smug look on her face. She wasn't even sure how to respond. The weekend had been weird enough without the added bombshell of Nadine's return. Now, Granny's behavior confirmed that she'd likely traveled to another dimension. It seemed the only explanation.

"Cat got your tongue?" Granny asked.

"Since when did you start supporting my friendship with Nadine?"

"Since after she left."

"That doesn't even make sense." Ivy crossed her arms over her chest. She just wanted to go back upstairs and take another nap. Better yet, go to bed and wake up in the morning.

"Me and your parents were wrong."

Ivy blinked. Definitely an alternate universe. "About what?"

"Nadine. She brought adventure to your life. Gave you spunk. At the time, we wanted you to be a good girl, but she gave you the courage to push the envelope." Granny shook her head. "I regret it now."

Ivy threw her hands up. "You're not making any sense. What is there to regret?"

"That we disapproved of her. That we didn't support the friendship more."

"You wanted me to be a *bad girl* like Nadine?"

"I do now."

Ivy's eyes widened. "Seriously? Are you feeling okay?"

"I'm fine." Granny waved her hand at Ivy. "I don't want you to always be our good girl anymore. I want to see you live your life. For you, not us."

Tears welled in Ivy's eyes. Did Granny understand more than Ivy realized? Being the oldest of the first batch of kids, she'd always been the responsible one. The one who took care of everyone and everything. She'd forgone college, so she could help on the farm and with the rest of the kids. The only time she'd rebelled was with Nadine's encouragement. "But you're my family."

"We all adore you, dear, but I want more for you than," Granny glanced around the room, "this."

Ivy's breath caught, and the walls closed in on her. She wasn't ready to have this conversation with Granny or anyone for that matter. Her family was enough. All she needed. Ivy stood and put her hand against her chest. "While I appreciate your concern, I don't need Nadine or anyone else to turn me into a bad girl."

Granny grinned. "Whatever you say." She pushed back in her recliner until she was in a prone position. "I'm going to take a little nap before dinner."

"Sleep tight," Ivy said. She wanted to escape the room and the conversation.

"Ivy," Granny called.

Ivy turned.

"Give Nadine a call when she gets back." Granny closed her eyes.

"Sure." *Never.*

Chapter Eleven

Ivy slid on her navy blue slacks and pulled her cream-colored sweater over her head. She hoped her parents wouldn't disapprove. Normally, she wore a dress to church, but tonight, she couldn't bring herself to do so.

She'd felt odd since the rally four days ago. Nothing new had happened. No more crazy or vivid dreams, but still she hadn't felt like herself. She couldn't be sure if it was the dream or Granny's revelation about Nadine that had her more troubled.

For whatever reason, she wanted to hide herself behind her clothing, and tonight, a dress seemed too revealing. She glanced at herself in the mirror, straightened her sweater, and picked a piece of lint off her shoulder. When she turned to leave her room, dread filled her heart. Maybe she could feign being ill. She scolded herself. Even though Devlin's sermons weren't like Pastor Armstrong's, it was still unlike her not to want to go to church. When they'd still had their little church in Mullins Creek, it was her favorite thing to do.

She'd loved Pastor Armstrong's sermons, but the singing was her favorite part. Not only had they sung the hymns she knew by heart, but Pastor Armstrong had encouraged the choir to sing modern Christian music.

The only sound at their new church was the

awful organ music and Pastor Devlin droning on and on. *Stop.* Her parents would be mortified if they knew she was having such thoughts. She was just being silly and hadn't adapted to the change. That must be it. After all, their church was one of the biggest in Illinois, so it had to be good. Didn't it?

※ ※ ※ ※ ※

Rain flopped onto the bed and let her calendar fall to her chest. She still wore her shoes, but she kicked them off, finalizing her decision. When was the last time she'd missed a rally? It had been over five years ago when she'd had the flu so bad that she couldn't stray far from the bathroom. Otherwise, she always found a way to make it no matter how lousy she felt.

She didn't want to let anyone down, but she couldn't find the energy tonight. It had been four days since the *incident*, and she still didn't feel quite like herself. Nothing more had happened after the hallucination, at least that was what she was calling it.

Despite her best efforts to put it out of her mind, she found her thoughts frequently returning to it. The theory she'd settled on was that it had been a shame-based fugue. After all, she'd never had flatulence during a romantic encounter before. While such a radical reaction seemed excessive, emotions could be tricky.

She clasped her calendar against her chest but couldn't bring herself to look at it. What once was her lifeline now felt like an anchor. Nearly every box was full of something, so why did she feel so empty?

Maybe she should just take the rest of the week

off from attending any rallies. The thought made her chuckle. Like that would ever happen. She'd been filling her calendar full for over a decade, so she doubted she'd change now. But tonight, she'd lie in bed and relax. Maybe watch a little television, but first, she'd close her eyes for a few minutes.

⚜⚜⚜⚜

Ivy leaned back against the soft cushioned seat, which should have made her happy, considering the hard uncomfortable pews at their old church, but it only made her feel emptier. She'd trade in the luxurious surroundings for the love that radiated from Pastor Armstrong. She willed herself not to slump like she did at the movie theater, or Mama would elbow her to sit up straight.

Pastor Devlin was in rare form. His amplified voice filled the church as he preached against the evils of the left-wing radical devils. The lighting hit him in such a way to shroud him in a soft glow and give the illusion that he was a much taller man.

Devlin's high-pitched screech pierced her eardrums. *Was it appropriate to bring ear plugs to church?* Somehow, she doubted it. She shifted in her seat, put her hand against her cheek, and pressed her fingers against her ear canal. She tried to do it nonchalantly so Mama wouldn't notice.

Devlin slammed his fist onto the podium. The microphone caught the reverberation and filled the church with what sounded like thunder. Ivy had to hand it to Devlin; his theatrics were impressive.

When she and her family first began attending Autumn Harvest Church, she'd been shocked at the level of anger in Devlin's sermons. Now she'd become mostly desensitized, but tonight, he seemed more extreme. Or maybe she'd still not fully recovered from the bout she'd had on Sunday.

Ivy glanced around the ornate yet modern church. Since the first service she'd attended, the stadium seating made her uneasy. It felt more like a sporting event than worship. It was a far cry from their little church that rarely drew more than a hundred people. She sneaked a glance over her shoulder. There must be well over a thousand people here tonight, probably closer to two.

Most of the faces were strangers, or at least people she'd only seen sitting in these seats. Only about half the people from their old church had come to Autumn Harvest. Tonight, she'd only noticed a handful in the crowd. She often wondered what they thought of Devlin's screeching.

Suddenly, the lights dimmed, and Devlin stopped speaking. Ivy could still hear him breathing into the microphone, but he remained silent otherwise. The lights continued to dim until he was barely visible. He held his hand high and bowed his head. A soft hum issued from the speakers before the lights were completely extinguished.

Without warning, the lights were brought back up, nearly blinding Ivy. She blinked several times to combat the spots dancing in front of her eyes.

"Jesus shall not let these devils win," Devlin practically screamed into the mic, causing Ivy to flinch. Then he launched into a tirade about sexual perversion.

Ivy squirmed in her chair and squeezed her legs together as she listened to him preach. She hoped she didn't look guilty. After her bizarre sexual dream Sunday, she could still feel the explosive orgasm. Warmth climbed up her neck to her cheeks. Church was the last place she should be thinking about these things. Besides, it was only a dream, so it wasn't anything she could control. At least that was what she needed to believe.

Devlin raised both hands toward the sky. "I know Jesus wants us to rid the world of these sexual perverts, these homosexuals, and men who want to become women. They will corrupt our children. They must not be allowed to live among us."

Ivy leaned forward. Did she just hear him right? Was he advocating killing gay people? She shook her head slightly. Obviously, she must have misunderstood.

Then he said, "They must perish."

Ivy leaned over toward Mama. "I thought Jesus taught about love—"

An electric charge filled the air.

Sulfur.

Chapter Twelve

I vy's eyes flew open. *No!* As much as she wanted to get away from Devlin's ranting, she didn't want to be back here at Rain's house. At least she appeared to be alone this time, which was a plus.

When she glanced down, she was relieved to see she was fully dressed. Rain's body was clothed in a pair of khaki chinos with a navy blue polo shirt. Once she got her bearings, she noticed the notebook she clutched to her chest.

Would it be wrong to look at it? If it was a dream, it wouldn't matter, and if this was real, then she had bigger problems than peeking at someone's planner.

Ivy gasped when she turned the notebook over and looked at the page it was opened to. *Holy cow.* Nearly every square in the calendar was chock full of writing. The writing was small and neat, which made the full squares even more impressive. Who does this much stuff?

Her finger played across the page. ASPCA. Trevor Project. Save Our Planet. Planned Parenthood. NAMI. Special Olympics. Doctors without Borders. ACLU. HRC. The list went on and on.

"Who are you, Rain?" Ivy said aloud.

Ivy knew most of the groups listed in Rain's calendar, and it confused her. How could this be the same woman who she'd fought with over an anti-Jesus sign? Ivy went to scratch her head but jerked her hand back when she rubbed against stubble instead of her long hair.

Her gaze returned to the calendar. A wave of self-consciousness hit Ivy. Somehow, it didn't feel right studying Rain's calendar in her personal space. Ivy scooted to the edge of the enormous bed and swung her legs over the side. She'd go into the kitchen. Her stomach rumbled. Did Rain ever eat?

Once she'd prepared herself a peanut butter sandwich, she sat at the kitchen island with Rain's planner and a pen. She stared down at the box for today. *Oh, no.* She glanced at the clock on the microwave and realized she was late for an appointment. Forty-five minutes late.

Her pulse quickened. Maybe she could still get there. She hated not being where she was supposed to be, so she jumped from the barstool in a frantic search for her shoes.

In mid-scurry, she stopped. The realization hit her. Rain was late, not her. Ivy plopped back down onto the bar stool and picked up her sandwich. She pursed her lips and rubbed her chin. According to the time, she was still sitting in church and would be for another half an hour.

Her mind raced. Was it possible that Rain was in her body? *No.* That was a crazy notion. Ivy was at the church, listening to Pastor Devlin. Somehow, she must be having a waking dream. Her breath caught in her throat. Or maybe she was having a psychotic break. Is this what the old saying "being out of your mind" meant?

Possibly, Devlin triggered it with his hate-filled sermon. Ivy snapped her fingers. *Dissociation.* That was it. Wasn't that the term psychiatrists used when stress caused people to escape from their own bodies? She needed to look it up.

She glanced around the kitchen, hoping to find Rain's phone. Something told her Rain was likely someone who kept her phone nearby, so Ivy hurried back into the bedroom. Sure enough, a cellphone sat on the nightstand.

Ivy's hand hesitated a few inches from the phone. Should she? *Really?* She needed to stop being such a rule follower. It wasn't like she was peeking in windows, for goodness sakes. She snatched the phone off the table before she could have second thoughts.

Ivy had never taken the time to set up the biometrics on her phone since she didn't have anything worth hacking anyway, but hopefully, Rain had set up hers. *Oh, no.* That meant Ivy's phone would be useless to Rain. Maybe she should set it up, just in case this was real.

She used her—Rain's—fingerprint to unlock the phone. She'd go straight to Google and look at nothing else. Rain's phone was much bigger than hers, so she fumbled holding it as she typed. D-I-S-S-O-C-I-A-T-I-O-N.

She read the definition aloud. "Disconnection and lack of continuity between thoughts, memories, surroundings, actions, and identity." As she read further, it said the symptoms may go away on their own, or she might need to seek psychiatric help.

Ivy dropped onto the bed and stared at the phone as she went down the rabbit hole of a Google search. *Trauma.* All the articles she read said trauma could bring it on. The rally certainly had been unpleasant, but she wasn't quite sure she could label it traumatic. Although, that weird old lady certainly was creepy.

Ivy sat up straighter and dropped the phone onto the bed. Until now, she'd practically forgotten about the crazy woman who kept chanting at them. She closed her eyes, trying to remember what she'd said.

Another thought popped into her mind. *Duh.* Why hadn't she figured it out sooner? She could use Rain's phone to call herself. Maybe Rain would answer. Her shoulders slumped. *No.* Her butt was in the soft cushy seats of Autumn Harvest Church, and she never took her cellphone into church.

She could still call. Leave herself a message. Let herself know she wasn't crazy.

She swiped Rain's phone and hit the phone icon. She typed in her cellphone number and hit send. After six rings, she heard her own voice, telling her to leave a message after the beep.

Beep.

Ivy took a deep breath, not sure what to say. She stared at the phone in a panic and hit the end call icon.

How absurd. Was she nervous about leaving a message to herself? Sure, she wasn't crazy about calling people and leaving messages, but she was calling herself, for God's sake.

She pushed out a huge burst of air and called again. This time when she heard the beep, she was ready.

"Hi, Ivy. Um, it's me...um, you. I mean, it's me, Ivy. If you're hearing this, I wanted to let you know you're not crazy. Well, you might be, but this is kinda real or something. Oh, shit. Um, sorry, I didn't mean to swear. I'm just not sure whose voice this message will be in. Since I'm using Rain's body, then it probably will be her voice, not yours...um, mine. Uh, you know what I mean. It's...." Ivy glanced at the clock. "It's seven fifty-three, which means you...I should be out of church soon. Well, I guess that's all I wanted to say. Have a good evening. Bye."

Ivy ended the call. Her face burned. That had to be one of the most cringe-worthy messages she'd ever left. *Have a good evening? Bye?* Who says that in a message to herself? *Ugh.* What if Rain was in her body and listened to it? *She'll think I'm an idiot.*

Ivy slowed her breathing. *No.* Rain wouldn't know her phone's password, so the only person who could possibly hear it would be herself. Maybe she should leave Rain a message. Ivy glanced at the phone. She wasn't sure how to leave a voicemail on a phone she was calling from.

She could write Rain a note. Ivy jumped from the bed and went in search of paper.

※※※※※

Rain found herself sitting in a cushy chair, looking at a man standing at a podium. He seemed to be yelling about something.

The lady sitting next to her put her hand on Rain's arm. "What did you eat for dinner?"

Rain's eyes widened as the question sank in, and she noticed the heavy smell of sulfur in the air. Several others seated around her had turned and glared at her before turning their gazes back to the man with the microphone.

Her face reddened. She glanced down at her frilly white sweater before she reached up and touched her long hair. No, it wasn't her face that reddened. It had to be Ivy's.

Where the hell was she? She glanced around the room and quickly ruled out a sporting event, even though the stadium seating gave her that impression. A play? Theater? Her gaze landed on a giant picture of Jesus. She groaned. Church. *Really?*

The lingering stench of sulfur drew her attention. Maybe she'd been right, her flatulence was pushing her into a shame-based fugue. First, she'd farted during sex and now in a group of people.

Dumbass. She hadn't farted in church. She didn't even attend church. Ivy was the one farting this time.

Thunder reverberated off the walls. Rain jumped, and her gaze darted around the room. What the hell was that? The man pounded on the podium again, creating another round of thunder.

Her heartbeat slowed. She needed to calm down, or she was going to jump out of her skin. Ivy's skin. *Hmm.* Maybe that wouldn't be a bad idea.

The word *homosexual* caught her attention. *Great.* She was sitting in church, listening to a preacher talk about queers. Could this week get any worse?

She took a deep breath and tuned into what he was saying.

"We must fight against the perversion that those people, those freaks, are shoving down the throats of our children. Thank Jesus that some of our politicians are fighting back against the evil. In Florida, it is now illegal for the homosexual agenda to be pushed on impressionable children."

Rain scoffed. *Homosexual agenda?* The term always irked her. The only agenda she had was to be left alone by crazies like this guy.

Several voices called out, "Amen."

"And in Texas, they're working to arrest parents

for child abuse when they mutilate children's genitals."

More calls of *amen* rose from the crowd.

"Transgender." As the man said the word, he looked as if he'd just taken a gulp of sour milk. "Ha. Transgender is a lie. God does not make mistakes." He pointed at the crowd. "Who here thinks he knows better than God?"

The crowd shook their heads in unison.

"Exactly," the man yelled. "These people—perverts—think they know better than God, and we must fight them. Defeat them."

Rain looked around in horror. What kind of church was this? She frantically gazed around trying to locate the exit. Could she just stand up and run out? Who'd stop her?

Her hand trembled. Maybe they'd know she was a lesbian. Did they still stone people? *Stop.* Now she was overreacting, although listening to this man, he likely favored stoning.

Rain flinched when a hand grasped her arm. She looked into the kind eyes of the woman sitting next to her. The woman with the pies. Ivy's mother, she deduced.

"Honey, are you all right? You're pale." Then she reached up and put her hand against Rain's forehead and then her cheek.

Rain stiffened but didn't pull back. Was this some kind of weird laying on of hands? Would she start chanting or speaking in tongues? Rain bit her lip and breathed in slowly, trying to calm herself.

Ivy's mother lowered her hand. "You don't have a fever, but you're a bit clammy."

Rain exhaled. She wanted to laugh. Of course, Ivy's mom was checking her temperature. It wasn't a gesture she was used to with her own mother, but Rain was confident it wasn't nefarious.

She needed to figure out her name, instead of thinking of her as Ivy's mom all the time. *No.* This nightmare needed to end. She didn't need to start learning these people's names. Anyone who attended a church like this must be one step from Satan, anyway. *Really?* She didn't believe in God, so why in the world would she invoke Satan? If she didn't get a grip soon, someone would come after her and lock her up. Rightfully so.

Not wanting to alert Ivy's parents that anything was amiss, she decided staying was the only option. She narrowed her focus, and her gaze locked on the preacher at the podium. If she had to sit through this, she might as well get a read on what the enemy was saying.

Ten minutes later, the preacher finished his sermon, and Rain's blood was boiling. She hoped Ivy's mom didn't feel her forehead again because her face was on fire.

No wonder queer kids from ultra-religious families were so messed up. How could anyone feel even slightly good about themselves when they were deluged with such hate-filled messages? Tears welled in Rain's eyes, but she blinked them back. She would not cry, but she would give the idiot a piece of her mind.

Her legs buckled as she rose from her chair. Adrenaline must have been coursing through her body. The tremble in her hand confirmed her theory. On unsteady legs, she pushed her way past the people who were going the opposite direction on the stairs.

Rain glared down at Ivy's slender arms. It would

take Rain some time to get used to this body. Ivy didn't have the same muscle and bulk to push through the crowd as Rain had with her own body. She shrugged. She'd have to make do with what she had. Instead of trying to muscle past, she turned sideways and slid between the oncoming people.

Ivy's mom called out, but Rain ignored her and marched toward the podium.

The preacher held court with several parishioners. Rain stopped in her tracks. The idiot from the rally, what was his name—Hankins? Haskin? —stood in front of the preacher espousing something that he'd likely consider wisdom. He turned before Rain could decide what to do.

"Ivy." He smiled. "Did you come to see me?" He winked, but his gaze never reached hers.

"No," Rain said tersely. "And my eyes are up here, dumbass."

He stammered, but she turned away before he could respond.

꙾꙾꙾꙾

Ivy crumpled the fourth piece of paper and threw it into the garbage can. What should she say to Rain? *Hi. I'm the crazy woman who thinks she's in your body.*

Ivy rolled her eyes. She ran her hand through the stubble on the side of her head. It was becoming a security blanket. She'd caught herself rubbing the short hairs, enjoying the tingling sensation on her fingertips. If she wasn't playing with Rain's hair, she was squeezing her large biceps or running her hand across her rock-hard stomach.

Enough. She needed to focus on the letter she'd been trying to write. Maybe she needed a snack to get her brain working.

❧❧❧❧

The preacher must not have heard her rebuke of Hankins, or whatever his name was, because he smiled and took a step forward. "Are you wanting to talk to me?"

"As a matter of fact, I am." Since Ivy's voice was normally softer, Rain put more oomph behind it, so her words came out in a near yell.

The preacher flinched but quickly regained his shroud of calm. "Apparently, my sermon has you fired up. Good for you." He smiled.

The toothy leer made her skin crawl, so she locked her gaze on him.

"It sure the hell did." She glared. "What kind of bullshit are you shoveling here? Do you know how dangerous your brand of hate—"

The floor shook.

Sulfur.

Chapter Thirteen

I vy blinked twice, hoping to get her bearings. She was no longer eating an apple in Rain's kitchen. *Crap.* She'd never gotten the note written. Obviously, she was still at church, but something was amiss.

Why was she standing by the podium? She and her family never ventured into Pastor Devlin's throng, but here she stood. She scanned the faces of those surrounding her. Everyone looked angry, except for her mother and father, who stared slack-jawed.

Oh, no. What had she done? She must have blacked out or dissociated again. And by the scowl on Devlin's face, she'd said something he didn't like.

"How dare you?" Devlin pointed his finger and thrust it toward her face.

Involuntarily, she flinched but didn't step back. She searched for a response. *How dare she what?* It would probably be inappropriate to ask him to elaborate.

"Pastor Devlin." Mama put her arm around Ivy's shoulder. "I'm not sure what has gotten into Ivy lately. She hasn't been herself." Mama turned to Ivy. "Honey, are you feeling okay?"

"Blasphemous," Devlin shouted, and spittle flew from his mouth. His face reddened. He ignored Mama and stepped toward Ivy. "I will not let a woman talk to me like that."

When he got to within a few feet of Ivy, Devlin raised his hand.

Ivy hadn't realized Papa was there until he stepped in front of her. Papa's broad shoulders blocked her view of Devlin. Judging by the muscles bulging in the back of Papa's neck, he was angry. "I'm not sure what's going on here." Papa's voice was low. "But no man will ever raise his hand to my daughter. And you, a man of God, should be ashamed of yourself. I suggest you take three steps back." When Devlin didn't move, Papa said, "Now!"

Devlin stumbled backward, and Ivy could finally see him past Papa's shoulder. His ruddy face held a mixture of contempt and fear. He glanced around at the parishioners as if they'd come to his aid, but most suddenly became interested in looking at their shoes.

Devlin skirted around behind the podium before he responded. "That girl. That heathen needs to atone for her sins," Devlin shouted into the microphone. Ivy suspected he knew it was still live.

Since most of the attendees had already made for the exit, Devlin's voice ricocheted off the walls.

Papa shook his head and frowned. "A good preacher needs to keep his head no matter what. Your anger concerns me. We'll have a talk with Ivy, and then we'll see you on Sunday." Papa never raised his voice, nor did he take his gaze off Devlin. He turned to Ivy. "I'm not sure what's going on, sweetheart, but I think we best get you home, so we can find out."

Ivy's eyes filled with tears. She wasn't sure what had happened here tonight, but the look of love and concern in Papa's eyes made it clear how much he adored her.

Mama put her hand on Ivy's back, and Papa

held out his elbow for Ivy to take. Ivy finally noticed Violet, who stood off to the side, her eyes wide. *Great.* The last thing she needed was for Violet to witness whatever just went down.

She'd just threaded her arm through Papa's when Mr. Haskins stomped toward them.

Ivy sighed. She just wanted to go home, but from the look of Haskins, he had other plans. Likely, she'd offended him, too, but she didn't know how.

Papa shook his head and began walking. Ivy followed, with Mama and Violet bringing up the rear.

"Wait," Haskins called. "She owes me an apology."

Papa turned. A vein throbbed in his neck. "Ain't nobody gonna be apologizing to you, Haskins. I suggest you back off."

Ivy straightened her back, held her chin up high, and squeezed Papa's arm as they walked up the stairs to the exit.

The ride home in the car was silent. When Ivy had tried to talk, Papa had raised his hand and said, "I think we all need to take some space and think on what happened tonight. There will be plenty of time for talking tomorrow."

Ivy read between the lines. Papa wanted to consult with Mama before he said anything, and, she suspected, he didn't want to talk in front of Violet. In typical Violet fashion, she'd not taken the hint, or maybe she did and simply chose to push the envelope. She'd shot several questions at Ivy, and when Ivy didn't answer, she began a recap of what had happened with Devlin.

Mama had finally had to tell her *enough.* This left Violet hunkered against the car door in a pout, which suited Ivy fine. She wasn't in the mood for Violet's incessant chatter. As much as she wanted to process all that had happened, she found she couldn't do it surrounded by her family. Her stomach churned and hands trembled. Whatever was going on with her had taken a toll.

Ivy shivered. The temperature in the car was frigid, or possibly the chill was coming from inside of her. Her sweater was doing nothing to stave off the cold. When they'd gotten into the car, James's letterman jacket had been crumpled up on the floor at her feet, so she'd folded it and placed it on the seat between her and Violet. She slipped it on, happy to be the benefactor of his forgetfulness.

For what must have been the dozenth time, she glanced at her purse, wanting to grab her cellphone. She longed to check for the message she'd left herself, but it would have to wait until she was alone in her room.

☙ ☙ ❧ ❧

Rain stared at the apple in her hand. This was starting to feel all too real, but she knew it wasn't possible. She believed in science not witchcraft or magic. She stiffened. *Fuck.* What was that book she'd read a few years ago? Something like *Girl on Fire?* Rain shook her head. *No.* That was from the *Hunger Games.*

She grabbed her phone and scrolled through Goodreads. There it was. *Brain on Fire.* Now she was beginning to remember. The woman had a rare form of encephalitis that made her go crazy. Was Rain's brain swollen?

Rain's heart raced. She touched her head, but she doubted she could feel anything on the outside. It wasn't like her skull would expand. Maybe she should go to the hospital. Her palms began to sweat, and she could feel her heart thumping in her chest.

She dropped her phone on the kitchen counter. She couldn't read any more about it, or she'd likely have a heart attack. Sleep was what she needed. *Benadryl.* If she were having an allergic reaction to something that was making her brain swell, then maybe it would help. Plus, it always made her drowsy. It was a win-win.

She dropped her half-eaten apple into the garbage, her appetite gone, and went in search of Benadryl. Things would be better in the morning.

⁂

As soon as Papa pulled the car to a stop, Ivy pushed open the door. She wanted to sprint toward Granny's house and never look back, but instead, she casually stepped out onto the driveway.

"Welp," Papa said. "I reckon I need to go finish working on that tractor. It ain't gonna fix itself."

Ivy shut the car door and edged her way backward. If she just slunk away, would they try to stop her?

"Benjamin, don't stay out in that barn all night," Mama said.

Ivy suspected that was for show since there was no way the two wouldn't want to discuss what happened in church.

"Course not. I'll be in shortly." He started to

walk away but turned. "Good night, Ivy. I heart you."

"I heart you, too, Papa." Tears welled in Ivy's eyes, but she refused to cry. She needed all her senses to figure out what was happening, and falling apart like an emotional wreck wouldn't help her any.

"Come on, Violet," Mama said. "Let's give Ivy some peace and quiet."

Mama's words sent a chill through her. Even though she wanted to be alone, having Mama voice it somehow caused an emptiness to bubble inside her.

"Thanks." Ivy wrapped her arms around Mama and squeezed her tight, hoping Mama would make her feel more grounded—stable.

When Ivy stepped back from Mama's hug, a flash of sadness crossed Mama's eyes. "Nothing worse for a mother than to have her children hurting." Mama patted Ivy's arm. "Why don't you go get some rest? I think this family... I have been asking too much of you lately. It's starting to take its toll."

Ivy's heart broke. She didn't want Mama blaming herself for whatever crackup she was having. "No, Mama. It's just been a long week."

"It's only Wednesday."

"Don't remind me." Ivy tried to put levity in her voice, but she wasn't sure how successful she was.

Normally, she'd rather slam her finger in a car door than make anyone feel bad, especially her family, but the only thing she could focus on was her cellphone. The cellphone that Ivy swore was as heavy as a brick in her purse.

Mama gently swiped a piece of hair off Ivy's face. "You're still my baby girl, even if you were the first born. I'm not sure what's going on with you, but I'm here should you ever want to talk."

Ivy resisted the temptation to fall into Mama's arms again and tell her everything. Until she figured out if she was losing her mind, she didn't want to worry her parents. They had enough to concern them, with the prospect of possibly losing the farm.

"Thank you," Ivy said. "I just need a good night's sleep, and I'll be fine in the morning."

As soon as Ivy entered the cottage, she stuck her head into the living room, said a quick hello to Granny, and promptly made her way upstairs to her room. She tossed her purse onto her bed and snatched her phone out.

She held it in her hand for a couple of beats, almost afraid to see what she might find. Would it be worse if there were no message? Not that it mattered, what would be would be. With a deep breath, she turned on her cellphone.

At the top of the screen, the icon for a missed call and voicemail flashed at her as if it were neon. Had she and Rain actually switched bodies?

Only one way to find out. She punched in her voicemail code. She listened slack-jawed as a voice, not her own, echoed back the words she'd spoken earlier.

Ivy flopped back onto her bed and listened to the message three more times before she set her phone down. Her mind raced. What did it all mean? Did it confirm she wasn't cracking up or just the opposite?

She balled her hands into fists and placed them against her forehead. Maybe if she pushed hard enough, her brain would start working again. Come up with a solution.

She put her hand against her chest and felt her racing heartbeat. Wasn't that what the saying "descending into madness" meant? It could happen at any time or place. Panic would get her nowhere. She needed to take charge of the situation.

With more confidence than she felt, she snatched the phone off the bed and called Rain.

After the third time with no answer, Ivy jabbed the end call icon. Why wasn't Rain answering? Surely, if she was having the same experience as Ivy, she'd want to talk.

Ivy's hands went numb, and she dropped the phone to the bed. If Rain wasn't answering, it could only mean one thing. Ivy was alone in this. She was the only one having the hallucinations.

She flopped back against her pillow. The only answer she had left was sleep. She closed her eyes and blocked out the world.

Chapter Fourteen

Ivy rolled onto her back and stretched. She blinked several times, trying to clear her blurry vision. Her eyes were gritty, so she had trouble focusing.

The events of last night flooded her thoughts. Had she really slept straight through until morning? Judging by the sunlight peeking through her blinds, she had. The last thing she remembered was unsuccessfully reaching out to Rain.

In exasperation, she'd flopped back onto her bed and, like the proverbial phrase, was asleep before her head hit the pillow. It was completely unlike her. Normally, she tossed and turned, unable to shut off her mind, but last night, it was as if a power switch was flipped. Her stress and exhaustion had gotten the best of her, and she'd powered down.

To her surprise, she still lay on top of the covers, not having pulled them back anytime during the night. She'd stayed warm, cocooned in James's letterman jacket. The only part of her that was cold was her hands, so she shoved them into the coat pockets.

Her hand bumped against something hard. She let her fingers play over the smooth surface of the slender box. As she explored it, she deduced it must be about four inches tall.

The distraction allowed her to forget the events of last night, so she absorbed herself in trying to figure out what it was. She rolled it around in her hand for several minutes, but she was no closer to having a guess.

Ivy felt a twinge of guilt as she pulled the box from James's pocket, but her curiosity won out. It looked as she suspected it would after she'd explored it with her hand. The only thing that startled her was how beautiful the wood grain was.

She turned it over several times, enjoying the craftsmanship. While pretty, it still didn't look familiar. She pulled it closer to her face and inspected it. The top looked to have a piece that she could slide back and look inside.

As soon as she did, a distinct odor hit her senses. She breathed in deeply. Was that what she thought it was? It couldn't be, could it? She tilted the box toward her and looked inside.

Her breath caught in her chest. *Marijuana.* That was what this had to be. Nervously, she glanced around the room, sure someone would see her. She looked inside the box again. One side held a small silver pipe, and the other compartment was filled with what she suspected was pot.

Her stomach gurgled. As if the week hadn't been bad enough, now she'd found James's stash. Granted, it was legal in Illinois, but she doubted Mama and Papa would be okay with it.

First their daughter caused a scene in church, and now their son was smoking pot. She groaned. They'd surely blame themselves for being bad parents.

She closed her eyes and willed herself to concentrate. Now, not only did she need to talk with her parents, but she'd also need to have a chat with James. She shoved the box back into his coat pocket. *One problem at a time.*

She glanced at her cellphone that sat on the nightstand. When she reached out, her hand hesitated over the phone. If she thought too much, she'd talk herself out of what she knew she needed to do. Without allowing herself any debate, she snatched it from the table.

It had been years since she'd called off work, but today warranted it.

❧❧❧❧

The Benadryl had kicked Rain's ass, and she'd slept like a log. Possibly, it was overkill taking four. What time was it anyway? She reached for her phone. *Shit.* It wasn't on the nightstand where she had always left it.

Last night flooded back into her mind. She reached up and grabbed her head. What, did she expect it to be swollen like the guy in *Mask?* She needed to get a grip. First things first, she needed to figure out what time it was.

When she stood, the room spun. Encephalitis or too much Benadryl? She walked to the kitchen, and her dizziness subsided. *Fuck.* It was already after eight o'clock. She'd slept for over ten hours, no wonder she felt so fuzzy.

She picked up her cellphone. *Jesus.* Her notifications had blown up last night while she slept. Ever since she'd been nominated to the SWAN board, her social media posts had been getting more traffic. If the trend continued, she'd become a social activist influencer yet. Six missed calls? *What the hell?* Two from Sasha. Three from a number she didn't recognize. Probably someone wanting to give her an extended warranty for her car. And one from Gilda.

Shit. She was late to work. The last thing she wanted to do was listen to Gilda give her shit about it, so she called and forced a message into her assistant's voicemail, letting her know she'd be in late, around lunchtime.

Besides, her morning was relatively light since it was the quarterly grant meeting this afternoon. She'd be sure to make it on time for that. The few appointments she had could be rescheduled.

The thought made her queasy since she wasn't one to shirk her duties. *Seriously.* It wasn't like she came in late all the time.

Her parents would be angry, but they'd have to get over it. Hell, recently, they'd been gone from their precious foundation more than they were there, and she was expected to pick up the slack, so she should be able to cancel a few meetings without feeling guilty.

She snorted. Sure, she could, but her insides didn't seem to agree as her chest tightened. *Ugh.*

༄ༀ༅ༀ

Ivy hung James's coat in her closet and left his stash in the pocket. She'd confront him later, but first, she needed to clean up the mess she'd made last night.

When Ivy left the house, she found Granny sitting on the front porch in her rocker. Steam curled up from the cup of coffee she sipped. A thick wool shawl was haphazardly draped over Granny's shoulders, but she didn't seem to notice that it only adequately covered one side of her body.

Granny chuckled as she watched the squirrels

chase one another around the base of the birdfeeders. She turned to Ivy with a look of concern on her face, "How are you this morning?"

She knew. Ivy doubted that Mama or Papa would have told her, but news traveled fast in a small town like Mullins Creek. "I'm good."

Granny looked her up and down before she spoke. "Um, isn't that the same outfit you wore to church last night?"

Ivy nodded.

"You gonna wear it to work?" Granny's gaze traveled to her rat's nest hair. "Don't you think maybe you should have brushed your hair?"

"I called in." Ivy decided the less said the better.

"I see." Granny narrowed her eyes. "Not feeling well?"

"You could say that."

"Shouldn't you go back to bed then?"

No doubt, Granny was baiting her. One or more of Granny's friends likely called her and told her all about the lurid scene at church. "Maybe, but I need to go talk to Mama and Papa first."

"Care to talk to your old Granny about it?"

She couldn't play dumb any longer, so she might as well get it over with. "What have you heard?" She considered sitting on the porch swing but thought better of it. That would only invite a lengthier conversation.

"Heard you let that moron have it." Granny chuckled.

Ivy's mouth fell open. That certainly wasn't what she'd expected to hear.

Granny laughed again. "You can pick your jaw up off the floor, dear."

"But...but I was rude to a holy man."

"Holy man." Granny snorted. "That man wouldn't know Jesus if he walked into that church wearing a crown of thorns."

"Granny!" What was going on? Ivy's life had been turned upside-down the past few days, and this conversation did nothing to put things back to normal. "You always taught me reverence. What's gotten into you?"

"I taught you that when it came to Pastor Armstrong. It doesn't apply to this buffoon."

Buffoon. Granny just called Devlin a buffoon. Ivy struggled with a response. "But you only went to Autumn Harvest that one time."

"One time was one too many." Granny pointed at a blue jay that swooped down and picked up a whole peanut from the bowl she left in the yard. "First blue jay of the morning. Peanuts won't last long."

Ivy nodded about the bird, but she was still stuck on what Granny had said before. "But you stopped going because of your hip. You said it hurt to sit that long."

"I lied." Granny had a gleam in her eye when she met Ivy's stunned gaze. "Did you really think I could sit on those hard pews all those years, but then those cushy matinée seats would bother me?"

"Knock me over with a feather," Ivy said, using one of Granny's favorite sayings. "Why'd you stop going?"

"It only took me one sermon to know I wouldn't find Jesus in that church." Granny pointed toward her birdfeeder. "Just sitting out here watching all God's critters, I feel closer to Him than anywhere else. When you all go to church, and I say that loosely, I sit out here and talk to Jesus."

It took Ivy a couple of beats to process what Granny told her. "But why didn't you tell me?"

"Wasn't my place." Granny took a sip of her coffee and rocked gently in her chair.

"Did you tell Mama and Papa?"

"Wasn't my place to do that, either."

"But—"

"Everyone has to find their own relationship with God. If you believed you could find God with that charlatan, who was I to tell you any different?"

"But you're always giving us a piece of your mind. I've never known you to be quiet about anything."

"There's a first time for everything." Granny chuckled. "It's a private thing. Everyone must find their own path, whatever it may be. It makes me heartsick every time you all trudge off to that house of disrepute."

Ivy stifled a giggle. "Don't you think house of disrepute might be a bit strong?"

"That's what happens when I've bottled up my opinion for too long. It's gotta come out somehow." Granny took another sip of coffee. "Does this mean you all have finally come to your senses?"

Ivy shrugged. "I'm not sure. Last night was pretty much a blur, but Papa told Devlin we'd be back on Sunday."

"That's a shame." Granny reached up and took Ivy's hand. "Your parents are good people. I think they're closer than you think to making some changes."

Ivy narrowed her eyes. "Have they talked to you about it?"

"Nope. But I watch and listen." Granny winked. "Sometimes, an old woman needs to rest her eyes, but it doesn't mean she's sleeping."

"I knew it." More than once, Ivy suspected that Granny wasn't asleep, but she'd never been able to prove it until now. "What is it you think you've learned during your *cat naps?*"

"That your parents don't always buy what that snake oil salesman is selling."

❧❧❧❧

Rain picked at her salad as she glanced through the stack of proposals. Despite being distractable the last few days, she'd still meticulously pored over the grant applications and could likely summarize all sixty-two of them without referring to her notes. The quarterly grant meeting was too important for her not to do her due diligence.

She thumbed through the requests again. It seemed they got more and more each year as more nonprofits heard about their foundation. A Bridge to the Future had started out funding organizations in Northern Illinois but soon encompassed the entire state. When they'd landed a handful of bigger bequeaths, they'd expanded their reach nationwide. Rain's parents were pushing to go global, but much to their chagrin, the board was being cautious.

A loud rap at the door caused her to jump. She'd know that knock anywhere. "Come in, Gilda," Rain called.

The tiny woman pushed into the room, and her gaze immediately went to the stack of files lined up around Rain. "Are you still poring over those?"

Rain nodded.

"What, you don't have page seventy-five on

proposal number twenty-six memorized yet?" Gilda
let out an easy laugh. "Come on, Rain, you know you
can't fund them all."

Rain tossed the folder she was holding onto the
desk. "It's just so frustrating. There's so much need
out there, and there's never enough money to go
around."

Gilda moved toward Rain and put her hand on
Rain's desk. "Give yourself a break. The last four years,
since your parents dumped all the responsibility on
you, you've nearly tripled the fund."

Gilda was never known to have a filter, so she'd
been vocal about Rain's parents' *excessive* travel
over the past few years. Still, Rain felt she should say
something in their defense. "They're trying to find
new funding sources."

Gilda snorted. "And exactly how much money
have they brought into the foundation? And during
that same time, how much have you brought in?
Without traveling all over Europe."

Rain squirmed in her chair. "It only takes one
to pay off," Rain said the line that she'd stopped
believing. "Besides, they're my parents, so I'd prefer
not having this conversation."

"Fine. But you know you can't single-handedly
end world hunger, don't you?"

"But I can try."

Gilda shook her head and turned toward the
door. "Even if you did, they still wouldn't notice you."

"What?" Rain said.

Gilda turned back with a sad smile. "I said, don't
kill yourself trying. There's more to life than your
job."

Rain narrowed her eyes. They both knew Gilda

was lying, but Rain didn't have the energy to have this conversation. "I'll keep that in mind." She held up a roll of colored stickers and nodded toward the clock. "I've gotta make sure I got the right stickers on the files."

Gilda smiled. "Such a high-tech system."

Rain returned the smile before Gilda exited.

She examined the three piles laid out in front of her. The pile to her left sported green dots and was the smallest. There were only three folders. These were the ones she'd fight to get funded.

She glanced at the pile on the right, which was thicker than usual. The red dots seemed brighter today, as if they were calling her out. Had her mood affected her decisions? Although she hated a poorly written proposal, especially ones that didn't follow the guidelines, she could usually separate the quality of the proposal from the cause, but she'd struggled to do so this time. If the group couldn't even write a decent proposal, how could they successfully tackle a problem? She turned over the files, so she didn't have to look at the dots any longer.

She turned her attention to the center pile with the yellow dots. Maybe she should skim through a few and move them to the green. *No.* She pushed the folders away. Let someone else go to bat for the others.

With a sigh, Rain lay her head on the desk, hoping to clear her mind, but the stressors continued to ding at her. A little focused breathing and mindfulness practice might reset her.

Chapter Fifteen

Ivy caught herself rubbing her chin or straightening her hair whenever anyone came near her on the sidewalk, as if it would hide her from their view. *Ridiculous.* It was nearly as bad as when children covered their own eyes and thought they couldn't be seen. Why did she feel so guilty walking downtown on a workday? It wasn't like she'd ever blown off work before today.

Despite feeling conspicuous, she had a bounce to her step. The conversation with Mama and Papa had lifted her spirits. Until this morning, she hadn't realized how much she detested going to church. It once was the highlight of her week and brought her comfort and joy, but with Devlin, it had become an unpleasant chore. It was good to know that Mama and Papa had experienced some of the same feelings.

While they hadn't made any long-term decisions, somehow knowing her parents didn't buy into his rhetoric was enough. Time would tell what Sunday would bring, but she no longer had a knot in her stomach.

To alleviate her guilt for playing hooky, and because Mama needed the help, she was running errands. She'd picked up Papa's medicine at the drugstore, popped into the grocery store for tomatoes since the ones Mama had on the windowsill had gone bad, and now she planned on treating herself to a sandwich at the deli.

She rounded the corner and smiled. Mr. Hooper had put out the bistro tables in front of the restaurant, so she could eat outside in the sunlight. She froze. If she ate outside, it would be more likely that she'd see someone she knew. She lifted her face to the sun and let the warmth wash over her. It was settled. She'd take her chances and eat outside where she wanted to.

Obviously, she was becoming a rebel. Causing a stir at church and skipping work all within twenty-four hours must mean she was turning into a *bad girl.* The theme song from the old TV show *Cops* ran through her mind. She couldn't help but chuckle at the thought. *Yep. Bad girl. Bad girl.*

Even her sandwich order had been risky, a turkey club with mustard, pepper jack cheese, and jalapeños, and she'd thrown caution to the wind and bought one of The Sandwich Hut's famous brownies.

The people she knew, which was most of them, who passed greeted her with a smile and a word. None of them gasped, clutched their pearls, or passed out seeing her here on a workday.

She'd finished her sandwich and was contemplating whether to eat her brownie or save it for later when a shadow blocked out the sun. She turned to see what caused it, and she came face to face with Nadine Forester.

Nadine's twinkly blue eyes hadn't changed much in the ten years since Ivy had last seen her, except maybe there was a bit more caution. The only thing that had changed drastically was her hair. Her once bright blue mop was back to its original brown, but it couldn't have been more than half an inch long.

Ivy hoped she wasn't as gap-jawed as she thought

she might be. She managed to smile. "Nadine. I heard you were in town. I'm sorry to hear about your mother. I hope she's doing well."

"Seriously?" If it were possible, Nadine's gravelly voice was even huskier. "The first time you see me in what...ten years...you sound like a damned Hallmark greeting card."

"Um...I'm sorry. I...um...I'm not sure what I'm... what you want me to say." Ivy's face burned as she stumbled over her words.

Nadine reached out her hand. "You can start by giving me a hug."

Before Ivy could think about it, she was on her feet and wrapped in Nadine's embrace. She melted against Nadine. She'd almost forgotten how healing a bear hug from Nadine could be. Nadine had at least four inches on Ivy and nearly fifty pounds, and her powerful arms held Ivy tight.

Ivy clung to Nadine. With all that had been going on in her life, it felt good to be holding on to her old anchor. Nadine gave her one last squeeze and let go.

"Are you okay?" Nadine took a step back and studied Ivy's face.

Ivy fought back tears. Nadine had enough on her plate. Dealing with her mom's cancer was much more pressing than Ivy's drama. Ivy nodded. "I'm good. Just a bit overwhelmed to see you."

Nadine's face transformed when she smiled. Ivy always teased her that her smile covered half her face. It took her from looking intimidating to cartoonish in the best possible way.

"Missed me, huh?" Nadine winked.

Ivy considered the loaded question. She'd missed

Nadine horribly when she'd left. Nadine gave her the courage that Ivy sometimes lacked, but she'd also left a huge hole in her life. A hole that Ivy had never really filled.

"I did," Ivy said in a voice barely over a whisper.

Nadine's smile left her, and the twinkle in her eye turned sad. "I'm sorry how things went the last time I was here. I was a jerk."

"No." Ivy shook her head hard enough for her hair to slap her in the face. "I was as much to blame. Probably more so."

Nadine smiled again. "What do you say we agree that both of us could have done better? Bygones?" Nadine held out her hand.

Ivy stared at it. *Bygones?* It was that simple? Of course, it was in Nadine's world, but Ivy wasn't sure it worked that way in hers. She'd been crushed for years, and still today if someone mentioned Nadine, her stomach did flip-flops.

Nadine slowly pulled back her hand and frowned. "I guess you're not ready to forgive me." She nodded. "I understand." She held up the bag she'd been holding. "I suppose I better get these to Mom. She ran out of her last pain pill earlier."

"Oh, god, of course, she needs her medicine." Ivy took a step back. "I don't want to keep you."

Nadine opened her mouth as if to say something but stopped and drew her lips together in a tight line. She studied Ivy for a few beats before she said, "It was nice seeing you again, Ivers."

Ivy's heart clenched at the nickname Nadine had always used for her. Violet had innocently called her that once. The optimal word being once. Ivy had laid into her so hard that Violet would never think of using the name again. She'd felt bad but couldn't bring herself to explain her reason to Violet, who'd never met Nadine. Some things and people were better left in the past.

Nadine took a few more steps back and waved the bag in the air. "Um, okay. Well, you have a good day. Maybe I'll see you around." Nadine bit down hard on her lip and began to turn away.

"No!" Ivy said much louder than she'd intended. When Nadine turned back, Ivy grabbed Nadine in another hug. Tears rolled down her cheeks. "I'm sorry. I'm so sorry."

Nadine hugged her tightly. "It was a fucked-up time," Nadine said, her mouth near Ivy's ear. "Two confused kids."

"We were twenty-three," Ivy said as she let go and stepped back.

"We're from Mullins Creek." Nadine smirked. "It takes us longer to mature."

Ivy laughed, and it felt good. Nadine could always make her laugh regardless of the situation. That was until the last time they'd seen each other. "Truer words have never been spoken."

Nadine glanced down at the pharmacy bag. "I really need to get these to Mom, but I'd like to grab a coffee with you sometime. Maybe talk out what happened. Come to some peace with each other." She looked down at the ground before she continued. "I miss you. You..." Nadine looked up and squared her jaw. "You were the best friend I ever had. And I miss the fuck out of you."

"I certainly miss your eloquence." Ivy smiled.

"So?" Nadine's eyes relayed caution with a hint of hope.

"I'd like to catch up." Did she just say that aloud? Judging by the huge smile that lit Nadine's face, she had.

꙰꙰꙰꙰

Ivy dropped her library books on her desk. One day, she'd learn to only request one or two, instead of the ten she normally got. She'd never get through them all.

Her gaze landed on James's coat, and she sighed. She walked over to it and picked it up. How had he grown so fast? She could still remember helping Mama feed him and change his diaper. Now she had to confront him about marijuana. She hugged the coat against her, and soon found herself slipping into it.

She sat hard on her bed and looked up to the ceiling. "What are you trying to tell me, God? Have I disappointed you?"

She lowered her gaze to her hands that were tightly clenched into fists. It had been nearly a week since that rally, and ever since, her life had gotten complicated. The old woman with the gray hair and eyes flashed across her mind. The moment had been surreal. Had she put a curse on Ivy?

Ivy wasn't superstitious, but she did believe God moved in mysterious ways. From the moment the woman had chanted at them, everything had spiraled out of control, and it wasn't just the weird out-of-body experiences she was having. Her church life was in a shambles, she'd played hooky from work, James was smoking weed, and now Nadine had returned to town and wanted to talk.

She lifted her head again and looked to the

ceiling. "Please, God. Did you send the old woman?
What did her chant mean? Love—"

Static.

Sulfur.

Chapter Sixteen

No. Not again. Ivy gaped at the giant mahogany desk she sat behind. It was nearly the size of a billiards table. She stretched out her arms and snatched the nameplate. It was ostentatious with the first letter of each word larger than the rest. Rain A. Hargrove. She giggled. RAH, how appropriate. Vice president. Rain was only thirty-two. *Impressive.* She'd done well for herself.

So what was it Rain was vice president of? A quick glance around the enormous office told her it must be a Fortune 500 company. The desk alone must have cost more than Ivy's car. A table with six leather executive chairs filled one corner of the room, while the other corner sported matching leather couches.

Modern artwork hung on the walls, except for the wall with a floor-to-ceiling bookshelf. From where she sat, the books looked to be mostly hardbacks, most the size of textbooks. She started to rise from the desk to check out the books when the large painting directly across from the desk caught her eye.

A Bridge to the Future was written in multicolored letters with an artistic rendition of a suspension bridge with sunbeams bursting from it. Ivy dropped back into the chair and studied the picture. *Interesting.* Perhaps this was an architectural firm, a modern one. It would have to be modern since the colorful sign didn't look like the cold precision that she would expect.

A knock on the door pulled her out of her thoughts. *Crap.* Maybe if she stayed really quiet, they'd think no one was here. Being in Rain's house or even with her girlfriend had been challenging, but she certainly wouldn't be able to pull off having conversations about building bridges or skyscrapers.

The knock came louder before the door opened. A harried middle-aged woman entered. "Do you want me to make copies of your spreadsheet for the meeting?"

Ivy glanced down at the desk and saw the colorful spreadsheet. If she gave it to the woman, she might be asked questions about it. "No."

"Uh, okay." The woman gave her a puzzled look.

"I'm trying something different this time." She needed to just shut up and not dig herself in deeper.

The woman gave her a slight smile full of skepticism. "The meeting starts in an hour. You know Jeffrey and Joyce don't like it if anyone's unprepared."

"I was thinking about skipping this one," Ivy said, deciding to test the water.

The woman's eyes widened, and then she laughed. "You almost had me going there for a second. Stop fucking with me and get your files together."

Ivy flinched. Did people in offices talk this way with one another? Apparently so. She needed to show that she could talk the lingo. "Tell Jeffrey and Joyce they can go fuc—" She couldn't do it. "They can go sit on it and spin." Her stomach lurched. Rain's body or not, she couldn't do it.

The woman snorted. "I'll let you tell your parents to sit on it and spin." She shook her head. "Sometimes, I don't know what in the world gets into you."

Her parents? Jeffrey and Joyce were Rain's parents? And they'd be at this meeting? No way could she go now. Surely, they'd figure out that Ivy had stolen Rain's body. Well, not exactly stolen it, but they'd have to know something wasn't right. "Honestly, I'm not feeling the best. I don't think my lunch is sitting well with me."

The woman marched across the office and pointed at the half-eaten salad pushed off to the corner of the desk. "A Greek salad, half-eaten at that, isn't something that should make you ill. Although, I still think you'd do better if you had a burger and fries every now and then like the rest of us."

Ugh. Rain was a health nut on top of it. That would explain her abs. Without thinking, Ivy ran her hand across Rain's muscular stomach. "I'll catch the next meeting," Ivy tried again.

"Cut the shit." The woman frowned down at her. "Let's go."

Ivy narrowed her eyes. "But you said the meeting doesn't start for an hour."

"Aren't you going to help me set up?" The woman glowered.

"Sure. Of course." Ivy reluctantly rose. She'd taken three steps around the desk when she noticed the woman was staring at her. Had she spilled food on her shirt? Ivy glanced down at herself. She wore a dark gray business suit with a white shirt underneath. It had a unisex feel to it. *Sharp. Classy.* She bet Rain... she...looked good in it. "Did I spill on myself?"

"The files." The woman pointed to the desk.

"Oh, yeah, the files." Ivy scurried around the desk and scooped up the pile sitting closest to the chair. The ones with a green dot on them. Her gaze shifted between the other two piles. *Crap.* Did they go, too? She'd already made enough blunders.

"Nice try." The woman laughed. "You can't just bring your favorites."

An answer. Good. She felt on firmer footing, so she picked up the other files and said, "You can't blame me for trying."

⃠⃠⃠⃠

"Fuck. Fuck. FUCK!" Rain said aloud as she looked around the room that was starting to become too familiar.

Not now. Not right before the quarterly meeting. What happened to her body when she went into one of these fugues? Did she run on autopilot, or did Ivy take over her body?

She glanced around the room in horror. Hopefully, it was autopilot. She couldn't imagine the little hayseed in a boardroom. She wandered over to the mirror behind the door and stared at Ivy, or herself as Ivy.

Oh, god. Now she was wearing a letterman jacket. In her thirties? That was just creepy. *James,* the script on the front read. Who was this James? A boyfriend? Was he still in school? That was even creepier, but she doubted someone as attractive as Ivy would have to cruise the local high school for a date. Maybe Rain should write her a note and tell her that adults didn't wear their boyfriend's letterman jacket. She glanced down at her hand, half expecting to find a class ring wrapped in angora.

Ivy's long fingers caused her to do a double take. Oddly, Rain was a sucker for hands, and Ivy could be a hand model. Her long slender fingers sported mid-length fingernails with a French tip. Rain studied Ivy's fingers. While the nails looked good, it was obviously an at-home job not the hundred-dollar manicures that Sasha sported.

She tore her gaze from Ivy's fingers and looked into the mirror. In all the chaos, she'd never taken the time to really look at Ivy, except for the brief time she'd changed out of Ivy's dress. Still, that had been so surreal she could barely remember, but now she could study her. *Damn.* She was good-looking.

Was it creepy to be checking Ivy out when she wasn't aware? Rain shrugged and continued to gaze in the mirror. Ivy's hair was silky. Rain was surprised how thick it was when she ran her hand through it. She'd avoided looking into Ivy's amber eyes. It wasn't as if she needed to, they'd been emblazoned in her mind ever since she'd first seen them at the rally nearly a week ago.

Ivy's face was slightly flushed, as if she'd recently been out in the sun. There was a hint of freckles around the top of her nose. No doubt, Ivy likely turned more than a few heads.

Rain held open the jacket and gazed at Ivy's ample breasts, encased in her tight T-shirt. They were about the same size as Sasha's. Although Rain knew she should resist, she couldn't help herself. Reverently, she cupped Ivy's breasts and lightly squeezed. Firm but with some give. She guiltily dropped her hands to her sides. They felt nothing like the ones Sasha's father's money had purchased for her.

What was wrong with her? All this craziness was getting inside her head and turning her into a pervert. She'd never think about walking up to a woman at a bar and touching her boobs, so on what planet was it okay to touch Ivy's breasts without permission? Did being inside her body count as permission?

"Ugh," Rain said louder than she intended. *Shit.* The last thing she needed was for the entire Nash clan to come stampeding into her room. They would probably come at her swinging Bibles. That wasn't fair. They'd been nothing but sweet to her. Well, they hadn't really been nice to her. It was Ivy, their daughter, they were kind to. She doubted they'd be as nice to a big dyke like her. They would probably throw her out of the house if they saw her touching Ivy's breasts.

It was official. She was cracking up, or the encephalitis was getting worse. She glanced at Ivy's cellphone, knowing it was useless since she didn't know the passcode. *Fuck.*

Rain's unfocused gaze darted around the room. She needed to calm down. The stack of books piled on the tiny desk caught her eye. Books had always been her escape, maybe they would do the trick. Although she doubted it. Ivy likely read Nicholas Sparks or some other cheesy romances.

She pulled out the desk chair and sat. The first book she picked up crinkled. She smiled at the library wrapping. It was her favorite place when she was a kid, but it'd been a long time since she'd been to one. She wondered why she'd stopped. Probably her e-reader.

One by one, she shuffled through the books. *Interesting.* Maybe there was more to Ivy than met the eye. Rain hadn't expected Ivy's choice of reading material. Talk about eclectic. Rain's edginess abated as she sorted the books into piles. Three fiction, two history, one self-help, two spirituality, and two biographies. Nothing in any of the piles was what she expected to find.

Was looking through Ivy's library books as intrusive as touching her boobs? *Nah.* Rain spread the three novels on the desk. Not a romance among them. One dystopian, one espionage, and one suspense thriller. The rest of the books were just as surprising. Both books on spirituality were on Buddhism;

somehow, Rain didn't believe the crazy preacher would approve. Brené Brown's new book was among the selections. One that Rain hadn't had the chance to read yet. The most head-scratching book, though, was *Untamed* by Glennon Doyle. Rain wondered if Ivy had a clue what it was about.

Her heart rate had returned to normal as she looked through the last book. Maybe she should take Ivy's car and go in search of herself, but if it was like before, it wouldn't be that long before she switched back. Besides, it might be dangerous hurtling down that road at seventy in the middle of a switch. She picked up the suspense thriller and stood.

≈≈≈≈

Rain awoke with a start, her heart beating out of her chest. She must have fallen asleep. The book she'd been reading had fallen to the floor since Ivy's bed was so narrow. She'd been dreaming, but she couldn't quite remember what about. How long had she been asleep?

Rain frantically glanced around the room, and her gaze fell on the pile of books on the desk. Her dream came back to her. There had been stacks and stacks of books around her, and each time she picked one up, three more appeared. The piles threatened to collapse on her. That was why she'd awoken with a start.

She took a deep breath. Her insides were vibrating. She'd had one other panic attack in her life, and she feared another one was coming on. The dream must have signified how out of control she felt. How long would she be stuck in this state? She kept ending up in her own body, but what if her mind finally completely snapped and she remained in Ivy's forever? Her hands trembled, so she shoved them in her coat pocket.

Her fingers banged against something solid. She wrapped her hand around a familiar-shaped container. *No way!* Was there more to the country bumpkin than met the eye? She pulled the smooth box out.

Yes. Finally, the universe was smiling on her.

"I'll be damned," Rain said as she pulled out the one-hitter pipe.

Maybe this was a dream. An ask and she shall receive type of thing. As if a woman with gorgeous hands, perfect breasts, and mesmerizing eyes wasn't enough, when she thought she was about to have a full-blown panic attack, the universe handed her pot.

She put the container up to her nose and sniffed. Slightly skunky, not near as smooth as what she normally smoked, but she couldn't be choosy.

She tamped the one hitter into the blend and twirled it around a few times. Her heartbeat had slowed by the time she found a lighter in the other pocket. With a flick of her thumb, the flame shot out, and she held it to the pipe. Assuming by the smell that this weed wouldn't be as potent as what she was used to, she took a huge hit.

It was harsh and almost caused her to cough, but she forced herself to hold it in despite the burn. *One. Two. Three. Four. Five.* She couldn't keep it in any longer. She blew out a stream of smoke.

Crap. Did Ivy normally smoke in her room? Rain hurried to the window and threw it open while she tried to wave the smoke out.

One more hit would help calm her nerves, Rain thought and brought the pipe to her lips.

❧❧❧❧

The beginning of the meeting had been a bit dicey when Ivy had nearly mistaken an older couple for Rain's parents. Luckily, someone had called the woman Clare right as Ivy was about to call her mom. She'd finally met Rain's parents when they materialized on the large screen through Zoom. They were in Europe, so they couldn't be there in person. It settled her a bit, knowing they couldn't interact with her one on one.

As more people filed in and every chair at the table had been filled, Ivy formulated a game plan. With nearly twenty people in attendance, she'd try to lay low and say as little as possible.

They were over an hour into the meeting, and she had started to enjoy herself. It hadn't taken long for her to discover that A Bridge to the Future wasn't an architectural firm but a foundation that funded various nonprofit projects. She'd become absorbed in her work—Rain's work.

The proposals were fascinating, and she pored over the files. She only wished she'd had more than an hour to read them beforehand. She was doing the best she could to get a handle on what the projects were about.

Even though she'd started out quiet, after getting several looks from those gathered around the table, she'd begun to participate more. Soon she forgot she didn't belong here.

The red-faced man across the table slammed his fist on the file in front of him. He'd made her uncomfortable much of the meeting because he was so loud and opinionated. The latest proposal had him fired up. "I can't even believe we accepted this application. We should have thrown it right back in their faces."

Ivy glanced down at the file folder with the red dot. She'd skimmed it again, hoping to figure out what had the man so stirred up, but she'd come up empty. "Maybe I'm missing something, but I don't see what's so wrong with this."

Several people's heads whipped around, and they stared at her. Obviously, she'd said something wrong. "Um, sorry. I...um...I obviously missed something." She held up the file and pointed to the red dot. She'd begun to sense they were Rain's color coding. "Of course, I had a red dot on it." The others around the table nodded. She was on the right track. "I was just playing devil's advocate."

"Damn you, Rain." The red-faced man laughed. "I thought you'd been body snatched there for a second."

Ivy tried to hide the surprised look on her face but faked a laugh instead.

From the big screen, Rain's father said, "Good one, Rain. You had me going, too. I've been surprised by some of the projects you've gotten behind today, but if you'd been serious about this one, I would have had to tell Joel to call the medics."

Everyone around the table laughed. She smiled and nodded, still not clear why an inner-city worship group would be looked at unfavorably. From the graphs she'd skimmed, the program had been successful in reducing delinquency in other states. She sighed and pushed the file aside, hopeful they'd find funding elsewhere.

"Now this is a project I can get behind," the red-faced man said. He held up a file folder. "Project number fifteen-twenty-two. Do we need to discuss this, or should we just take a vote?"

Ivy's heart sank. It was one of the three with green dots on it. "I think we should talk about it." She glanced around the room for support and met a few friendly faces.

"What's there to talk about? These guys are doing some radical things. They're going to revolutionize policing in this country," one of the men at the far end of the table said.

A few others sitting near him nodded.

"Yeah," red face said. "Get those bastards to stop killing people."

"Bastards?" Ivy cringed as soon as the word crossed her lips. "Who are you referring to?"

"Seriously?" Red face scowled. "The police."

Ivy took in a deep breath. Her sister Rose had been a police officer for the past eight years, and it broke her heart to see her struggle with being an officer. Of course, Ivy couldn't share those experiences with the group, or could she?

Ivy shifted in her seat and sat up taller. "While I understand there are bad police officers as there are in any profession, I feel that the verbiage in this proposal is divisive not healing."

"Divisive my ass," said the petite woman beside her. "You have to be divisive when the idiots go around shooting innocent black people."

Ivy's heart ached. She and Rose had had many conversations about this. She still remembered the night when one of Rose's fellow police officers had been shot in the line of duty. She'd responded to a simple call at a hotel about a disturbance—a dog barking. She and her partner had been shot in cold blood. Rose had been nearly inconsolable and had considered quitting the force.

"I agree. It's horrible. But that doesn't mean we should lump all police officers into the same category." She held up the report. "How can we support a program that speaks of defunding the police?"

Red face laughed. "Back the blue. Is that what you're saying, Rain? I don't know what the hell's gotten into you."

"Yes, we should back the blue." Ivy heard a few intakes of breath from those around the table, but she continued. "We can't solve a problem by turning on a whole group of people. People who risk their lives every day to protect us."

"So you're okay with them going around shooting black people?" Leslie, the lone black woman in the room, asked.

"God, no." Ivy put her hand against her chest. She met Leslie's gaze. "Of course not. It breaks my heart." She pulled the top sheet out of the folder. "I pray that someone can come up with an answer. But this isn't it."

Red face let out a loud laugh. "Shit. Now Rain has started praying. What the hell is going on? Did hell freeze over?"

Ivy didn't react. Instead, she kept her gaze on Leslie.

Leslie never broke her gaze, even when others around the table began to murmur. "So what do you find wrong with their proposal?"

"The language. The anger."

"So you don't believe we have a right to be angry?" Leslie's eyebrows rose.

"You have every right to be angry." Ivy held her gaze. "I can't pretend to know how you feel. How angry it must make you. I'm not arrogant enough to claim that I can."

Leslie narrowed her gaze. "I ask you again, what is wrong with the anger in the proposal?"

"I might be naïve." Ivy fiddled with the button on her shirt, suddenly feeling self-conscious. Why had she gotten herself into this conversation? She should have kept her mouth shut, but Rose's face kept flashing in her mind. "The best way to fight darkness isn't with darkness but with light."

"Jesus Christ, do we have to listen to this bullshit?" red face said.

"And the best way to fight hate is with love," Leslie said, never breaking her gaze with Ivy.

"Yes." Ivy's voice came out little more than a whisper. "Does that make me naïve?"

"As fuck," red face said, but the rest of the room remained quiet.

Nobody spoke for several beats before Leslie nodded and said, "You've got my attention. You said you don't have the answers, but something tells me you have a suggestion."

Ivy held up a file with a red dot on it. "Have you looked at this one? Seventeen eighty-two."

The only sound in the room was the shuffling of papers. Ivy waited until the noise quieted before she continued. "It's a group of retired police officers who—"

"Let the fox into the chicken coop." Red face slammed the file onto the table. "No thank you."

"Henry, would you shut up?" Leslie said and shot him a look. "Let Rain speak."

He crossed his arms over his chest and glowered at Ivy, but he didn't say anything further.

"Please, continue," Leslie said.

Ivy glanced up at the screen at Rain's parents. They hadn't spoken during the entire exchange. Rain's mother's expression was unreadable, but her father's face was full of irritation.

She'd come too far now, so she looked away from the screen. "As I said, it's a group of retired police officers. Eighty percent are people of color. Who better to address the issue than them? I don't claim to have the answers, but I do know who I'd like working on the problem."

Ivy looked up from the file and slowly gazed around the room, making eye contact with each person, even those who'd reacted with hostility earlier. The last gaze she met was Leslie, who gave her a subtle nod as if to say *go on*.

"The other proposal we're considering is made

up of professors of criminology, which on the surface sounds good, but from a quick look at their bios, none of them have ever worked in law enforcement." Ivy put her finger on the sheet. "Plus, only ten percent are people of color. If we're going to put money toward someone to solve the problem, I know where I'd place my bet."

"Agreed," Leslie said.

The vote went quickly with only three members voting against Ivy.

Leslie winked at her when the vote passed.

֍֎֍֎

Fuck. Rain wasn't sure if it was the quality of the weed or Ivy's body not being used to smoking it, but she hadn't felt this high in years. She'd been staring in the mirror watching Ivy's face melt, and then she'd push it back into place and laugh.

Damn, that was cool. But she needed music. Getting lost in it was one of her favorite things to do when she was high. Tracie laughed at her when she'd sworn she could hear every instrument distinctly. It was almost as if the pot slowed the entire song down so much that she could hear every note.

Rain found Ivy's phone on the nightstand. She didn't have high hopes for Ivy's playlist, but any music would do right now. Even if she had to listen to some twangy country music.

Fuck. How was she supposed to get in? On a whim, she typed 1-2-3-4. *Nothing.* She rummaged through Ivy's purse.

"Dude," Rain said aloud. "Where the hell is your ID?" She located it and punched in Ivy's birthday. *Eureka.* The screen unlocked. Bad passcode but good for her.

Rain's eyes widened when she opened Ivy's

music app. The most recently played were Jenna Blake, Megadeth, Slipknot, and Anthrax.

"What the fuck?" Rain walked to the mirror and gazed into Ivy's beautiful eyes. The amber color sparkled like gold, or maybe it was just the pot. "Who are you, Ivy Nash?"

Rain giggled and pointed at the mirror. "Ivy— dude—it's not like I'm talking to myself because I'm not here."

Ivy's eyes widened in the mirror, and Rain pointed. "See, you know it, too. But wait, that can't be. If I'm not here, then you got high all by yourself." Rain shook Ivy's head.

Rain pointed at the mirror again. "See, you agree with me. I knew it." Rain scrunched up Ivy's face in thought. "So since my mind's here and your body is...that means...like both of us are here. We're like hanging out together. Cool."

She turned away from the mirror. Maybe she should take another hit. Ivy's hand grabbed her shirt. Did Ivy grab her, or did she grab herself? *Deep.*

Rain gazed down at the hand that still held on to the front of her shirt. *Pretty nails.*

"No. No. No," Rain said aloud. She was heading down the wrong path. Last time she'd admired Ivy's hands, it had led to her groping Ivy's breasts. "Bad, Rain. No boobies."

She giggled again at the sound of Ivy's voice saying boobies. What had she been going to do? Another hit. *No.* She was high enough. Ivy's stomach growled. Food. She needed food.

Rain sauntered back to the mirror and sucked in Ivy's cheeks. She needed food, or she could get arrested for starving Ivy. That wouldn't do. Rain paused. Something was wrong with that thought. *Music.* She'd almost forgotten the music.

Music. Then food. That was good. She had a

plan.

She giggled again. And then again. "He-he. Food and music. Now all we need to do is dance, Ivy, then it'll be a date."

The thought broke her into a new round of giggles. She needed to focus, or Ivy would surely starve. The thought sobered her slightly, but then she giggled again. *Sobered.* She wasn't drunk, just high.

After considerable effort, she'd found earbuds and plugged them into the phone. She only put one in, so she could hear what else was going on around her. She wavered between Jenna Blake and Anthrax before settling on heavy metal. *Rock on.*

Just as she was about to hit play, the phone vibrated in her hands. She threw it on the bed as if it had bitten her and then laughed. *Dumbass.*

A text had come in from someone named Nadine.

It was great to see you today. I'd love to meet up for dinner if you aren't busy tomorrow night. Talk about old times.

Rain stared at the phone. She should stay out of Ivy's business. She giggled, and her thumbs flew over the keyboard.

I'd love to!! Where? Time?

Awesome. Should we go classy or casual?

Rain glowered at the phone. Too many choices, and she was hungry.

Surprise me. Granny needs me. Gotta go. Text me the deets.

She pushed open Ivy's bedroom door. The house wasn't big, so it shouldn't take much to find the kitchen.

❧❧❧❧

As Ivy was leaving the boardroom, Leslie moved up beside her. She put her hand on Ivy's arm. "Thanks for being a voice of reason in there. Sometimes, I question why I'm here, so I really appreciate it."

Ivy smiled and then wondered if it looked different than Rain's real smile. Her family always said her eyes practically disappeared when she smiled. Did she make Rain's eyes disappear? She pushed the thought out of her head. "I just want to do the right thing. Thanks for backing me."

"Keep making common-sense decisions, and you'll keep getting my backing."

Other members began milling around, so Ivy made her exit. She didn't want to be drawn into a one-on-one conversation for fear she'd be discovered. In her distraction, she'd not noticed that Rain's assistant had followed her until she swung open her office door.

"Shit," Ivy said, startled when her assistant pushed in behind her. "Did you need something?"

"What got into you today?"

Apparently, she hadn't pulled it off as well as she thought she had. Ivy shrugged, hoping it would suffice.

"You surprised me a couple times. I think you surprised your parents, too."

Ugh. She didn't want to talk about it, or she would only bury herself worse. "I did what my heart told me to do."

Rain's assistant stared.

❧❧❧❧

Rain spread the feast out on the kitchen table while Anthrax blared through the earbuds. This was the life.

She wrapped her arm around the large mixing bowl and held it against her chest. With a spatula, she stirred through the thick brownie mix. Her mouth watered at the chocolaty smell.

There were still clumps of powdered mix, but she couldn't wait any longer. She dipped her finger in like Winnie the Pooh when he scooped honey.

The bite was only inches from her mouth when Ivy's grandma walked into the room and gasped.

"Ivy June, what in the world are you doing?"

Rain squinted as her marijuana-addled brain tried to make sense of what Ivy's grandma was asking. Somehow, it seemed too deep, so she flashed the old woman her best rock and roll symbol and said, "Peace, love—"

The air crackled.

Sulfur.

Chapter Seventeen

By the perplexed look on Granny's face, Ivy, or more likely Rain, had done something to cause it. Ivy looked down in horror at her chocolate-covered fingers. What in God's name had Rain been doing?

Through the sulfur smell, she got a whiff of chocolate rising out of the bowl she hugged to her chest. *Yum.* Ivy put her nose closer and inhaled deeply.

It was as if a magnet pulled her hand upward. She shoved all three fingers in her mouth and sucked off the sticky goo. *Heaven.* Granny said something, but she wasn't listening because the brownie mixture called to her. She stuck two fingers deeply into the sludge, trying to avoid the spot the egg hadn't been completely stirred in.

She miscalculated and only managed to get half of the bite into her mouth before the other half fell to her shirt. A little spill wasn't enough to deter her, so she raised her shirt to her mouth and gobbled the gooey mix.

Granny marched toward her as Ivy sucked on her shirt. She stared at Granny in horror, unsure what had gotten into her, but it didn't stop her from licking the remaining chocolate off her T-shirt.

"Ivy June, hand over that bowl. Right. This. Second." Granny stood in front of her with one hand on her hip and the other outstretched toward the bowl.

Should she try and make a run for it? She giggled. Surely, she could outrun Granny. Images of Granny chasing her as she carried the bowl like a football flashed in her mind. She giggled some more. Then she saw Granny tackling her and the bowl flying through the air. Now she couldn't stop the giggles.

What was wrong with her? Everything was surreal. If the smell and taste of the chocolate didn't seem so real, she'd swear she was having a dream.

Granny grasped the bowl. A tug-of-war with an old lady would be wrong, wouldn't it? Of course, it would be. Ivy dipped her hand into the bowl one last time and scooped up a handful of the batter before she let Granny take it.

Ivy flinched when Granny looked at Ivy's hand. *Crap.* Granny might take it away from her. Ivy crammed the goo into her mouth, not caring that some of it squished onto her cheek and trickled down her chin.

Granny backed away from Ivy with the bowl clutched in both hands. It wasn't lost on Ivy that Granny seemed reluctant to turn her back on Ivy. "Honey, I know you've been stressed lately, but you've got me worried."

Ivy had been too distracted by the sweets to pay close attention to anything else, but she finally realized someone was screaming. She stared at Granny, whose mouth had stopped moving. *Oh, no.* What if Granny had been afflicted with whatever was making Ivy lose her mind? *Aliens? Pod people?* Granny's lips had stopped moving, but the screaming continued.

"Stop screaming at me," Ivy tried to yell but feared it had come out low and slow.

"What in the world are you going on about?" Granny asked. "I'm not yelling at you."

Granny's lips had stopped moving, but the screaming continued. More than screaming, something else. Pounding? A buzz saw? Ivy pointed. "You're lying. I still hear you screaming, even if your lips aren't moving."

Granny slammed the bowl down near the sink and marched back toward Ivy. Her normally rosy cheeks were bright red. She reached toward Ivy's head.

Ivy shrieked and closed her eyes. Then all the screaming and pounding stopped. She cautiously opened one eye. Granny stood over her holding a cord. What was she going to do with it? Ivy reached for her neck to protect it.

Granny dropped the cord on the table. "You have your music so loud no wonder you couldn't hear anything. Now will you tell me what's going on?"

Ivy stared at the cord, trying to make sense of what Granny was saying. A tinny sound came from the table. *Earbuds.* Of course, she must have been listening to her music. She picked up the earbud and moved it toward her ear. The strains of a heavy metal guitar solo assaulted her senses. *Holy hell.* No wonder she felt like ripping her face off. It was unpleasantly loud.

"I think I need to go lay down. I'm not feeling well."

"Honey, you're under way too much stress. It's starting to take a toll."

Ivy nodded. She needed to be alone. She was having trouble concentrating on Granny's words because she was fixated on the tiny piece of pepper between Granny's two front teeth. Ivy narrowed her eyes but then quickly turned away. She couldn't stand to see it. It kept getting bigger and bigger, and it would soon be the size of a golf ball. *Gross.*

"I can't talk now. I need to rest." Ivy went to leap from her seat, but instead, she slowly rose. She moved her arm toward her hair and was shocked that it seemed to move in slow motion. Fascinated, she waved her hand in front of her face, but it moved past as if she were doing tai chi.

"Bugs?" Granny said.

"Where?" Ivy's eyes widened. "Not spiders I hope."

"No...I...Oh, never mind. Go take a nap. And clean off those grubby hands of yours. You don't need chocolate all over your sheets."

Potato chips. Where the hell did that come from? She *needed* potato chips. An unopened bag of Doritos sat on the table. *Wow!* Had she just manifested them from her mind? She snatched them up and held them like she would a baby, hoping Granny wouldn't take them like she had the brownie mix.

An open bottle of Gatorade sat on the table, too, which reminded her she was thirsty. She coughed. *Ouch.* Her throat was raw like someone had scrubbed it with sandpaper. The Gatorade was soothing as she gulped it.

She gazed over her shoulder at Granny as she exited the room, just to make sure Granny's alien form didn't take hold when Ivy turned her back. As she walked through the living room, she gaped. She'd never noticed all the mismatched furniture before. It was as if the various pieces made a kaleidoscope. She closed one eye and then the other to make the pieces move just like turning a kaleidoscope. *Cool.*

When she entered her room, she gasped at the mess. Her books were strewn all over her desk with one on the floor. James's coat was in a heap in the middle of her floor.

The blinds clanked against the screen as a stiff breeze blew them inward. A storm appeared to be brewing. She hurried to the window and closed it, sure she hadn't opened it in the first place.

As soon as the wind from outside stopped, she caught a skunky whiff. *Odd.* She smelled it after she closed the window not before. She sniffed again. A little smoky, too.

She'd torn open the Doritos earlier when she

climbed the stairs. She stared at the bag. The entire time she'd been examining her room, she'd been shoving chips into her mouth. She licked her fingers and closed the bag.

Suddenly feeling extremely tired, she turned toward her bed. She'd made it before she'd left, but the comforter was askew and bunched in the center. Then her gaze landed on the small container on her pillow.

Her mouth fell open, and she stared. Was that what she thought it was? The silver pipe sat on the bed, and the crushed pot leaves had spilled.

Realization dawned. "Damn you, Rain. You got me high."

❧❧❧❧

Rain's hands shook. She'd been trying to calm down since she'd *come to* at her desk. She longed for Ivy's pot stash, so she could get high and forget everything. Whatever was going on had her seriously freaked out. She'd tried to call Tracie but had gotten her voicemail. If she wasn't afraid of driving in this state, she'd jump in her car and head to Wisconsin.

An email alert popped up on her screen. Work might distract her. She loved modern technology. The minutes for the grant meeting were already being disseminated. She'd wanted to quiz Gilda on what they'd funded but couldn't figure out how to do so since she was supposed to have been at the meeting.

She clicked on the link for the minutes, and her mouth fell open. *What the hell?* She ran through the list again; she had to have read it wrong. *Nope.* They hadn't funded her favorite project; instead, they'd funded the one for the retired police. *Damn it.* Had she been sleepwalking through the meeting, or worse, had Ivy had a hand in what happened?

Her phone broke her concentration. She smiled at the sound of Bon Jovi's *It's My Life.*

"Hey," Rain said.

"Sorry I missed your call, kid." Tracie said. "Damned phone. Jeannie made me get a new one, and I don't know how to use the fucking thing."

"Flip phones went out with the Beatles."

"I didn't have a goddamned flip phone and neither did the Beatles."

"Then what? A Galaxy 10?"

"Nine," Tracie mumbled.

Rain laughed.

"Shut up." Tracie tried to put rage into her voice, but Rain could hear the smile. "So what the hell did you want?"

"An invite."

"To what?"

"To come see you and your lovely wife."

"Door's always open. You should know that by now." Tracie paused for a beat before she said, "Is everything okay?"

Rain straightened the papers in front of her as she considered her answer. "I'm not sure."

"Decisive as always, I see." When Rain didn't respond, Tracie said, "Hey, I was teasing. What's going on?"

"I'd rather talk to you in person."

"Now you have me worried."

"No, no. Nothing to be worried about. I just need a good dose of Jeannie." Rain smiled, awaiting Tracie's reaction.

"What the fuck? That's just wrong. What does Jeannie have that I don't?"

"Other than a pleasant personality?" Rain

chuckled. "She's a bit more maternal."

"I'm as maternal as a fucking titty."

Rain nearly spit out the drink of water she just put into her mouth. After she swallowed, she coughed before she spoke. "You can't say shit like that when I'm drinking."

"When you coming?"

"I'd like to drive up after work tomorrow. Stay the weekend."

"Perfect. We're going to a neighborhood barbecue on Saturday afternoon, but I'm sure everyone will be thrilled to meet you."

Rain inwardly groaned, but she couldn't complain since she'd invited herself. "I'll try to leave the office around three. Hopefully, beat the traffic."

"Sounds good. I'll tell Jeannie to make sure we have all the fixins for Bloody Marys."

"Awesome. I'll see you Friday."

"Later," Tracie said and then was gone.

Rain shook her head and smiled. *Typical Tracie.*

After her call with Tracie, Rain felt as if she could breathe again. Whatever was going on, a weekend with Tracie and Jeannie would cure her. It was probably stress from trying to run the foundation all on her own while keeping up her schedule. She needed to get used to it because she didn't suspect her parents would return anytime soon.

Chapter Eighteen

Rain trudged up the sidewalk, willing her feet to keep moving. Even though she'd packed for only two days, her suitcase pulled heavily on her weary arm. Lack of sleep was starting to take its toll.

Before she arrived at the front porch of the quaint cottage, the bright blue front door flew open. Jeannie rushed out with a huge smile on her face, followed closely by Tracie.

Holy shit. Rain hadn't seen her friends in nearly a year and was shocked that Tracie's hair had gone from salt and pepper to one hundred percent salt.

Tracie must have registered the look on Rain's face because she laughed and ran her hand through her buzzcut. "Ya stunned at how gorgeous I'm looking?"

"Yeah, sure. That must be it."

Jeannie sidled up to Tracie and put her arm around Tracie's waist. "I think she looks sexy." Jeannie licked her lips for emphasis.

Rain shook her head. "You two are so cute it's sickening."

Jeannie smiled and winked at Rain.

"I still have no idea how you scored someone as beautiful and sweet as Jeannie," Rain said to Tracie. It was true. Even in her sixties, Jeannie could still turn heads.

"How many times do I have to tell you, kid? It's my sunny disposition."

"Plus, she's got a nice ass." Jeannie patted Tracie's backside.

Rain laughed. Her earlier fatigue lifted. Just being in their presence gave her a sense of hope.

Tracie grabbed the suitcase out of Rain's hand. "Get your ass inside, so you can tell us what the hell's going on."

"What she meant to say," Jeannie said, "is please come in, Rain. Get comfortable. We'll make you a drink, and then you can tell us what's going on with you."

∿∿๊∿∿

The setting sun shimmered off the lake, and a cool breeze swept across the water. A speedboat streaked past and drowned out the chattering birds and the distant sound of a lawn mower. Tracie and Jeannie's patio was one of Rain's favorite places, so if she was going to be able to tell her crazy tale, this would be where it would most likely happen.

Tracie had turned on their outdoor heaters, so she didn't have to mess with starting a fire, while Jeannie hauled snacks out and laid them on the table. Snacks was a misnomer. The spread was more like a feast. Rain had already grabbed a beer out of the refrigerator and was over halfway through it.

Jeannie went to sit but stopped. "Oh, my. Looks like I better grab you another one."

Rain thought of protesting but smiled instead and took a large pull from her bottle.

"Slow down, slugger. We've got all night." Tracie pointed at the water. "We have baby ducks. Check it out."

They watched in silence. Rain chuckled as the ducklings shoved their heads under the water. "Baby duck butts."

"What about duck butts?" Jeannie asked when she returned.

"Just Rain being her mature self," Tracie answered.

Rain wasn't ready to talk about the strange incident, so she said, "I want to hear all about the conference you went to."

Tracie groaned and covered her face with her large hand. "Ugh. I've just about recovered. Do we have to talk about it?"

"After that reaction, yes. My curiosity is piqued."

Jeannie patted Tracie's hand. "Do you think you can talk about it without shouting?"

"Shouting? You're only making me more interested. What was this conference anyway?" Rain was happy to shift the focus from her problem for a bit.

"LGBTQ nonprofit leadership conference."

"Cool. That had to be uplifting," Rain said.

Tracie snorted. "I wouldn't call it that. More like a shit show."

Jeannie shook her head. "Let's just say, Tracie came back a little frustrated."

"Frustrated? Try mad as hell." Tracie's face turned crimson. "I came away convinced we're gonna lose all our rights because we're too fucking idiotic to know who the real enemy is."

Tracie took a pull from her beer before she continued. "We have to wake up and smell the fucking coffee. Fifty-one percent of the population lost the right to control their own bodies, and we spent over two hours debating who the fuck should be allowed in the room. Trans men? Trans women? Bi? Pan? Non-binary? And some terms I'd never even heard of. I don't give a shit, as long as we can get on the same page."

"You know that sounds insensitive, don't you?" Rain took a deep breath and waited for Tracie's reaction.

"Fuck insensitivity. Weren't you listening?"

"I know your heart," Rain said. "But others might think you're transphobic or don't support diversity."

"Ya know what? I'm tired of walking on eggshells. We're so focused on creating a safe space for everyone—well, guess what, Rain—while we've been worried about that, the country's gone to hell. We're under siege, and instead of picking up arms—figuratively, not literally—we're worried about hurting someone's feelings. Meanwhile, the other side is destroying us, and we play right into their hands by all this petty infighting."

Rain cringed. She hated when Tracie got like this. At least, it was only her and Jeannie hearing Tracie's rant, but it made her nervous that Tracie would say something to the wrong people. "You need to be careful." Rain knew it would incite Tracie, but she loved her too much to see her walk down the wrong path. "You don't want people to mistake your words."

"Bring 'em on!" Tracie crossed her arms over her chest. "I won't keep quiet any longer." Tears welled in Tracie's eyes. "I ran into two of my oldest friends, both nearing seventy. They've been in the fight for nearly fifty years, but they were afraid to speak—paranoid. Hear that, Rain. They were silenced because they didn't want to be treated like dinosaurs, so they kept quiet. We lose all the history—the wise voices because they don't want to have the mob jump on them."

Rain held up her hands, hoping to calm Tracie, while Jeannie continued to rub Tracie's back. "I can tell you're upset."

"Damned right I am." Tracie pointed at Rain. "And I don't think you truly understand."

Did she? If she were honest, lately, Tracie's opinions seemed to be going a little off the rails. "I'm trying to, but...you seem so angry. I don't want you to be labeled something that I know you're not."

"And that's the problem." Tracie snorted. "People are so afraid of being slapped with a label that we don't discuss the issues anymore. We laugh at all the right-wingers who blindly waved their flags for the *big election lie*, while we're doing the same damned thing. We're shaking in our boots that we might inadvertently say something that will get us labeled, canceled, and then shunned before we're even given a chance to speak."

Tracie slammed her hand against her knee and scowled, her face the color of a lobster. "Screw that. We need to learn to have tough conversations. Messy conversations. Talk strategy. Be willing to listen to each other."

Rain's chest ached. "But when you say things like that, you open yourself up for labels."

Tracie's jaw stiffened. "Let me say this loud and clear. Racism is wrong. Transphobia is wrong. Not respecting someone's identity is wrong. But labeling people without gathering all the facts is also wrong. Shaming people on social media is wrong. Joining a Twitter mob is wrong. Not allowing healthy debate is wrong."

Good. At least Tracie wasn't completely lost, but Rain still worried that her fiery speech would get her in trouble one day. "I know people get upset on social media, but it's because we've had enough. We're tired of taking it."

"Just listen to what you said." Tracie laughed, but by the tone, it wasn't in good humor. "You sound like one of the twenty-somethings I was talking to." Tracie had a look of disgust on her face as she shook her head.

"Ah, you're in one of your 'kids today' moods." Rain hoped her joke would lighten the tension. She glanced out over the water as the sun broke the horizon.

"Nope. Just this one kid. She was twenty-three and said she was worn out from the fight. I just about spit out my gum. Twenty-fucking-three, and she's tired of the fight, so I thought I'd educate her."

Rain groaned and glanced at Jeannie for support. Jeannie just shook her head and squeezed Tracie's hand.

"I asked her if she knew about Don't Ask, Don't Tell, DOMA, Matthew Shepard, Stonewall..." Tracie sighed. "She couldn't get away from me fast enough. She was tired. Really? I've been fighting this battle for over forty years, so I wasn't receptive to her being too tired to continue the fight."

"Not all young people are like that."

Tracie's face softened, and she smiled. "You're right. I met two amazing young women. They were out in the community, meeting people. They took their message to churches, synagogues, community centers, colleges, and even high schools. Changing one heart and mind at a time. They're the ones that will change the world, not the Twitter warriors."

"On that note." Jeannie clapped her hands together. "Why don't we find out what brings Rain here?"

"Definitely. Definitely." Tracie nodded. "Sorry, I just get worked up."

"And so does your blood pressure." Jeannie rubbed Tracie's leg. "And the doctor said that's not good for you."

Tracie winked at Rain. "She wants to keep me around, but she still hasn't figured out that I'm too ornery to die."

Jeannie shot Tracie a glance. "Don't even joke about things like that."

Tracie lowered her gaze to her lap. "Sorry. Bad joke." She glanced at Rain and said, "Tell us why you look like you've been hit by a freight train."

"Do I look that bad?"

Tracie nodded with vigor, so Rain turned to Jeannie.

"You've looked better, sweetie," Jeannie answered.

Confirmation that she looked like shit. "I'm gonna tell you something, and I know you're going to think I've lost my mind."

"Great way to preface a story." Tracie chuckled and rubbed her hands together. "This should be good."

Jeannie shot Tracie a look before she said to Rain, "You seem troubled. There's nothing you can't tell us."

"What if it's something so unbelievable that I'm not even sure it's real?"

Tracie choked on her beer. "Oh. My. God.

You've fallen in love with a man."

"No! Jesus, why would you think that?"

Tracie shrugged. "You said it was something unbelievable."

"Think unbelievable like in the supernatural kind of way."

"Like that TV show?" Tracie asked.

Rain shook her head. "Not really. I mean it's not about the TV show, but I suppose it's something that could happen on the show."

"You've fallen in love with a werewolf?"

"Would you let her talk?" Jeannie said.

Tracie scowled. "Uh, sorry. Go on."

"And for the record, I haven't fallen in love with a werewolf or a vampire."

"Good." Tracie glanced at Jeannie and clamped her lips together.

"It all started after the minor altercation at the rally on Saturday. The one I told Tracie about."

"Tracie gave me the highlights, but I'd like to hear it from you," Jeannie said.

"I thought we weren't supposed to interrupt her," Tracie said.

Jeannie raised her eyebrows but didn't say anything.

"An argument. It was dumb," Rain said and continued to relay her confrontation with Ivy and the old woman who stepped between them. "I swear it was a clear day one minute and then thundering and lightning the next. Followed by a downpour."

Rain grabbed a handful of cheese curds while she paused to let her friends take in the story.

Tracie's eyes narrowed. "I'm not getting why it's causing you such distress. Am I missing something?"

Rain sighed and took a slug of her beer. She put another cheese curd into her mouth, hoping to delay. Her friends stared at her with anticipation.

Rain finished her first beer and opened the new one Jeannie had brought out. She held up her hand. "Before I tell you the next part, I don't want any lectures."

"This doesn't sound good," Tracie said.

"I just know you can't stand Sasha."

"Are you still seeing that whiny Kardashian?" Tracie asked.

"Seriously," Jeannie said. "Would you stop calling her a Kardashian?"

"Uh, sorry. I shouldn't insult the Kardashians like that."

"Just ignore her," Jeannie said. "I try to most of the time."

Rain smiled, knowing the two were trying to lessen her nervousness. While she appreciated their effort, her insides fluttered, and she thought she might throw up.

"Anyway, later that night, after the rally, I was in bed with Sasha...you know...um..." Heat rose up Rain's neck. She tried to avoid the subject of sex with Tracie, but this needed to be said. "Let's just say that I was just about at that point. Uh, ya know."

"You were about to come?" Tracie said.

Kill me now. Rain shifted her gaze to the water and stared out at the ball of orange that had just about disappeared beyond the horizon. "Yes. But before I did, the strangest thing happened. I heard this crackling noise and smelled sulfur. Then I was holding a tray of pies surrounded by a bunch of strangers."

Tracie and Jeannie had identical slack-jawed

expressions, but neither spoke. As Rain waited for a response, every sound around her seemed amplified. The pleasant crackling of the fire registered as a blaze in Rain's mind the longer the silence dragged on. "Are you going to say something, or are you just going to call the ambulance to haul me away?" Rain practically shouted.

Jeannie recovered first. She smiled. "Wow. That was a lot to take in."

Even though Rain wanted to get on with the business of figuring out the problem, she knew she had to give her friends time to process what she'd told them. With the ice broken, they began to ask questions, and Rain told the rest of her story.

"The last time it happened was yesterday afternoon," Rain said. "I missed the entire quarterly board meeting. Apparently, I was off my game, or on it, depending on who you talk to." Rain snorted. "I still can't believe some of the proposals I voted yes on. They were clearly ones I'd put a red sticker on."

"If you end up in Ivy's body, do you think she's in yours?" Jeannie asked.

"Would I sound crazy if I said yes?"

"Holy shit. You really believe this, don't you?"

Rain looked down at her lap, and her shoulders sagged. She would not cry. "I don't know what to believe anymore. Either it's real, or I need to be locked away in the psych ward." She brought both hands up to her forehead and grabbed on to her hair.

She felt an arm around her shoulders. *Jeannie.* Rain could tell by the scent of sandalwood. The gesture made it harder for her to hold back her tears. All she wanted to do was wrap her arms around Jeannie and sob against her chest. Jeannie squeezed her one last time and went back to her seat.

"Okay, kid. That's some story. Now I get why you look like shit."

Rain smiled. Leave it to Tracie to state the obvious.

"Have you Googled her?" Tracie asked.

"Nah."

"Why the hell not?" Tracie grabbed her cellphone off the table.

"No," Rain practically shouted. "I'm not ready."

Tracie's lip rose in a sneer. "What do you mean you aren't ready?"

"I've thought about it a million times."

"But?"

"Even if she's real, am I gonna just show up on her doorstep and ask her if she's been having out-of-body experiences?"

"She's got a point," Jeannie said.

"And if she's not real, then what?" Rain brought her beer to her lips but stopped. "I'm not ready to deal with it yet."

"Come on, you can't just bury your head in the sand," Tracie said with her usual surety.

"Tracie," Jeannie said. "Leave her be. It's not even been a week. Not everyone moves at the same speed you do."

"I'm just trying to help," Tracie muttered.

"Oh, and there's this." Rain pulled out the paper she'd been carrying, unfolded it, and set it on the table. "I found it this morning when I was taking the garbage out. There were several crumpled-up notes."

Tracie snatched the paper and read it.

Rain-

I know who you are. I know where you live.
I'm going to get you

She whistled. "Whoa. This isn't good. Shit, has your stalker reappeared?"

Rain shook her head. "I don't think so. That was all online."

Jeannie had taken the paper and appeared to be studying it. In the fading light, it was getting harder to see, so she used her cellphone flashlight. "Did you see this?" She held the page out to Rain and Tracie and put her finger at the end of the sentence. "No period."

Rain took the page and looked at where Jeannie pointed. "You're right."

"Maybe you wrote it yourself when you were in one of your states," Tracie said.

"That doesn't come close to matching my handwriting."

"Much too flowery," Jeannie said.

"I heard somewhere that people with multiple personalities have completely different handwriting," Tracie said. "Sometimes, they even write with the opposite hand."

"Not helping," Jeannie said. "Ivy?"

"Why would she threaten me?"

"Maybe it's not a threat." Jeannie put her finger on the page. "It could mean she's trying to tell you that she knows who you are."

Rain nodded. She'd wondered that herself, but there was no mistaking the "I'm going to get you" part. "The end certainly sounds like a threat to me."

"Perhaps it wasn't finished." Jeannie narrowed her eyes. "Maybe it was supposed to say, I'm going to get you proof of who I am."

"Or I'm going to get you a pony," Tracie added.

Jeannie rolled her eyes. "In what universe would someone leave a note to someone living in the middle of the suburbs, saying they were going to get them a pony?"

"Hmph, I was just making a point." Tracie stuck her lip out and frowned.

"A bad one," Jeannie said.

"I don't know." Rain's shoulders slumped, and she picked at her fingernail. She wanted the thoughts swirling in her head to stop.

"Chin up. We'll think of something," Tracie said.

Rain still didn't look up when she said, "Do you believe me?"

"I believe that you believe it," Tracie answered immediately.

"Meaning?"

"Meaning, I don't think you're blowing smoke up our asses. No doubt it feels real to you."

"But is it real?"

"Damned if I know."

Chapter Nineteen

Ivy ran the brush through her hair one last time before turning from the mirror. She either had Rain to blame for this or her own alter ego. Unfortunately, she still hadn't been able to figure out which.

After the effects of her foray into pot smoking had worn off, she'd discovered the texts from Nadine. Had she agreed to the meeting or had Rain?

It didn't matter now; she'd decided she'd go. After everything that happened between the two, it wouldn't be fair to cancel. She chuckled to herself. Granny might barricade her in the house after the incident with the brownie mix.

She'd convinced Granny that she'd had a bad reaction to the Benadryl she'd taken for her allergies. Whether Granny believed her was still up for debate.

If dealing with Granny wasn't bad enough, then she'd been confronted by a frantic James, who'd realized his stash was missing. Ivy had soon dampened his righteous indignation, but having the conversation behind her parents' back had left her feeling unease. She pushed the thought of her family from her mind. It was time to focus on herself.

It had been a long time since she'd gone out to a bar, not that The Tap House was anything special. Just your run-of-the-mill bar and grill.

After rejecting wearing a dress, she'd settled on

a pair of faded blue jeans and a tailored button-down shirt. Casual yet classic.

"How pathetic," she said aloud. At her age, it shouldn't be such a big deal to go out to dinner with a friend. Other than a few work events and church, she'd not been out in years. Even when she was married to John, they rarely went anywhere.

More pathetic, the most excitement she'd had in a long time was sitting in Rain's quarterly meeting. If that was even real.

She sighed. Maybe the rally truly had been the turning point she needed. In a week's time, she felt more alive than she had in years. How sad that it took living someone else's life to feel it.

⁂

Ivy sat in her car outside the restaurant and tried to muster the courage to go inside. It wasn't seeing Nadine that had her worried the most. It was the fear that she'd have another episode of leaving her body. The thought even sounded crazy to her.

She pushed open her car door. It was now or never. Her boots clicked on the asphalt as she made her way across the parking lot. With each step, her heart raced faster as if she were doing wind sprints, rather than walking into a restaurant.

The hostess greeted her at the door, but Nadine had already risen from the booth and waved her arm. Ivy smiled at the hostess and gestured toward Nadine. With more confidence than she felt, Ivy strode across the restaurant. She looked straight ahead, not wanting to see any of the patrons for fear she'd see someone she knew.

Since her outburst in church—or rather Rain's—she was sure the entire county was watching her and whispering behind her back.

Nadine stood when Ivy reached the table. She gave Ivy a quick hug before she returned to her seat.

"I wasn't sure if you were going to show," Nadine said. "If I remember right, you're always early."

"I wasn't sure, either. I've been sitting in the parking lot for the past twenty minutes."

"There's nothing to be afraid of." Nadine smiled. "I promise."

Nadine always had a way of putting Ivy at ease, and tonight was no exception. The tightness in her chest lessened, so she could nearly breathe normally.

Ivy gazed down at her hands that she'd rested on the table. She fought the urge to pick at her fingernails. "I'm sorry. I didn't mean to keep you waiting."

"No biggie." Nadine waved her hand toward the rest of the restaurant. "I've been people watching."

Ivy smiled. "That was always one of your favorite pastimes."

"Still is." Nadine leaned in. "That couple over there under the TV hasn't spoken to each other since they walked in. And that pair over there in the corner, I'm pretty sure they're having an affair."

"And you figured all this out in five minutes?"

"Eight, but who's counting?"

Ivy laughed again. She'd almost forgotten how much she enjoyed Nadine's company.

After a waitress drifted over and took their drink order, Nadine said, "Thanks for agreeing to come."

Ivy had no intention of telling Nadine that it wasn't her who had accepted the original invitation. She wondered if she'd let Nadine in on what had been happening the past week. If there was anyone in the world she'd trust to tell, it would be Nadine. But then again, it wasn't like she really knew her anymore. Even so, sitting across the table from her, it felt like no time had passed.

"So tell me what you've been up to these past ten years," Nadine said.

"You first." Ivy surprised herself with her quick response. Maybe it was simply self-preservation.

"Fair enough." Nadine flashed one of her patented smiles before she continued. "After I finished college, I started a successful business. Got married. Had two kids. Sold the business and now here I am."

Ivy stared. *Got married?* That wasn't what she expected to hear. Nadine stared across the table at her. She needed to say something. As she struggled with how to respond, the waitress arrived with their drinks. She said a silent prayer at the additional time she had to think.

Once the waitress left, her thoughts still were a jumble, but she had to say something. "Got married? Who's the lucky guy?"

Nadine's eyebrows shot up. "Guy? Who said anything about a guy?"

"Oh, um...I just—"

"You know gay marriage is legal in this country, don't you? Since 2015."

"Of course." Ivy's face heated. "It's not something I think about since there's not much of that to see in Mullins Creek."

Nadine winked. "You'd be surprised."

"Really?" Ivy regretted the shock in her voice. "I mean, I'm sure there are. I've just not been...you know...around it." Ivy wanted to crawl under the table, but she needed to stop digging herself a deeper hole. Nadine's arm rested on the table, so Ivy patted it. "Congratulations to you and your...um...do I say wife?"

"Wife is good."

"And two kids, too. How old?"

"Six."

"Twins?"

Nadine laughed. "We call them twins, but they're not. They were born a week apart."

"Oh, adoption. How nice."

"Nope, not adoption, either."

Ivy crinkled her nose as she tried to make sense of what Nadine told her.

Nadine pointed and laughed. "God, that face is priceless. Haven't been able to figure it out yet?"

"No."

"Spoken like a straight girl." Nadine winked. "My wife had our son, and I had our daughter."

"You were pregnant?" Could she be any more insulting? "Sorry. I never thought of you having a baby."

"Trust me. I didn't, either." She turned up her nose. "Don't get me wrong. I love our kids, but I would never do that again. Especially having two hormonal lesbians in the house at the same time."

Ivy laughed at the look on Nadine's face. "Sounds like it took bravery or stupidity, one of the two."

"Definitely stupidity." Nadine laughed. "And a false belief that love conquers all."

"Oh, no. Did you and your wife divorce?"

"Nope." Nadine grinned. "But we darned near killed each other."

"Where is she and the kids?"

"Staying with my sister in Joliet."

"Why not with you? Your mom's house is huge."

"I'd never subject Kari to the homophobe."

"Your mom hasn't changed?"

Nadine shook her head.

"Then why did you drop everything to come here?"

"Because she'll be dead soon."

"Oh." Ivy was sure shock showed on her face.

"Sorry." Nadine rubbed her forehead. "That was crude. Gallows humor. I'm not sure how to deal with it, so I say shit like that. I guess I hoped she'd have a come to Jesus moment since she's dying. It hasn't happened."

"I'm so sorry." Ivy didn't know what else to say.

Nadine's expression suddenly turned serious. "Are we going to talk about the kiss?"

There it was. The moment she'd been dreading. She knew she should say something, but instead, she picked at the label on her nearly empty beer bottle.

Sizzling came from Ivy's left, and she stiffened. Her heart raced. *Shit.* Not now. She couldn't switch now. Her gaze darted around the room until she saw the waitress carrying a sizzling plate of fajitas. She let out a loud exhale.

"I shouldn't have brought it up," Nadine said.

"No, I want to talk about it," Ivy answered. Poor Nadine, Ivy could only imagine the look that had just crossed her face. "Seriously, I do. I just had a moment of panic." It was true, but she wasn't panicking about what Nadine thought.

"Do you need another one?" Nadine motioned to Ivy's beer.

"As long as we're planning on staying here long

enough for it to wear off."

Nadine waved for the waitress and ordered another round before she continued. "I just want to tell you that I'm so sorry." Nadine slumped against her chair. "I've been wanting to say that to you for ten years." Tears welled in her eyes.

"No." Ivy grabbed Nadine's arm but then thought better of it and pulled back. "I mean, it wasn't all your fault. There were two of us involved."

Nadine shook her head adamantly and frowned. "No. You're straight. I had no business kissing you."

How could Ivy ever explain it to Nadine when she had a hard time understanding it herself? It had been the best kiss of her life, but she wouldn't tell Nadine that. Especially since she had a wife. Still, she needed to be honest. "You weren't the only one doing the kissing."

Nadine's eyes widened. "You mean you kissed me back?"

Ivy smiled. "You were there. What do you think?"

"I thought I imagined it." Nadine ran her hand through her hair.

Ivy understood, especially in light of what was happening in her life. She'd learned all too well how much someone's mind could play tricks on them. "You didn't imagine it."

"Well, I'll be damned. You mean I spent the last ten years beating up on myself, and you were the tramp that kissed me back?"

Ivy laughed, happy that Nadine had decided to lighten the moment. "Afraid so."

"But you're not...I mean you're—"

"Straight? Yes. But you were my best friend. I had so many feelings for you."

"So it wasn't horrible?"

Ivy smiled. What a loaded question. Ivy wouldn't lie, but she certainly wouldn't tell her the entire truth. "No, it wasn't horrible, but I'm straight."

"Hot damn. I'll take it." Nadine winked at Ivy and stopped talking when the waitress brought their beers.

Once she'd left, Ivy asked, "Does your wife know about it? The kiss?"

"Of course. I tell her everything."

"And she knows you're here?"

"Duh. I don't keep things from her." Nadine took a swig of her beer.

"And she's okay with it?"

"One hundred percent. She trusts me. I'd never do anything to jeopardize my family, even for my first love."

Ivy's cheeks burned. "I was your...your first—"

"Love. Yep. You were my perfect woman. Well, except for your big flaw."

"Hey, now. What's my big flaw?"

"You're straight."

Ivy laughed. Nadine's deadpan delivery made her laugh even harder. "I suppose that does create a dilemma."

"Undoubtedly." Nadine's smile faded, and a serious expression took its place. "Are we okay?"

"More than okay." Ivy felt lighter than she had in a long time, despite all the other craziness swirling in her life. "God, I've missed you."

"I missed you, too. That's why my wife said I needed to come. I had to make peace with you. I hope it won't be another decade before we talk again."

"She sounds like a special woman."

"She is. Oh, and one other thing."

"Why don't I like the sounds of this?"

"She's dying to meet you."

Ivy groaned. "Why didn't I see that one coming?"

Chapter Twenty

The cloying smell of brownies baking filled the kitchen. Rain giggled to herself, remembering the brownie batter incident. If Ivy was real, something that at the moment seemed questionable, Rain would likely have a lot of explaining to do if they ever met.

"It's been over forty-eight hours since your last out-of-body experience." Tracie knocked on the nearby door frame. "I'm beginning to think it might just have been stress."

"I sure the hell hope so. Or maybe it's just an Illinois thing, and I'm immune in Wisconsin."

"Clean honest living." Tracie smiled.

"I guess you're gonna have to clean out your office, so I'll have a nice room to live in."

"No way." Tracie shook her head. "You'd cramp our style."

Jeannie walked past with a sheet of brownies and thunked Tracie on the back of the head with her hand. "Behave yourself."

"You're gonna deny that you're a screamer?"

Jeannie's face colored. "That is not the point."

Tracie chuckled and leaned toward Rain. "I'd say her face says it all."

"Keep that up, and you're not getting any of these." Jeannie waved the tray under Tracie's nose.

"Fine." Tracie thrust out her bottom lip. "I'll be

good."

"Shouldn't you be mixing up your Bloody Marys?" Jeannie glanced at the clock. "Party starts in an hour."

Tracie let out a long exhale before she got to her feet. "You work me like a dog, woman."

"I can help." Rain wasn't exactly looking forward to the block party tonight, but it had been on Tracie and Jeannie's calendar long before she barged into their weekend.

"We wouldn't be allowed in if Tracie didn't bring Bloody Marys," Jeannie teased.

"Whoa." Rain held up her hands as if in surrender. "I don't want to mess it up and get you kicked out."

"They're a pretty forgiving lot," Tracie said.

"For Republicans," Rain said without thinking. Even though she was curious about the people Tracie talked so much about, she couldn't help being concerned about being in a deeply red part of Wisconsin.

Tracie glared but then said, "The vodka's in the pantry."

"On it," Rain said. It was probably best that Tracie chose to ignore her snide comment.

Tracie opened the refrigerator and began pulling out ingredients. "Hey, where's the garlic?"

"It's in there, just look," Jeannie said.

Rain plucked the bottle off the shelf and carried it to the island where Tracie had discarded several containers. She picked up a large bottle of tabasco. "Holy hell, you're going to load these suckers."

"Only way to serve them." Tracie pushed the refrigerator door closed with her elbow and dropped another armload of ingredients. Tracie stopped and looked at Rain. "Um…I wanted to say I'm sorry about my outburst last night. I just get fired up."

Rain caught Jeannie smiling and nodding out of the corner of her eye, but Rain's gaze remained on Tracie. "I'm afraid I was pretty rattled last night with all this body-switching stuff, so I'm not sure if I completely understood why the conference had you so angry."

Jeannie groaned and set a large pitcher on the island next to Tracie's pile. "Do you really want to get her going again?"

"I'm calmer today." Tracie smiled and blew Jeannie a kiss.

Jeannie chuckled. "You're on your own, Rain. I'm going to jump in the shower." She gave Tracie a peck on the lips before she sauntered out of the kitchen.

"Damn, she's hot," Tracie said after Jeannie had left.

Rain smirked and pointed to the doorway where Jeannie had just exited. "One day, I'm going to have that."

"Hey, now." Tracie stood up taller and glared. "She's taken."

Rain laughed. "You know what I mean."

"You ain't gonna find someone like Jeannie if you keep seeing Malibu Barbie."

Tracie had a point, but Rain wasn't going to admit it. "Back to my earlier question, what set you off about the conference?"

Tracie poured a generous amount of vodka into the pitcher. "I suppose it was the rabble-rousers that—"

"What the hell is a rabble-rouser?" Rain asked.

"A shit stirrer. An instigator."

Rain nodded. "Okay. Go on."

"There were these two young women who were fixated on how we worded our mission statement, wanting to make sure our language was inclusive enough."

Rain narrowed her eyes and studied Tracie. "What's wrong with that?"

"Nothing on the surface. I get that we need to do better, but then I found out their story, and it pissed me off." Tracie pointed at the jar of garlic. "Open that and throw a few scoops in."

Rain picked up the jar. "Are you gonna tell me what their story was?"

"Oh, yeah." Tracie shook a generous amount of Worcestershire sauce into the pitcher. "They're so deep in the closet that they're standing next to their eighth-grade cheerleading outfit."

Rain stopped mid-scoop and turned to Tracie. "What the hell does that mean?"

Tracie chuckled. "The analogy sounded much better in my head. I meant they're so deep in the closet that hardly anyone in their *real* life knows they're gay. Not their family. A few friends. And certainly not their work."

"There's lots of people who aren't comfortable being out or don't feel safe." Rain plopped the garlic into the pitcher.

"You call that a scoop?" Tracie took the spoon and heaped it full. "This is more like it." She handed it back to Rain. "Day in and day out, for the last forty years, I've been out there getting my ass kicked. I've put more blood, sweat, and tears into this movement than those two will ever understand. I've seen some pretty ugly things. Dealt with a lot of bullshit. So while

I'm out in the world getting pummeled, the only time those two join the fight is to attack their own."

Tracie grabbed the bottle of vodka and poured more into the pitcher.

Damn. Rain made a mental note to drink the Bloody Marys in moderation. "Maybe by speaking up in that group, they'll gain more courage to stand up in the larger community." Rain hoped her positive spin would curb Tracie's agitation.

"Bullshit."

Nope, didn't work.

Before Rain could speak, Tracie continued. "We're taking a beating in this battle, and we're clawing each other apart from the inside. Bit by bit, we're losing ground. Losing our allies and not gaining any more. Now more than ever, we need to hold on tight to our community, but that's not happening. We're fighting among ourselves. It makes me sick."

"But what about the old guard who want to push out trans people, non-binary—"

"That makes me sick, too. We need to sit down at the table and talk it out. Hear each other for a change instead of shouting each other down. Let the old-timers speak their peace. Be heard."

Rain had heard this argument before at some of the rallies she'd attended, mostly by people who wanted to deny everyone a seat at the table, so she couldn't let it go. "So the trans people should sit down, shut up, and listen?" Rain tried to keep the bite out of her voice but suspected she'd not been successful.

"All sides should sit down, shut up, and listen for a change. Seek first to understand and then to be understood. One of the seven habits from my man Covey."

Rain rolled her eyes. Tracie had been spouting wisdom from Stephen Covey since she and Rain met. "I saw that eye roll." Tracie smirked.

Jeannie breezed into the kitchen with a robe wrapped around her. She glanced at Rain and then Tracie before she frowned. She waved her finger in the air. "No more politics. We're going to have fun today."

Tracie looked away and busied herself with putting the ingredients back into the refrigerator.

"Good try." Jeannie put her hand on Tracie's back. "Enough politics. Rain's here to de-stress. Looking at your faces, this conversation is far from relaxing." She pointed at Rain. "You have permission to tell her to zip it."

"Yes!" Rain raised her fists over her head.

Tracie spun around from the refrigerator. "Just for that, no Bloody Marys for you."

Rain put her hand against her chest. "I'm crushed, but my liver thanks you."

❧❧❧❧

Ivy used a large stick to push one of the logs back onto the bonfire. It was their first of the season and one of her favorite events. The first get-together of the year and the last were always the most special because everyone made a point of being there, despite their busy schedules. Later as the warm weather wore on and summer vacations took hold, some of the Nash clan would be unable to attend. She'd not missed one in ten years.

As the darkness settled, the kids had scattered to play some of the same games she'd played when she was younger. Kick the can had always been her favorite, but now they'd taken some of the fun out of it as the kids texted their location to outwit the can guardian.

She glanced over at Violet, who was huddled with three giggling teenage girls. Ivy choked back her sadness. It wasn't too many years ago that Violet was right in the middle of the games, but now at fourteen, she'd grown too old for that sort of thing.

Where had the years gone? Ivy sighed and tuned back into the adults' conversation.

"I think Ivy did the right thing," her sister Rose said. "There's something off about Devlin."

"You only went once," Max said. "How did you make an assessment so fast?"

"I'm trained to analyze a situation quickly," Rose shot back.

Max laughed and turned to his wife. "She's going to play the policewoman card again."

"Officer." Rose stuck out her tongue.

"Mature," Max said. "And they let you carry a gun?"

Ivy smiled. She'd always envied Max and Rose's bond. Being two years older than Rose, he'd always played the big brother. Insanely protective of her, but also her biggest tormentor.

"Well, I say good on Ivy," Max's wife, Didi, said.

Ivy was glad it was getting dark, so Didi couldn't see the amusement dancing in her eyes. Didi watched way too many British TV shows and was always spouting British sayings. Occasionally, her Tennessee drawl was infused with a touch of Brit.

"It wasn't on purpose, it just kinda happened," Ivy said. She stared into the fire. "I'm not sure what came over me."

"God works in mysterious ways," Mama said. "We just need to keep praying, and maybe he'll send us some answers."

"Enough of this talk." Papa slapped his hands against his thighs. "Who's in for a game of cornhole?"

Max and Rose were the first on their feet. Ivy sighed. She'd sit this one out. She just wanted to stare into the fire and try to make sense out of the past week.

❧❧❧❧

Rain gazed into the fire. Her cheeks hurt from laughing so much. It was what she'd needed. Over forty-eight hours without a switch. Finally, maybe she could get back to her regular life.

Tracie and Jeannie had been right. Their neighbors had rolled out the red carpet for Rain and treated Tracie and Jeannie like royalty. Even though it made Rain cringe every time someone called Tracie and Jeannie *the girls*, it didn't seem to bother her friends.

Rain rubbed her overfull stomach. It was nearly ten o'clock, so they'd eaten hours ago. Unfortunately, Rain had wandered up to the heaping food table more times than she'd like to admit. She'd have to spend most of her life in the gym if she ate like this at home.

Many of the guests had already left, so it was down to a more intimate group. During the evening, some conversations had made Rain cringe, but she'd vowed to stay clear. Tracie and a couple of the guys were in a spirited debate over gun control. Then one of the men turned to Rain.

"Do you hunt?" he asked.

"No." She smiled and shook her head. Did she

look like someone who hunted?

৶৶৶৶৶

Ivy carried two giant glasses of ice-cold lemonade toward the fire. It had become her and Papa's tradition to end the evening with his favorite beverage. It was just after ten, and the last of the family had left. Cleanup had gone quickly. It was one of the nice things about such a large family. Now that they'd gotten older, everyone made sure Mama and Ivy didn't get stuck with a mess.

"Here you are." Ivy handed him his glass before she sat in the lawn chair beside him. "Just the way you like it, extra sour."

He laughed. "Better not be, or I'm gonna throw it on the fire."

Ivy smiled at their ongoing joke. Papa liked sweets more than anyone she'd ever met. Maybe he was perpetually high.

"What's that twinkle in your eye about?"

Oops. He'd caught her. "Nothing. Just happy to be out here with you. It was a nice party."

He nodded and took a drink of his lemonade. "Ah. Perfect. It was a nice party. I can't believe how quickly they grow."

"I was thinking that, too. Frank's shaving, and Violet's got breasts now."

"Stop. I don't want to hear anything about my baby girl having those things."

Ivy stifled a chuckle. Papa couldn't even bring himself to say breasts. "Max and Rose's kids are growing like weeds, too."

"I remember when you used to sit on my lap

roasting marshmallows." Papa sighed. "Seems like it was only yesterday. Those were the good old days."

There was something in his voice beyond nostalgia. "You seem weary tonight. Is everything okay?" Ivy asked.

He turned and met her gaze. "Sometimes, I think I'm just getting too old to understand the world anymore. I never wanted to become a relic. I've embraced technological advances and use them on the farm—when I can afford it." He shrugged. "I know most people probably believe we're backwards here in Mullins Creek, but I've tried really hard to break that stereotype and never be that guy."

Ivy put her hand over the top of his. "I certainly wouldn't call you a relic. Who do you think taught me that learning is the most important thing anyone can do?" Ivy pointed toward Granny's house. "I have a gigantic stack of library books on my desk to prove it." She hoped her attempt at levity would lighten his mood.

He sighed. "I reckon you're right."

"Spill." She could always read Papa. "Something's happened that put you in this melancholy mood."

"It's nothing."

"Don't give me that." Ivy smiled. "When extra sugary lemonade doesn't do the trick, something's wrong."

"It's extra sugary now, is it?"

"Maybe." Ivy averted his gaze and stared at the fire.

"I'll be damned." He laughed. "You've been slipping extra sugar into my drink for all these years, haven't you?"

"Busted." Her decade-long secret had just been

blown. "This was always our time, so I wanted it to be extra special."

"So you loaded me up with sugar." Papa let out a belly laugh. "I always wondered why the lemonade around the fire was the best—"

"An extra spoonful of sugar will do it."

Papa laughed again. "Aren't you full of surprises? Does your Mama know?"

Ivy smirked. "I'll never tell."

"Well, I'll be dipped in shit. I've been played all these years."

"In Mama's defense, she's only known for a few years. She caught me putting in the extra spoonful a while back, but I swore her to secrecy. She said she didn't mind since it made you less drowsy at the end of the night, so you didn't fall right to sleep."

Papa's eyes widened. In that moment, the meaning of Mama's words registered, and Ivy's face burned from more than just the fire.

"The vixen." Papa laughed hard and pointed at Ivy. "You should see the look on your face."

Ivy turned away, sure she'd remain red for the rest of the evening. "Can we get back to what we were talking about? What's got you so down?"

Papa wiped the tears of laughter from his eyes. "After that, I'm not sure I'm down anymore."

"Very funny." Ivy continued gazing at the fire, still not ready to meet his eye. "Tell me."

"It was something silly. Happened a couple of months ago, but I haven't been able to shake it. And now this thing with Pastor Devlin has me asking myself questions. All sorts of questions is all."

"Still as clear as mud." Ivy squeezed his hand.

"What do you know about white privilege?"

His question took her off guard. It was nothing they'd ever discussed before, but by the serious look on his face, it weighed heavily on his heart. She measured her words, wanting to say something profound. "I know it's something we should pay heed to, but to be honest, I'm not so sure how to do it. And sometimes, it makes me feel ignorant."

"You too?" He turned to her and smiled before he looked back into the fire. "I thought you youngsters had it all figured out."

"Afraid not."

He squeezed Ivy's hand. "Am I a racist?"

Dang it. He was full of tough questions. Of course, she'd never believe her Papa was a racist, but she didn't think he wanted her to outright dismiss it, so she said, "What do you think?"

He shook his head. "I didn't used to think I was, but now I don't know." He turned to her. "I read things from both sides, ya know."

She hadn't known. Her conservative father never ceased to amaze her. "I didn't," she said.

"I didn't used to," he admitted. "But with all the divisiveness in our country and everyone being so angry...more hateful...I wanted to find out for myself what was making everyone so mad. I didn't want some TV personality telling me what to think."

"Wise." It was all that Ivy could think to say as she processed what Papa was telling her.

He rubbed the stubble on his chin. "I haven't even told your mama about this. It would only upset her. I went into the city for that car show. Afterwards, me and a few of the guys went downtown for dinner. Walked past a Black Lives Matter rally. One of the guys, I didn't know him very well, he was a friend of

Joe's, came up from Missouri. Well, this guy yells out, 'All lives matter.'"

"Oh, Papa. Why'd he do that?"

"I don't know. The marchers weren't doing anything or bothering anyone. But he thought it was necessary to stir things up." Papa swallowed hard.

"For you to be so upset, something more had to have happened."

"I kept walking. I just wanted to get to the restaurant. I wasn't looking for any trouble." He tilted his head back and looked up at the stars. "Then this young black woman stepped in front of me. Couldn't have been much older than twenty-one. She pointed at me and called me a racist." He stopped talking and continued to stare at the sky.

After several beats, she said, "What did you do?"

"Something dumb. I should have kept walking and left well enough alone."

Ivy's heart raced. Did Papa, the man she respected more than anyone, do something to be ashamed of? She wanted to change the subject but knew she couldn't. "Can you tell me?"

"I told her I wasn't racist, but I never should have said anything."

Ivy's stomach clenched. By his demeanor, she knew there was something more to his story, so she said, "How did she respond?"

"She laughed at me. Said my privilege was showing and that she could spot a racist a mile away." He shook his head. "I tried to tell her about Sam." Papa's eyes glistened like they always did whenever he mentioned Sam.

Sam had been in the service with Papa and died in Papa's arms when an IED had taken out the Jeep they were riding in. Papa escaped with his life. Sam hadn't been so lucky.

Papa dropped his gaze to the fire. "She looked at me with more contempt than I've ever seen. I thought she was going to spit on me for a second. I wish she would have."

≈≈≈≈

Rain bit her tongue. She wouldn't get into a political debate with Tracie and Jeannie's neighbors.

"People kill people not guns," the man said.

Ugh. Why did he have to say the stupidest line in the world? "So now you're going to resort to clichés and sound bites?"

"Come on. Let's talk about something less divisive, like religion." Tracie laughed, obviously hoping to cut the tension.

"No, I want to hear what Slick means by that."

Slick? Now he'd resorted to name calling. Should she retaliate and call him *Bubba?* It would be justified but still not a good choice. She'd met so many bearded men in T-shirts and baseball caps that they'd all started to look the same, so she couldn't remember his name. She took a deep breath. "All I'm saying is that's a simplistic way of looking at things. An argument used to cut off any logical debate."

"Ha," he said loudly. "Logical debate. I've not heard anything logical from your side in forever. Your version of logic is do as we say because we know better. Well, no thank you, ain't no ivory tower snowflake going to tell me what to do with my guns. You do know about the Second Amendment, don't you?"

Rain bit her tongue. If she weren't sitting here

with her friends, she'd school him on what a fool he was, but she'd need to pick her words more carefully. Plus, he'd been hitting Tracie's Bloody Marys hard, so that wouldn't help the situation. How could she nicely tell him he was an idiot?

Jeannie jumped up from her chair. "I'm going to get another brownie, anyone want one?"

"I'll take one," the man said. "I think Slick needs one, too, might sweeten her up."

Rain fumed, but she didn't want him to know he'd gotten under her skin. "Sure, Jeannie. I could use another."

While Jeannie scurried off, the man stared at her. "Ya gonna answer my question?"

"Do you even know the basic tenets of sensible gun control?"

🙢🙢🙠🙠

"Oh, Papa. What could have been so bad that you wished someone would spit on you?" Ivy asked.

He stood and put more logs on the fire. They crackled as they lit. He didn't speak until he sat back down. "She said that Sam was my token...token..." He shook his head. "I won't say the word she used, but I was shocked. Sam was like a brother to me. I would have gladly given my life for his. The color of his skin didn't make no difference to me." He looked down at his lap.

Ivy reached out and took one of his hands. In a soft voice, she said, "I can tell there's more."

He brought her hand to his lips and kissed it before he lowered it back to the arm of the chair, but he didn't let go. "She asked me how many black friends

I have. I just stared at her dumbfounded 'cause I don't have any. A couple of acquaintances but none I could call friends."

"But we live out in the middle of a cornfield. There's not much diversity in Mullins Creek." Papa's gaze dropped to the ground. "That's exactly what I said. It wasn't for being racist, it's just the opportunity isn't there. Her laugh was so cruel. And then she said, *Spoken like a true racist.* I've heard that argument before when I've read up on it. Convenient to claim there's no opportunity for it. But maybe I'm just lazy. Disrespecting Sam's memory."

Ivy's heart broke for him. His pain permeated the air, but she didn't know what to say to make it better. "You're the hardest-working man I know. There's nothing lazy about you."

"I feel lazy. I've spent my life raising you kids and trying to put food on the table. Now it all seems selfish. Not only did I not make an effort to have more diversity in my life, but I also didn't do it for you kids, either. Maybe she was right about me."

"No, she—"

"Wanna hear the worst part?"

No. She really didn't, but she said, "What's that?"

"We went into the restaurant, and Joe's loud-mouth friend wouldn't let it go. He went on and on about the protesters. Said horrible things. One other guy joined in, while the rest of us sat around uncomfortably trying to change the subject. I didn't buy into what he was saying. I don't think any of us did, but we sat there like wimps not saying a word. I left there feeling so ashamed. It was a quiet ride home."

He squeezed her hand tighter and drank the last of his lemonade.

In all her years, she'd never seen him like this. "You're a good man. A bad man wouldn't even question it, but you've been carrying this weight around with you for months. A selfish and lazy man wouldn't do that. If anything, I love—"

The fire cracked.

Sulfur.

Chapter Twenty-one

*F*uck. Rain had been sure she'd been cured after two days, but she certainly wasn't in Wisconsin anymore. The fire burning in front of her was much bigger than the one she'd been sitting around.

She flinched when she realized the man next to her was holding her hand. It took all her willpower not to snatch it away from him.

"What in the world was that?" the man said.

Ivy's dad. She wasn't sure if that made her feel better or weirded her out. She hadn't held hands with her dad since she was five. Ivy's dad's hands were large and calloused and engulfed Ivy's tiny hand.

She took two centering breaths. "What was what?"

He turned to her with a puzzled expression and pointed to the fire. "Didn't you hear that boom coming from the fire?"

"Oh, yeah, that. Yeah, I heard it." Rain hoped she sounded convincing.

"And that smell." He held his nose. "Probably one of Max's kids. Threw a stink bomb in there."

She glanced around the area. She didn't see any kids. It was just her and Ivy's dad.

He chuckled. "Probably a slow-acting one. The shell has to burn away before the center's ignited. Those kids are something else."

Rain laughed, too, unsure what else to say. "Now that the excitement's over, where were we?"

Shit. She had no idea what they'd been talking about. This could get awkward fast. Her mind flashed to Ivy, and she inwardly groaned. If they did switch bodies, Ivy would be right in the middle of a gun debate with Bubba.

When Rain didn't speak, he said, "Thanks for listening to my story. I prefer you not saying anything to Mama."

"It's our secret," Rain said, hoping that was the right answer.

"So back to my original question. What's your thought on white privilege?"

Fuck. From gun control to white privilege. Someone must hate her. And how was she supposed to have this conversation with him? Her first thought was to flood him with everything she knew, but somehow, she doubted it would be Ivy's style. Why did she care? She'd already caused Ivy enough problems with the dickhead preacher and then got her high, so she felt she owed Ivy better this time around.

Rain cleared her throat. She needed to channel the woman she'd been getting to know the past week. "That's a pretty complicated subject, Dad." That should be a safe enough answer.

His head whipped around.

Shit. Not safe enough.

"Dad? Did my story upset you so bad that I'm no longer Papa?" The hurt in his amber eyes, the ones that matched his daughter's, was clear.

"Sorry, Papa," she said, hoping to fix the mess she was creating. "White privilege is such a tough subject that I temporarily forgot myself." That even sounded lame to her ears, but maybe he'd buy it.

He continued to study her. Unconsciously, she squeezed his hand. It was as if Ivy's body took over since it was certainly nothing she'd have thought to do.

It worked. He smiled and turned back toward the fire.

"I was listening to NPR the other day," he said.

Her eyebrows shot up. That wasn't something she'd expected to come out of his mouth. "And?"

"They were talking about it. I'm trying to wrap my mind around the concept, but sometimes, it's hard."

Rain bit her tongue. Normally, she'd unload on someone who made such a comment, but out of respect for Ivy, she wouldn't. "What makes it so hard to understand?"

He waved his hand toward the barn. "I don't feel privileged. I've worked this farm since you were a baby, trying to give you and your brothers and sisters a good life. But after all that, I still could lose it all. The equipment's getting older and older. Seems like I'm repairing it more than it's running." He chuckled. "I've just about run out of duct tape and chewing gum to hold it all together."

Surely, he was joking, so she let out a short laugh. "I might have a little chewing gum in my purse, but I normally don't carry duct tape." Where in the world had that come from?

His belly laugh startled her, but then she sat back and enjoyed the sound of it.

"I'll keep that in mind when I run out." He sighed. "I'm just feeling sorry for myself. I know there's some things I don't have to worry about, which is probably what they're talking about. For instance, I don't worry what could happen to Jimm...James if the cops pulled him over. As a father, I can't imagine how that must feel." He ran his hand through his hair. Some of it remained standing and cast odd shadows from the fire.

She glanced at him and could feel his anguish. It shocked her when she realized her heart went out to him. What was wrong with her? She sat here feeling sorry for a white cis male. This body swapping was starting to do weird things to her.

He glanced at her, apparently waiting for her to respond.

How could she explain it to someone like him? Her thoughts jolted her. When did a simple man, trying to raise his family become *someone like him*? She didn't have time to analyze herself, she needed to come up with an answer before he got suspicious.

Her mind flashed to something she'd seen a long time ago. It might work. "Ya know, Da... Papa, I saw this really interesting video on YouTube one time."

He nodded and met her gaze.

"It was a race with a bunch of kids. A hundred-yard dash, so the coach had them all stand at the starting line. Then he told the kids that lived in a home with two parents to take a step forward. Told them to step forward if they'd not went to bed hungry or if they'd not known anyone that died of an overdose. Anyone that hadn't experienced racism. I can't remember all the things he said, but the point was that by the time the race started some of the kids were halfway to the finish line."

He snapped his fingers. "I saw that on Facebook

one time."

"So that's the thing. It doesn't mean that white people like us never have hardships, but it means that most of us probably started the race a lot closer to the finish line."

He smiled and nodded. "When did you get to be so wise, Ivy June?"

"I was taught by a good man," Rain said. *Wow.* She kept pulling statements like that out of her ass. Something about the fire, the farm, sitting here holding this man's hand was having a weird effect on her. She could feel his pain and his goodness, but she couldn't say how. All she knew was that she wanted to help erase some of the pain etched on his forehead.

He squeezed her hand. "Thanks for the talk. I heart you, Ivy."

Oh, god. Another possible trap. Should she respond in kind or tell him she loved him? She took a leap of faith and said, "I heart you, too, Papa."

He smiled. She must have given the right answer.

He held up an empty glass. "I better get inside to Mama. She'll be mad if I let the extra sugar go to waste." He winked at her.

Rain had no idea what he meant, so she decided returning the wink was the safest choice.

❧❧❦❦

No! Ivy had been having such a nice conversation with Papa, but Mullins Creek was long gone. She glanced around the small fire and at the faces sitting around it. One face caught her eye. She'd seen the woman in pictures in Rain's house.

Judging by the surroundings, she wasn't in Oak

Brook at Rain's house, but where was she? She didn't have time to consider it further because an angry-looking man stared at her from across the fire.

"Since you want to talk about gun control, let's." His eyes bore into Ivy, making her want to crawl under her chair.

"Pardon," Ivy said, wanting to buy herself time to figure out what was happening.

"I said—" the man started.

A woman carrying a plateful of brownies inter-rupted. Ivy had seen this woman in Rain's pictures, as well. She seemed a little overly enthusiastic about passing out dessert, but who was Ivy to judge? She took a brownie and smiled. The woman winked at her before she made her way around the rest of the circle.

Ivy set the brownie on her lap and broke off a piece and put it in her mouth. She sensed someone staring, so she looked up, expecting it to be the angry gun control man, but he was busy with the woman with the brownies. Ivy turned to her left and met the gaze of Rain's friend.

Her hair was grayer than in the picture, but her square jaw and penetrating eyes were unmistakable. But why was she staring?

Before Ivy could address her, the angry man said through a mouthful of brownie, "I'm waiting for your answer, Slick."

"About gun control?"

"I'm pretty sure that's what we were talking about. You were about to school me on how you and your kind want to take away my Second Amendment rights."

Ivy gazed into the man's eyes. Ironic that she and Papa were just talking about how angry people were nowadays. "I see something I said made you angry. Can you explain that to me?" That should buy her time to figure a way out of this.

The vein in his forehead stood out. She suspected that it likely throbbed, but the glow of the fire didn't cast enough light for her to say for certain. "Damn right I'm pissed. You people are like broken records. Every time something happens, the first thing you want to do is take my guns away."

"I understand that upsets you. Can I ask, do you have children?"

"Oh, here it goes." He crossed his arms over his chest. "Gonna start telling me that I don't care about my kids because I want them to get shot up in school."

"No, sir." Ivy shook her head. She kept her voice level when she continued, "I was curious, if you have children, what have you taught them about guns?"

The man sat up straighter in his chair and thrust out his chest. "I have three, two boys and a girl. I started teaching them when they were ten. Their mom wanted me to wait until they were teens, but I won that argument." He smiled. "All three can shoot better than me."

Ivy smiled. "I bet your papa taught you, too."

"That he did. He had some of the sweetest guns, but he wouldn't let me touch 'em until he put me through my paces."

"And you did the same with your kids?"

"I did." He narrowed his eyes. "I'm not sure what this has to do with gun control."

"You're a good dad, as was your dad. Sounds like you had gun control in your family."

He frowned. "We didn't have no gun control."

"You just told me your papa put you through

the paces before you could touch them."

"Of course. But I don't need no government putting me through the paces."

"And from what you told me, I would probably agree. Unfortunately, every father isn't as responsible as you." She shrugged. "Some of these kids getting guns don't even have a dad. I for one would feel safer if I knew someone was putting them through the paces."

The man stared for several beats, and he nodded slightly. "The government would probably screw it up."

Ivy pursed her lips. "I won't deny that. That's why we need sensible gun owners like you at the table, coming up with the right policies. But everyone has dug in their heels, not even willing to sit at the table and talk. In the meantime, innocent people—children—are dying."

A shadow crossed his eyes. "Guns ain't the problem. Crazy people are the problem. Bad morals are the problem. And what about those violent movies the liberals are making money on hand over fist? What about those?"

"And therein lies the problem," Ivy said.

Rain's friend shifted in her seat next to Ivy. She moved to the edge of her chair and said, "Don't you think we've had enough of this discussion? I'd like to end the evening on a positive note."

"Let her finish," the man said. "This should be good."

Rain's friend sighed and sank back in her chair. "Go ahead, kid."

Ivy turned to her and smiled. "Thanks." Ivy thought she caught a puzzled look from Rain's friend, but she couldn't be sure.

The man had a satisfied smirk on his face when she turned back. "Tracie's given her permission. Let's hear what you've got."

"The problem is that we try to solve complex problems with simple solutions. We let the politicians convince us that there is one and only one thing that needs to be fixed. The right screams about mental health and the left about guns. Did you ever think we need to look at all the factors and do something about all of them? Instead, we sit here over a fire arguing amongst ourselves while nothing's ever done. And then we all lose."

"I'll be damned. A liberal with half a brain."

Ivy smiled to herself. She believed that was a compliment.

"Well, look at that, Jeannie." Tracie said to the brownie woman. "We put Tim and Rain's half a brain together, and they finally have a full brain to work with."

Tim laughed, so Ivy joined in, hoping it signified the end of the conversation.

Tracie leaned over and put her mouth near Ivy's ear. "Ivy, we need to talk."

Ivy's eyes widened. Did Tracie just call her Ivy?

Chapter Twenty-two

Rain flopped onto Ivy's bed with a library book she'd taken from Ivy's desk. She might as well make herself at home since she didn't know how long she'd be here. Hopefully, Tracie and Jeannie were observing her and would have some answers.

In a strange way, it was almost starting to feel like home. There was something warm and inviting about the room, despite its flaws. It was tiny compared to Rain's master suite, and the walls were nicked and marred. The wood trim appeared to be rotting in places, and the dark brown carpet should have been replaced a decade ago.

On the other hand, it had so many more personal touches than her modern, almost sterile, décor.

Rain rolled off the bed and wandered over to the pictures on the wall. She smiled at the goofy poses and the joyful faces. If only she knew who they were. She considered pulling them off the wall to see if there were names on the back, but something stopped her. She didn't want to mess up Ivy's room.

As she moved back toward the bed, a large book caught her eye. She pulled it off the shelf. It weighed a ton. When she dropped it onto the mattress, the springs squeaked.

She climbed back onto the bed and sat with her legs crossed. The decorative cover showed vines—no, it was ivy—growing up the side of a tree. *Clever.* Rain stared down at the book. Was it wrong to look at it?

She stared for some time before she carefully opened it. The first picture made her smile. A little girl with amber eyes, probably not much older than five, with a gap-tooth smile covered the page. No doubt, it had to be Ivy.

Rain took her time flipping through the pages, stopping to read all the captions. By the time she finished, she knew the names of all five of Ivy's siblings, along with a few of her high school friends.

Once finished, she closed the book and stared at the cover. There was something intimate about looking through someone's memories. She only wished Ivy was here to explain the pictures.

Whoa! Where the hell did that thought come from? Like she and Ivy would ever sit around and look at scrapbooks together. It was official, she was losing it. Maybe she should try to call Tracie. *No.* Something held her back. *Fear?* If she called, she might find out she was truly losing her mind. She opened the cover of the scrapbook and started the journey through Ivy's life again.

⚘⚘⚘⚘

Ivy followed Tracie and the brownie woman, who she'd discovered was named Jeannie. A feeling of dread descended with each step. They knew who she was.

It hadn't taken long before they'd said their goodbyes at the party. Tracie's eager look was unmistakable. No doubt she couldn't wait to question Ivy.

After Tracie told her they only lived a block and

a half away, they'd walked in silence. Ivy calculated they'd nearly reached their destination. Her heart rate accelerated when they turned down a path toward a cottage.

Maybe she shouldn't go into the house with these people. She could still take off running down the street. She doubted they could catch her if she did. *Seriously?* What did she think they were going to do to her? Besides, anything they did to her, they'd be doing to Rain. *Ugh.* Everything was so complicated.

Instead of being paranoid, she should be excited. Hopefully, she was about to get some answers. She squared her shoulders and followed them with a purposeful stride. Things would be okay.

After they entered the house, Tracie invited her to sit on the couch while Jeannie brought her a bottle of water. They both sat on the couch across from her.

Once they were situated, Tracie narrowed her eyes and let her gaze move from Ivy's head to toe. She pointed at Ivy and waved her hand up and down. "You even carry yourself different than Rain. Uh, I mean you carry Rain's body different than Rain does." She looked toward Jeannie. "Help me out here."

Jeannie patted Tracie's leg. "What she's trying to say is that even though you look like Rain, you carry her body different. More feminine."

Tracie laughed. "Oh, god, wait until Rain hears that. She'll be afraid she'll lose her butch card."

Ivy drew her shoulders in and crossed one arm over her chest and grabbed her opposite elbow.

"Stop it." Jeannie lightly slapped Tracie's leg. "You're making her uncomfortable." Jeannie moved to the edge of the couch. "It's okay, Ivy. I know you have to be a little scared."

Ivy glanced up from her lap and met Jeannie's kind eyes. Where Tracie came off gruff, Jeannie had a more maternal air. "How do you know who I am?" She tried to put strength into her voice, but she was sure she'd failed. Her insides felt like jelly, and she fought the urge to cry.

"Rain told us about you," Tracie said. "And... um...I'm sorry if I frightened you. I didn't mean to."

Ivy finally let herself hold Tracie's gaze and was surprised by what she saw. The large woman with the gruff exterior had softer features than she'd realized. Her face was weathered, but her crow's feet showed a lifetime of laughter. While her eyes weren't as kind as Jeannie's, they still held a warmth that Ivy wasn't expecting.

"What can we do to make you more comfortable?" Jeannie asked when Ivy still didn't speak.

Ivy took a deep breath. She needed to say something. "I'm just a little overwhelmed is all. It's been an interesting...a difficult week."

"That's an understatement if I've ever heard one," Tracie said with a chuckle.

Ivy smiled. "I suppose it is." Her smile faded. "Do you...does Rain know what's happened?"

"Afraid not," Tracie said. "She wasn't sure if she was losing her mind or if it was real. Obviously, it's real."

Upon hearing Tracie's words, tears welled in Ivy's eyes.

"What's the matter, dear?" Jeannie said.

"I don't know. Maybe I'm relieved or scared or both." Emotions welled inside of her, and she struggled to breathe.

"You're breaking my heart." Jeannie scooted

closer to the end of her seat. "Would it be okay if I come sit with you?"

Ivy bobbed her head up and down but didn't trust herself to speak.

Jeannie was across the room in a second and sat close to Ivy. "Is it okay if I put my arm around you?"

"Please," Ivy managed to croak out.

Jeannie wrapped her in a hug, and the floodgates opened.

≈≈≈≈

The faint sound of music drew Rain's attention away from the scrapbook. She glanced around the room, trying to find where the sound was coming from. The windows appeared to be closed, so it wasn't likely someone was playing their music too loud.

It sounded a bit like heavy metal, so she doubted if Granny was jamming out. The sound stopped, so she went back to looking at the book.

Not more than five seconds later, the sound came again. She turned her head from side to side, trying to figure out where it came from. Then it stopped.

This time, she stood, waiting for it to happen again. It didn't take long before the music returned. She traced it to the desk. To Ivy's purse. *Duh.* It must be Ivy's phone.

The music stopped once more. Rain reached into Ivy's purse and pulled out the phone. Just as she did, it went off again.

Rain looked down at the familiar number. One of the few she had memorized.

"Tracie?" Rain said into the phone.

"What the hell took you so damned long to

answer, kid?"

"Oh, god. Are you there with Ivy...with me...I mean Ivy in me. Not in me. In my body."

"Good god. Would you stop already? Ivy's gonna think you're a lunatic."

"Um, is she hearing all this?"

Tracie chuckled. "Did I forget to tell you I had you on speakerphone?"

"Asshole!"

᪥᪥᪥᪥᪥

Goose bumps ran up Ivy's arm as she heard her own voice say *asshole*. It sounded like her, but in a way, it didn't. The delivery was off. Now she understood how Tracie knew almost immediately when Ivy entered Rain's body.

"Hi, Rain," Ivy said, sure the voice came out more timid than what Rain would expect.

"Ivy? Wow. So glad to meet you. Well, not exactly meet you but hear you. I guess I've heard you, so it's good to hear you as me...did that—"

"Rain, put a sock in it." Tracie laughed. "Ivy's about to take your body and jump off a cliff if you don't stop babbling."

"Uh, yeah. Sorry. So it's real, we haven't lost our minds?" Rain asked.

"Nope, we haven't lost our minds." Ivy chuckled. "Just our bodies."

Rain laughed.

It was strange hearing her own laugh come from the other end of the phone, but Ivy pushed her racing thoughts aside, so she could focus on the phone call with Rain.

"Shit like this only happens in the movies," Rain said. "How did we get into this mess?"

"That's what I've been trying to figure out. I imagine it has something to do with the old woman at the rally."

"Like a curse or something?" Rain asked.

"Sheesh, that sounds pretty melodramatic," Tracie said.

Jeannie tapped her on the back of the head. "Not helping."

"Just saying." Tracie vigorously rubbed her head as if Jeannie had smacked her hard.

Ivy couldn't help but smile. In just the short time with them, she found them endearing.

"What the fuck, melodramatic," Rain practically shouted. "You try being shoved into a gorgeous blonde's body and tell me how you handle it."

Tracie raised her eyebrows. "Sounds heavenly to me. What are you complaining about?"

Jeannie glowered at Tracie and tapped the back of her head again.

Ivy's face burned. She couldn't believe they were having this conversation.

"I'm so sorry," Rain said. "I didn't mean...well, you are beautiful, Ivy, but that was so out of line."

"As was Tracie's comment," Jeannie added.

Rain groaned. "I'm tired and confused and obviously not thinking straight."

"And keep your hands off her body," Tracie said.

"Jesus," Rain said. "Jeannie, can you put her outside, so the adults can talk?"

Ivy laughed despite herself. Normally, talk like this would make her uncomfortable, but something about Tracie's unfiltered personality strangely put her at ease. An image of a gigantic teddy bear with the mouth of a sailor came to mind.

"And if it wouldn't be too much to ask, do you think you can refrain from smoking pot in my body?" Ivy smirked. She had no idea where her newfound courage came from, other than how at ease she felt with Rain's friends.

"What?" Tracie turned to Ivy. "Rain conveniently left that part out of the story."

"Um, well, I must have forgotten."

"Bullshit. I have to hear this." Tracie smirked at Ivy. "Now you see why I told her to keep her hands off you. She's a sly one."

"Goddamn it. Would you stop?" Rain practically yelled.

Ivy ignored Rain. "I thought my Granny was going to have me committed. When I popped back into my body, I was elbow deep in a bowl of brownie mix." Ivy exaggerated, enjoying Jeannie and Tracie's smiles. "I'm surprised I hadn't shoved my whole head into the bowl. I didn't have any idea what was wrong with me until I found the marijuana on my bed."

"You'd never been high before?" Tracie said.

"No, ma'am."

"Ugh, would you stop calling me that?"

Rain's laughter came through the phone. "You better relish it because you'll never hear it when I'm in my own body."

"I think I like this version of you better." Tracie winked.

"That's so cold," Rain said.

"She is sweeter than you," Jeannie said with a snicker.

"Ouch, now I'm mortally wounded," Rain said,

but her grin was evident in her voice.

Jeannie lightly touched Tracie's shoulder and nodded.

Tracie cleared her throat. "I suppose we better talk about how to address this little dilemma."

Ivy's chest swelled. The subtle exchange between Jeannie and Tracie confirmed her suspicions that they were trying to bring levity to the situation. It had worked. Ivy felt much more ready to handle the conversation now. She hadn't quite gotten used to her voice coming from Rain, but it wasn't nearly as jarring as it had been at first.

"It sucks that you guys are all together," Rain said. "And I'm stuck here."

Stuck. Something in the word cut into Ivy. Despite everything, she'd felt freer than she had in years. Was her life stuck in a rut?

"Are you okay, Rain?" Jeannie asked.

"Um, yeah. I hate—"

Sizzle.

Sulfur.

Chapter Twenty-three

*F*uck. Rain shook her head and glanced around Tracie and Jeannie's living room. She swore it was more jolting each time they switched. It didn't exactly hurt, but it was weird. Almost as if she were slime that had been sucked through a straw and then plopped into a container that she slowly oozed into.

Wow. Where had that imagery come from? If she didn't know better, she'd have thought Ivy had gotten her body high.

"Rain. Honey," a voice said. She felt a hand on her arm. "Are you back?"

Rain blinked several times and finally focused on Jeannie's concerned face.

"Yeah." Rain shook her head. "It's me." She frantically looked around the room. "Ivy?" She practically shouted.

"Relax," Tracie said. "She's probably back in her body. Ivy, you there?" Tracie called into the phone.

"I'm here," Ivy's soft voice came through the phone.

Rain's heart skipped a beat. Hearing Ivy's voice in this way was so much different than when she was in her body. Her tone was even more melodic than Rain had thought. She wondered if Ivy would look different in person, too. *Stop.* Now was not the time to think about those amber eyes or that sweet smile.

"Are you struggling to settle into your body like

Rain is?" Jeannie asked.

"Ah, I think so. It seemed different this time. More intense somehow," Ivy said.

"Yes. That's exactly it," Rain said. "I almost feel like something's missing. Uh, a piece of me."

"Empty?" Ivy's voice sounded far away.

Yes! It was almost as if her body missed Ivy, but she had no intention of saying that aloud. It would come out way too creepy, and they had just met. Kinda.

"Any clues to what caused it?" Tracie asked.

"Maybe because Rain wanted to be here. She was frustrated and wished herself here," Jeannie said.

"The sulfur smell is thick," Ivy said.

"Sulfur?" Rain sniffed the air. She looked at her friends. "Do you smell anything?" They shook their heads. "But you smell it, Ivy?"

"Yeah, it's about to make me gag. I need to open a window."

"We're on to something." Rain snapped her fingers. "I never thought about it, but sometimes, I smelled sulfur, and sometimes, I didn't."

"Do you think," Ivy's voice held a note of excitement. "Do you think that whoever caused the switch gets the smell?"

"That makes sense," Tracie says. "Kinda the origination of the detonation."

"Holy fuck." Rain laughed. "That was a mouthful. How about we just say the source?"

Tracie's lip curled. "Fine. Source works, too."

"It's a start. We've got one puzzle piece in place," Rain said. "Jeannie, do you have a paper and pen? I want to take notes."

❧❧❧❧

Ivy's frustration rose. They'd been talking for another half an hour, but they'd not come any closer to unlocking more of the mystery. Most of that time they'd spent going down a rabbit hole that led nowhere. She gazed down at the list she'd written. Still no pattern emerged.

1. Rain sex with Sasha (sulfur)
   Ivy brunch with family
2. Ivy on phone with Rain's parents (sulfur)
   Rain asleep in Ivy's bed
3, Ivy in church (sulfur)
   Rain asleep in own bed
4. Rain in church telling off Devlin (sulfur)
   Ivy in Rain's kitchen
5. Ivy in bedroom by herself (sulfur)
   Rain at desk before quarterly meeting
6. Rain high talking to Granny (sulfur)
   Ivy in Rain's office
7. Ivy with Papa around fire pit (sulfur)
   Rain at barbecue
8. Rain in Ivy's room on phone with them (sulfur)
   Ivy in Wisconsin with Tracie and Jeannie

"How about," Rain said. "Maybe it happens when we're both experiencing something similar. Like just now, we were both frustrated, and earlier, we were both sitting around a campfire."

"Hey, you may be on to something," Tracie's voice came through the phone.

A twinge of sadness pinged in Ivy's chest. She wished she were back with the others. *Ridiculous.* She needed to focus on solving the problem not longing for a coffee klatch or slumber party.

Ivy sighed. The first switch contradicted the theory, but she didn't want to talk about it. She took a deep breath, willing herself to just say it. At least in this instance she was glad she was alone in her bedroom. "I don't think that holds up in light of the first switch."

"Hold on." Tracie chuckled. "I think we need to hear it from Ivy's point of view."

"No, we don't," Rain said.

"I'm afraid I'm going to have to side with Tracie on this," Jeannie said. "We can't leave any stone unturned."

"Ugh," Rain said. "I don't think we need to go there."

Heat rose up Ivy's neck. "I can do it."

Rain groaned. "I don't know which will be worse, hearing you tell it or having Tracie gape at me with her ugly mug while you do."

Ivy launched into the story. After the first couple of minutes, she was able to ignore the burning in her cheeks as she filled in the details.

Tracie's laughter echoed from the phone. Ivy thought she detected the faint sound of Jeannie trying to stifle her laughter, as well. And there was no mistaking Rain mumble-swearing in the background.

"Poor Ivy had to be subjected to you doing the nasty, with Sasha of all people."

"Really? The nasty? Are you in junior high?" Rain asked. "It wasn't like I knew we were going to switch. I thought it was a private moment."

Ivy grinned, something about Tracie brought the devil out in her. "Trust me, I could have gone a lifetime without being *thrust* into your private moment." She made sure to emphasize the word thrust.

"Good one," Tracie said with a laugh. "So were you like in the middle of it, or—"

"If you must know, I was just about to orgasm," Rain huffed.

"So, Ivy, did she? Or did you? Ugh, did one of you arrive at the big O?" Tracie asked.

Ivy put her hand against her red-hot face. She'd likely have crawled under the table if she were still with the others. The memory of that first time flooded back, and she felt a stirring inside. She shifted positions, so her pillow was no longer pushing against her groin. "Um, let's just say, the mission was accomplished."

Tracie burst out laughing.

Ignoring Tracie, Rain said, "See, there's nothing similar about the two situations."

"I think we need to look at it a little more closely," Jeannie said. "I think both could be considered joyful times."

Tracie laughed. "Leave it to Jeannie to spin together a wholesome family gathering with Rain's sleezy orgasm."

"It was not sleezy," Rain said.

"Whatever," Tracie replied. "But I can at least follow the logic train. Do the other times fit?"

"Smoking pot and the quarterly meeting doesn't hold," Rain said.

"Now wait," Ivy said. "Euphoria?"

"Euphoria?" Rain said. "At a quarterly board meeting?"

"I thought it was kinda fun since I don't get to do anything like that working as an aide in the school. For a minute, I felt like I had a career. Something I'd always wanted, but it wasn't in the cards." Ivy stopped, suddenly feeling exposed. When no one spoke, her discomfort grew. "Stupid, I know, but I thought I should be truthful."

"Not stupid at all," Rain said with conviction. "From what I heard, you were a hit. Everyone was raving about how on I was, or I guess you were."

"We have two potential matches," Jeannie said. "What about the rest?"

Ivy ran her finger down her list. "Nope. Some of the others don't hold."

"Back to the drawing board," Tracie said.

"Ivy, do you remember what the old woman said to you?" Jeannie asked. "Rain said she couldn't remember since she was so freaked out by the whole thing."

"I remember it perfectly. It rings in my head all the time," Ivy said. "She kept pointing at us and saying, love—"

Electricity.

Sulfur.

♫ ♫ ♫ ♫

Rain jerked and reached toward her chest. *Breasts. Bigger breasts.* She was back in Ivy's body. She looked down at her hand in horror and jerked it from Ivy's chest.

"Looks like it's happened again," Tracie said.

"Yeah," Rain answered and fell back against the pillow on Ivy's bed.

"Hold on," Jeannie said. "Ivy, tell me again what the old woman said."

"Love or hate. Hate or love," Ivy said.

"Damn, nothing. I thought I had it," Jeannie said. "Earlier, I remember Rain had just said hate when it happened, and now Ivy said love. I thought maybe."

"Good thought," Rain said. "But obviously another dead end."

𝒩𝒩𝒩𝒩

Ivy yawned. It was nearly two a.m., and the day had taken its toll. She wanted to find a solution, but they were going in circles, and her focus was waning.

She was about to ask if they could call it for the day when Rain said, "I have a kooky idea."

"We're all ears," Tracie said.

"Ivy, humor me," Rain said. "Could you say one of the words that the old lady said?"

"Why don't you?"

"I want to be able to monitor the sulfur."

"I don't even know what that means, but I'm too tired to argue." Ivy stifled a yawn. "Here goes. Love—"

Sizzle.

Sulfur.

𝒩𝒩𝒩𝒩

Rain pumped her fist in the air. "That's it. Love or hate is the key."

"No, or you would have switched," Tracie said. "You're still here."

"I will be until the sulfur dissipates."

"What? This old brain is fuzzy this late at night," Tracie said.

"Do you get it, Ivy?" Rain said.

"If I'm following your train," Ivy said. "There's

a time lag between when it can happen, so we can't switch back and forth in rapid succession. Once the sulfur subsides, it's like a reset."

"Exactly." Rain smiled. Somehow, she knew Ivy would get it. She'd already begun to appreciate her brain—her intelligence.

Chapter Twenty-four

Ivy changed into her pajamas, more tired than she'd been in years. They'd switched back and forth a couple of times to prove Rain's theory. They'd discovered it took about ten to fifteen minutes before they were recharged for the switch.

Now back in her own home, she was finally alone. Somehow, her room seemed different than it had. Smaller. Dingier. That wasn't fair. She loved her room and her life, but being in Rain's body made her long for something more.

Ridiculous. She was tired and not thinking straight, just like a two-year-old who needed a nap. Before she got into bed, she picked up the scrapbook on the comforter. She hugged it to her chest. This was her life.

Rain's face flashed in Ivy's mind. Had Rain been looking at her scrapbook? What had she thought? Ivy snorted. Rain probably hoped she wouldn't get trapped in some country hick's body forever. Rain was worldly, and her parents were in Europe. She had an exciting career, while Ivy still lived with her Granny and worked as a teacher's aide.

Ivy put her scrapbook on the shelf. Embarrassment washed over her. For a few hours tonight, she thought maybe they could be friends. That she could hang out with Tracie and Jeannie in Wisconsin with Rain. Yeah, right, like they'd want her there.

Despite her mood, she couldn't help but smile as she thought of Tracie giving Rain a hard time. There was no doubt how much Tracie loved Rain, just like an older sister who couldn't help but pick on her.

She snatched her phone off the charger as if it was the enemy. It had been her connection to the others when she switched back and forth. Now it mocked her. Reminded her that she was the outsider. She carried it to her purse and shoved it inside, no longer wanting to look at it.

She crawled into bed. Everything would look better in the morning after a good night's sleep. She pulled the covers over her head and closed her eyes.

※ ※ ※ ※

Rain had said her good nights to Tracie and Jeannie, but Rain knew sleep would be a long way off for her. The night played in her mind in an endless loop.

She shivered as she crawled into bed, even though it wasn't cold. She'd spent countless nights in Tracie and Jeannie's spare bedroom, but for some reason, it felt foreign tonight. Normally, it brought a sense of comfort, possibly the only place that had ever felt like home to her, so why did she want to jump in her car and travel back to Illinois?

A quick glance at the clock told her if she left now, she'd get home near dawn. That wouldn't be fair to Tracie and Jeannie for her to just up and leave. She fell back against her pillow and stared at the ceiling.

Ivy's face, or more accurately, her eyes, were stuck in Rain's mind. She wanted to meet her—

needed to. Several times, she'd almost asked if they could meet up, but she'd held back. Ivy would think she was crazy. They had nothing in common. Ivy was surrounded by a loving family who adored her, while Rain had spent her life trying to prove herself to her parents. Ivy's parents were proud of her for just being Ivy, while no matter what Rain did, it never seemed to be enough. One cause after another. One more rally, in hopes that she'd be deemed worthy. Worthy of love. Worthy of attention. But at thirty-two, her only true friends were two lesbians in their sixties. Everyone else in her packed calendar didn't know her outside the cause she was championing. Lately, she'd not been able to keep track of her causes or the people running them.

Ugh. She was just tired and stressed. Things would look better in the morning. She rolled over to turn out the lamp, and her gaze fell on her cellphone. The one Ivy had held earlier to talk to her. She cradled it in her hands. A lifeline. Foolish, she knew, but somehow, it tied her to Ivy.

Would Ivy have gone to bed? She closed her eyes and imagined Ivy's bedroom. *Shit.* She'd left the scrapbook out. Would Ivy think it creepy that she'd been looking at it? Maybe she should apologize.

Rain sighed and unlocked her phone. She scrolled through her recent calls and smiled when she saw that Ivy had put her contact information into Rain's phone. That had to mean something, didn't it?

She clicked on the message button. What would she say? She typed and erased several messages until she finally settled on:

It was great to finally meet you. I'm sorry about

the scrapbook. I hope you didn't think it was creepy. I just wanted to get to know you better. Not in a stalker way. I thought it was important to know more about the person whose body I was sharing. Um, that probably came out wrong, too. I should probably stop while I'm behind. I'm sure we'll be in contact since one of us will slip up and say one of "the words." I wonder what happens if we write them. I won't try it now, just in case you're asleep. That's about it. Again, it was great meeting you. Good night, Ivy.

Rain hit send before she could erase another message. She lay in bed for a long time watching her phone in case an answer came in. Nothing. Ivy had likely fallen asleep, or maybe she didn't want to talk to Rain.

An hour later, Rain finally shut off the light and buried her head under the covers.

Chapter Twenty-five

The incessant buzzing of the alarm filled Ivy's tiny room. She rolled over and groaned as she tried to find the offending noise. Her hand traveled across the surface of her nightstand with no success.

Crap. Where was her phone? Ivy opened one eye and looked at the table. Bottle of water. Lamp. And a book.

She finally remembered she'd stuffed it into her purse last night, and the purse sat across the room on her desk. The offensive alarm continued to squawk as she glared at the distance between her and her phone.

She debated snuggling into the warm covers but thought better of it. Mama and Papa shouldn't have to deal with church alone, with whatever fallout might come from her outburst. Reluctantly, she pushed the covers off and made a dash to the desk.

Ivy had left the window open, believing sulfur permeated all the fabric in her room, even though she knew it wasn't true. This time of year, nights still got cold, and her room proved it.

She plunged her hand into her purse, grabbed the phone, and sprinted back to bed. Once under the covers, she hit snooze. With her teeth chattering from the chill of the air, it was unlikely she'd be able to fall asleep.

At least she could lie here a bit, check her email,

and maybe take a spin around social media. As soon as she unlocked her phone, she noticed a text message alert. Probably her cellphone company wanting to sell her an upgrade.

She hit the message icon and smiled. *Rain.* Then she frowned. The little circle with an R in the middle would never do. She needed to see Rain's smiling face when she opened the message.

She did something she'd been afraid to do the entire week: She Googled Rain Hargrove. Ivy stared at a long list of entries. Most of them revolved around Rain's work at the foundation and her activism.

Impressive. As she scrolled through, Ivy's heart grew heavier, but she pushed it aside. Rain had much to be proud of, so Ivy certainly wouldn't rain on Rain's parade. She giggled at her pun.

Ivy searched through the images. Most showed Rain in business attire, standing at a podium or around a board table. Several professional head shots popped up, but they looked too formal and stiff.

Her finger moved quickly over the screen, and photos sped past. She abruptly stopped and scrolled back to find the one that had caught her eye. It was a picture of Rain wearing a flannel shirt and backward baseball cap, but it was Rain's huge smile that captured Ivy's attention. This was the one.

The caption showed it had been taken during Rain's volunteer work with Habitat for Humanity. Ivy studied the picture. Rain looked so relaxed—so happy.

She'd been so focused on the pictures that her alarm went off before she'd read the text message. There wasn't much time, but she could at least find out what Rain wrote. Probably a reminder not to say one of the dreaded words.

Ivy opened the message. After finishing, she read it through two more times, each time her smile grew larger. Was Rain just being polite, or had she truly enjoyed talking with her? Ivy touched her cheeks. Despite the circumstances, she'd laughed a lot. Rain and Tracie's antics, with Jeannie as the straight man, had made what could have been a traumatic experience not only less traumatic but fun.

She needed to get ready for church, but she wanted to at least respond. Her thumbs hovered over the keyboard, but she stared at the blank screen.

"Just write something," Ivy said to herself.

Mama would be hopping mad if Ivy made them late to church since everyone would likely be staring when they walked to their seats.

She dashed off a message and hit send before she could overthink.

≈≈≈≈

Rain felt like a truck had hit her. She'd tossed and turned for what seemed like hours after she'd shut off the light. The clock read nine, so at least she'd managed a few hours of sleep. To avoid the traffic coming from the Wisconsin Dells, she needed to get on the road within the next hour or two.

She stretched and reached for her cellphone. It wouldn't hurt for her to lie here a little bit. In all the excitement of yesterday, she'd not checked her email, which was unheard of for her.

Her breath caught when she saw that Ivy had responded. She stared at Ivy's picture, the one she'd found last night while she couldn't sleep. In the picture, Ivy wore a sleeveless shirt; more than likely, it was a sleeveless dress. Ivy had been named the teacher's aide of the year, and the photo was of her accepting the award.

As soon as Rain had come to the picture, Ivy's huge smile and amber eyes leapt off the screen. Rain had looked no further.

She took a deep breath before she opened the message.

Sorry I missed your text. I was exhausted and fell asleep as soon as my head hit the pillow.

Rain tried not to read anything into Ivy's words. Just because Rain couldn't sleep didn't mean Ivy should be burdened by the same affliction.

It was great meeting you, too. I know this might sound silly, but I had a really good time last night.

Rain's chest swelled. Maybe she hadn't been being sappy after all. Ivy had enjoyed herself.

I know we still have things to figure out. Since we'll likely say one of those two words again, no matter how hard we try not to. Even though we just met, would it be wrong to tell you I look forward to working with you to find a solution?

I've probably already said too much, but why stop now? :) Something's happened to me since that day at the rally. It may sound crazy, but I don't think I'm the same person I was last week. And I hope we get the chance to get to know each other better.

I have to go now before I'm late for church.

Whatever you do, please don't switch bodies with me this morning. I don't want you to get me kicked out of church :) :) HA HA... that was a joke.

Have a great day. And if you're not too busy, maybe you can call me when you get home. Please at least text, so I know you made it home safely.

Rain smiled like an idiot as she reread the message. The only people who ever asked her to text when she got home were Tracie and Jeannie. Her parents didn't even know she was in Wisconsin.

Maybe she should text back. *No.* Ivy had specifically said to reach out when she got home. She wouldn't bother Ivy while she was trying to get ready for church.

Rain bounded out of bed, suddenly ready to tackle the day.

Chapter Twenty-six

Rain stared at her calendar but wasn't really seeing it. She needed to get a handle on her agenda for next week, but she'd not been able to focus. The last hour, the clock seemed to be moving in slow motion. This was the third time she'd checked it, and it had only moved two minutes.

She still had nearly forty-five minutes until she was scheduled to call Ivy. As soon as she'd gotten home, she'd texted and let Ivy know she'd made it. She hadn't wanted to disturb Ivy's family time, so she'd asked if she could call her at eight tonight. Ivy had responded, *Sure,* with lots of exclamation points and emojis. Rain took it as a good sign.

Giving up, she tossed her calendar onto the counter and stood. Maybe she should take a walk around the neighborhood to burn off some excess energy.

Her phone dinged, and she snatched it off the counter. Maybe Ivy wanted to move up the time of their call. She hit the message icon and squinted at the screen. What did that mean? She read the text again.

Want to come out and play?

When she didn't respond right away, another text came through.

I'm horny.

Rain's eyes widened. *What the fuck?* Maybe Ivy was accidentally texting the wrong person, although the Ivy she knew wouldn't be texting things like this. She rolled her eyes and said aloud, "Sure, because you're such an expert on Ivy in a week."

Another text came through.

I'm rubbing my pussy now. You better come quick.

Rain slapped herself on the forehead. *Dumbass.* She'd had Ivy so much on the brain that she'd not paid close enough attention.

Her fingers flew over the keyboard.

Not tonight, Sasha.

Fine. But just so you know what you're missing.

A picture came through, and Rain promptly deleted it without looking. Would she have done that a week ago? She shrugged. She wasn't the same person she was then, so who knew?

❧❧❧❧

Ivy had already slipped into her pajamas and told Granny good night. It was almost as if her family sensed that she needed a break, or maybe as strange as she'd been acting, they feared she was heading for a breakdown.

Either way, she'd been able to come to her room

early and prepare for Rain's call. Not that she needed to prepare for it, but she wanted to wind down from her busy day. It had been a good day. She'd felt more content than she had in months. Throughout the day, she'd looked forward to her call from Rain.

To get her mind off Rain, she'd sat at her desk and picked up one of her library books. She'd reread the same passage for the third time when the phone rang. She jumped.

"Hi, Rain," Ivy said into the phone.

"Hello. Is this still a good time to call?"

"Perfect." Ivy got up from her desk and made her way over to her bed. "I was just reading."

"You mean from that enormous pile of library books?"

"How did..." Ivy laughed. "Oh, yeah, I guess you would know."

"I might have to say one of the dreaded words because I really want to know what happens in that thriller."

Ivy leaned back against the headboard. Her fears that there would be awkward silence dissipated. "Don't you think it would be easier to check out your own copy from the library?"

"Where's the challenge in that?"

Ivy smiled. "I'll make you a deal."

"Cool, I like deals. What is it?"

"You get your own copy, and then we can read it together."

"Like a book club?" Rain asked.

"No, like a book accountability club."

Rain laughed. "What the hell is a book account-ability club?"

They'd bantered about the accountability club

for a bit before Rain asked, "How did church go?"

Ivy groaned. "It was okay. Devlin wouldn't look in our direction, and his sermon was about straying from the flock. Somehow, I think it might have been directed at us."

It surprised Ivy when Rain asked several poignant questions about the service and seemed to be interested in her answers.

"I don't want to come off rude," Ivy started to say.

Rain laughed. "Which means you're planning on saying something rude."

"Oh, god, you're right. That's the only time people say something like that, isn't it?" Ivy smiled. The interaction was surprisingly easy.

"Afraid so, but go ahead. Hit me with your best shot."

"You just seem to know a lot about church, and um, you don't seem like you're all that religious. I was just curious is all." Ivy hoped Rain didn't take offense.

"Wanna know something else that will likely shock you?"

"Sure."

"I've read the Bible cover to cover—twice."

"Wow." Ivy's face flushed. "I'm embarrassed to say I've never read it cover to cover."

"I bet a lot of churchgoers haven't," Rain said. "Oh, shit. I didn't mean to imply anything negative."

"No offense taken," Ivy said. "After you witnessed the worst of my church, how could you not have some negative feelings?" The statement made Ivy uncomfortable, so she turned the conversation to Rain's trip to Wisconsin.

They talked for over an hour without a lull in
the conversation. Ivy had stretched out on her bed
and rested her head on her pillow. Another sign she
was relaxed.

Ivy tried unsuccessfully to stifle a yawn.

"Sounds like I'm keeping you up past your
bedtime," Rain said.

"Nah. Having to get up for church this morning
after the late night is catching up with me. I'd hoped
for a nap, but Mama talked me into helping her with
her vegetable garden. If everything we planted grows,
we'll have a feast."

"I've never had a garden," Rain said. "I had a
couple house plants, but they died. I've never grown
any food, though."

"Not even herbs?"

"Nope, nothing."

"You'll have to come check it out when
everything starts growing." *Oh, no.* Did she just invite
Rain to the farm? Ivy braced herself for Rain's polite
rejection.

"That would be awesome." The smile in Rain's
voice was contagious.

They'd talked for another half an hour when Ivy
yawned again.

"Shit, I'm sorry," Rain said. "I was going to let
you go a while ago. Then I started yammering again."

"I like to listen to you yammer."

"Gee thanks, I think."

"It was a compliment," Ivy said.

"I was just wondering...um...well," Rain said,
stumbling over her words. "Since we still have this
predicament and all. That maybe we should talk
regularly?"

"I'd love—"

Crackle.

Sulfur.

⚜⚜⚜⚜

"Oh, shit," Rain said, now in Ivy's body. She glanced around Ivy's bedroom and grinned. She was stretched out in Ivy's body on the bed, just like Rain had imagined she'd be.

"I'm so sorry," Ivy said in Rain's voice. "I didn't mean to."

"Another reason we need to talk on the regular," Rain said.

"Can this be our time?" Ivy asked. "Maybe check in at eight o'clock every night. Debrief."

"That's a great idea."

Chapter Twenty-seven

Ivy pulled her car to a stop in front of the familiar house. Maybe she shouldn't have agreed to this. Just because they'd shared a body didn't mean they had anything in common. Their lives were polar opposites. Rain was a city girl through and through, while Ivy was pure country. Besides, what did a conservative Christian have in common with a liberal activist?

Her hands shook. Yeah, this was a bad idea. Even though the past two weeks, they'd fallen into the routine of talking every night and had accidentally switched bodies multiple times, it didn't mean they'd have anything to talk about. Likely, the evening would be filled with them awkwardly staring at each other. She should leave and call Rain and tell her she'd changed her mind.

Ivy reached for the gearshift just as the front door flew open. Rain appeared sporting a huge smile. As soon as she spotted Ivy, she waved and bounded down the three steps. *Shit.* Too late, Rain had seen her and loped toward the car. In person, when Ivy wasn't in Rain's body, she looked taller and her shoulders broader.

Ivy needed to stop gaping, but she sat frozen. Her heart raced, and her stomach clenched. She tried to smile but was afraid it came out a grimace.

Rain arrived at the car, threw open the passenger

door, and climbed in beside Ivy. "Hey you," Rain said with an even bigger smile, if that was possible. "I can't believe we're finally meeting in person."
"We met at the rally," Ivy reminded Rain.
"I don't think that counts."
Ivy shook her head. "Me either."
Rain narrowed her gaze. "You're freaking out, aren't you?"
Damn her. It was as if sharing a body helped Rain read her, or maybe that was just who Rain was. Ivy nodded but couldn't find any words. Tears welled in her eyes, making her even more annoyed with herself. This was a crazy reaction. If she kept it up, Rain would doubt her sanity.
Rain reached out to Ivy but stopped and pulled her hand back. "Um...I was going to pat your arm, just to you know...offer you reassurance or something, but after all the talk of Haskins...I didn't want to give you the creep factor."
Ivy glanced at Rain out of the corner of her eye before she turned back and looked out the windshield. She bit her tongue to stifle a giggle. An image of Rain as an overzealous puppy flashed through her mind.
Seeing Rain so enthusiastic and vulnerable was what Ivy needed. The butterflies churning in her stomach subsided as Ivy unhooked her seatbelt and turned fully to face Rain. Ivy smiled, a genuine smile, for the first time when their gazes met. Rain's blue eyes were even more expressive in person, and her eyelashes would be any woman's dream. "Sorry, I'm a bit nervous." Ivy held up her hand as proof. It still trembled slightly. "But hey, look, it's better than it was a few minutes ago."
"May I?" Rain motioned toward Ivy's hand.

"Please."

Rain sandwiched Ivy's hand between hers. The warmth and the strength were reassuring. "It's okay. What has you so on edge?"

Good question. Unfortunately, she didn't have a good answer. Ivy shrugged.

"Okay, good. Now that we have that cleared up." Rain smirked. "Would you like me to serve you dinner out here until you feel more comfortable?"

"Oh, god, I'm so sorry. You've got dinner waiting for me inside, and I'm sitting here like an idiot."

"No pressure. We can sit out here for as long as it takes. No need to apologize for how you're feeling. This is all a bit overwhelming."

"Aren't you nervous?" Ivy asked, hoping she didn't sound as hopeful as she felt.

"I was up until about an hour ago." Rain met her gaze. "But then I got so excited to see you. To meet you face to face that I forgot to be nervous."

Ivy chuckled. "How does one forget to be nervous?"

Rain shrugged. "It's a talent, I guess. For the past hour, I've been playing out in my head how our first meeting would go."

Ivy grinned. "In any of your scenarios, did it involve sitting in my car, trying to convince me not to slam it into gear and peel out of here?"

Rain laughed. "I have to admit. That wasn't one of my scenarios. Pretty short-sighted of me, don't you think?"

"I'd say." This time, Ivy smiled fully.

Rain's forehead creased. "But can we go back to throwing the car into drive and escaping? Were you planning on letting me out first?"

Ivy looked up at the roof of the car and pretended to think. "Hmm, I hadn't thought that through."

"What do you say you turn off the car and come inside?" Rain patted Ivy's hand. "And if after that, you still want to get the hell out of here, you can. But at least have some dinner first."

❧❧❧❧

Rain pulled the pan of vegetarian lasagna from the oven. It smelled divine. Too bad she hadn't made it herself.

After a quick tour of the house, Ivy excused herself to wash up before dinner. Meeting Ivy in person had left Rain unsettled. Rain hadn't recognized her own discomfort until they'd come inside. She'd been so focused on putting Ivy at ease she'd not had time to think of anything else. But as she gave Ivy the tour, Rain couldn't help but notice her reaction to Ivy.

Damn it. She couldn't—no, wouldn't—be like the leery Haskins. In person, Ivy's amber eyes were even more mesmerizing. They held a softness and genuineness that Rain rarely saw.

As if on cue, Ivy entered the kitchen. Her shoulders curved in slightly, and her gaze remained on the floor. Her long blond hair was swept to the side, but it looked slightly different than what Rain had grown accustomed to. Rain narrowed her eyes and studied Ivy before she figured out why. She was used to seeing Ivy's face in the mirror, so it appeared different from this perspective.

Ivy's blue maxi dress brushed against her sandaled feet. Despite its simplicity, it was possibly the most sensual dress Rain had ever seen.

Stop. She needed to get a grip on herself. What a creep. This was her friend. Her straight friend, so she needed to stop acting like a hormone-infused teenager. *Stop acting like Haskins.*

"Everything smells delicious," Ivy said but still didn't meet Rain's gaze.

"Courtesy of Whole Foods," Rain admitted.

"You mean you haven't been sweating over a hot oven all day?" Ivy smiled.

"Trust me. It's better this way. I want you to come back."

"Oh, so my embarrassing moment in the car hasn't dissuaded you from inviting me again?"

"Quite the contrary." Rain removed the garlic bread from the oven and turned it off.

"Do you want some help?"

"Sheesh. I just took the bread from the oven. Is it that obvious I don't know what I'm doing?"

Ivy chuckled and motioned toward the stove. "Since you just turned on the stove burner and left the oven on, my answer would be yes."

"Oh, shit." Rain set the bread on the counter and punched buttons on the stove.

Ivy hurried across the kitchen and in one motion snatched up a dishtowel and picked up the pan. "Um… this is too hot to set on the counter without something under it. Do you have any trivets?"

"I'm not sure."

Ivy narrowed her eyes. "How can you not be sure if you have a trivet?"

"Probably since I don't know what a trivet is." Rain smiled sheepishly and pointed to a drawer. "There's all kinds of stuff in there. I'm not sure what, though. Most came from my housewarming party."

"How long ago was that?"

"Seven or eight years."

"Seriously?" Ivy held the pan of garlic bread with one hand while she tried to rip the plastic off of whatever she'd found in the drawer.

Rain wandered over and stood helplessly watching. She should probably do something but feared she'd only get in the way.

They were only a couple of feet apart when Ivy glanced at her. "Mind opening this package?" Ivy handed her a set of what looked to be giant coasters.

"On it." Rain randomly yanked a knife from the knife holder.

Just as she was about to cut through the plastic, Ivy called, "Stop. Do not use a good bread knife. You'll ruin it."

Rain looked down at the serrated knife, the one she used for almost everything. "Bread knife?"

"Don't tell me you didn't know that."

"Um, is that a trick question?"

Ivy groaned, but amusement danced in her eyes. "If you tell me you cut your steaks with that, I'm going to...."

Rain gazed at her expectantly, but Ivy had stopped talking. "I need to know what you're going to do before I decide whether I should plead the Fifth."

"Oh, good lord, you do, don't you?"

"Maybe." Rain gave Ivy her best innocent look. The one she used often when picking up women. *Oh, god.* She shouldn't use that look.

Ivy peeked into the drawer and pulled out a pair of scissors. "These should work."

Rain took the scissors and sliced through the plastic before triumphantly slapping the largest coaster onto the cabinet. "Which knife should I use to cut the lasagna?"

Ivy pulled a knife from the holder. "This will do."

Rain studied the lasagna and put the tip of the knife in one spot but then moved it to another before she lifted the knife again. "Uh, how big should I make these pieces?"

Ivy held out her hand, and Rain relinquished the knife.

Now that the initial awkwardness had passed, having Ivy here felt so natural. "Do you think with everything that's happened, we have some kind of cosmic connection or something?" Rain asked. "Things with you just feel...I don't know..."

"Familiar?" Ivy pointed to a spatula, and Rain handed it to her. "We need plates, too."

Rain went to pull two plates from the cabinet and noticed the salad bowls on the shelf above. "Shit. There's Caesar salad in the fridge."

Ivy chuckled. "You really don't do this often, do you?"

"No, that's why I offered to take you out for dinner." Rain pulled down two salad bowls. "You're pushing me outside my comfort zone."

"Good." Ivy had retrieved the salad from the refrigerator and peeled back the plastic. She started to say something and then shook her head. "Never mind. I'll look myself."

"What do you need? Maybe I can help."

Ivy rifled through a couple of drawers before she held up a contraption. "Got it."

Rain stared. "Isn't that for making meatballs?"

Ivy stopped midstride and stared at Rain. "With

this?" She held up the utensil. "Holy cow. How big of meatballs do you intend on making?"

"Let me show you." Ivy handed her the contraption.

"See right here." Rain held it up and pointed to the two big scoops on each end. "I thought you put the meat in here, and then..." Rain used the handles to clamp the scoops together. "Then you form the meatball in between."

Ivy laughed. "Or you use the *salad tongs* to pick up salad."

"Oh." Rain's face warmed. "Yeah, or I guess you could do that, too."

"Remind me never to ask you to cook meatballs."

"How about you remind me never to cook?"

"Oh, no." Ivy shook her head. "You're going to learn to cook." Ivy's face reddened. "I mean, if you keep me around."

"Now I'll have to if I'm going to become the next Rachael Ray."

Ivy smiled. "Okay, Rachael. How about we start with you learning basic kitchen utensils?"

Rain shrugged and rolled her eyes. "I guess even Rachael had to start somewhere."

Once they'd sat at the dining room table, Rain said, "Our earlier conversation got derailed by the impromptu kitchen lesson."

"Which conversation was that?" Ivy took a bite of the lasagna and closed her eyes. "Not bad. My compliments to Whole Foods."

"Why do I think you could do it better?" Rain took her first bite. *Yum.*

"I've always believed homemade is the best. Mama's lasagna is to die for, although she uses beef, so you wouldn't be able to eat it. But I'm sure she could whip up a vegetable one."

Rain's chest filled. The thought of visiting Ivy's home, as herself, made Rain surprisingly happy. "Do you cook?"

"With Mama around, I'm mostly the sous chef, but I can hold my own. I learned from the master." Ivy waved her hand. "But enough about that. Why can't we ever finish a conversation?"

"Huh?" Rain tore off a piece of garlic bread and dipped it in the lasagna sauce.

"It's like we have three conversations going at once. We start one. Then we chase down another path that branches into another before we circle back to the original topic."

"We do that, don't we?" Rain smiled. "That's why I have to keep a notepad on my nightstand."

Ivy frowned. "To answer your question about cosmic telepathy, after that comment, I'm pretty sure we don't have it."

"I'm not following." Rain searched her mind for an answer but found none.

"Exactly." Ivy grinned. "I have no idea how you went from a cosmic connection to your nightstand."

"Ah. I have this notepad I keep by my bed. That's where I usually am when we talk at night. So if we get off on a tangent, I write down the topic, so I can circle back to it."

"I should have guessed." Ivy slapped her hand on the table. "And here I thought you were just hanging on my every word and remembered to circle back on your own."

There was probably more truth to Ivy's statement than Rain cared to admit. Eight o'clock had become what got her through the day. She'd bowed out of more than one evening meeting or left early, so she'd be available at eight o'clock.

"Sorry. My mind's not that good, regardless of how scintillating the conversation."

"Wow. I've never been called scintillating before. I love—"

Sizzle.

Sulfur.

Chapter Twenty-eight

Ugh. Ivy had let down her guard and blew it. She looked across the table at herself. "Now this is creepy," Ivy said.

Rain, in Ivy's body, stared slack-jawed. "You got a little sauce on your...uh...my cheek."

"Seriously, that's your first reaction?" Ivy swiped at Rain's face with a napkin.

"It's bad enough sitting across the table from myself without having to look at pasta sauce dripping down my face."

Ivy looked at the napkin and held it up. She pointed at a tiny red spot. "I would hardly call this enough sauce to be dripping. I'm not sure how you even saw it."

"I've got good eyes...er, or I guess you do." Rain rubbed Ivy's upper chest above her breasts. Ivy suspected Rain was trying to soothe away the tightness if it was anything like what Ivy was experiencing.

"Hey, are you touching me?" Ivy raised her eyebrows, hoping to lighten the weirdness of the moment.

Rain looked down at her hand—Ivy's hand—in horror. "Uh...no. Sorry, I—"

Ivy burst out laughing, and Rain joined her. *Weird.* She never thought she'd be sitting across from herself watching herself laugh. "I was joking. I wanted to wipe the look of horror off your...ugh...my face."

Rain looked away. "This is too fucked up for words. Maybe if I don't look at you or me with you in me. What the fuck? That sounded wrong."

Ivy chuckled. "It's a bit more disconcerting than I might have imagined." Ivy started to reach out to take Rain's hand but realized she would be taking her own and pulled back.

"Is this just too big of a mind fuck, or does this feel different?" Rain uncovered her eyes.

Ivy stared into her expressive amber eyes. Many people had said they were her best feature, and in this moment, she could understand why. But when she gazed into them, something felt different. There was something she didn't recognize as her own. "I think I understand what Tracie meant. When she said she knew immediately it was me in your body." Rain had averted her gaze, so Ivy said, "Look at me."

Rain took a deep breath. "I'll try, but this is strange."

Their gazes met.

"I don't k—"

"No," Ivy said. "Don't talk. Give me your—my—hands." Rain obliged, and they linked hands across the table. "No words. Just look at me. Feel me."

After they sat like this for several minutes, Rain broke the silence. "Wow. That's wild."

"What are you feeling?" Ivy knew what she felt as her chest filled with emotion, but she wanted to hear from Rain.

"I'm looking at me." Rain shook her head, and her cheeks reddened. "But I'm not. My expressions are different. My eyes are softer."

Ivy wondered if she blushed the same way, or if this was only how Rain blushed as her. "How do you feel about it?" Ivy asked.

"This is gonna sound totally crazy, but I like me better."

Ivy cocked Rain's head and stared.

Rain pointed. "That's the look. It's not a Rain look. It's sweeter. More genuine."

"Less guarded?"

"Exactly," Rain said.

Ivy's mind was running in overdrive. She was trying to listen to Rain's words, while she studied herself across the table. "I have an idea. Let's focus on you first because I can't do both at the same time."

"You can go first," Rain volunteered.

"No, I'd rather you."

Rain motioned toward their nearly empty plates. "What do you say we go sit in the living room where it's more comfortable?"

"We should clean up first." Ivy stood and began to gather up the dishes.

"Um, I think just this once we can leave them and do it later."

Ivy glanced at the plates, uncertain how she felt about it. "Compromise. We at least clean off the table and set it in the kitchen."

Rain laughed. It startled Ivy, and she jumped. Hearing her own laugh made everything more surreal. She gathered as many dishes as she could, needing time to think.

Rain collected the rest of the dishes, which was fewer than what Ivy had, but still Rain held them awkwardly. She'd perched the wine glasses precariously in the center of the lasagna tray.

Ivy pointed. "You might not want to do that. I'm thinking we're gonna need another glass of wine, so breaking them wouldn't be a good idea."

"I've got more."

"Not the point."

Ivy stepped back and watched herself walk toward the kitchen. God, she hoped she had more grace than that. It was apparent that Rain wasn't accustomed to wearing dresses. Her legs were spread too far apart and her strides too long.

When they entered the living room, Ivy sat in the recliner and crossed her legs underneath herself.

Rain hid her smile. She was pretty sure she hadn't sat that way since she was five and had a tea party in her room with her stuffed animals. Rain sat in the other recliner.

"Um...you might want to close your legs," Ivy said.

"Oh, god. Sorry." Rain looked down in horror and clamped her legs together. She sat as she always did with her knees spread wide. Not a good idea when she was wearing a dress.

"Much better." Ivy smiled.

To hide her embarrassment, Rain said, "It's not like you haven't seen your own panties before." She motioned toward her lap.

"True." Ivy smirked. "But I prefer you learn to sit in a dress, so you don't do that with my body in public some time."

"Good point." Rain sighed. "Let's talk about how fucking weird this is."

Ivy chuckled. "Seeing myself say the F-word is throwing me off."

Adorable. Ivy hadn't even been able to say fuck. "I'll have you swearing like a sailor in no time." Rain winked.

"I can think of some of your better traits that I'd like to pick up instead of swearing."

"Such as?"

"Your confidence," Ivy said without having to think about it.

Ivy's response caught Rain off guard. "Wow. I like that answer."

Ivy ran her hand along Rain's shoulders and across her chest. She let her hand run across Rain's washboard stomach. "Your body is so powerful. I guess you could say a bit masculine." Ivy blushed. "I hope that's not offensive."

"No, not at all," Rain replied. "It's something I've worked hard at. I never wanted anyone to look at me as a helpless female."

"Is that how you see me?" Ivy asked.

Rain swallowed hard. How could she explain how she saw Ivy? The one thing she knew was she wouldn't lie. "Not helpless but certainly a lot softer than me. Feminine. I'm embarrassed to admit, if I was in a boardroom with you, I'd probably have biases." Rain smiled. "Although that's burned me on more than one occasion."

"Burned you?"

Rain nodded. "Some of the most hard-nosed competitors I've ever gone up against are the really feminine women. The big burly guys are usually the easiest."

"Isn't that stereotyping?"

"I suppose, but it doesn't make it any less true. It's unfortunate, but it's almost like the more feminine-looking women have to work twice as hard to be taken seriously, so they develop this insanely hard shell. I've made the mistake of crossing a couple in my day. Big mistake."

Ivy smiled. "The confidence I'm picking up from you isn't real?"

"No, it's real, for the most part. I'm comfortable in my own skin." Rain laughed and took a handful of Ivy's dress and shook it. "I'm not so comfortable in your skin or your dress."

"I can tell. I certainly hope I don't look that awkward in my dresses. If I do, I need to get a new wardrobe."

Rain smiled. "You wear your dress well. You even make my body look better."

Ivy scrunched up Rain's nose.

Rain pointed. "That look alone isn't one I'd give. It's adorable, though." *Crap.* Did she just call Ivy adorable or herself? This was too much of a mindfuck.

"Was that a backhanded compliment?"

Rain laughed. "I was just thinking the same thing. See, I'm telling you there's some weird cosmic connection."

Ivy ran her hand through the short hair on the side of Rain's head. "This conversation is fascinating, but I'd prefer to have it in my own body. This is giving me a headache."

"Agreed." Rain sniffed the air. She couldn't detect any sulfur. "I'd love—"

Electricity.

Sulfur.

⚜⚜⚜⚜

Ivy shifted on the couch and recrossed her legs.

Odd how unnatural it felt to be in the position Rain had been sitting in. For some reason, the switch was more disconcerting when they were together.

"Damn," Rain said as she uncrossed her legs and squirmed in her seat. "That was intense."

"If it's all right by you, can we be really careful? I'd prefer to stay me while I'm here." Ivy smoothed the wrinkles from her dress.

"Definitely." Rain ran her hand down her face and rubbed her eyes. "Seeing me but not quite me is jacked."

"Where were we?" Ivy asked, hoping they could return to the conversation. It was fascinating to see how much their experiences were similar.

"Talking about the good and the bad of switching. You like my confidence, while I like your softness."

"Maybe we have something to learn from each other." Ivy had thought this all along but had never voiced it.

Rain pursed her lips. "Two people who'd never be sitting in a living room across from each other if this hadn't happened."

Rain's words stabbed into Ivy's chest. She knew they weren't meant to be hurtful, but they hurt just the same. "I know you're right, but it makes me sad."

"Why?"

Ivy looked down at her hands that rested in her lap. "It doesn't make you sad?"

"I didn't say that. I just asked you why it made you sad."

Ivy raised her eyebrow and gazed at Rain. "So does that mean it does make you sad?"

"Maybe." Rain smiled.

Ivy took it as enough encouragement to

continue. "I enjoy you. I enjoy this." Ivy waved her hand between them. "Talking. Getting to know you. Discovering who you are. Even though it's been crazy, it's been good, too."

"I feel the same." Rain averted her gaze. "I've got a lot of like-minded people in my life...."

Ivy's heart dropped to her stomach. Rain was about to tell her that she was a strange anomaly that didn't fit in her life but was something to study.

"But," Rain continued. "This past month, you've become my go-to person. When something good happens, I think *I can't wait to tell Ivy*. Or when something bad happens, too."

Ivy's spirits soared. She put her hand against her chest. "I feel the same." She looked away. "Well, it isn't like I have a lot of people in my life like you do."

"Ha. Are you serious? You've got the tightest-knit family I've ever known."

"That doesn't count." Ivy smoothed her dress.

"To hell it doesn't." Rain grimaced. "I bet every one of them would come running at the drop of a hat if you needed them."

Ivy nodded. "But you have a bunch of friends that would do the same."

"Debatable." Rain glanced at the window, not wanting to meet Ivy's gaze. "The relationships are different."

Was Rain just trying to make her feel better since she had no close friends? "Come on," Ivy said. "I've seen your calendar. You know more people than what lives in the entire town of Mullins Creek."

Rain shook her head. "Mostly acquaintances with a narrow focus."

Ivy looked at Rain blankly. She wasn't sure she

even knew what that meant.

"By the look on your face, that made no sense," Rain said. "We get together for causes. My friends Jodi and Lisa are big into gun control. Sarah, Gina, and Maddie, women's reproductive rights. Tessa and Jen are all about immigration. And—"

"Where does Sasha fit into that mix?"

Rain laughed. "A big mistake one night when I drank too much."

"No. I mean what cause?"

"She's only got one cause—herself."

"Ouch. And you're with her why?" Ivy hesitated to prod about Sasha, but she wanted some answers. Whenever Sasha's name came up when they talked on the phone, Rain quickly diverted the conversation. Would she do it again tonight?

"Weren't we talking about how it feels to be in each other's bodies?"

"In other words, mind my own business." Ivy tried to say it lighthearted, but Rain's unwillingness to share stung.

"No, no. Nothing like that." Rain slid to the edge of her seat as if she was trying to get closer to Ivy. "That's one of the things I'm enjoying about this friendship. We talk about everything, whereas with my other friends, we tend to stick with our narrow common interests. This feels like a whole friendship."

"All right then. Since it's a whole friendship, shouldn't you tell me about Sasha?"

Rain groaned. "Honestly, it's the most boring story in the world. Plus, it makes me look bad."

"Makes you look bad and boring? I'm not buying it." Ivy smirked. "If it makes you look bad, it should at least be interesting."

Rain chuckled. "You know for someone sweet, you have a dark side."

Ivy shrugged. "Stop stalling."

"Fine." Rain crossed her arms over her chest and pretended to scowl.

"The icy scowl won't work, either."

"Let's just say, Sasha might be classified as friends with benefits, except—"

"Except, what?" Ivy studied Rain. "Do you want her to be more?"

"God, no," Rain practically shouted. "This is going to make me look so bad, but I don't like her enough to consider her a friend."

"Oh." Ivy hoped her mouth hadn't fallen open. She felt naïve. How had she missed it? With as little time as Rain spent with Sasha, she'd not expected it was a serious relationship, but this surprised her.

"Do you think I'm awful?"

"No." Ivy shook her head. "I just think it's kinda gross."

"Whoa. Tell me how you really feel."

Ivy put her hand over her mouth. "I shouldn't have said that."

"But it's what you were thinking?"

Ivy reluctantly nodded. She wouldn't lie to make Rain feel better.

"I guess I should have expected that out of a conservative Christian." Rain's tone held a note of bitterness.

Ivy's shoulders stiffened, and she sat up straighter. Several biting responses flooded her thoughts, but instead she said, "Yeah, I guess it shouldn't have come as a surprise."

The tension in the room rose. They'd been

having such a good time; she never should have brought up Sasha. Maybe it was better that their differences derailed their friendship now before Ivy got any more attached to Rain. *Oh, god.* Judging by the feeling in the pit of her stomach, she was already attached. A wave of panic washed over her.

Rain stared at her with a look that was a cross between irritation and concern. When Ivy met her gaze, Rain said, "Did you hear a word I just said?"

"No," Ivy admitted.

"Mind telling me where you went? What you were thinking about?"

Ivy shrugged, but Rain continued to stare. "I was thinking how sad it was that I'd only been here a few hours, and I'd already screwed up our friendship." Ivy looked down at her hands. "And that I was starting to get attached to you, and maybe I should have just kept my mouth shut about Sasha."

The hard set in Rain's jaw lessened, but her eyes still held an edge. "I just didn't think me being gay made a difference to you. I thought you were one of those accepting Christians."

"It has nothing to do with you being gay." Ivy frowned. "It has to do with you sleeping with someone you don't even like, let alone love."

"Don't you think describing my relationship with Sasha as gross was a bit harsh?"

"Yucky then. Is that better?"

Rain glared for a second but then burst out laughing. "Damn. You're not going to let me get away with anything, are you?"

Ivy shook her head. "Afraid not. I know you think I'm being judgmental, and maybe I am. You don't have to do anything I say, but I'd be going against my principles if I acted like I think it's okay."

"And why do you think you have a right to judge me? Isn't that reserved for God in your worldview?"

"I wasn't judging you."

"Gross and yucky sounds pretty judgmental to me."

"You asked my opinion, so I gave it."

"I see. I thought you struggled with your confidence. Your response seemed pretty confident to me."

"I'm confident when it comes to my principles not my abilities."

Rain rubbed her chin and looked toward the ceiling. "That's pretty profound. What is the principle you're confident about?"

"I believe sex is something sacred. It should communicate love and affection."

❧❧❧❧

Rain stretched out like a starfish on her bed. Ivy had left over an hour ago, but Rain continued to stare at the ceiling no closer to sleep.

Other than the one tense moment when they talked about Sasha, they'd had an amazing time. They talked nearly nonstop. How was it that she felt more comfortable with someone who shared such different viewpoints than she did with some of the friends she'd had for years? Friends who shared her beliefs. This body switching was beginning to feel more like a body snatching. Her thoughts had been so jumbled since it began. Was it possible that bits of Ivy were being left behind in her own mind with each switch? As she pondered the thought, her eyes grew heavy, and she drifted off to sleep.

Chapter Twenty-nine

Rain groaned. It was her own damned fault that she was surrounded by a horde of sticky six-year-olds. Would she ever get it right and not say the words love or hate?

How did Ivy do this every day? They were swarming around her, demanding all sorts of things, and they kept touching her with their sticky hands.

The phone in her pocket vibrated. She pulled it out only to see her picture on the screen. *Duh.* Ivy must be calling her.

"I know. It was my fault. I need to erase those words from my vocabulary," Rain said into the phone.

Ivy laughed. "I promised the kids they'd get an extra recess today if they worked well with each other."

"Did they?"

"Yes, that's why I'm calling. Just take them out for recess. I'll switch us back as soon as I can."

"Recess?" Rain whispered into the phone, hoping the little beings around her wouldn't hear. "I don't know what to do at recess."

Ivy laughed again. "Wow. You can handle a boardroom but not first-graders?"

"They're scary."

"You were a kid once. Just remember what you liked to do at recess."

One of the kids yanked on Rain's arm. "You're

not supposed to be on the phone, and I haveta pee."

Ivy laughed. "Sounds like you've found Eugene."

"How the hel....How should I know?"

"Ginger-headed with freckles and Coke bottle glasses?" Ivy asked.

"Yep."

"That's Eugene."

"Great, I know one name. Care to tell me the rest?" The growing swarm whined and demanded her attention.

"Sounds like you better get them outside before you have a mutiny on your hands." Ivy laughed.

"You are so going to pay for this."

"What did I do? You're the one that switched us."

"Details." Rain gasped. "Oh, god, someone just hit someone over the head with a book bag."

"Let me guess, an angelic little girl with blond curls that would rival Goldilocks."

"You're good, how did you know?"

"She hit an adorable olive-skinned boy with big brown eyes."

"Right again."

"She's got a crush on him. That's Sylvia and Javier."

Rain chuckled. "Aggressive woman who knows what she wants. I like it."

"That's all I can help you with." Ivy chuckled. "I'm late to your meeting."

"I'm gonna need a stiff drink after this," Rain said before they ended the call.

Rain stared at her phone as if it would make Ivy come back. She sighed. How hard could wrangling a few first-graders be anyway?

One of the kids screamed. When Rain turned,

she found him on the floor holding up a bloody elbow.

࿆࿆࿆࿆

Ivy glanced at her watch. For the past ten minutes, she'd been trying to switch back and save Rain, but it hadn't worked. For some reason, it seemed longer this time, or maybe it was just her impatience.

Damn. Or maybe it was because she'd been whispering under her breath. Perhaps she needed to say it more forcefully. She frowned. If that was the case, why hadn't Rain just done it herself?

Ivy took a deep breath. "I love—"

Sizzle.

Sulfur.

࿆࿆࿆࿆

It worked. Ivy's eyes widened. What in the world had Rain been doing? The landscape around her whizzed by faster and faster. Ivy laughed and clung to the metal pole.

The children gathered around the merry-go-round and seemed to push it faster with each revolution.

"Stop. Stop," Ivy called out but laughed as she did. She shifted from her butt into a crouching position, ready to get off as soon as she thought it was safe.

The children laughed and clapped as the wheel lost momentum.

It was still turning, but it had slowed. She partially stood and made the leap. When she landed, she stumbled but managed to catch herself. As soon as she took a step forward, she weaved and nearly fell over. *God.* She was so dizzy she felt drunk.

The children laughed as they swarmed her. Hopefully, she didn't tip over and land on one of them. She hugged them against her as she steadied herself.

"Can we do the slide again?" Javier asked.

"Yeah," several other voices called out.

"That was a blast," Jocelynn said. "Please."

What in the world had Rain been up to? Ivy smiled to herself. As each day passed, she learned more and more about the woman she shared a body with and was surprised how much she'd already grown to like her over the past couple of weeks.

Ivy was looking forward to this evening's call to hear Rain's take on her experience with first-graders. Ivy chuckled to herself as the children pulled her toward the slide.

♋ ♋ ♌ ♌

"The kids said it was the best recess. *Ever,*" Ivy said.

Rain smiled and stretched out on the couch, ready for their nightly call. "What can I say? I'm fun." Rain chuckled. "Any time you need me to fill in, just say the word."

Ivy laughed. "Nice pun."

"Pun?" Rain crinkled up her nose, trying to figure out what she'd inadvertently said.

"Seriously?" Ivy groaned. "Say the word. Like in say one of *the* forbidden words."

"Duh." Rain laughed. "Good one, if I hadn't been too stupid to figure it out."

"You said it. Not me."

Rain smiled. She loved Ivy's playful side. "What did the kids tell you?"

"They said they were glad to know I didn't have a stick lodged so far up my ass that I couldn't have fun."

Rain gaped at the phone. "They did?"

"No!" Ivy laughed.

"By the way they were swarming you when I popped into your body, I don't think they consider you a boring adult."

"Probably not. We have fun, but I've never joined them on the playground equipment before."

"Why not?"

"Hmm, good question." Ivy took several beats before she spoke again. "I've been a little more reserved with this class. A little more careful."

"Why?"

"Umm...I don't know...I guess...um, ya know, I'm getting older."

Rain frowned. "Something's wrong. I can tell."

"But you've only known me for a minute, so how would you know?" Ivy's voice was soft and didn't hold any note of defensiveness.

"But I'm the only one you've ever shared your body with." Rain coughed and sat up on the couch. "Shit. That came out *way* wrong."

Ivy rewarded her with a laugh. "Do you want to try that again?"

"I'd prefer not to. But I'd like you to tell me what's going on, or at least tell me if what I'm picking up is right."

"You're not wrong."

"Is that like a double negative thing that means I'm right?"

"Possibly." Ivy sighed. "I can't believe I'm going to tell you this."

Rain grabbed a nearby pillow and hugged it to her chest. Something in Ivy's voice made her uneasy. She didn't say anything as she waited for Ivy to continue.

"I'm not comfortable with Mr. Haskins. You know, the lovely man you met at the rally."

"What does he do that makes you uncomfortable?" The hairs on the back of Rain's neck stood up. The bastard better not be laying a hand on Ivy.

"Nothing really. I'm just being silly. I shouldn't have said anything."

"Ivy, if he's doing something inappropriate, you have every right to say something."

"It's not like that. He's never touched me. Well, not that way."

"What way?" Rain suspected she knew the answer but wanted to hear it from Ivy.

"Nothing sexual."

"But he touches you, and it makes you uncomfortable?"

"Just in a friendly way. Like everyone does when they're talking to each other. You know, touching my arm, taking my elbow while we walk, or patting my knee."

"Do you think he'd do that with one of his male colleagues?"

"Oh, god, no. But I'm probably overreacting."

Rain's heart went out to Ivy. Just talking about Mr. Haskins seemed to be making her edgy. "Even if he does touch other people, if it makes *you* uncomfortable, it's still not okay."

"Pastor Devlin says this trend has gone too far

and made it impossible for a man to be a man in our society."

"That's bullshit," Rain said before she thought it through. "Sorry, I just don't understand how you and your parents can go to that church."

"My parents are good people." There was no doubting the edge in Ivy's voice. "I think we should end this conversation."

Rain's chest clenched. She hadn't wanted to upset Ivy, and she didn't want to end their call. "I'm sorry. I didn't mean to be offensive."

"Well, you were." Ivy's voice no longer held an edge. "I know you probably think my folks are uneducated rednecks, but they're some of the smartest, kindest people I've ever known, and I'm not just saying that because they're my parents."

Guilt washed over Rain. Was she biased? Even prejudiced? If she were honest, she likely was, but her conversation with Ivy's dad flooded into her mind. She didn't want to lie to Ivy, but how could she tell her the truth? "I'd like to say that you're mistaken, but I respect you too much."

"Meaning?"

"I'd be lying if I said I don't have preconceived opinions of people like your parents."

"And like me?"

Shit. This conversation was getting more uncomfortable by the minute. "Yeah, I suppose, but—"

"So why do you continue calling me every night if I'm some backwards hick?" Ivy's voice held more hurt than anger.

"That's what I was trying to explain. If you asked me a month ago, no doubt I would have written you all off as right-wing religious zealots." Rain stopped.

"I should just shut up. That sounded so terrible."

"Please, continue." Ivy's voice was soft. "It's hard to hear, especially from you. But I like honesty." Ivy's sweet voice gave her a note of encouragement. "You could have lied to me. It would have been easier. Most people would have, but you've been honest."

"Would it help to tell you that it's scaring the hell out of me?"

"Scaring you? Why?"

"I look forward to eight o'clock. It's the highlight of my day. You're intelligent, funny, and I enjoy talking to you. I value the friendship we've been building. So I'm in a catch-22." Rain sighed. "The best relationships are based on honesty, and I respect you too damned much to lie to you."

"That may have been the sweetest thing you've ever said."

"What, that I like you so much that I'm willing to call you a redneck hick?" Rain hoped that Ivy was ready for levity.

"Putting it that way, I rescind my statement."

"But I...I was just—"

Ivy laughed. "Just messing with you. Payback."

The tightness in Rain's chest released. "I've spent time with your family. Granted they didn't know they were spending time with me."

Ivy chuckled. "There's that, but go on."

"I really like them, so I struggle to understand how they got tied up with the likes of Devlin."

"Our old preacher died, and we had to find a new church."

"I don't know much about churches, but couldn't you have gotten a new preacher?"

Ivy sighed. "We tried, but we couldn't get

anyone who wanted to come out to Mullins Creek.
Besides, Devlin had been raiding our church for years
and swooped in when Pastor Armstrong died. I heard
rumors he was giving a signing bonus." She shook her
head. "But I think that was just talk."

"But why'd you go?"

"We followed the others." Ivy let out a burst
of air. "Maybe we never should have stayed, but we
did. I've been a part of a church community all my
life, so have my parents. Without one, I feel empty.
No excuse, but Devlin knows how to play on people's
fears."

"But how?"

"He uses the divisiveness in this country
to his advantage. He speaks to the fears of rural
Americans who feel like they're under attack. We're
too conservative. Not woke enough. Which translates
into dumb. He stirs up the congregation."

Rain sighed. "It's complicated, isn't it?" Every
time she talked to Ivy, she began to understand more
of the complexity that created division. Sometimes, it
made her sad, and other times, it just overwhelmed
her.

"I'm afraid so." Ivy let out a loud breath.

"Back to the original conversation." Rain smiled.

"What is the original conversation?" Ivy laughed.
"You've taken me down several other rabbit holes."

"Mr. Haskins."

"Can we talk about something else?" Ivy asked.

"As a matter of fact, I had something I wanted to
talk to you about. A proposition."

"You're propositioning me now, are you?"

"No!" Rain practically yelled, hoping that it
didn't blast Ivy's eardrum.

Ivy burst out laughing. "Sheesh, you're almost too easy."

Rain snorted. "Sure, you call me out for propositioning you, then you go around calling me easy."

"Are you going to tell me about this proposition?"

"Nah, never mind." Suddenly, Rain felt self-conscious. "It was a bad idea."

"Let me be the judge of that."

"I know it's a bit last minute," Rain said, "so I understand if you can't make it. But I've got tickets to the Cubs game on Monday, and I wondered...would you like to go with me? You could come stay with me for the weekend. Maybe go to Brookfield Zoo on Saturday. Or something." Rain knew she was rambling but was afraid to stop because then she'd have to hear Ivy's answer. "It's Memorial Day weekend, so it'll give us plenty of time to explore the city. Or maybe it's a dumb idea."

"Do you think you could take a breath, so I can answer?"

"Uh, yeah, sorry. It's just...it's not just a get-together since we need to do a little experimenting."

"Now you're propositioning me to experiment."

"Shit. That's not what I meant." Heat rose up Rain's neck and settled on her cheeks.

"Who could resist such a passionate offer? I'd lo— I mean, I'd like to. I just need to make sure someone will be around to keep an eye on Granny."

Chapter Thirty

Ivy leapt to her feet as the baseball sailed over the vine-covered wall in centerfield. She cheered and waved her arms around wildly as the batter circled the bases.

Rain snatched the hot dog out of Ivy's hand before she slung ketchup all over the surrounding fans. She smiled at the older gentleman sitting behind them when he mouthed *thank you.*

Ivy continued to scream, seemingly oblivious to having been relieved of her hot dog. It was refreshing to see a Cubs game through Ivy's eyes. Rain had spent so much time at Wrigley Field it had lost its magic, but watching Ivy's enthusiasm reignited Rain's passion, so she rose to her feet and yelled alongside Ivy. She was careful not to sling the hot dog on an innocent bystander.

Once the home run hitter had tipped his hat to the crowd from the dugout, the pair sat back in their seats.

"Hand it over." Ivy reached out.

"I didn't think you even noticed I took it." Rain grinned.

"Do you really think I'd lose track of my ballpark frank?"

"I'm not sure why you'd want it back after you ruined it." Rain tried to put on her best sneer.

Ivy snatched the hot dog. "Are you still going on

about the ketchup?" She shoved the half-eaten hot dog into her mouth.

"No self-respecting Chicagoan would ever put ketchup on a hot dog."

Through a half-chewed bite, Ivy mumbled, "Good thing I'm not a Chicagoan."

"Isn't everyone that lives in Illinois a Chicagoan?"

Ivy shook her head. She finished chewing and swallowed before she spoke. "Have you forgotten I'm a small-town girl living in the middle of a cornfield? We do things different there."

Rain's chest tightened. Something as simple as a hot dog reminded her that she and Ivy came from different worlds. It had been so easy to forget this weekend as they'd fallen into an easy interaction. But what would happen next?

"Are you okay?" Ivy asked as she studied Rain's face.

"Yeah. Sure." Rain shrugged. "I was just thinking about how much fun we've had this weekend."

The crowd groaned as the umpire called a third strike on the Cubs batter to end the inning. Ivy joined the crowd in their catcalls before she responded to Rain. "It's been the best." She squeezed Rain's knee. "I can't remember when I've had so much fun."

"You're not just saying that?" Rain wished she could take it back as soon as it was out of her mouth. The last thing she wanted was to come off needy and insecure.

"Of course, I'm not just saying it. The zoo, kayaking on the Chicago River, and now a Cubs game. How could we go wrong?"

Rain frowned. "I thought maybe you'd say the company you were with."

When Ivy turned and smiled, the sun caught the highlights in her hair. "The company hasn't been so bad, either. I wish I didn't have to go back home tonight."

"Stay." *Damn it.* What had gotten into her? She needed to find a filter, fast.

Ivy gave her a sad smile and sighed. "I'd lo— Oh, shit. I almost did it again."

Rain laughed. They'd accidentally switched twice during their time together. "I never realized how often we use the L and the H words until now."

"No kidding." Ivy clapped as the Cubs player made a diving catch in short left field. "Back to our conversation. Unfortunately, I have to work in the morning."

"Me too." Rain frowned. An internal battle raged. Should she say what she was thinking or let it go?

Her decision was delayed when the Cubs recorded the last out of the inning, and the familiar strains of *Take Me Out to the Ballgame* began.

Ivy clapped and was on her feet in an instant. She reached down and pulled Rain up. Most times, Rain remained silent or at best mumbled the words of the song but not this time. Soon she was belting out the lyrics as if she were at an Irish pub.

Ivy draped her arm over Rain's shoulder, and they swayed back and forth as they sang. Rain raised her hand high as she motioned for one, two, and three strikes. At the end of the song, they cheered wildly, and Ivy wrapped Rain in a hug.

Rain stiffened for an instant but then melted into Ivy's embrace. She held on to Ivy's slender figure, enjoying how well they fit together. When they let go,

Rain hoped the flush she felt in her face didn't show. Luckily, Ivy was too busy cheering for the upcoming batter to notice.

Rain leaned over and put her mouth near Ivy's ear to be heard over the lively crowd. "Do you want to leave after this inning?"

Ivy whipped around, her face only inches from Rain's. Caught off guard, Rain snapped her head back and stared into Ivy's intense eyes.

"Why would we leave now?" Ivy scrunched up her nose. "Are you insane? We're still down by two runs."

"Um...well, that's what some people do," Rain stammered. "I mean, to beat the crowds."

Ivy put her hands on her hips. "That's not what this person does. I stick around to cheer my team on until the bitter end."

"Sorry, bad idea." Rain held up her hands as if in surrender. "Forget I even mentioned it."

"Mentioned what?" Ivy winked.

"You know it'll take us at least three times longer to get out of here, don't you?"

"Got somewhere else you need to be?" Ivy raised her eyebrow.

Rain shook her head.

"The longer it takes for us to get out of here, the more time we get to spend together," Ivy said.

Rain smiled. "I like the way you think."

❧❧❧❧

Ivy dropped her bag onto the floor and slumped against the train seat. Rain had been right, it was a madhouse after the game, but it was worth it. Judging by the garb worn by the other passengers crammed onto the train, many had been at the game with them. The boisterous and likely drunken crowd was loud, making it difficult to hear anything, so she leaned against Rain.

Ivy rested her head against the taller woman's shoulder. "Thank you for letting us stay."

Rain smiled. "No, thank you. We would have missed an epic win if we'd listened to me."

"And we wouldn't have gotten to sing one of my favorite songs."

"Seriously?" Rain laughed. "*Go, Cubs, Go* is one of your favorite songs?"

Ivy widened her eyes. "How could it not be?" She softly broke into song, singing it directly to Rain, but soon some of the surrounding passengers picked it up. Before long, the entire train car had joined in.

When they exited the train and were walking toward Rain's car, Rain turned to Ivy. "Do you want to stop for something to eat on the way home?"

Ivy touched her stomach. She'd eaten more ballpark food than she probably should have, but the hopeful expression on Rain's face gave her pause. It would also delay her having to leave for home. "What did you have in mind?"

"Sushi. After how much you ate at the game, I doubt you'd be up for much more."

"Sushi?" Ivy crinkled her nose.

"Don't tell me you've never had sushi."

"I bought some at the gas station once, and it was pretty disgusting."

"Ugh. Seriously?" Rain shook her head. "It should be illegal for gas stations to sell sushi."

Ivy smirked and bumped her hip against Rain's

as they walked. "I bet you could join a group that protests gas station sushi."

"Are you insinuating that wouldn't be a meaningful cause?" Rain put on a scowl, but Ivy could see the amusement dancing in her eyes. Over the weekend, Rain had shared the insane number of causes she championed. It had become their running joke that Rain could find a cause for anything.

Ivy pulled out her cellphone and pretended to scroll. "Let's see. There's MAGSS. Mothers Against Gas Station Sushi."

"Really?" Rain glanced over her shoulder.

"No!" Ivy laughed. "And you say I'm the naïve one."

Rain joined her laughter. "That's it. The choice is out of your hands. We're getting sushi."

☙ ☙ ❧ ❧

"Oh. My. God. That was amazing," Ivy said as she licked a drop of sauce from her finger.

"Are you ready to march against gas station sushi then?" Rain's smile lit up her face. The color on her cheeks and her slightly disheveled hair from being outside all day made her even more attractive.

"Sign me up." Ivy ran her finger along the plate, gathering up the tiny pieces of rice that had fallen from the sushi.

"Nobody's looking. You could probably pick up the plate and lick it."

"Stop!" Ivy gave Rain her best glare.

Rain's eyes held a look that Ivy hadn't seen before. *No*, that wasn't true. It was just more intense than what she'd experienced so far this weekend.

She probably shouldn't say anything, but Ivy couldn't help her curiosity. "What's that look for?"

"I've really enjoyed this weekend." Rain blushed and looked away. "I mean...um...the look you saw. I guess you might call it affection." Rain stopped for a beat, and her eyes widened. "I mean, I really like you... for a friend and all, and this weekend has been great. But, well, I was just thinking how much...um...you know we're so different and all, so maybe you..." Rain picked up her glass of water and took a large gulp. She took a deep breath before she continued. "Oh, fuck it. Apparently, I've forgotten how to form sentences." She waved the waiter over and asked for their check.

Ivy bit her bottom lip. Fear gripped her as she tried to interpret what Rain was trying to say. "Does it bother you that we come from different sides? From different worlds?"

Rain's brows came together, which created a deep crease in her forehead. "Is that what you think I'm trying to say?"

Ivy nodded. "I know I'm not who you're used to hanging out with. I doubt if you have any friends like me."

Rain fidgeted with her wallet but abruptly slammed it onto the table. "This is all so confusing." A pained look crossed Rain's face. "I mean, I've enjoyed the hell out of this weekend, out of the past month, but I probably shouldn't." She rubbed her forehead. "Am I making any sense?"

"I'm not sure," Ivy answered honestly.

Rain threw her hands in the air, but a smile lit her face. "Well, it seems we've got this communication thing just about down to a science."

"Science like quantum physics or something

equally as confusing?" Ivy put a smile on her face, despite her unease.

"Apparently." Rain laughed and shook her head. "I'm usually not this inarticulate."

"I wish you'd find your words." It wasn't like Ivy to speak up, but something inside made her push on. "Because right now you're scaring me."

Rain leaned across the table toward Ivy. "I'm not trying to scare you."

Damn it. Why did she feel so vulnerable? "It's okay, Rain. I get it. We come from different worlds. Just because we had a fun weekend doesn't mean we'll become fast friends. Our values don't mesh. I get it."

Rain reached out and put her hand on top of Ivy's but then drew back. "No. That's not what I'm saying. Is that seriously what you took from my ramblings?"

Ivy nodded. "You said you enjoyed this weekend. *But.* When someone says *but*, they say you should ignore the first part because the second part is the only thing they really mean."

Rain shook her head. "Sorry, I'm not getting it."

Ivy let out a deep breath, frustrated that she couldn't get her point across. "When someone says, 'That's a pretty dress you're wearing, but it would look nicer if it were blue.' It means they really didn't like the dress. They just said it to soften their real message. So you should always disregard anything they said before the but."

"So are you the dress or am I?" The groove in Rain's forehead deepened.

"I'm the dress." Ivy glared. "Why would you be the dress?"

"How the hell should I know?" Rain threw her hands in the air. "I can't figure out why you'd be the dress, so I thought maybe I was."

Heat crawled up Ivy's neck. The more they talked in circles, the more frustrated she became. "Fine. Do you want me to lay it on the line?"

"Please."

"You said you enjoyed this weekend with me, but... To me, that meant you only said the first part to be nice. And then you said you shouldn't have enjoyed it, so I'm thinking that means you can't imagine being friends with someone like me."

Rain's mouth dropped open, and she stared for several beats before she spoke. "That's what you thought I was saying?"

"No. I just made it up." Ivy crossed her arms over her chest. "Of course, that's what I thought. Why else would I have said it?"

"Whoa. Okay." Rain made a calming gesture with her hands. "I understand how you could think that. I apologize. It's not what I meant."

Ivy hadn't realized she was holding her breath until a burst of air pushed through her lips. "You're not just saying that because I lost my shit."

"No offense," Rain smiled, "but I'd hardly call that losing your shit."

"So you did mean offense?" Ivy smirked.

Rain studied her for a few seconds before she grinned. "Ah, the old but thing again. Disregard everything I said before the but?"

"Exactly." Ivy shot Rain a satisfied smile.

Rain nodded toward the waiter, who'd circled the table twice. "How about we finish this conversation at my house?"

Chapter Thirty-one

Rain was glad they had the short drive back to her house to process the conversation at the restaurant. It only took ten minutes, but it had given her time to get her thoughts in order. Even though it was almost eight o'clock, Ivy didn't seem to be in a hurry to leave, which Rain took as a good sign.

"Do you want something to drink?" Rain asked.

Ivy held up the bottle of water she'd already pulled from the refrigerator. "I'm good."

Rain dropped onto the couch opposite Ivy. The freckles at the top of Ivy's nose were more pronounced after a day in the sun. Rain squeezed her eyes shut for a few seconds to reset her thoughts. Now wasn't the time for her mind to go down that path. "Are you sure you're okay sticking around? You have to work in the morning."

"It's fine, Rain." Ivy stretched. "Thank god there's only two more weeks left in this school year. I'm ready for a break."

"Do you get the entire summer off?"

"I pick up an odd job or two or three." Ivy laughed. "I usually do some part-time waitressing and help out with my brother-in-law's landscaping business. Riding around on a lawn mower all day isn't such a bad way to spend the summer."

"Wow. That sounds like a lot."

Ivy met Rain's gaze. "We didn't come back here

to talk about my summer jobs."

Rain sighed. "I'm sorry that I wasn't communicating well earlier."

Ivy's eyes were wary, but she shook her head. "You don't need to apologize. I just want to better understand what happens next." Ivy glanced down at her hands that rested in her lap. "Until we figure out this curse or whatever it is, we don't have a lot of choices, but we do have some."

Rain took a deep breath before she spoke. "What I meant to say earlier is that I really enjoy your company. This weekend is one of the best I can remember." Rain smiled. "You make me laugh, but... no, not but...and you also make me think. While we might not share all the same opinions, I never once felt like you weren't open to listening to my viewpoint."

Ivy nodded. "Agreed. I always feel heard, too."

"In fact, at times, I thought we were closer aligned than I'd have imagined." Rain scratched her head. "It kinda blows my mind."

"You mean I'm not the enemy you want to march against?" Ivy's smile hid a hint of defensiveness.

Rain pursed her lips and put her hand against her chest. "You feel that I'm...that my side is against you?"

Ivy nodded. "How could I not? I watch CNN. I read the news."

"But it's your side that's always on the attack— trying to take away rights, not mine."

Ivy pulled her legs against her chest and wrapped her arms around them. "You believe that, don't you?"

"Of course." Rain's heartbeat quickened, but she vowed to remain calm. "How can you think your side is under attack?"

"The H word goes both ways."

Having a heated debate about love and hate while needing to be careful not to say the words was making an already tense conversation more difficult. Rain shook her head. "Not at the same level. Or intensity. You'd never believe the number of nut jobs I've seen carrying signs that say God hat—damn it—I almost said it again. God detests fags."

Ivy cringed, and her eyes widened. "Do you think that's who I am? That I believe that?"

"I've been to your church, remember?"

Ivy ran her hands through her hair, which left it splayed in several directions. She bit down on her bottom lip. "That's not who I am. I know there's things wrong with Autumn Harvest, but that's not the way it was at Mullins Creek Church."

"But Mullins Creek Church is gone."

A pained look crossed Ivy's face, and she sighed. "I know."

Rain moved halfway down the couch and stopped a few feet from Ivy. "I want to marry who I want to marry. That shouldn't have any effect on you or anyone else from your church."

Ivy shook her head. "I don't want to take away who you can marry."

"But don't you understand that people like Devlin do?"

Ivy's gaze dropped to the floor. "But your side wants to stop me from worshiping how I want to."

"That's not true. We just want a separation between church and state."

Ivy clenched her hands together before she looked up and met Rain's gaze. "Right. That's convenient to hide behind. Did you ever think it's gone too far?"

Rain crinkled her nose. "I don't see how it has."

"Of course, you don't." Ivy's jaw tightened.

"Besides, it's part of the First Amendment."

"Let me ask you, do you think we should do something about guns?"

"Of course, but what does that have to do with religion?"

"Besides, it's part of the Second Amendment," Ivy said, mimicking what Rain said about the First Amendment. "I guess it's your side that picks which amendments should be reconsidered and which shouldn't."

Wow. Ivy's response was like a gut punch. Rain slid back toward her own side of the couch. "I didn't realize you were...were one of..."

"One of what?" Ivy's face was flushed, and she looked as if she could cry. "Go on, Rain, tell me what you really think of me."

Rain shook her head. "I just never suspected you'd be like that with guns." All the energy drained out of Rain. The thought of Ivy marching on the side of the NRA made her stomach roil.

"I'm not." Ivy glared. "I'm just making a point, but I can see by your reaction what you think of me."

"Fuck." Rain put her head in her hands. "How did we get to this point?"

"We got to this point because you've lumped things into *your* side and *my* side. You think you have it all figured out—me all figured out. For the record, I believe we need sensible gun control, but you're too busy labeling me to have known that." The vein in Ivy's forehead throbbed.

"I'm sorry." Rain's heart ached. "I don't want it

to be this way." She slid back down the couch toward Ivy. "Do you know what Tracie said to me the first time I told her about you and the rally?"

Ivy shook her head, but her eyes softened at the mention of Tracie.

"She told me that maybe I needed to sit down and talk with you. To listen to what you had to say—your ideas—and share mine with you."

"Can we do that?" Ivy asked. Rain sensed hope in her voice.

"I want to." Rain swallowed the lump in her throat. "I enjoyed this weekend so much. I enjoy you. I can't wait for eight o'clock every night because that's Ivy time." Rain put her hand against her chest. "We have to find a way."

"Why do you hate religion so bad?"

"Because of people like Devlin."

Ivy smiled. "I think you and Granny would get along famously." Ivy let out a sigh, and her smile faded. "But Jesus is about lo—the L word."

"Not the Jesus Devlin is hyping. I can't believe in the God your church is selling. Most of the people I know don't. Especially if they're gay."

"That may be the saddest thing I've ever heard." Ivy's eyes filled with tears. "Don't you realize there are so many good Christians out there?"

"And that's why you worship with Devlin?" Rain regretted the words as soon as they came out of her mouth. By the look on Ivy's face, they landed like a slap. "Sorry, that wasn't fair."

"I pray every night for an answer." Ivy held Rain's gaze. "But you probably think that's silly."

Did she? If she were with her friends, they'd probably laugh at Ivy's naïveté, yet there was something so sincere in Ivy that it gave Rain pause. "I admit, I don't think I've prayed since I was five. One of our teachers used to have us pray before lunch, but some of the parents caught her and stopped it."

Ivy flipped her hand open toward Rain. "And you just proved my point. That's probably the reason we stay. The lesser of two evils. Either stick with Devlin who at least believes in Jesus or risk being overrun by the people that wouldn't let a five-year-old pray in school. It's a choice my family's had to make."

Rain let Ivy's words sink in. Ivy's admission left Rain feeling cold.

"I see that look of disgust on your face." Ivy rested her head on her knees and stared at the floor. "Contempt."

"Whoa, that's going a bit far." Rain knew there was some truth in Ivy's assessment, but Rain didn't want to feel that way about Ivy.

"Then what would you call it?"

"Disappointment." The word fell from Rain's mouth before she could censor herself.

Ivy looked up and met Rain's gaze. Rain was surprised to see tears welling in Ivy's eyes. She was even more shocked that she wanted to comfort Ivy.

Ivy nodded. "I feel the same."

Rain clenched her jaw. "So you're disappointed in me?"

"No. I'm disappointed in me." Ivy broke eye contact with Rain. "And my family," Ivy said in a soft voice.

The admission caught Rain off guard. She searched for something to say but instead sat staring, probably with her mouth hanging open.

"Granny always says if you roll around in shit,

then you're gonna get shit on you," Ivy said. "I know
that what Devlin preaches isn't right...it's full of the
H word. My mama and papa know, too, but we keep
going back."

"I don't understand." Rain tried to soften her
eyes in hopes that Ivy wouldn't feel attacked. "You and
your parents seem to be good people, so I'm struggling
to make sense of it. Isn't there another way?"

"Who the hell knows?" Ivy threw her hands into
the air. "I hate—"

Sizzle.

Sulfur.

⁂

"Fuck," Rain said from Ivy's body. "Could we
have any worse timing?"

Ivy clutched Rain's chest. The pain nearly overwhelmed her. They'd switch multiple times, but it had
never hurt like this before. Maybe it was becoming
more dangerous each time they switched. Ivy's heart
rate soared.

"Are you all right?" Rain asked.

Ivy blinked several times. It was weird looking
into her own concern-filled eyes. "I don't know," she
admitted. She rubbed Rain's chest harder. "I think
there might be something wrong with your body."

"Yours too," Rain said and clutched Ivy's stomach.

Ivy pointed. "Wait. My stomach's bothering you?"

"Yeah. But you're grabbing my chest." Rain
snapped her fingers. "When you're upset, what happens
in your body?"

"My stomach churns." Realization dawned, and

Ivy smiled. "And your chest hurts."

Rain nodded and took several steps toward Ivy. She reached out her hand but stopped. "When I feel that feeling in my chest, sometimes, it helps to put my hand on it. Something about the warmth calms me. May I?"

Ivy nodded. She didn't let herself think too much about Rain touching her. She just wanted the pain in her chest to go away.

Rain put her hand on Ivy's chest, or rather her own.

Ivy put her hand over the top of Rain's and closed her eyes. Rain had been right. The tightness in her chest subsided a little. "Thank you. I can't handle us arguing."

"I can tell by your intestines," Rain said with a smile in her voice. "Um, do you think I should go into the bathroom?"

Ivy threw her head back and laughed. "You'll be fine. I've never pooped myself."

"Thank god, I'd hate—"

Sizzle.

Sulfur.

৯৷৯৷৶৷৶৷

Ivy shuddered. They'd just switched; surely, they couldn't have switched back so quickly. She gazed at Rain, who still had her hand over Ivy's hand that rested on Rain's chest.

"Holy shit. That was fast," Rain said.

"What just happened?"

"I'm not sure." Rain rubbed her chin and glanced at the ceiling. "I have a thought."

Ivy did, too. "We felt what the other was feeling. We were understanding each other."

"Exactly." Rain's gaze locked on Ivy.

Ivy wasn't sure what happened next, but she was in Rain's arms. Rain cupped her cheek, and their lips met.

Ivy's eyes flew open, and she pushed away from Rain. This couldn't happen. Her pulse raced. She needed to get out of here.

Chapter Thirty-two

Rain dramatically flopped face-down onto the couch. Her cheek chafed against the rough fabric, but she didn't care.

After their kiss, they'd awkwardly tried to brush it off as too many body switches in short succession, but Ivy had practically bolted from the house shortly after. To make matters worse, it was nine o'clock, and Ivy still hadn't called.

Fuck. With each minute the clock ticked past eight, it had been harder and harder for her to breathe. Today, Rain had barely been able to concentrate on work, wondering how their conversation would go tonight. Her thoughts churned. She'd come up with so many clever opening lines to start a phone call with Ivy, but she'd dismissed them all as inadequate.

She twisted slightly on the couch and pulled the tattered Post-it Note from her pocket. It had been lying on her desk when she'd returned to her body this afternoon after accidentally body switching with Ivy.

She'd pulled it out of her pocket more times than she'd care to admit. The scribbled-out words taunted her. She'd almost convinced herself that it said, *I miss you,* but it was likely only wishful thinking.

If anyone had seen her, they would have thought her crazy. She'd put a piece of paper on top of the note and lightly colored over it with a pencil, hoping the original words would come through. The only letter she could clearly make out was an S.

In her desperation, she'd taken packets of sugar substitute and spread it over the note, thinking the sugar would fall into the indentations of the words. It had only served to make the note sticky, and now her pocket would likely attract bugs.

She stared at the note, willing the words to pop to the surface. When they didn't, she dropped her face back onto the scratchy cushion.

Rain ran her hand through her hair. She'd not bothered to put product in it today. She'd gotten several sideways glances in the hallway. Her hair had always been a source of pride, but now she didn't care that it drooped to the side. *Fuck it.* After all, it was just hair.

Possibly, Ivy felt as rotten as Rain did. Rain huffed out a breath of air into the pillow. But what if she didn't? After all, Ivy hadn't called. Obviously, Ivy didn't want an agnostic lesbian in her life. What better way to let Rain down than by not calling?

Or she could say one of the words and switch places. Then she could feel if Ivy's stomach was churning like it had been on Sunday night. If they switched, Ivy would feel the breathtaking tightness in Rain's chest. Would that make Ivy understand?

No. That wouldn't be fair. If she wanted to talk to Ivy, she needed to *woman* up and call her.

After several more minutes of wallowing, Rain rolled off the couch and plopped onto the floor. She hugged her knees against herself and stared at the clock. It was still before ten. Not too late to call. It didn't matter that it wasn't her day. She could still call.

She inhaled deeply. Her phone was on the

counter in the kitchen. It was probably a sign she
shouldn't call. How could it be a sign when she was
the one who left it there? Now she was just being
ridiculous. But if she called Ivy, what should she say?

Rain was still contemplating an opening line
when her doorbell rang. She glanced at the clock. Who
the hell would be at her door this late on a Tuesday
night?

Her heart rate quickened. *Shit.* Her parents were
flying to Australia. Didn't the police always show up
when a plane went down? She watched too many
movies, but then again, how else would they do it?

She jumped to her feet and hurried to the
door. As soon as she threw it open, she immediately
regretted her decision.

"It's about time I find you at home. *Alone,*"
Sasha said and pushed her way inside.

"Um, Sasha. This isn't a good time." Rain tried
to keep the irritation from her voice. It wasn't Sasha's
fault she felt so lousy.

Sasha eyed her from head to toe. "Jesus. Have
you been on a bender or what?" She reached up and
tried to straighten Rain's hair.

Rain stepped back. "It's just not a good time."

Sasha reached out again, but Rain moved her
head away. "What the fuck's gotten into you?"

A hurt look crossed Sasha's face before she
frowned. "You look like hell."

"Even more reason to leave me be. I'm not up
to your standards." It was a low blow, but Rain just
wanted her to go away.

"Oh, babe, it would take more than a little
mussed-up hair to make me not want you." Sasha
pushed her body against Rain's and ran her hand

up the side of Rain's leg and around to her buttocks. Sasha kneaded it and pulled Rain toward her.

Rain stumbled backward and bumped into the corner of the table. It caught her on the outer thigh. "Fuck. That hurt." She moved away from the table and took several steps back from Sasha.

Sasha winked. "Gonna play hard to get? You know that turns me on." A seductive smile played on her lips.

Normally, gazing into Sasha's lust-filled eyes was all it took for Rain to give up the pretense that it was over between them. That she no longer wanted to be fuck buddies, but tonight, something was different.

She felt nothing when Sasha touched her. No, that wasn't true. Revulsion. She'd felt disgust. At herself and at Sasha.

"Come on, Rain. You've been saying never again for months, but...." Sasha licked her lips and moved toward Rain. "But we both have needs. I'm throbbing right now. Don't leave a girl hanging."

Guilt coursed through Rain. She'd been playing this game with Sasha for too long, but she wanted it to end. She took several steps back. "I don't want to hurt you, Sasha, but I can't do this anymore."

Sasha threw her head back and laughed.

Whatever reaction Rain was expecting, this wasn't it.

"Seriously. You must think you're pretty fucking special, huh?" Sasha clenched her teeth as she spoke. "But you're as vanilla as they come, and trust me, I have many more flavors than you."

Rain narrowed her eyes. *What in the hell is Sasha talking about?* "Vanilla?"

"Yeah. The most boring flavor there is. You're

one step up from my vibrator." Sasha smirked. "Don't look so shocked. Did you think you were the only one?"

Rain hadn't really given it much thought. A quick scan of her body told her she felt nothing from Sasha's jab. She couldn't come up with a retort that wouldn't come off insulting, so she remained silent.

"Don't get me wrong." Sasha wriggled her eyebrows. "You're easy on the eyes and know all the right buttons to push, but you're about as passionate as a robot." Sasha laughed. "I still remember the time I pulled out those handcuffs. I thought you were going to pass out."

Rain had had about enough of the insults. Her day had been lousy enough without listening to Sasha's barbs. "I'm glad you have other outlets."

"I knew it." Sasha took a step forward and pointed. Her finger was only inches from Rain's face. "It's that fucking blondie, isn't it?"

Rain took another step back. *Blondie?* She hadn't thought Sasha was drunk, but now she wondered.

Sasha let out another cruel laugh. "Don't play dumb with me. I saw her."

"Saw who?" Rain's patience was nearing its end.

"That little blond bitch you took out on Saturday. The one wearing that hideous muumuu."

Realization dawned. Sasha had seen her with Ivy. "She wasn't wearing a muumuu." Seriously, that was the best retort she could come up with?

"That's a pretty lame defense of your girlfriend."

This time, it was Rain's turn to laugh. "I can assure you that she's not my girlfriend."

"Funny, her car seemed to be parked outside your house all weekend."

Rain's eyebrows shot up. "Were you watching me?"

Sasha waved her hand. "Don't flatter yourself. I drove by hoping for a quickie on Saturday and saw you walking her to your car."

"And you knew about Sunday and Monday, how?"

"I was still horny on Monday." A mischievous glint shone in her eyes. "I'd had plenty of other flavors all weekend, but I was craving a little vanilla. Still am." She moved toward Rain.

Rain held up her hand. "Just stop. I'm done."

"Aww, how sweet. Gonna stay faithful to Blondie. Looking at her, I bet she's even more vanilla than you are." Sasha laughed.

Ivy in bed flashed through Rain's mind. *Fuck.* This was so not the time to be visualizing something like that.

Sasha pointed. "Oh, god, you're blushing. I'm right. Your girlfriend just lays there while you have your way. Is she just a taker?" Sasha licked her lips. "I'd be willing to give you a little if she isn't."

Rain walked past Sasha and opened the door. "It's time for you to leave."

"Hit a sore spot, did I? Blondie isn't ringing your bell?"

Sasha's crudeness was bad enough, but directed at Ivy, it angered Rain. "Please, just go."

Sasha sashayed toward the door. When she came up beside Rain, she ran her finger across Rain's nipple. "Don't say I didn't warn you. I can read frigidity from a mile away, and that one is as uptight as they come."

Rain wanted to defend Ivy, but anything she said would just prolong the conversation. Besides, talking about sex and Ivy made her uncomfortable. Rain pushed the door open farther.

"Where'd you find her? Certainly, none of the places we hang out. The nineties called and want their dress back." Sasha laughed again.

For the first time since Sasha walked in, Rain studied her. Her tight designer jeans clung to her ass. Likely, her jeans cost more than Ivy made in a week. Her tailored shirt was unbuttoned almost to her navel, and it was apparent she wasn't wearing a bra.

Sasha stepped across the threshold and glanced over her shoulder. "Don't come crawling back to me when Blondie leaves you unsatisfied."

Rain bit her tongue. *Not a snowball's chance in hell* didn't need to be spoken aloud. "I wish you the best, Sasha. Good night."

"Fuck you, Rain." Sasha held up her middle finger as she walked down the sidewalk.

Rain quickly shut the door and twisted the lock.

She glanced at the clock. *Fuck.* It was nearly ten thirty, so she couldn't call now. Was this the sign from the universe she'd been looking for? If so, apparently, she wasn't supposed to contact Ivy.

Rain sighed and double-checked the lock. She plodded to the couch and let herself fall back onto it, face first.

Chapter Thirty-three

Ivy ran her hand down the side of her red dress and turned sideways to look at herself in the mirror. She'd not been entirely herself since she'd met Rain, and her choice of dresses proved it. When was the last time she'd worn red, especially to church?

Besides, it wasn't like it was Sunday. She'd never wear red to Sunday service, but Wednesday evening had to have different rules, didn't it?

What would Pastor Devlin think? She shrugged, realizing she didn't care.

She'd been unsettled since she returned from Rain's late Monday. They'd tried to brush off the kiss as nothing, and Ivy had practically fled from Rain's house. But it hadn't felt like nothing. Her thoughts had gone to Rain so many times over the past two days. It was as if she could think of nothing else.

She'd not been so drawn to a friend since Nadine, but she quickly pushed that thought away. Another friendship that had been ruined by a kiss. Obviously, she needed to keep her lips to herself.

The lack of phone calls the last two days should tell her everything she needed to know. The kiss had been a mistake, and after spending the weekend with Ivy, Rain obviously found her distasteful. Did Rain find Ivy boring, or was she repulsed by Ivy's views?

Ivy glared at herself in the mirror and said, "Or maybe it's your own damned fault."

Tuesday night, her night to call Rain, Ivy had been tense. Since they hadn't talked about it, she wasn't sure if she should make the call. What if Rain didn't answer? It would be an obvious sign that Rain wanted nothing to do with her, and she wasn't sure if she could handle it.

In a panic at around seven, instead of sitting by the phone debating, she wandered over to her parents' house. She figured it would calm her before she went back home to make the call.

As soon as she walked in, a frazzled Mama had grabbed her by the hand. Violet had ensconced herself in her bedroom and had refused to come out. All Mama had been able to determine was that there was a boy involved.

Like a dutiful sister, Ivy had gone to Violet's room and, after much cajoling, had convinced her to open the door. Dealing with a teenager experiencing her first heartbreak wasn't for the faint of heart nor was it a quick affair.

Nearly three hours and a trip to the ice cream shop later, Ivy returned to her room. It had been way past her time to call Rain. She'd snatched up her phone in hopes that Rain had reached out. Nothing. Was that a sign? For the next hour, Ivy had constructed an apology text, but it remained unsent on her phone.

Embarrassingly, she'd waited all afternoon for her phone to ring. Rain always gave her a quick call before church. She'd been willing it to ring for the last few hours. It hadn't. It had been a long shot. After she blew off yesterday, would Rain really call her the next day?

Ivy sighed and ran her hands down her dress one last time. She knew she looked good, especially with the tan she'd gotten over the weekend with Rain. She cringed and studied her own eyes. They'd lost their sparkle. No way could she hide her sadness. Ivy pushed her hair off to the side and spun from the mirror.

Mama's eyes widened when Ivy walked into the kitchen, but she didn't say anything. No doubt, the red dress came as a surprise to her, but Mama would keep her judgment to herself...for now.

The drive to church was a quiet one. Ivy knew it wasn't fair, but lately, she'd answered their questions with as few words as possible until they stopped asking her any. How could she explain everything that had been happening in her life without them wanting to have her committed? Would they understand if she told them she was questioning everything she once believed?

They were only about ten minutes from church when Ivy said, "Do you think our church fosters division?"

"Whoa," Papa said. "Where'd that come from?"

Ivy's eyes welled. "I'm sorry. I've just had a lot on my mind. Confusing things."

"Is one of them questioning your religion?" Mama asked.

Ivy made eye contact with Papa in the rearview mirror and shook her head. "Not my religion but my church."

"I see," Mama said. "Care to tell us what brought this on?"

Ivy's shoulders sagged at the harshness in Mama's voice. "Never mind."

Papa put his hand on Mama's knee and patted it. "Let's let her speak. No judgment."

Mama nodded. "You're right." She turned in her seat and looked at Ivy. "Go on, honey. I'm just not used to our good girl being so sullen." She grinned. "We expect it from Violet but not you."

Ivy smiled. "Honest, I haven't meant to treat you badly. It's—"

"No, no," Mama said. "You haven't treated anybody bad. You just seem a million miles away most times, and we don't know what to do about it." Mama put her hand over her heart. "It's hard for a mama to see and not be able to help."

Ivy looked down at her lap and picked at her fingernail. "Autumn Harvest and Devlin don't feel like Mullins Creek Church." She stopped, waiting to see if her parents would respond. When they didn't, she continued. "I used to walk out of church feeling uplifted. Closer to Jesus. Now I just feel heavy and full of...of...I don't know..."

"Anger? Hate?" Papa said.

Ivy's head snapped up, and she met his gaze in the mirror. His expressive eyes held the same sadness she'd seen in her own earlier. "Yes! How did you know?"

Papa shot a glance at Mama, who gave him a nearly imperceptible nod. "'Cause we've been feeling the same thing."

"Most Sunday nights," Mama said, "your papa and I read Bible verses to each other in hopes to feel closer to Jesus again."

"Does it work?" Ivy asked.

"Sometimes." Mama sighed. "But we miss the community we had at our old church."

"We keep hoping things will die down," Papa said. "That the political rhetoric will go away, and our country will go back to what it used to be before it became okay to spew hate at one another. And then maybe Devlin will calm down and stop spewing his brand of the gospel."

"Do you believe that?" Ivy said softly, not wanting to make Papa feel that he was being challenged.

He pulled the car into the nearly full lot outside of the church. "I haveta." His voice was low.

"Meaning?"

Papa ran his hand through his hair, leaving it slightly mussed. "I grew up in the church. I believe in Jesus more than anything. I just don't know what's happening anymore. Love has turned to hate."

Ivy cringed at the words but quickly relaxed. It only mattered if she or Rain spoke them, but she feared she had PTSD when she heard the words.

"Did Papa say something to upset you?" Mama's gaze bore into her.

Ivy was quick to shake her head. "This whole situation upsets me. I want better for us. For our community. For our country. For the world."

Papa's shoulders dropped. "But we're just three tiny people in the middle of nowhere. I'm not sure how we do it."

Mama reached between the seats and patted Ivy's leg. "You've always been the sensitive one in the family. I see how much this is weighing on you. Pray, honey. God will help you find your way."

Ivy smiled when she gazed into Mama's kind eyes. There was still good in the world. She knew that every time she spent time with her family. They were far from perfect, but they were good solid people. *But why did they let Devlin push them around?*

"Whelp." Papa slapped his hand against the

steering wheel. "I suppose we better go in before we're late."

The seats were nearly full when they entered the church, or as Ivy had taken to calling it, *the arena*. Ivy kept her gaze straight ahead, but she could feel the stares and heard the whispers as she walked past. Red was not a popular color here.

She sneaked a glance at Mr. Haskins as she walked past. His eyes nearly popped out of his head before he gave her a cheesy grin. She averted her gaze without a reaction. *Dumb*. Why had she even looked his way?

Devlin had just entered the stage, and his gaze locked on her. *Shit*. She'd wanted to sit before he saw her. His eyes narrowed until they were barely slits, and his pointy nose turned up even farther. She was pretty sure a sneer played on his lips. She looked away, but Devlin's face filled the large video screens around the church. It was definitely a sneer.

Why had she decided to wear such a rebellious dress? Was she just looking for trouble?

They slid into their customary seats. She opened her hymnal and pretended to study it. Mama knowingly patted her on the leg. She glanced up and smiled. It reminded her that she needed to be grateful. No matter what happened, they would always be by her side.

Wouldn't they? Ivy scowled. Where had that thought come from? What if Violet turned out to be *different*, would they still accept her?

Before she could explore her thoughts further, Devlin stepped to the podium. "Good evening, my flock. Let us start with a prayer to rid our congregation of the immorality that continues to knock at our door.

That threatens to destroy our community."

Ivy swore he stared at her the entire time, but she was likely being paranoid. *Wasn't she?* She bowed her head, so she'd no longer have to look at him. Instead of following his words of condemnation, she silently prayed for strength and love.

As if he sensed her disobedience, he said, "You are not praying hard enough. I can barely hear you." His booming voice bounced off the walls, and he continued.

The congregation returned his volume as they prayed, but Ivy stubbornly continued her own silent prayer. Maybe it was wishful thinking, but she couldn't hear her parents' voices mixed in with the others.

When Devlin finished his prayer, he launched into his sermon. Ivy tried to tune out his hate-filled rhetoric as he spoke of the left-wing adulterers, pedophiles, and baby killers.

He pounded the lectern, which drew her from her thoughts. "And coming up is the worst month of all. June is when the sinners take to the streets, but we must be there to push back. They call it Pride. We call it an abomination, certainly nothing to be proud of. We must disrupt this decadence before our children are lost."

He paused and stared out at the crowd. His gaze swept the congregation, but still, he didn't speak. Suddenly, he lifted his arm and pointed. "Will you go to battle with me in June? Will you help me save our children?"

The man Devlin pointed at stood and cried out. "Yes, Pastor Devlin. I will stand with you."

Devlin moved on to another worshipper and another, and each stood and vowed their support.

Ivy's hands had begun to sweat, and her gaze darted around the room as more people stood in solidarity. She wanted to look away from Devlin, but she found she couldn't.

Suddenly, his gaze landed on her. The corner of his mouth turned up as he pointed at her. "Will you join me in the battle to save our children?" His voice filled the room. Maybe it was her imagination, but she swore there was a collective inhale as he stood with his finger outstretched at her.

She wasn't aware of standing, but she found herself on her feet. When she didn't speak, he repeated his question. She could sense Mama and Papa beside her, but she didn't turn to them.

This was something she had to do on her own. Devlin's Jesus wasn't the Jesus she learned about in Mullins Creek Sunday school. This wasn't the Jesus she prayed to every night. This wasn't the Jesus her parents taught her to follow. This was something else. Something that made her skin crawl.

She stood as tall as she could make herself and called out, "No! I will not join you." She pointed back at him. "And you, sir, do not speak for the Jesus I know...and lo—" *Damn.* She couldn't say love, or Rain would be plopped into the middle of her fiasco. "The Jesus I exalt is merciful and kind."

She looked down at Mama and Papa and mouthed, *sorry,* before she slid in front of the others to escape the row. When she reached the aisle, she ran. Her sandals slapped against the carpet, but she couldn't hear it over Devlin's loud protestations. She heard her name called. She heard her family name ring out, but she continued to run up the aisle.

She pushed past the double doors into the lobby

and finally let out the breath she'd been holding. A quick glance around the commercialized area told her she hadn't escaped far enough. Ivy ran to the front door and burst through. The evening held a bit of a chill, and she shivered. Or maybe it was her. All the negative energy she'd absorbed all these months trying to break free of her body.

Standing outside the front doors was no longer enough. She ran across the parking lot toward their car. Maybe that would be far enough away from the church. She laughed out loud, or perhaps she'd keep running all the way home.

Ivy laughed louder. Twenty miles in a dress and sandals. She could make it.

"Ivy." She heard her name called, but she kept running. She couldn't believe Devlin would chase her. Her heart rate increased. Would it be like the horror movies she'd watched where the entire congregation would chase her with pitchforks and torches?

Jesus. She needed to get a grip. Nobody chased fallen women with pitchforks anymore, did they?"

"Ivy June! Would you please stop?" the familiar voice called.

She skidded to a stop. *Mama?* Slowly, she turned to see both her parents jogging across the parking lot toward her.

Had they been sent to drag her back inside? *Wow.* When had she become so paranoid? She took several deep breaths, willing herself to calm down.

As her parents approached, she could see that Papa's face was red. Was it from running or anger? Likely, she'd soon find out.

"For the love of God, girl," Papa said. "Your old man can't run like he used to, so could you please not bolt again?"

Ivy's gaze dropped to the pavement. Shame flooded over her. She didn't care what she'd done to herself, but she'd just embarrassed her entire family. "I'm sorry," she muttered.

A pair of arms wrapped around her. *Mama.* Then both were engulfed by Papa's strong arms. He held on tight, and the tears she'd been fighting for so long ran down her cheeks. Suddenly, she was sobbing and couldn't stop.

Chapter Thirty-four

Rain had hoped the weekend would bring her relief from the horrible week, but it hadn't. At least, she'd been at a rally most of the day on Saturday, but when she'd returned to her house last night, she'd never felt worse.

She'd slept little. She tried to blame it on Sasha, who'd continued to barrage her with texts. But it wasn't Sasha who had kept her up. No matter what she did, she couldn't get Ivy off her mind.

She'd been up since five a.m., trying to decide what she should do. Despite knowing it would be better to call, she couldn't bring herself to do it. The coward's way was better than nothing.

Rain crumpled up another piece of paper and threw it onto her growing pile. She poised her pen over the fresh sheet and stared. How hard could it be to come up with a witty text? Something that would catch Ivy's eye, make her want to respond.

She brought the tip of her pen to the page, but her hand didn't move. A tiny spot of ink spread out where the tip rested. She could almost laugh at herself if she didn't feel so terrible.

Perhaps she was making it too hard. Something simple might be the best way to go. Her tongue stuck out between her teeth as she concentrated on her writing.

Hi. I've missed you.

She glowered at the simple sentence before she scratched it out.

Sorry I haven't reached out. I've been busy.

She shook her head. Too dismissive. She scribbled across the words and moved to the next line.

I have no excuse for why I haven't reached out. I've missed you and would like to talk.

Rain dropped her pen onto the table and stared at the words. Despite its simplicity, it was all true. She glanced over at the pile of discarded papers. This was as good as any.

She picked up her cellphone, and her fingers flew over the keys. She only reread it once to check for errors before she hit send. If she waited any longer, she would likely erase it.

She dropped her head onto the kitchen table. There was no turning back now. Unfortunately, she didn't know for sure when Ivy got out of church on Sundays, so she'd just have to wait.

Rain picked up her phone to check the time. Eight a.m. If memory served her, Ivy wouldn't be home for at least another hour. She sighed and went to put down her phone when it vibrated.

A text message had come in. Probably Sasha, but she had to check.

She swiped her phone, hit the message icon, and was greeted by Ivy's picture.

Her hands shook when she tapped the message folder.

I've missed you, too.

Rain read the message several times. With each reading, more emotions welled in her chest. Ivy hadn't said anything about meeting, though. What did that mean? As she contemplated her response, another message came through.

I'd love to meet, but...ha ha...seriously, I would love to meet.

Rain smiled. Ivy remembered their *but* conversation. That had to be a good sign, didn't it? Before Rain could respond, another message came through.

It's family brunch day. Normally, I would ask to be excused, but it's been a bit of a shit show this week, so I should stay.

Ivy would think Rain had disappeared if she didn't respond soon. Rain's fingers moved across the phone. *Is everything okay?* It wasn't a masterpiece, but at least it was something.

I think so. I'd rather tell you about it in person.

Rain's shoulders stiffened. What did that mean? She shouldn't push. Ivy clearly didn't want to talk about it via text. *When and where would you like to meet?*

A text came back from Ivy a moment later. *Would you be willing to come here?*

Rain stared at the screen. Ivy wanted her to come to her house. Obviously, she'd been there before but not in her own body. Her pulse quickened. Ivy always came to her, so it was only fair, but was it a good sign or a bad one? She could read it either way. *Sure, what time?*

⚜⚜⚜⚜⚜

Ivy cradled her phone in her hand. She was sure she had a goofy grin on her face, but she didn't care. She felt right for the first time all week. Rain was coming to visit her.

Ivy looked up from her phone and discovered

Papa staring at her. She hadn't seen him come into the kitchen since she'd been so preoccupied by her conversation with Rain. "Everything all right?" Papa asked.

"It is." Ivy's smile widened.

Mama turned from the batter she was mixing and glanced down at Ivy's phone. "Good news?"

"Yes. Remember my friend Rain, the one I visited last weekend?" She didn't wait for them to respond. "She's coming out to the house."

"Oh, good. Will she be here for brunch?" Mama asked.

Ivy shook her head. "No, she'll be here this afternoon. We don't want to scare her off."

Papa chuckled. "A Nash Sunday brunch certainly isn't for the faint of heart. Maybe next time she can come back for the full experience."

Ivy's chest swelled at the thought of having Rain at their family gathering. *Odd.* She wasn't sure what that reaction was about, but she didn't have time to think about it because Mama had just said something. "I'm sorry. Could you repeat that, Mama?"

"I said, grab some butter out of the refrigerator."

❧ ❧ ❧ ❧

Although Ivy always enjoyed Sunday brunch, today it seemed to drag on for hours, and she couldn't wait for the others to leave. She'd given up worrying about what it meant.

All she knew was that she missed Rain.

Possibly, she was being paranoid, but she swore that either Papa or Mama, or sometimes both, watched her most of the meal. Of course, it might have had more to do with the topic of conversation since it was the first brunch that they'd had since she and her parents had quit Autumn Harvest. They'd spent extra time praying before the meal, and during, the entire family had a lively discussion about what happened next. In typical Violet fashion, she'd pumped her fist in the air and tried to give Ivy a high-five, until Mama had shot her a look. She'd feigned innocence, saying Devlin had always given her the creeps.

Ivy's heart was warmed when Rose's and Max's families agreed that their time at Autumn Harvest had been a failed experiment. They wanted a church that was more aligned with Jesus and love, not the hate that Devlin sowed. They'd look for a new church, but in the meantime, they'd have Bible study every Sunday at home.

As Ivy helped Mama clean up, she glanced at the clock on the microwave. Rain would be there in about fifteen minutes.

Mama snapped her towel at Ivy.

Ivy shrieked and laughed. "What was that for?"

"I've been trying to get your attention for the last few minutes, but you're somewhere off in la-la land. I said, why don't you go ahead and freshen up before your friend gets here?"

Ivy glanced down at her red dress. She'd put it on this morning as a statement. She thought of it as her power outfit. The one she'd declared freedom in. Besides, she felt pretty in it and didn't want to take it off.

"You don't have to change out of your dress," Mama said as if reading her mind, "but I thought you'd want to comb your hair and wipe some of the flour off your nose."

Ivy swiped at her face. "You let me walk around with schmutz on my face all morning?"

Mama laughed. "No. I just wanted to see what you'd do."

"You've been living with Papa too long." Ivy laughed. "His bad habits are rubbing off on you."

"I don't have any bad habits," Papa said as he entered the kitchen.

Mama patted him on the arm. "Sure you don't. Whatever you need to believe to get through the day."

Papa laughed. "Haven't you been listening to Devlin, woman?" A twinkle danced in Papa's eyes. "A wife should never talk back to her husband."

"Then I guess it's a good thing we quit." Mama gave him a sideways hug and stood on her tiptoes so she could give him a peck on the cheek.

He spun Mama around until she was in his arms. "I think an occasion like this requires a proper kiss."

Ivy smiled and turned away. After all these years, they still adored each other. Hopefully, someday, she'd find someone like that.

"What are you doing in here?" Mama asked.

"I wanted to make sure we rolled out the red carpet for Ivy's friend."

"And how do you propose we do that?" Mama asked.

Papa opened the cupboard and pulled out a pitcher. "You need to make your super-secret lemonade."

"You mean the one loaded with sugar?" Ivy asked.

"That'd be the one." He smiled.

"And I suppose you think you need to test it."

Mama playfully swatted his arm.

"Quality control. We wouldn't want to serve bad lemonade."

Ivy chuckled. "I'll leave you to it. I'm gonna take Mama up on her suggestion to freshen up a bit."

Chapter Thirty-five

Holy hell. Rain had expected the lemonade to have a twinge of sour, but instead, it was as if she was drinking cotton candy.

Mr. Nash held up his glass after he'd taken a big gulp. "Best damn lemonade in the state." He brought the glass to his lips and guzzled more.

Rain raised her glass, as well, and took a tiny sip. She'd end up in a diabetic coma if she drank it like he did. "My compliments to the chef."

She'd been sitting on the front porch chatting with Ivy's father for the past fifteen minutes. He was as nice as she remembered from their chat around the campfire when he believed he'd been talking to his daughter. Rain was a little uncomfortable with the deception, but it wasn't like she could do anything about it.

As soon as Rain had arrived, Ivy pulled her aside and said her parents wanted to meet her. It hadn't surprised her that Ivy's mother had requested help with Granny before Ivy could even sit down. Rain had seen Granny outside pulling weeds when she'd driven up, so Rain doubted Granny needed much help. Especially help that took two people. Ivy had given her a helpless smile and winked when her mother had pulled her away.

She'd fallen into an easy conversation with Ivy's father. Suddenly, he paused and fixed Rain with a serious expression. "I'm glad you're here. I think it might do Ivy some good."

Rain considered how she should answer. What did he mean? Hope soared inside of her. Did it mean that Ivy was struggling, too?

Before Rain could come up with a response, Mr. Nash continued. "Our Ivy's not been quite right this week, but she won't tell us what's wrong." He shook his head. "And then after what happened Wednesday night, I just don't know."

"What happened, sir?"

"For Pete's sake, how many times do I haveta tell you, it's Ben. Not sir or Mr. Nash."

Rain smiled and held up her hands. "Okay, okay, I get it, Ben."

He smiled. "It's not mine to tell. I'll leave it for Ivy to tell ya." He sighed. "She's such a good girl. The best." He met Rain's gaze. "She's always taking care of everyone else, the family. Never takes any time for herself, so I'm glad she has a friend she can talk to."

Warmth spread across Rain's chest. She was glad that Mr. Nash approved of their friendship. She wasn't sure why it was so important to her since they were adults, but for some reason, it was. "Ivy's a great person. I'm glad she's in my life, too."

Looking into Mr. Nash's eyes was a bit disconcerting since they looked so much like Ivy's. He held her gaze for several seconds, as if sizing her up. He nodded, as if satisfied with whatever he saw in her. "Me and her mama feel bad that we've held her back. She's such a bright girl and should've gone to college. She needs to forge her own life, but we've been selfish since she's such a help around the farm and with her brothers and sisters." He shook his head and spread his arms out toward the vast expanse of land around them. "It's getting harder and harder to keep this place going."

"How many acres do you have?"

Mr. Nash smiled. "Four hundred eighty-two. The original farm was two hundred acres when my family came here in the seventeen hundreds, but we've accumulated more land over the years."

"You farm it all?"

"Except for where the buildings are." He turned and pointed toward Granny's house but held his hand high. "And way out yonder, there's about ten wooded acres. It's hilly and a creek runs through it, so we've always kept it as it is. When the kids were little, it was their favorite place to play." He smiled. "You'll have to have Ivy take you out there."

"I'd like that." She nodded toward the barns that were east of the house. "What do you do with those?"

"We used to use them all, well, at least my dad did. But now all but the big one is pretty empty."

Rain narrowed her eyes and stared at the buildings. Why would they have barns they didn't use?

As if reading her mind, he said, "My dad used to raise livestock. That's what those four buildings were for. But when I took over, I just didn't want to do that. Still have a few chickens for eggs and goats for milk, but that's about it."

Something about him put Rain at ease. She'd always reacted to energy, and his seemed pure and decent. If someone would have told her that she'd be sitting on a porch, drinking lemonade, and talking to a farmer about his chicken and goats, she'd have said they were crazy, but here she was.

Even more astonishing, there wasn't anywhere else she'd rather be. Well, except for having Ivy there, too. "You mentioned it's hard to keep it going, what's changed?"

"I ain't getting any younger." He laughed. "Plus, corporate farms are gobbling up all the farmland. Anytime someone dies, if their heirs don't want to farm, then they normally sell to the highest bidder." He winked at her. "That's how I got the last eighty-two acres."

"High bidder?"

"Hardly." He chuckled. "Old man Turner sold it to me in 2012. He said if his kids didn't want to take over the farm, then screw 'em." Mr. Nash blushed and put his hand on his chest. "Pardon my language."

"I've heard worse." Rain smiled.

He returned the smile. "So Turner sold it to me for half what he probably could have gotten. Oh, man, the kids were hopping mad. They threatened to sue me after he died." He looked into the sky with a sad smile. "He was a smart man. The sale was ironclad. I went to school with his son, but he still won't talk to me to this day."

"I'm afraid I don't understand why the corporate farms are a problem then."

"It's hard to get help to keep her going. There's not enough here to support multiple families, so Max went and got a job working on cars at the dealership. He still helps out when he can, but with a family, it gets harder and harder."

Rain nodded, starting to get the picture. "Don't you have two younger sons?"

"They're good kids, but they're involved in so many things—sports, band, clubs—that they don't have a lot of time." He tipped back his head and drank the last of his lemonade. A sugar trail clung to the inside of the glass. "Ivy's the most helpful. Did she tell you that she helped me fix the tractor?"

"I'd heard that rumor."

He chuckled. "It's true."

"Does she drive the tractors, too?" Rain asked.

"She's been driving them since she was thirteen." He grinned. "Sometimes, I think my girls will be the ones to take over the farm. Our youngest, Violet, loves driving the combine."

Rain was about to ask another question when Ivy returned. She'd changed out of her dress and wore a pair of faded blue jeans. An unbuttoned flannel shirt was opened to reveal a Mickey Mouse T-shirt. Her feet were clad in a pair of sturdy boots that looked made for farm life.

Mr. Nash looked up at Ivy with an enormous smile. "There you are. I was just getting to know Rain a bit better."

"And teaching her about farming, I hear." Ivy shook her head and turned to Rain. "He'll have you helping with the harvest if you aren't careful."

"That would be so cool."

Ivy groaned and pointed at her dad. "Now see what you've done."

His eyes twinkled. "I'm always on the prowl for good help."

Rain shifted her gaze to Ivy, and as soon as she looked into Ivy's amber eyes, she was lost. Rain would have agreed to harvest the crops by hand if it meant spending more time with Ivy. She pushed the thoughts away. Sitting on the porch with Ivy's father was no time to be sizing up his daughter. Although

Ivy's red dress had made it hard for her to concentrate on anything else. Maybe Rain could focus now that Ivy had changed for the tour, but Rain doubted it.

Ivy patted her dad's shoulder. "You've had her long enough. She's mine now." Ivy reached down and pulled Rain to her feet.

Mr. Nash stood, as well. He clamped his large hand on Rain's shoulder. "It's been nice talking with you, Rain." His eyes narrowed. "You still seem so familiar. Are you sure we haven't met?"

Before Rain could find a comeback, Ivy kissed her father on the cheek. "I don't think you two run in the same circles."

Mr. Nash grunted, but he still had a look of concentration on his face. "I reckon, but I just feel like I know her."

꧁꧂

Ivy had been showing Rain around the farm for nearly an hour but still hadn't mentioned the big news that Ivy and her father had alluded to. Rain decided not to push since Ivy seemed content to give the grand tour. Rain was thrilled to get the chance to get a deeper glimpse into Ivy's world, so the news could wait.

When they'd first started walking, Ivy had grabbed Rain's hand, squeezed it, and confessed how happy she was to have Rain there. The gesture filled Rain's chest with warmth.

Now they were walking toward the back of the property, where the wooded area lay. The path was dirt and hugged the edge of the field where tiny plants poked through the soil.

Rain pointed. "What's growing here?"

"Corn."

"Yummy." Rain rubbed her stomach for emphasis.

"No, not so yummy." Ivy laughed. "This is feed corn, not sweet."

Rain narrowed her eyes and glanced at Ivy. "Are you messing with me?"

"No." Ivy shook her head, and her hair shimmered in the sunlight. Rain looked away, so she could concentrate on Ivy's words. "This is feed corn. Used to feed livestock. Most of the fields you see around here are either seed corn or feed corn."

"Wait, now there's three different kinds of corn?"

"Yep. The seed corn is used to grow more corn. Lots of science goes into creating hybrid corn for the best yields."

"Ugh." Rain pretended to pull her hair. "This farming stuff is confusing. I just want corn that I can slather with butter and dive in."

Ivy patted Rain on the shoulder and leaned toward her. "I'll let you in on a little secret," Ivy whispered. "We have a patch of sweet corn up near our family garden. When it's ready, I'll make you some." A huge smile lit her face. "You won't believe how much better it is than store bought."

"And tomatoes?"

"Yep, we have tomatoes, too."

Rain spread her hands out in front of her as if she were holding a plate. "A huge plate of tomatoes and six ears of sweet corn?"

"Six? Holy hell, you'll get a stomachache."

"But it'll be worth it." Rain grinned.

When they neared the woods, Ivy said. "I hope

you enjoy it as much as I do." She stopped walking, so Rain stopped, too. "I don't get out here as much as I used to. It's only about a mile walk, or I could drive Papa's truck."

"If you enjoy it so much, why don't you come out here more?"

"I'm not sure." Ivy shrugged. "I suppose it brings back too many memories."

"Bad ones?" Ivy's response had taken Rain off guard since she'd assumed the woods held happy memories.

"No, good ones. That's why it's so weird." Ivy pushed her hair away from her face.

"Maybe not weird. Confusing, yes, but not weird." Rain narrowed her eyes. "Well, at least not in the true sense of the word."

"So just weird in the untrue sense?"

Rain laughed. "Yeah, that's it." They'd reached the edge of the woods where the field ended. Rain turned and squared her shoulders, so she was facing Ivy. "Maybe it reminds you of things that you've lost."

"That's one of my theories." Ivy held Rain's gaze. "Or maybe the dreams that never came true." Ivy shook her head and abruptly looked away.

Rain rolled Ivy's words around in her mind and bit her lip in concentration. "What dreams?"

"Silly ones." Ivy turned away and began walking into the woods.

Rain hurried to keep up. She wanted to know more but sensed that Ivy would answer in good time, so Rain followed.

They weaved through the woods. Several times, Ivy held back branches, so they didn't swing and hit Rain in the face. Rain hadn't expected the overgrowth.

"Is it always this thick?"

"We used to have a better path cleared, but it's become overgrown." Ivy held up a branch, so Rain could walk under. "My favorite spot is just a little farther."

Leaves from past seasons crunched under foot, and with the sunlight blocked by the trees, the air grew colder. Rain glanced behind them and realized she couldn't see the field anymore. Panic washed over her. "How do you know where you're going? It all looks the same to me."

Ivy chuckled. "Spoken like a city girl."

"You seriously know where you are?"

"Yup. Right around the bend, we should be at my log by the creek."

They'd walked for another two or three minutes, and the overgrowth gave way and they stepped into a clearing. A small creek gurgled off to the left.

Ivy pointed to a giant log that sat a few yards from the bend in the creek. "That's it." She turned to Rain and smiled, but it didn't reach her eyes. "That's where I did most of my daydreaming."

On impulse, Rain reached out her hand. "Mind if I join you?"

Ivy took Rain's hand and led her toward the log. A spot of sunlight spilled through the trees and landed on half of the fallen tree. Ivy squeezed Rain's hand. "See that? The sun still shines on it."

"It's pretty here. Peaceful."

When they arrived at the log, Ivy motioned toward it. "Have a seat." Ivy sat but didn't let go of Rain's hand.

As much as Rain wanted to continue to enjoy the warmth of Ivy's hand, she reluctantly let go.

She'd have to sit much too close to Ivy if she didn't.
Tentatively, Rain lowered herself. "This is your spot?"
"One of them." Ivy pointed across the creek.
"One log would rot, so then I'd find another. Max,
Rose, and I played out here all the time when we were
kids." She wrapped her arms around herself as if she
was cold, but Rain suspected that wasn't the case.
"Then when we got older, I'd sneak out here by myself.
I'd sit on a log or against a tree and read for hours."
"And dream?"
Ivy nodded. "And dream."
What did Ivy dream of? Probably typical things.
A husband and kids, Rain thought.
"I wanted to travel the world," Ivy said. "See
things. See all the places I read about in my books. Go
to college and learn about all those things." Ivy sighed.
"But sometimes, life takes you in a different direction.
The family needed me. When you're the oldest of six,
there are added responsibilities."
Rain shook her head. "Six. I'm an only child, so
I can't even imagine."
"Yep. When I was nineteen it was a full house.
A sixteen-, fourteen-, four-, and two-year-old with
Violet on the way."
"But you can still do those things now." Rain
put extra conviction in her voice when she recognized
Ivy's slumping shoulders. "You're only in your early
thirties."
Ivy dismissively waved her hand. "Why are we
talking about my foolish dreams? Don't all kids have
dreams? What was yours?"
Rain kicked at the peeling bark at her feet.
Maybe she should just make something up. *No.* That
wouldn't be fair after Ivy opened up to her. "I wanted

a family."

Ivy shifted on the log, so she was turned toward Rain. Her face showed surprise. "Somehow, that wasn't what I was expecting. You wanted, uh...uh...a husband and kids?"

Rain grinned. "No husband. I knew I was gay from a young age. Probably eight or nine. Well, I knew I liked girls, so it was always a wife and kids. I didn't know where kids came from at that point."

"I'll tell you the same thing you told me. You still have plenty of time."

Rain shrugged. "I suppose, but I'm probably too busy."

Ivy patted her hand. "Is that another *but?*"

"Damn, you don't miss anything." A loud splash came from the creek, causing Rain to jump. "Jesus. What the hell was that?"

"Just a frog." Ivy playfully pushed Rain's shoulder. "Don't worry, it won't attack you."

"That had to have been one big-ass frog. It sounded more like an alligator."

Ivy shook her head and rolled her eyes. "Alligator? Really?"

"Ya never know."

"Tell me more about this family you wanted."

"Not much to tell." Rain smiled. "I just thought it would be kinda cool to have kids to take places. The zoo. The Cubs game. And go see all their softball games and band concerts." Rain met Ivy's gaze. "I bet your parents did all of that."

"Yeah, don't all parents?"

Rain bit her lip and tried to keep a poker face. Such a loaded question.

Ivy frowned. "I'm sorry. That was insensitive."

"Nothing to be sorry about. My parents were busy saving the world, so they couldn't always make those things." Rain gave a nonchalant shrug. "Enough about me. Are you going to tell me the big news of the day?"

Ivy brought her hand to her chest. "Oh, god, I almost forgot. I walked out of church on Wednesday night. Quit. My family followed suit."

Rain's head whipped around. "You did what?"

"You heard me. Don't look so shocked." Ivy grinned. "It was the best feeling ever."

"But why?"

"You were right. I can't claim to follow Jesus if I let all that ha— oops, I almost said it. If I let all that negativity into my heart. On Wednesday, Devlin started going on and on. So full of the H word. Then he started talking about gay people, and your face," she put her hand against her forehead, "your face was right there in my mind, so I stood up and walked out."

"Wow." Not the most brilliant thing to say, but Rain couldn't think of anything else. "And your parents?"

"After I walked out of the church, my parents followed me. When we got home, we talked. They agreed this isn't who we want to be. This isn't the church we want to be a part of."

"What happens next?"

"Dunno. We eventually find a new church, but for a little while, we'll worship at home. When it's time, God will lead us where we need to be."

"I can't believe you waited all this time to tell me."

Ivy gazed down at her hands and played with the seam at the bottom of her shirt. "It was just nice having you here...after, you know...after we haven't talked. I wanted to show you the farm not talk about Devlin."

Rain studied Ivy who continued to look down at her shirt. "I really missed you. I just didn't think you wanted to talk to me."

"Why would you think that?" Ivy's voice came out loud enough that several birds flew from a nearby tree, squawking as they went.

"You didn't call on Tuesday. It was your turn, so I figured you didn't enjoy the weekend."

"God, no. It was the best weekend I've had in a really long time." Ivy finally looked up. "I panicked. Then Violet needed me, and after that, I didn't know how to fix it."

"It was one of my favorite weekends, too." Rain smiled. "You don't know how many times I picked up the phone to call, but I kept chickening out."

Ivy laughed. "Me too. We're a pathetic lot, aren't we?"

"You could say that. What do you say we make a promise...you know, so it won't happen again?"

"Go on," Ivy said, finally making eye contact.

"We promise that we'll talk things out. No disappearing on each other. Even if our differences become too much. We tell the truth, not just leave each other hanging."

"I don't think our differences should be a problem," Ivy said. "But I'll still make the promise."

Chapter Thirty-six

M rs. Nash waved from the porch as Rain and Ivy came around the side of the barn. The sun was getting lower in the sky and shone in their eyes, but Rain could still make out Mrs. Nash's huge smile.

"I thought I was going to have to send Papa out after you two," Mrs. Nash called. "Supper is almost ready."

Ivy turned to Rain and smiled. "That's code for you're staying for dinner."

Rain patted her stomach. "If it's anything like the meal I had last time I...um...popped in, I'm not complaining."

"Just know, you'd better bring an appetite to Mama's table, or she'll be offended."

"You've got nothing to worry about on that front since I didn't eat lunch."

"You shouldn't skip meals," Ivy said in a matter-of-fact tone.

"I wasn't hungry." Rain hoped the explanation would suffice since she didn't plan on telling Ivy why she had no appetite.

"Me neither." Ivy gently touched Rain's arm. "When I'm upset, I don't eat."

Of course, Ivy would be honest about it, while Rain tried to maintain her bravado. When she gazed into Ivy's sincere eyes, Rain was compelled to tell the truth. "Same here. Are you sure it's okay? Your mom hadn't planned on a guest."

"Trust me, nobody ever leaves Mama's table hungry." Ivy grinned. "Besides, she'd hunt you down if you decided to leave now."

Rain held up her hands in surrender. "Then who am I to argue?"

When they reached the porch, Mrs. Nash had already gone inside. Ivy reached for the door handle but stopped. "I need to warn you that Violet doesn't always have a filter and neither does Granny, but it's your lucky day because James and Frank are playing baseball with their friends."

"Oh, good, only one teenager to contend with. I'm getting to the age that teenagers think I'm old, and I hate—"

Sizzle.

Sulfur.

～～～～～

"Fuck," Rain said, now in Ivy's body. "I can't believe I just did that."

"Great. Dinner just got a whole lot more interesting." Without thinking, Ivy went to sweep back her hair, but her fingers entangled in Rain's hair. "How much product do you use to get your hair to stay up like this?"

"Obviously not enough." Rain squinted and examined the mess Ivy had just made. "You're gonna have me looking like a clown if you don't keep your hands out of my hair." Without giving it a thought, Rain reached out and began straightening the hair.

Rain froze and yanked her hand back. She

shouldn't casually touch Ivy like that, even if it was her body.

"Ouch," Ivy said and then scowled. "Why'd you do that? You just pulled a clump of my..." Ivy laughed. "I guess it's your hair you pulled out, not mine."

"Um, sorry. I shouldn't like...um...I shouldn't touch you when you're me."

Ivy rubbed her chin. "Oh, lord, that's a conundrum. Are you touching me or yourself?"

"Exactly." Rain hadn't given much thought to it until now.

Ivy ran her hands along Rain's stomach. "Sorry, but every time I'm in your body, I have to touch your stomach muscles."

Rain suddenly felt warm. Maybe a change of subject would be her best bet. "Maybe it'll be like last time. Remember, we switched back quick."

Ivy's eyes lit up. "Hopefully. I would love..." Ivy waited. Nothing happened. "Nope, it didn't work."

"Maybe I should say I have to go home and can't stay."

"Bad plan," Ivy said. "First, since you're in my body, you'd have to stay, and I'd be the one leaving."

"Oh, crap, I hadn't thought about that. And second?"

"I'm starving. You weren't kidding when you said you hadn't eaten." Ivy smiled.

Rain sighed. "I guess we have no choice then. Let's do it."

"There you are," Mama said when they entered the dining room.

"About time," Violet said. "I'm starving and Nazi mom wouldn't let us eat without you."

"Violet," Papa said in a stern voice. "We've got

company, so mind your manners."

Violet dropped her head and stared at the table but not before she wrinkled her nose at Ivy. Or at Rain in Ivy's body.

"Knock it off, Violet. Be nice to Rain or she won't come back again," Ivy said, forgetting she was in Rain's body.

Violet looked up and frowned. She shifted her gaze between Rain and Ivy. "Is that some weird city thing, talking about yourself in the third person?"

Shit. Rain didn't want Ivy to make her look like a pompous ass, so Rain tossed Ivy's head back and let out a loud laugh.

Everyone in the dining room stopped and looked at Rain in Ivy's body. She needed to rectify the situation. With a sheepish grin on her face, she said, "Rain's just such a jokester."

"I am. Never mind me," Ivy said. Apparently satisfied, her family went back to bringing the food to the table. Ivy leaned in close. "Please, don't make that face with my body," Ivy whispered. "You make me look like I'm constipated."

Rain couldn't resist and made a similar face.

"Stop," Ivy said under her breath. "Two can play at that game." She crossed Rain's eyes and let her tongue loll from her mouth.

"Seriously?" Rain glowered but was secretly amused by Ivy's antics. "Are you ten?"

Ivy doubled down and pulled Rain's cellphone from her pocket and snapped a couple of selfies. "For posterity."

"I'm ignoring you now." Rain turned away and said to Mrs. Nash, who'd just walked in carrying a steaming bowl of mashed potatoes, "Is there something

I can do Mrs...um...Mama?" *God, that felt weird.* The only thing Rain had ever heard Ivy call her mother was Mama, so she'd have to go with it.

"Are you okay, honey?" Mrs. Nash eyed Rain as she set the potatoes on a hot pad.

The caring look in Mrs. Nash's eyes was unsettling to Rain, so she muttered, "I'm okay," as she looked away.

"Why don't you and Rain sit down?" Mrs. Nash said. "I think we have everything."

Rain looked helplessly at Ivy. She had no idea where anyone sat.

"Is it okay if I sit here?" Ivy said from Rain's body.

"Perfect," Rain said a little too enthusiastically from Ivy's mouth. Better the family think Ivy was losing it than to focus on Rain.

"I bet one of these seats are yours," Ivy said. She tilted back her head and placed her hand on her forehead. "Let me guess." Ivy pointed to the chair to the left of Rain. "I think that one is it."

Rain clapped Ivy's hands, finally getting the hang of Ivy's cues. "Got it on the first try." This could be a long meal. Several times already, Granny had given them both strange looks. Something told Rain that Granny didn't miss much.

Rain bit Ivy's lip when she realized how absurd she was being. Like the family would guess that they'd switched bodies. *Dumb.* She didn't have to fear being found out. Her stomach dropped. What she did have to fear was Ivy's family not liking her because of Ivy's strange behavior in Rain's body. The unsettled feeling gave her pause. It wasn't like she planned on spending a lot of time here, did she?

"Oh, darn it, Ivy, I forgot to get the drinks. Do you mind getting them?" Mama asked.

Rain stood tentatively in Ivy's body and was soon followed by Ivy, who launched Rain's body from the chair she was sitting in. "I'll help you."

"Don't be making Rain help, she's a guest," Mrs. Nash said.

"I'd enjoy helping," Ivy said from Rain's mouth.

Perfect. Ivy just scored Rain points. Before Mrs. Nash could protest further, they scurried to the kitchen.

They'd barely cleared the door when the mouth-watering scent reached Rain's nose. The unmistakable smell of roast filled the air. Her reaction surprised her since she rarely ate meat anymore. Maybe it had something to do with being in Ivy's body.

Mr. Nash stood over the piece of meat with an electric knife expertly cutting it into thin slices. He smiled at them when they entered. "Mama putting you to work?"

Ivy opened Rain's mouth to answer, so Rain said loudly, "Just getting the drinks."

Mr. Nash started and nearly dropped the knife. "Jeesh, inside voice, Ivy." He chuckled and looked at who he thought was Rain. "I haven't had to tell her that since she was ten."

Rain and Ivy both smiled. This was harder than Rain imagined. Hopefully, they could get through the meal without Ivy's family thinking they were on drugs.

Once they were seated, Mr. Nash turned to Rain. "Would you like to say grace?"

Shit. Shit. Shit. He thought she was Ivy. She'd never said grace in her life. This could go so wrong.

She'd seen it done on television before, but what if that wasn't the way they did it? *Shit.* Somehow, rub-a-dub-dub thanks for the grub probably would be wrong. She felt everyone's gaze on her, but she'd frozen.

"Ivy? Did you hear me?" Mr. Nash said.

Rain turned and looked at Ivy. "Rain, would you mind doing the honors?"

Ivy smiled at her, which was still hard to get used to. Seeing herself smiling from across the table was a little creepy. Even thinking that made her head spin.

"If it's okay with your family, I'd be happy to," Ivy said from Rain's body.

Hopefully, Ivy knew that it would be a yes, or it would be right back in Rain's lap.

Mr. and Mrs. Nash smiled and nodded.

Rain stared as Ivy bowed her head. Rain wanted to take it all in should she ever end up in this position again. Ivy began the prayer as Rain watched.

She glanced at the rest of the family, who had their heads bowed, except for Granny, who stared at her with interest. Rain quickly bowed Ivy's head and didn't raise it until several beats after the final amen.

Ugh. This was so confusing. Maybe if she just focused on her meal and said as little as possible. Hopefully, Ivy would carry the conversation and, in the process, make Rain look good to the family. The prayer had been a hit, now if only Ivy could keep it up.

The conversation was light as the dishes were passed and plates were filled. Granny passed her a large bowl of Brussels sprouts. *Yum.* She rarely got Brussels sprouts, but she loved them. She took a heaping spoonful and debated taking another, but she didn't want to be greedy.

She passed the bowl on to Ivy, who had an unreadable expression on her face. *Damn it.* She'd never had to read expressions on her own face before, especially with a hint of Ivy mixed in. Ivy passed the bowl on to Violet without taking any.

The table had suddenly gone quiet. Something was wrong, but Rain couldn't figure out what. Ivy's entire family stared at Rain's plate. What kind of faux pas had she made now? Sure, she didn't like any of her food touching, so she kept it separate, but surely, that couldn't be it.

With a quick glance around the table, she noted that no one else seemed worried about their food items touching.

In a panic, Rain picked up her fork and scrambled the food on her plate, mixing the meat, potatoes, and vegetables into a big pile.

"For the love of God, girl, what is wrong with you?" Mrs. Nash said.

Ivy patted Rain on the shoulder. "The jig's up, Ivy," Ivy said from Rain's mouth. "Thanks for trying to protect me from the Brussels sprouts."

When Ivy's family stared, Ivy continued. "Rain *detests* Brussels sprouts, too, so I told her that I'd eat some. You know take one for the team, so she didn't have to eat any."

Ivy's explanation sounded lame to Rain's ears, but Ivy's family nodded as if understanding. All except for Granny, who narrowed her eyes, leaned forward, and gazed directly into Rain's eyes, or what she thought was Ivy's.

Rain squirmed. It was as if the old woman was looking into her soul. Rain grabbed her fork and speared a Brussels sprout and shoved it into her mouth. *Shit.* It was bigger than she thought. Where'd they find Brussels sprouts the size of kiwis? She tried to chew without choking.

Violet laughed and pointed at Rain. "Wow, that's epic." She reached into her back pocket and pulled out her phone. "I need a picture of this."

Rain looked toward Violet with Ivy's cheeks bulging as she chewed. She couldn't say anything through her mouthful, so she grunted.

Violet snapped a few more pictures before she turned to her parents. "When are we going to have Ivy committed? First, she sticks it to Pastor Devlin and then this. I think she might be possessed."

"Violet!" Mrs. Nash glowered. "You will not talk about that at this table, or you will be eating your supper in your bedroom."

"Fine." Violet snorted. "I was just trying to make a point."

"A point you'll be making alone in your room if you don't listen to your mother," Mr. Nash said.

The exchange gave Rain time to chew the Brussels sprout enough to be able to swallow part of it. She might develop Ivy's hatred of sprouts after she'd nearly choked on the mouthful.

Ivy put her hand on Rain's arm and leaned toward her, while Violet continued to plead her case. "Careful. I'd prefer you not choke me." Ivy winked.

Rain wanted to laugh but feared she'd end up snorting the Brussels sprout into places it shouldn't be. She concentrated on chewing and was finally able to swallow another portion.

Mr. Nash laughed. "When Ivy decides to take one for the team, she does it with gusto. Next time, I'd recommend cutting it in half, maybe even quarters, before you eat it."

Rain shrugged and swallowed the final bit. "Inexperience."

The others laughed, and the spotlight lifted from Rain. She'd just begun to feel more confident, when Mrs. Nash turned to Ivy and said, "So, Rain, tell us a little about yourself."

Rain just wanted to get through the meal in peace, so she said, "There's really not much to tell."

Rain realized her error as soon as she saw the horror on Mrs. Nash's face. "Ivy June. I don't know what's gotten into you today, but that was rude."

Ivy cleared her throat and patted Rain on the back. "It's okay, Ivy. I feel comfortable with your family, so I don't mind answering."

Rain relaxed. Ivy seemed to be handling the situation much better than she was, which in some ways was for the better. At least, Ivy was making a good impression on her family for her.

It was odd hearing about herself in Ivy's words but coming from her own mouth. The things Ivy decided to share and focus on were different than how she would have presented herself, which left Rain fascinated.

"All in all, I just want to make the world a better place. A better place for everyone," Ivy said on behalf of Rain.

By the smiles and nods from around the table, Ivy had scored her more points.

"That's so admirable," Mrs. Nash said. "No wonder our Ivy thinks so highly of you."

Granny's gaze shifted between Rain and Ivy, her eyes alert, even though she was pretending to cut her meat.

"Oh, and by the way, um...Mrs. Nash—" Ivy

said.

"Young lady, our names are Ben and Joan, not Mr. and Mrs. Nash."

"Sorry." Ivy smiled. She shot a quick glance at Rain before she held up a bite of the roast beef and said, "I just wanted you to know I love—"

Electricity.

Sulfur.

Chapter Thirty-seven

The table had been cleared, the kitchen cleaned, and the dishwasher started. Ivy and Rain were finishing washing the pans that Mama wouldn't put into the dishwasher. It had taken a little persuasion to convince Mama to let them do it, but she'd finally conceded. Ivy was thankful the rest of the meal had gone well after they'd switched back. Rain had charmed her family, even Violet, which depending on the day could be challenging.

"What are you thinking?" Rain asked as she rinsed the suds off a pan.

Ivy thought of making something up, but then said, "About how confident you are. How I hope some of that will rub off on me."

"Don't let me fool you." Rain smiled. "I'm not confident about everything."

The answer took Ivy by surprise, and she was about to ask for an explanation when Violet bounced into the kitchen. "I'm going to ride my bike to Sarah's. I just wanted to tell Rain it was nice to meet her."

Ivy gaped. Her kid sister was growing up, and somehow, Ivy had missed it, or maybe she just didn't want to see it.

Rain smiled. "It was nice to meet you, too."

"Um...I hope you visit again sometime...soon." A slight blush colored Violet's cheeks.

Ivy blinked a couple of times. Did her baby sister

have a crush on Rain?

"I'd like that." Rain continued to smile. "Have fun at Sarah's house."

"Thanks," Violet muttered as she scurried from the room.

Teenagers. "Apparently, you have a fan."

"That's good." Rain's eyes sparkled. "I can use all the support I can get here. I'm not sure what Granny thinks of me."

Ivy stopped drying the pan she had in her hand and looked at Rain. "Why do you say that?"

"She was eyeballing us most of the time. Something tells me she doesn't miss much."

"It's one of Granny's superpowers. She sneaks around disguised as a little old lady, but her mind is as sharp as a tack."

"Trust me, I figured that out in the first few minutes."

Ivy dried the final pan and put it into the cupboard. "Shall we go see what the others are up to?"

Rain put her hand on Ivy's arm. "I was hoping we could talk about...about...um...what happened the other day."

"You mean the elephant in the room that we've been stepping around all day?" Ivy grinned. She knew they needed to talk about it, but they'd had such a pleasant afternoon she feared it could ruin everything.

"That would be the one." Rain smiled back at her.

"Let's see if Mama and Papa will let us slip away without a fight."

When they emerged from the kitchen, Mama said, "Do you girls want to play some cards? I'm not sure we'll be able to pull Papa away from the Cubs game, but we can try."

"I was telling Rain about a book that I'd gotten from the library," Ivy said. It wasn't a lie. "I thought I'd show it to her."

"You and all your books." Papa laughed and glanced at Rain. "She reads anything she can get her hands on. I keep expecting the library to start charging us."

Rain smiled. "I'm a bit of a bookworm myself."

Mama smiled. "It's so nice for Ivy to find someone who's as curious as she is. You haven't had a friend like that since Nadine moved away."

Ivy shifted from one foot to the other. She'd not mentioned Nadine to Rain, and she sensed that Rain was looking at her, but she just wanted to move off the topic. "We'll leave you to your baseball game then."

"Can you walk Granny next door?" Mama said.

Before Ivy could respond, Granny practically threw herself into a nearby chair. "I think I'll watch the game for a while."

Papa was too absorbed in the game to notice, but Mama's head whipped around. "You want to watch the game?"

"I've been getting into it lately." Granny hated all sports. Ivy met Granny's gaze. The twinkle in her eye was unmistakable when she winked. "I'll let the girls have the house to themselves."

Ivy fought against letting her jaw drop as she pulled Rain from the room.

As soon as they'd cleared the front porch, Rain said, "Did I just see what I think I saw?"

"If you mean Granny's wink, wink, nod about leaving us alone, then yes, you saw it."

"What the fuck?" Rain said. "Do you think she

knows...knows what happened?"

Ivy shook her head, still trying to make sense of it herself. "I have no idea."

꙳꙳꙳꙳

They walked in silence to Ivy's room. Rain's curiosity was piqued. Nadine was clearly an important person in Ivy's past. Why hadn't she told her more about her?

As they made their way up the steps toward Ivy's bedroom, Rain tried to push thoughts of Nadine from her mind. She needed to focus on the conversation they were about to have. Her heart had already begun to race, and it wasn't from climbing the stairs.

Ivy turned to her once they'd entered the bedroom and closed the door. Suddenly, Ivy's tiny room felt even smaller. Rain grabbed at the collar of her shirt, hoping it would help her from feeling so warm.

Ivy's gaze darted from the bed to the desk chair. By the look in her eyes, Ivy had finally realized they were alone in tight quarters.

Rain stepped back until she bumped into the desk chair. "Where would you like me to sit?"

"Um..." Ivy looked at the chair and then the bed. Rain held her breath. The answer might reveal much. Ivy pointed to the bed. "We might be more comfortable if we sat here."

Rain wanted to leap onto the bed, but instead, she was nonchalant as she took the short three steps. It wasn't as if she wanted to ravage Ivy, but she wanted to be close to her and possibly be able to get another kiss.

Ivy had already sat at the foot of the bed, so Rain sat near the head, leaving a few feet between them. She kicked off her shoes and put one leg underneath her while the other dangled over the side.

"I've missed you," Rain said without thinking. It certainly wasn't what she'd intended on saying, but it was the truth. "And we need to talk about what happened."

"I missed you, too." Ivy fidgeted with her shirt.

"Well." Ivy slapped her hand against her leg but said nothing further.

Rain smirked. "Now that we have that cleared up, should we go to a movie or something?"

Ivy laughed, and some of the tension left her face. "Thank you." Her gaze bore into Rain's. The intensity in her eyes almost caused Rain to look away. "You can always make me laugh, regardless of the circumstances."

Rain tried to put on a confident air, even though she felt like an awkward teenager at her first dance. "I'm sorry I kissed you. I crossed a line I never should have." The words fell out of Rain's mouth in a rush.

Ivy pursed her lips before she responded. "Who said you were the one that kissed me?"

Rain stared slack-jawed. "What did you just say?"

"I said, who said it was you that initiated the kiss?"

"It wasn't me?" Rain tried to hide the dumb-founded look that she was sure was on her face.

"You didn't know?" Ivy looked at her like she had five heads. Of course, she'd look at her that way. Who didn't know when they initiated a kiss?

"It was all so jumbled with the body switches

and all. Um...I just assumed I must have. Since...you know...since I'm a lesbian, and well, you're not."

"I've kissed a girl before." Ivy sat up taller and jutted out her chin.

Wow. This conversation was getting more interesting by the minute. "Nadine?"

It was Ivy's turn to look shocked. "How did you know?" Before Rain could answer, Ivy jumped from the bed and hurried to her desk. "Did you read my journal?" A scowl creased her brow.

"No." Rain held up her hands. "First, I didn't know you had a journal, and even if I did, I would never do that."

Ivy stopped before she opened the drawer and turned back. "You promise?" Ivy stepped back to the bed.

"I promise." Rain smiled.

Ivy sat. "Then how did you know it was Nadine?"

"The look on your face."

"And what look would that be?" Ivy delivered the line with a slight hint of defensiveness.

"Part affection, part guilt, and another part I couldn't quite identify."

"Fear."

"Fear? What were you afraid of?"

"You finding out," Ivy answered without hesitation.

Rain scratched her head, trying to make sense of Ivy's words. "What did you think I would do?"

"Not want to kiss me again." A tiny vein throbbed near Ivy's temple as if inviting Rain to kiss her there.

Rain looked away and focused on Ivy's eyes. *Big mistake.* They were slightly misty and held a hint of vulnerability. *Damn.* Rain had slept with plenty of women in her time, but this was by far the sexiest look she'd ever seen. *Fuck.* She needed to snap out of it.

Worry lines formed in Ivy's forehead and around her eyes. "Was that the wrong thing to say?"

"No." Rain practically lunged at Ivy as she reached out to pat her leg.

Despite Rain's over-the-top reaction, Ivy didn't flinch. She smiled instead. "Then what are you thinking?"

"That I want to kiss you again." Rain couldn't believe she'd said that.

"Then what are you waiting for?"

"Um, well, um...Nadine—"

"Whoa. I'm not into threesomes."

"Oh, god. That's not what I—"

Ivy laughed. "Sorry, I couldn't resist."

Rain stared at her in shock for a couple of beats before she burst out laughing. "Damn you. Seems like you're full of surprises today. Here I thought you'd be freaked out by everything, but instead, you're fucking with me."

"You should have seen the look on your face." Ivy broke into a fresh round of laughter.

Once Ivy regained control, Rain said, "So what about Nadine? I'm not sure I should go around kissing you if you have a girlfriend."

Ivy shook her head and smiled. "First off, I would never have kissed you if I had a girlfriend. And second, Nadine is happily married with two kids."

The tightness in Rain's chest lessened. She hadn't even realized how tense she was until her body relaxed. "And you want to kiss me?"

"I think so." Ivy leaned back slightly.

"You only think?"

Ivy shook her head hard enough for her hair to whip across her face. "I know. It's just...um..." Ivy waved her hand between them. "What is this?"

"This is just us." Rain wasn't sure what else she was supposed to say.

A look of frustration crossed Ivy's face. "I don't want to be another friends with benefits situation."

"Oh, god, no. That's not what I'm suggesting."

"You probably think I'm old-fashioned, but I'm not comfortable with it like you are."

Rain studied Ivy's face. Her worry lines had deepened. "Are you asking to be exclusive?"

Ivy's cheeks immediately reddened. "We shared one kiss. I can't ask that of you."

Rain picked up the cue. "How about if we have two?"

"Two?"

"I'm all right dating exclusively after a second kiss." Rain grinned. "Well, that is, if it's good."

Ivy rubbed her chin and looked toward the ceiling. When she returned her gaze to Rain, she said, "Do you think I'm up for the challenge?"

Rain moved down the bed toward Ivy and put her hand on Ivy's arm. "If the first kiss was any indication, I don't think you have anything to worry about." Rain gazed into Ivy's eyes and put her palm lightly against Ivy's cheek.

Rain felt a slight tremble under her fingertips and wanted to pull Ivy against her but held back. "Are you okay?"

Ivy nodded. "Just a little scared."

"Of me?" Rain moved back slightly.

"Of this."

"We don't have to do anything you aren't comfortable with." Rain took Ivy's hand in hers.

"Oh, I want to." Ivy smiled. "No doubt I want to. I just worry that it isn't wise with our...er...our problem."

"Ahh, now I understand." Rain smiled. "It could complicate our body switching thing if it didn't work out."

"Exactly." Ivy squeezed Rain's hand.

"Because this body switch thing is so not complicated as it stands."

Ivy laughed, and the light in her eyes danced. "Good point." Ivy leaned toward Rain.

Rain moved in closer. Ivy's lips were only inches from hers. Despite the heat burning inside of her, she reminded herself to move slowly.

Rain's lips lightly brushed over Ivy's. Being the second kiss, she wasn't surprised by the softness of Ivy's lips as they played against Rain's. Ivy's lips moved in perfect rhythm with her own.

As if by some special agreement, their kisses remained light and tender, despite the desire raging inside of Rain. She didn't want to rush anything as much as she longed to let her hand slide underneath Ivy's shirt. Instead, she lightly rubbed her thumb over the back of Ivy's hand.

Ivy moaned into Rain's mouth and almost caused Rain to come undone. Rain pulled back, and their lips parted. She gazed into Ivy's eyes. The desire burning there threatened to overwhelm Rain, so she brought her lips to Ivy's again.

Sometime later, Rain wasn't sure how long, they pulled apart. When Rain got her bearings, she realized they'd fallen back against Ivy's pillows, and Ivy's leg was draped over Rain's.

Ivy dropped her head to Rain's chest. Her

breaths came out hard and deep. "Holy shit," Ivy said. "I think we need a cold shower." She started to roll off Rain.

"Wait. I like the feeling of you in my arms. If I promise not to kiss you again, at least for a while, can we stay like this?"

Ivy dropped her head back onto Rain's shoulder and put her arm across Rain's midsection. Ivy touched Rain's firm stomach. When Rain quivered, Ivy pulled her hand back. "Sorry. I adore your abs. They're yummy."

Rain laughed. "Yummy, huh?"

"Yep." Ivy snuggled closer to Rain.

"Are you sure we should do this?"

"Do what?" Ivy's voice came out sleepy.

"Cross these lines." Rain knew she should put some distance between her and Ivy, but instead, she held her a little tighter.

Ivy shrugged. "Who knows? But it feels nice, doesn't it?"

Really nice. Rain settled on something more casual. "It does. We just come from such different worlds, and this...this whatever it is complicates things."

"Uh-huh." Ivy twitched.

Damn. Was Ivy falling asleep in Rain's arms? She should probably get up, but instead, she pulled a corner of the bedspread up over Ivy's shoulder.

Ivy let out a contented sigh and nestled into Rain's side.

Chapter Thirty-eight

R ain turned on her stereo, trying to drown out thoughts of Ivy. Brandi Carlisle's smooth voice filled her car. Rain stabbed at the selector key. This was the last thing she needed to listen to. She flipped through her music. There had to be something that wouldn't bring her thoughts back to Ivy. Maybe something old school that didn't focus on romance and relationships. She settled on Black Eyed Peas and cranked the volume.

The fields flashed by as she sped down the country road. She let her foot off the gas as dusk approached, so she wouldn't hit any of the animals that dodged across the road. Where she lived, there were always squirrels, but here she just might see a raccoon or opossum. She laughed at herself. Ivy would say she was citified thinking raccoons and opossums were rarities.

Shit. The Black Eyed Peas weren't cutting it since she was back to thinking about Ivy. She sighed and gave up her battle. She might as well get this over with. She'd thought of doing it last week, but something had held her back.

Rain punched a couple of buttons on her steering wheel and said, "Call Tracie."

"Calling Tracie," the robotic voice responded.

The phone was picked up almost immediately. "Hey, kid."

Rain smiled. "Hey, Tracie."

"What's up?"

"Maybe I just called to say hi."

"Not likely. It's eight o'clock on a Sunday night. Not your usual call time."

She had a point, but Rain wouldn't give her the satisfaction of admitting that she was a creature of habit and had a pattern when it came to her phone calls. "Um, just driving home and thought of you with all the cornfields flashing past."

"Cornfields? Where the hell are you?"

"Just outside of Mullins Creek."

Tracie laughed. "I see. Visiting the little cutie, are you?"

Rain bristled. "Yes, I've just left Ivy's house."

"Relax. It wasn't an insult." Tracie chuckled. "I swear sometimes your generation is much too sensitive."

"Whatever." She knew Tracie hated it when she used the word, so that should even the score. Tension melted from Rain's shoulders.

"What is your...um...Ivy up to? Still trying to figure out how to stop your Freaky Friday shit?"

Wow. Tracie's comment made her realize that she'd not given much more thought to stopping the body switching. Maybe she didn't want to. If she did, would it mean that they'd go their separate ways? Rain pushed the concern from her mind; she needed to answer Tracie. "Something happened."

"Is she all right?" Rain could hear the concern in Tracie's voice.

"She's fine...um...I guess."

"What the hell does that mean? How can someone be fine, you guess?"

"Actually, something happened last weekend. Ivy and I hadn't talked about it, but we really need to."

"Did you do something bad when you were in her body?" Tracie groaned. "She didn't catch you touching her or something like that, did she?"

"Eww, you can be such an idiot sometimes." Rain stopped at a stop sign, but since there were no cars around her, she didn't pull away. "I wouldn't touch her without her permission."

"How do you pee?"

Ugh. Leave it to Tracie. "I try not to. I only had to do it once, and I didn't look."

Tracie's laughter filled the car. "Oh, god, that's priceless. How long did it take you to get up enough courage to take a piss?"

Rain glowered. She knew Tracie had taken the crudity level up a notch just to stick it to Rain more. "You can be such an ass sometimes."

Tracie continued to chuckle. "But you love me."

"Sorry, I can't say the word. It'll get me in trouble." Rain smirked. A blip of headlights shone in her rearview mirror, so she let off the brake and drove through the intersection.

"So back to the original question. How long did you try and hold it?"

No way would she give Tracie the satisfaction of knowing that she'd nearly peed Ivy's pants before she finally took the plunge, after she'd said love and hate multiple times without success. "I couldn't very well let her bladder burst, now could I?"

"Good no answer, kid, but I'll let you off the hook because I think there's something bigger here than wiping Ivy's ass."

"Jesus. Do you have to be so crude? Maybe you

could order a filter from Amazon or something. They sell everything."

"Jeannie's tried, but none of them work."

"I believe that." As much as Rain liked to complain about Tracie's lack of filter, it was one of her most endearing qualities. She always knew she'd get the truth from Tracie.

"Are you going to stop stalling and tell me what's going on?"

"I kissed Ivy. Twice." Rain hunched her shoulders in toward her body, waiting for Tracie's reaction.

"Good for you."

Rain's mouth dropped open, and she nearly drove through the stop sign she'd come to. "What did you say?"

"I said, about time you found a good woman."

"You approve?"

"Of course, I approve. Why wouldn't I?"

"Um, lots of reasons."

"And what would those be?" Rain could almost hear the eye roll in Tracie's voice.

"She's straight."

"Hmph. They're only straight until they're not. Give me a better reason."

The car behind Rain honked since she'd been too busy gaping at Tracie's words to pay attention to anything around her. She pushed the gas—hard. The car shot from the stop sign. "She's also a Christian."

"What's that have to do with anything?"

"She's not exactly on our side."

Tracie let out a loud exhale. "And what is our side? And when did all Christians become the enemy?"

"They aren't exactly accepting of us."

"Hmm, funny, it seems like Ivy has accepted you

just fine. How accepting of her have you been?"

Rain glowered. Of course, Rain was accepting of people, the entire rainbow of people. "What bug crawled up your ass?"

"Deflecting. I get it, but it ain't gonna work." Tracie let out a chuckle, but there was no joy in it. "How many Christians work for you? Are a part of your *little foundation*?"

Rain's hackles rose. It wasn't lost on her the condescending tone Tracie used when she mentioned the foundation. "We do good work. We don't tolerate bigotry of any kind."

"Unless it's toward people like Ivy. Pull your head out. If you want true diversity, you have to include people with opinions different than your own."

"But I bring people to the table that have been excluded forever. That's what it's all about."

"I couldn't agree more, but it's about having *everyone* at the table. Not throwing out the people that once had a seat to put others in their place. Build a bigger fucking table, Rain."

"That's not why I called." Tracie could be infuriating, but Rain didn't want to have a political debate. She wanted advice on Ivy, so she dropped the fight.

"Oh, yeah, we were talking about the kiss. How was it?"

"It was nice." Rain grinned.

"Oh, my god, you're falling for her." It sounded like Tracie slapped a table by the loud bang that came from the other end of the phone.

"How the hell did you get that from me saying it was nice?" Heat rose in Rain's cheeks. *Damned Tracie.*

She always cut through the bullshit right to the point. "Too respectful."

"How the hell can I be too respectful?" Now Tracie was just trying to goad her.

"Any of your other...um...conquests..."

"You mean girlfriends?" Rain snapped.

"Yeah, girlfriends." Tracie chuckled. "Or should I say fuck buddies?"

What the hell was Tracie's problem today? She seemed edgier than usual. Come to think about it, she'd been that way the last few times Rain had spoken to her. "Why are you so damned cranky?"

"Ah, nothing—I'm still trying to process that damned conference. I've been working on a piece for my blog. Probably piss everyone off."

Rain groaned. "You wouldn't be you if you didn't. But seriously, be careful there's a lot of haters out there, and you don't need to stir them up."

"Maybe we all need to be stirred up. It might get people talking to each other again. Bring both sides together." Tracie sighed. "Speaking of both sides, let's talk about Ivy."

"I'm not sure what happens next. It's probably a bad idea."

"I don't agree. Just because you haven't had much relationship success doesn't mean you can't."

"Relationship?" Rain practically yelled. As they'd talked, she'd noticed her speed had been increasing, so she let off the gas. She was nearly to the highway and didn't need to get a ticket out in the middle of nowhere. "I'm talking about a kiss not a relationship."

"You're thirty...what? Three?"

"Not for a couple more months."

"So you're thirty-two, maybe it's about time you

think about a relationship."

Ugh. This conversation was not going as she'd planned. She'd expected Tracie to tell her to pull her head out of her ass and not get involved with someone like Ivy, but instead, Tracie seemed to be voicing approval. "And you think a relationship with Ivy would be a good idea?"

"How long have I known you?"

"I dunno, fifteen years? What does that have to do with anything?"

"You haven't exactly had the best track record. If anything, your choices have gotten worse. Culminating in Sasha. Wow. That one's a piece of work. I still don't know what you see in her."

"She's..."

"Never mind. I don't need to hear about her body or what she likes in the sack. I rescind my comment of what you see in her. My point is that she's not relationship material."

"Maybe I'm not looking for a relationship." Rain knew her tone was defensive, but she didn't care.

"Then you better keep your lips off Ivy."

Rain paused, contemplating her response. "Why am I detecting anger?"

"Because Ivy's too good to be treated like one of your throw-away toys."

The words stung, but Rain bit her lip. "You haven't even met her, so where's this hostility coming from?"

"I've met her."

"In my body. That doesn't count."

"It does so." Tracie chuckled, lessening some of the tension building in Rain. "She was a hell of a lot nicer than you. Besides, I follow her on Instagram, and she's texted me a few times."

"You what?" Could this day get any stranger?

"We follow each other on Instagram."

"And how is it that I didn't know this?"

"Because you're too hip to be on Instagram. Too busy tweetering and tic tacking."

"Tok'ing."

"Yeah, whatever. Anyway, I've been keeping my eye on Ivy. Sweet girl."

"Back to this texting her. When did that start?"

"Uh, a few weeks ago. She texted me to congratulate me for winning my 5K race."

"You ran a race?" What the fuck? "And you won? Since when did you start running?"

"About a year ago, when I had that health scare. When my blood pressure spiked."

A slight twinge of hurt coursed through Rain. "Why didn't I know you'd taken up running?"

"Stop being butt hurt. I knew you'd have a million pieces of advice. They might work for someone in their thirties, but this old body didn't want to try and keep up."

As much as Rain hated to admit it, she would have tried to tell Tracie how to train. "Obviously, you're doing something right if you won."

"It wasn't that impressive." Tracie laughed. "It was the sixty and older category. But I passed the eighty-year-old woman and her walker like a boss."

Rain laughed. She suspected Tracie had done better than that. "Well, congratulations, anyway," Rain said and meant it. "I think that's pretty fucking awesome. I guess I'll have to keep an eye on Instagram more often."

"You'd get to see more of your girl Ivy, too. She's

a looker with her country girl charm."

Tracie didn't have to tell Rain that. Rain had been drawn to Ivy's simple beauty from the beginning. "She's even prettier in person." Rain wasn't sure why she'd said that. She hated it when women were reduced to their looks. "Inside and out," she added.

"Back to this kiss. Tell me about it."

Rain spent the next several minutes telling Tracie the story.

"I'll be damned. Have you ever kissed a girl without getting into her pants?"

"Yes!" Rain responded, her voice full of indignation.

"In the last decade?"

Damn it. Maybe if she avoided the question. "I wasn't trying to get into her pants."

Tracie let out a loud laugh. "In other words, the answer is no. Priceless."

"Fuck you," Rain said with a chuckle. "Can we get back to the topic at hand?"

"Sure. And if I'm not mistaken, the topic would be that you're falling for Ivy and have no idea what to do about it."

"Goddamn it. That's not what I said."

"Didn't have to. I wasn't born yesterday." Tracie snorted. "The lady killer, Rain Hargrove, doesn't go around kissing girls without a payoff, unless they have her hooked."

"You're such an asshole. Tell me again why I called you."

"Because I'd give it to you straight."

She had a point, but Rain wasn't about to admit it too easily. "You're still an asshole."

"Compliment accepted." Rain could hear the

smile in Tracie's voice. "She's different, so don't approach her like you normally would."

"What's that supposed to mean?"

"I'm betting she's a little old-fashioned, so you may need to court her."

Rain groaned. "The fifties called and want their decade back."

Tracie chuckled. "You don't have to listen to the ramblings of an old woman, but I've spoken my peace. It's up to you what you do with it."

"You're missing the point of this phone call." Rain pounded the top of the steering wheel.

"And what was that?"

"To convince me that kissing Ivy was a *very* bad idea, and I need to stop right away."

"No can do."

Chapter Thirty-nine

Rain turned her cellphone over and over in her hands, waiting for it to ring. She thought of turning on the television but stared at the ugly painting on her hotel room wall instead.

Normally, she enjoyed traveling for work, but this conference had been too long, probably because she'd not been able to see Ivy since their last kiss. She hoped they could get together this weekend, but Rain still hadn't worked up the courage to ask her.

Dumbass. How many women had she asked out over the years? Now she was afraid to ask out someone she'd already kissed?

Her thoughts were interrupted by the phone.

"Ivy!" Rain said.

"Rain!" Ivy said back and laughed. "Must be a good conference, judging by your enthusiasm."

"It's all right. I've been looking forward to hearing from you all day. It's what kept me going."

"Aww, that's sweet," Ivy said. "Sorry I had to call early. I hope it's not an inconvenience."

"Not at all. Sessions ended at five. But you never said why you needed to call early."

"Since this is our first Wednesday without church, my parents decided tonight we needed to have a game night."

Rain smiled. "How fun."

Ivy let out a heavy sigh.

"What's the matter?" Rain asked.

"Oh, nothing, I should be grateful. Game night is always fun, but I'm exhausted. I forgot how exhausting waitressing can be. The breakfast crowd expects you to hustle. At least, I got to mow lawns this afternoon, but all that fresh air and sunshine made me tired. I just want to curl up with a good book."

Rain thought for a second. "You could. I've got my Kindle with me, and it's chock full of books."

"That was mean, Rain Anne Hargrove."

Rain smiled. "You sound just like your mama."

"Oh, god, I do." Ivy laughed. "I guess there could be lots worse people I could sound like."

"True. Why'd you call me mean?"

"Taunting me like that. I can imagine you sprawled out in that glorious hotel room reading all evening. I'm envious."

"I'd certainly not call it glorious." Rain glowered at the ugly painting. "But I wasn't taunting you. We could switch."

"What?"

"Switch. You know...bodies."

"I know what switching means, geesh. You'd do that?"

"Yeah, you sound tired. It could be a mini retreat for you. Just as long as your family doesn't play Bible trivia or something."

Ivy laughed. "There won't be any Bible trivia. Do you really want to?" Ivy's voice held a note of hopefulness.

"Yeah. I'm kinda tired of staring at the hotel walls and networking with a bunch of strangers. It'd be fun to play games with people I know." *Wow.* That was unexpected. Since when would she rather hang out in an old farmhouse playing games than rubbing elbows with some of the biggest players in the foundation world? "I only wish you could be there, too."

"Oh, that would be fun. Let's see if you survive this one first, though."

"You're gonna let me do it?" Rain was surprised and excited.

"I think I am." Ivy yawned. "The thought of an evening by myself sounds too heavenly to pass up."

"Sweet." Rain grinned. "This should be fun."

"Be forewarned. The group can get competitive, especially Granny."

"I'm up for the challenge." Rain jumped from her bed, suddenly full of energy. But what would she wear? She laughed. "God, I'm a dumbass. I was just trying to pick out an outfit for tonight. I guess I won't need one."

Ivy chuckled. "Any requests for what you'd like to wear as me?"

"Yes. Please, no dress. I don't want to go flashing your private bits around, even to your family."

Rain laughed. "So what time's game night?"

"Seven."

"Okay. I better go get some dinner, so I'll be ready for you to lounge around in my body."

"I really appreciate this, Rain. More than you may know."

Rain's face heated. "It's my pleasure."

"Um, one other thing," Ivy said. "Before I forget."

The hesitation in Ivy's voice gave Rain pause. "What is it?"

"What are you doing Friday night?"

Damn it. She'd wanted to ask Ivy out, but now it seemed Ivy was going to beat her to the punch. "Um, nothing."

"Good." Ivy's voice brightened. "Would you like to accompany me to dinner with Nadine and Kari?"

᠕᠕᠘᠘

Ivy waved her hand in front of her face, trying to get the sulfur smell to dissipate. She glanced around the hotel room and smiled. This would be her sanctuary for the next couple of hours.

It was perfect, except for the hideous painting on the wall, but she'd take it. A note sat on the bed next to her, so she picked it up. She smiled at Rain's meticulous handwriting.

Greetings! I hope you enjoy your evening at the glorious Hotel de Rain.

The concierge would like to point out a few notable items for your stay. To your left, you will find the door to the balcony. The view of the Rocky Mountains is highly recommended.

Also, on the patio table, you will find a bottle of our finest Riesling chilling over ice. In the mini refrigerator, there is a cheese and fruit platter for your dining pleasure. You will also find a pint of gelato from the local creamery.

Ivy rubbed her chest and fought back tears. She couldn't believe Rain had gone to so much trouble. She scanned the room and noticed a large bouquet of flowers on the table. Tiger lilies. Her favorite. She returned to the note.

There are lavender and sage oils on the ledge of

the Jacuzzi tub, along with several types of bubble bath. (I wasn't sure of your preference). Along with candles.

Ivy chuckled. She was pretty sure Rain hadn't thought that one through. She could only imagine how red Rain's face would turn when she realized that she'd invited Ivy to bathe with her body.

For your reading pleasure, I have purchased the thriller you've been waiting to get from the library... forever. Your words, not mine. I also downloaded Brené Brown's newest book, in case the thriller turns out to be a dud.

I've also clad your/my body in the most comfortable PJs. I thought of dressing up for you but thought comfort would be more to your liking. And the concierge gives you permission to touch the ab muscles as much as you would like. :)

Enjoy,
Rain

Tears flowed down Ivy's cheeks as she clutched the note to her chest.

Chapter Forty

Rain glanced at her hands clenched on the steering wheel. She'd been parked outside the restaurant for nearly ten minutes. Maybe this was a bad idea. On what planet was it a good idea to meet Nadine and her wife? Sure, lesbians did it all the time, but Ivy wasn't your typical lesbian, if she was one at all.

Rain nearly jumped out of her skin when a sharp rap on her window brought her out of her thoughts.

Ivy waved. She sported a huge smile. *Damn, she looks good.* Rain had only ever seen her in the casual dresses she wore during the day or her church clothes. Rain wasn't prepared for the tight black dress that clung to her. While it was longer than most she'd seen at the clubs and came to just above her knees, it was still sexy as hell.

Rain let go of the steering wheel and pushed her thoughts away. She still wasn't clear on what they were doing, but this was kind of a date. Although, meeting with the only other woman Ivy had ever kissed made it seem less like one.

Ivy stared into the car at Rain. "Do you plan on coming out? Or are you going to shove it into drive and take off?"

Rain laughed. "How the tables have turned."

Ivy gave her a quizzical look.

"Remember the first time you came to my house?

I thought I was going to have to serve you dinner in your car." Rain turned off the ignition and stepped out of the car.

"Don't remind me." Ivy laughed and wrapped Rain in a hug.

Rain returned the hug, enjoying the warmth that spread across her chest. She could hold on to Ivy all day, but she suspected people would start to stare if she didn't let go.

When they separated, Ivy said, "I wanted to thank you again for letting me borrow your body Wednesday night."

Rain groaned and covered her face. "I still can't believe I did that. In my defense, a bubble bath is supposed to be relaxing. I just forgot you would've taken it in my body."

Ivy ran her hand across Rain's stomach. "It was so tempting."

"Stop." Rain's face warmed.

Ivy winked. "I'm just glad you enjoyed game night."

"It was great. Except I think Granny cheats."

Ivy laughed. "We've always suspected it."

"Should we go inside?" Rain asked.

Ivy took a step back and didn't hide that she was looking Rain up and down. "I was so busy chattering I didn't get a chance to take a good look at you. You look amazing." Ivy reached up and straightened Rain's collar. She'd worn her tightest button-down shirt since she knew it showed off her broad shoulders and washboard stomach.

Rain held her hands over her head and turned around. "Will I pass?"

"Nobody should have a bum that tight."

"Did you just say bum?" Rain spun around. "When did you become British?"

Ivy laughed. It was a sound that was becoming Rain's favorite, especially when she caused it. "It sounds less crude than ass," Ivy said.

"Booty," Rain offered.

"Rump."

Rain scowled. "That sounds like a roast."

"Fine, how about fanny?"

"Ugh, that's even less sexy than rump." Rain turned up her nose. "Sounds like something my grandma would have said."

"Buns? Derriere? Tush? Caboose? Keister?"

"Keister?" Rain tried to look over her shoulder at her butt. "Do I look like a gnome to you?"

"What are you talking about?" Ivy cocked her head. "What does a keister have to do with a gnome?"

"I don't know." Rain threw her hands in the air. "Ask Granny."

The look in Ivy's eyes went from puzzled to amused, and then she laughed. "Is that why Sven was in my room?"

"Who the hell is Sven?"

"My garden gnome."

Rain groaned. "So Granny was telling me to get my ass in the house? She must have thought I...uh... you lost your mind."

"Yep. She was telling you to bring your buns, derriere—"

Rain laughed and covered her ears with her hands. "Stop. I stand corrected. Bum is just fine. Although strangely, tush isn't so bad, either."

Ivy winked. "I knew you'd see it my way. Are you ready for this?"

Rain held out her arm. "As I'll ever be."

Ivy linked her arm through Rain's and smiled up at her.

Damn. Her smile went straight to Rain's chest. Danger bells went off inside of Rain's head, but she ignored them as they walked into the restaurant.

ꙮ.ꙮꙮꙮ

Nadine waved from across the bar when they entered. Ivy waved back, but her gaze was on the woman sitting beside Nadine. She was smaller than Ivy had imagined. While most women would look small next to Nadine, Kari appeared more petite than Ivy would have guessed.

"I'm assuming that's them," Rain said as she leaned down and spoke into Ivy's ear.

"That's Nadine. I think that's her wife, Kari, next to her, but I've never met her." When Ivy met Rain's gaze, she was surprised by how wide Rain's eyes were. "Everything okay?"

"Yeah," Rain said almost too quickly. She must have recognized the puzzled look on Ivy's face because she said, "Nadine's...um...she's bigger than I thought."

Ivy stopped herself from laughing or even smiling. Was Rain feeling threatened? "Six-foot-one, I believe."

"Oh." Rain swallowed. "You never told me."

They weaved around a couple who was blocking the aisles. "Sorry, I didn't think it was important." Ivy glanced at Rain out of the corner of her eye. They were almost to Nadine and Kari, so she wanted to make sure everything was okay.

"No, no, of course it isn't." Rain stood up

straighter as she said it and squared her shoulders.

It was almost as if Nadine had seen the gesture because she too straightened her back as they approached.

Good god. Rain and Nadine were like peacocks meeting each other for the first time. Rain already walked with a confident stride, but now she grew in front of Ivy's eyes. Her muscular chest puffed out as far as it would go.

Ivy met Kari's gaze. Kari smiled and rolled her eyes. Ivy smirked. Obviously, it wasn't just her who was witnessing this dance.

Nadine spoke first. "Ivy." She turned to Rain. "And you must be Rain."

Rain reached out her hand to Nadine. "Nadine. Nice to meet you."

Nadine winced slightly when Rain grabbed her hand but quickly covered it with a smile. They pumped each other's hands a few more times than necessary before they let go.

Ivy groaned inwardly. This could be a long night. She turned to Kari. "And you must be Kari. I'm so glad to meet you."

Kari surprised Ivy when she wrapped her arms around Ivy and pulled her in for a hug. Kari stood a couple of inches shorter than Ivy, so her mouth was near Ivy's ear when they hugged.

"If we aren't careful," Kari said into Ivy's ear, "those two will be peeing on everything or whipping out their dicks."

Ivy laughed. She already liked Kari. She whispered back, "We can always escape to the bar and have a drink."

Kari smiled as she let go and pointed at Ivy. "I

like the way you think."

Ivy wouldn't exactly call Kari pretty, but there was something magnetic about her. A dynamic energy surrounded her, and her blue eyes twinkled. Tiny crow's feet had begun to show around her eyes, which made them more enticing. Her auburn hair was likely not natural, but the color suited her.

"What would you like to drink?" Nadine asked.

≈≈≈≈≈

Ivy knew she shouldn't have another drink, but she wanted one. The waiter continued to stare at her, awaiting her reply.

Rain leaned over. "Go ahead. We can pick up your car tomorrow."

"We can drive it back to our place," Nadine offered. "Then you can pick it up anytime."

Ivy smiled and looked at the waiter. She pointed to her empty glass. "I'll have another."

Dinner had gone well. After her initial discomfort at having Rain and Nadine at the same table, she'd relaxed and allowed herself to enjoy the evening.

Rain and Nadine had circled each other a bit before they found they shared a deep love of the Cubs, and both had championed many of the same causes. Ivy was glad they had bonded, but their alpha dance had been fun to watch.

Rain had been adorable strutting around with her chest puffed out and her neck extended to give her the greatest height. It hadn't been until Rain finished her first beer before she stopped flexing her forearm muscle every time she reached for her bottle.

"I can't believe this woman," Rain said and put

her hand on Ivy's arm.

Ivy blinked away her daydream. *Shit.* What couldn't Rain believe?

Nadine shook her head. "And I can't believe Rain. We had so much in common, and then she dropped the bomb."

Crap. What had she missed? She'd drifted away at the wrong time. She hoped whatever they were arguing about didn't derail the entire evening.

Kari laughed. "I don't think Rain believing *Star Wars* is better than *Star Trek* qualifies as a dealbreaker for us hanging out again."

Ivy's stomach unknotted, and she laughed. "Let me throw down the biggest dealbreaker. I don't like either."

"Yes. You tell them." Kari held out her hand for a high-five.

Nadine groaned, and Rain covered her face.

"I'm so sorry." Nadine patted Rain on the back and gave her a solemn look. "I thought you and Ivy's relationship had potential, but I understand if you have to break it off. There was no way you could have known she's secretly a monster."

Ivy's stomach did a flip-flop at the word relationship. Sure, they'd talked about dating exclusively, but was it a relationship? *Ugh.* That was kinda what it meant. She glanced at Rain.

Rain had the same startled look on her face as Ivy felt. Nadine and Kari were too busy laughing to notice.

"Oh, Rain, I hear congratulations are in order," Kari said. "Being asked to sit on the board of SWAN, what an honor."

"No shit," Nadine added. "Pretty impressive. It's

not often that they let someone in their thirties on."

"Thanks. I was shocked when they asked me." Rain blushed. Ivy couldn't help but smile at how adorable she looked. "The first meeting was surreal. I didn't say much. I was too busy gaping."

"That would have been amazing," Nadine said. "I want to hear all about it."

"How about we have Rain give us the scoop over some celebratory dessert?" Kari said.

"Perfect." Nadine waved for the waiter.

※.※※.※

"Oh, god," Rain said. "Who thought dessert was a good idea?" She leaned back in her chair and looked at her distended stomach. She'd have to do crunches for hours to find her abs.

Nadine pointed at Kari. "It was her."

Kari shook her head and glanced at Ivy. "You get married, and the honeymoon is over. They just throw you under the bus."

Rain groaned and patted her stomach.

"You'll be fine." Ivy put her hand on top of Rain's.

Rain had noticed that during the evening, Ivy had become more and more comfortable touching Rain. She'd probably taken her cue from Nadine and Kari, but Rain wasn't complaining. She liked it but fought the urge to grasp Ivy's hand and hold on.

"Shit," Nadine said. "I almost forgot to tell you that your parents have my mom stirred up."

"My parents?" Ivy put her hand against her chest and frowned. "What did my parents do to her?"

Nadine chuckled. "Not to her. To Devlin."

"I forgot. She worships that man." Ivy stuck out

her tongue and made a vomiting gesture.

"You should have heard her ranting that your family is single handedly going to bring down Autumn Harvest."

Ivy grinned. "Maybe not bring it down, but who knows, we might be able to pull a few back from the dark side."

Rain tried to hide the surprise from her face. Ivy hadn't mentioned any of this to her. Should she be hurt?

"Last week, Nadine said you had nearly fifty people reaching out to you. Any more this week?" Kari asked.

Jesus. Kari knew about this, too?

Ivy must have sensed Rain's tension because she shifted in her seat and shot Rain a glance. Ivy went to pat Rain's hand, but Rain intentionally reached for her glass instead. Immature, probably, but Rain's hurt had begun to turn to anger.

Ivy's neck reddened, but she turned her focus back to Kari. "I think at last count they're at nearly one hundred. I was shocked at the outpouring."

"Do you think you're going to be able to resurrect Mullins Creek Church?" Nadine asked.

Ivy crossed her fingers on both hands and held them up. "I'm going to keep praying."

Rain continued to stare at the side of Ivy's head. By the way Ivy nervously fiddled with her hair, Rain suspected she knew but was ignoring her. Why hadn't Ivy shared any of this with her?

Rain's chest ached. Had she mistaken the connection they'd been developing? They talked every night, but she'd mentioned none of this.

"If you do, that's one church I might be willing

to attend," Nadine said.

Ivy pointed at Nadine. "I'm going to hold you to that."

Nadine held up her hands. "I'm serious." She nodded toward Kari. "She had me going to a church before we came here."

"Seriously?" Ivy's head snapped in Kari's direction. "How'd you manage that?"

Kari smiled. "She's not as uncivilized as she acts."

Ivy chuckled.

What the hell? Ivy's laugh that was normally music to her ears caused her jaw to tighten.

"What about you?" Kari said to Rain. "Any chance you'll join us?"

Fuck. She'd been hiding in the background during the conversation, but now they were all staring at her. Likely, the vein in her neck throbbed as she tried to hide her irritation. She knew Ivy had already picked up on her mood, but she wondered if the others had, too.

Ivy waved her hand, probably to draw Nadine and Kari's gazes away from Rain. "She's not into those kinds of things."

And there it was. Rain wasn't into those things, so Ivy must have decided to keep it from her. It sounded like it was a big part of what was going on in Ivy's life, and she'd not uttered a word about it.

"I didn't think I was, either." Nadine's eyes narrowed when her gaze landed on Rain's face. "There's something comforting about it, if you find the right one. You might be surprised."

Fuck. Rain was sure Nadine had picked up on her mood. She needed to respond, but an internal battle raged. It wouldn't do any good to show her irritation, but she crinkled up her nose and shrugged anyway. "I doubt it." She should probably leave it at that, but instead she said, "I'm really not into that crap."

Ivy visibly winced beside her. Nadine glared at Rain, and Kari's gaze darted among all three as if trying to figure out the puzzle in front of her. *Asshole.* Rain's chest tightened. Ivy didn't deserve this just because Rain's feelings were hurt. Rain turned to Ivy and went to pat her hand. Ivy turned the tables and reached for her glass of water. *Touché.*

Rain knew she deserved Ivy's reaction, but it still stung. All attention was on her. She had only a few seconds to decide how to react. She dropped her head and then glanced at Ivy from the corner of her eye. "I'm sorry. That was a jerk comment."

Ivy's eyes glistened, and she bit her lip but said nothing. There was no hiding the pain. She finally said, "Why'd you say it?"

Nadine stared at Rain and didn't try to hide her anger. There was no disguising the protective feeling Nadine had for Ivy.

Rain stood at a crossroads. She could feed on Nadine's anger and react in kind, or she could choose differently. When she looked into Ivy's eyes, her decision was made. "I was hurt that you hadn't talked to me about any of this." Rain couldn't believe that she was saying this, especially in front of Nadine and Kari, but she couldn't stop now. Her gaze locked on Ivy's, and everyone else at the table disappeared. "We talk every day, and I thought we shared everything, but it made me realize you hold me at arm's length sometimes." Rain looked down. "And it hurt. It hurt a lot." She looked back up. "But that's no excuse for lashing out at you. For being hurtful to you. And I'm sorry."

"Oh, Rain." Without warning, Ivy leapt to her feet and wrapped her arms around Rain's neck and hugged her.

Rain put her hands on Ivy's forearms and squeezed, doing her best to return the gesture. *Fuck it.* Rain didn't care if people stared. She stood and gave Ivy a proper hug. As they embraced, Rain said softly into Ivy's ear, "I'm so sorry."

"Shh," Ivy said. "It's okay. Admitting that in front of everyone took guts. And it just might have been the sweetest thing anyone has ever done for me. At least, someone I'm dating."

Rain's heart skipped a beat. "So we're dating?"

Ivy laughed and hugged Rain tighter. "I think so. That is, if you'd ever ask me out on a proper date."

When they broke their embrace, Rain glanced at the table. Nadine and Kari were intently studying the check, obviously trying to give them privacy.

After they sat, Rain smiled and said, "Well, that was awkward."

The others laughed, and the tension was broken. Nadine made eye contact and gave Rain a slight nod. Rain held her gaze and nodded back. The communication was clear. *Don't hurt Ivy.* Inwardly, Rain groaned. Not only did Ivy have five siblings to watch out for her, but she also had Nadine.

From the table, Rain's phone vibrated. She couldn't help but smile when she glanced at it. *Tracie.* It was as if the universe was speaking to her and wanted her to know that Tracie could be added to the list of people who would kick her ass if she hurt Ivy.

Rain swiped the call away. She'd call her later.

"Who was that?" Ivy asked.

"Tracie. She always has the worst—"

Ivy's phone sounded, and she snatched it out of her purse. She held it up and said, "Tracie." She handed her phone to Rain. "I think you should answer it."

"Hello," Rain said into Ivy's phone.

"Thank god," Jeannie said.

Rain's heart raced. "What's the matter?"

"The ambulance is here. They're getting ready to take Tracie away." Jeannie's voice quivered as she spoke.

"Ambulance? What the hell's going on?" Rain practically shouted.

Fear filled Ivy's eyes, and she grabbed Rain's hand and squeezed. The gesture was comforting as she waited for Jeannie to respond.

"Hold on," Jeannie said.

Rain could hear voices in the background, probably the paramedics.

She didn't realize she'd been holding her breath until Jeannie said, "I'm back. They're taking her to the hospital in Madison. They think it might be her heart."

"What happened?"

"She just collapsed. Oh, god, Rain, it was awful."

Rain bit her tongue. She wanted to ask a million questions, but she knew that would be too much for Jeannie. "But the paramedics are there, so that's good," Rain said in a soothing voice. "Is she...um...is she... uh...alert?" How else could she ask if she'd coded?

"She's in and out."

The tightness in Rain's chest loosened a little. *Tracie wasn't dead.* The thought nearly took her breath away.

"I have to go soon," Jeannie said. "They're about

to take her. I hate fucking social media."

Rain flinched. Jeannie wasn't one to swear or at least not to say *fuck*.

Social media? Before Rain could respond, Jeannie said, "I've gotta go. Will you come?"

"Of course."

"Ivy too?" Jeannie asked.

"She's right here. We're on our way."

Ivy was nodding. She likely could hear Jeannie's louder-than-normal voice.

"I love you," Jeannie said, and then the line went dead.

≈≈≈≈≈

"Do you mind if I turn on some music?" Ivy asked.

"That's fine," Rain said but didn't look in her direction.

"Any preference?"

"Nope."

They'd been driving for nearly an hour, and Rain had said little. She kept her hands at ten and two and stared out the windshield. That level of driving diligence seemed unnecessary since the traffic had thinned. Ivy had tried to engage Rain in conversation, but the lack of response had Ivy edgy. She wanted to comfort Rain but had no idea how. Maybe a little music could break through the tension.

Ivy scrolled through the choices and stopped when she ran her finger over Anthrax. Heavy metal always helped her relax; hopefully, it would do the trick for Rain. Ivy hit play, and the hard driving beat filled the car. Ivy bobbed her head and danced in her seat as the guitars screamed.

"Jesus. Are you trying to push me over the edge?" Rain asked.

"What?" Ivy turned down the volume.

"Is that shit supposed to relax me?"

"It does me."

"Well, it's more likely to cause me to run off the road. It's like a spike through the middle of my skull." Ivy turned off the music.

"You didn't have to do that." Rain shot her a look but quickly shifted her focus back to the road.

"A spike in the middle of your skull isn't exactly a ringing endorsement."

"At least I didn't say a rusty spike."

Ivy smiled. "I know you're worried sick about Tracie. I wish there was something I could do."

A tear rolled down Rain's cheek, which wasn't what Ivy expected. "I'm so sorry, I didn't mean to take it out on you. I don't know what I'd do if something happens to Tracie."

"I understand." Ivy put her hand on Rain's knee. "But please, don't push me away or shut me out. I'm here for you."

"Thank you." More tears streamed down Rain's cheeks as she put her hand on top of Ivy's. "Can you just hold my hand for a bit?"

Ivy tightened her grip on Rain's hand.

They'd been driving for another fifteen minutes when Rain's phone rang.

"Jeannie," Rain said as soon as she accepted the call.

"She's okay." Jeannie's voice came through the speakers. "She's going to be okay, the damned fool." Jeannie's words came out in a rush.

"Thank god," Ivy said.

"What's wrong with her?" Rain asked.

"They think it was a panic attack. All the stress of the day got to her, and then she hyperventilated, which caused her to pass out. They're going to run a few more tests, but they expect to let her out within the next hour or so. Which in hospital speak means three hours."

Rain let out a deep sigh. "I'm just thankful she's okay. We should be there in about forty-five minutes."

"That's the other reason I'm calling. Can you just go to the house?"

"But we want to see Tracie."

"I know." Jeannie sighed. "She's a little embarrassed and pretty tired. I think it would be better to talk about what happened in the morning after she gets a good night's sleep."

Chapter Forty-one

Rain looked up and smiled when the door to the patio slid open. "About time you climbed out of bed."

Tracie glowered. "The idiotic hospital didn't spring me until after two."

Jeannie came through the door, carrying a tray of fruit and bagels. She held them up. "I'm sure you two already found something to eat, but I brought these out." She gestured toward Tracie. "She needs to eat."

Ivy jumped up from the table. "Do you need any help?"

Jeannie smiled. "You could grab the orange juice off the counter."

"Throw some champagne in 'em or a little vodka," Tracie said.

"She doesn't need any." Jeannie glared at Tracie.

"Easy for you to say. You weren't just poked and prodded half the night."

Rain cleared her throat. "Do you think you can stop whining and tell us what happened?"

"Fine." Tracie scowled. "As soon as Ivy gets back."

Once everyone was seated, Rain said, "Let's hear it."

"I let the trolls get to me." Tracie sighed and looked at Jeannie. "It's embarrassing."

Jeannie took Tracie's hand. "Don't let her fool you. She can handle the haters. It was when they came after me that it got to her."

Rain's back stiffened. *Someone had gone after Jeannie?* "What the fuck's going on?"

"I'm getting there, kid. Just slow your roll." Tracie scowled. "Did you get a chance to read my blog post?"

"Yeah, but what the hell has that got to do with anything?" Rain glowered. Now wasn't the time to have a political debate.

"It caused quite a stir," Jeannie said.

"I'm sure." Rain smiled. "Tracie covered some pretty sensitive topics."

"With great care," Tracie added.

Rain raised her eyebrow. Tracie's piece had been thoughtful, at least for her, but Rain could see why it might stir some people up. In places, even Rain had bristled. "I'm still not getting how this has to do with trolls, Jeannie, and being hospitalized."

"The Twitter mafia came at me with a vengeance. Started a campaign to get me fired from my job. They wanted Tracie Bennett canceled."

"That sucks." Rain scowled. "It was an opinion piece, for fuck's sake."

"Yep." Tracie shook her head. "No matter how much of myself I've given to this community the last forty years, they wanted to shut me up. Silence me. They didn't want me to raise the questions that our community needs to wrestle with—to have a conversation about."

"What did your board say?" Rain asked. "Did they censure you?"

"We had a pretty tough meeting. It got loud at times, but they're standing by me." Tracie shook her head. "It gave me flashbacks to 1997."

Rain leaned over to Ivy. "That's when she was kicked out of the Army."

Ivy's eyes widened. "Why?"

"I joined the Army right out of college in 1982," Tracie said. "I wanted to be career military, just like my dad." Tracie's face softened, and she grinned like she always did when she talked of her father. "I won't bore you with all the details."

"Don't let her fool you," Jeannie said. "She was a decorated service member."

Tracie waved Jeannie's words off. "I served in the Gulf War in the early nineties. I came back with some mild symptoms of Gulf War Syndrome but nothing that would derail my career." Tracie sighed. "And then in 1994, things were supposed to be made better by the enactment of Don't Ask, Don't Tell." Tracie let out a bitter laugh. "Right. Leave it to the politicians to fuck it up. I was dishonorably discharged in 1997."

"Oh, god," Ivy said. "What happened?"

"That's not important," Tracie said.

Jeannie gave Ivy a sympathetic look. "She doesn't like to talk about it."

Ivy nodded. "I understand."

"Over thirteen thousand gay service members were discharged from 1994 to 2011," Tracie said.

Ivy's mouth fell open. "Wow. Why did I think it was a long time ago and only lasted a couple years?"

"Most people don't realize it lasted seventeen years and did a whole lot of damage." Tracie looked down at her hands. "Destroyed my career. My dream." She shrugged. "So at the age of thirty-seven, I had to reinvent myself. Went back to school and got my master's degree in social work. When I got my job with the county working with young people, I found my salvation."

"Then those sons of bitches tried to destroy her again," Jeannie said.

Whoa. The venom in Jeannie's voice made Rain sit up and take notice. It wasn't like Jeannie to get so fired up or swear.

"I couldn't believe it," Tracie said. "When they came after me in 1997, it didn't surprise me all that much. But when my own side turned on me, that's a bitter pill to swallow."

"But your board stood by you, what am I missing?" Rain asked.

Tracie's eyes turned to steel. "They crossed the line when they went after Jeannie." Tracie pointed to her tablet, and Jeannie handed it to her. She scrolled and then handed it to Rain. "See for yourself."

Rain took the tablet and moved closer to Ivy so she could see the screen, too.

Ivy gasped, and her face went white. "What is this?"

"Screenshots of some of the worst comments," Tracie said.

Ivy moved closer to Rain, and Rain draped her arm over Ivy's shoulder. Rain's chest tightened as she read the hate-filled comments.

"These are despicable," Ivy said. "Disgusting."

"Yep." Tracie snorted. "And they're supposed to be my allies."

"What the fuck?" Rain's jaw clenched. "You need to show this to the police."

"We already did," Jeannie said. "They told us we should probably buy a gun."

"Are you serious?" Heat rose up Rain's neck.

"We already have a gun," Tracie said.

Rain looked up from the tablet and gave Tracie a sideways glance.

"Don't look at me like that," Tracie said. "I'm ex-military. I know how to use one."

Rain couldn't deny she was glad Tracie owned a gun after reading the comments. "Isn't there something else they can do?"

"Probably now that one of the fuckers followed Jeannie to work." Tracie's face was crimson. "And tried to run her off the road."

Rain stared in disbelief. Would someone seriously do that over a blog?

"Your blood pressure's going up again." Jeannie put her arm around Tracie. "We don't need another trip to the ER."

Tracie took several deep breaths.

"Why didn't you tell me all this was going on?" Rain asked.

"It wasn't like you could do anything." Jeannie gave Rain and Ivy a big smile and motioned between them. "Besides, we wanted you to enjoy your budding relationship, not be worried about us."

"This is so messed up." Rain studied Tracie. Her coloring had returned to normal, but the bags around her eyes were heavy. "But you'll be okay, right? It was just an anxiety attack?"

Tracie rubbed her chest. "Now I know why so many people have anxiety. They're afraid of getting it wrong, so they're constantly walking on eggshells. They don't want the Twitter mob or the keyboard brigade to come after them." Tracie's volume rose as she spoke. "For fuck's sake, I've been to war, marched through hostile crowds. Been screamed at, spit at, and had things thrown at me, and I'd never had a fucking panic attack. Until now! They all want their safe zones, but where the fuck is Jeannie's?" She grabbed Jeannie's hand and kissed it.

Anger bubbled up inside of Rain. "Our side needs to focus our energy on fighting the right-wing idiots who are bombarding us with their religious bullshit, not attacking our own."

Ivy shifted in her seat next to Rain, so their arms were no longer touching. Rain glanced at her from the corner of her eye, but her attention was drawn back to Tracie, who'd slapped her palm to her own forehead.

"And look what you just did." Tracie pointed at Ivy.

Rain turned and saw the hurt in Ivy's eyes.

"What did I do?" Rain asked.

"My religion is a big part of who I am." Ivy stared at the ground. "When you talk bad about it... it's hurtful. It makes me feel like there's a part of me you don't accept...that you don't like."

Rain struggled to breathe. She stared at Ivy, not sure what to say.

Before Rain could respond, Tracie said, "You're alienating the wrong goddamned people. Ivy is not the enemy."

Rain blinked and shifted her gaze between Tracie and Ivy. "I never said Ivy was the enemy."

"Sometimes, it feels that way," Ivy said in a voice barely over a whisper.

"What? I don't know what you two are talking about."

"Jesus Christ, Rain," Tracie said. "Every time you mention religion, it's accompanied by a pompous sneer." Tracie flipped her thumb toward Ivy. "You're not going to hang on to her very long with that attitude."

"I'm not talking about Ivy when I talk about the nut jobs." Rain crossed her arms over her chest.

"I'm not trying to beat you up," Tracie said. "But while there are some over-the-top religious people, there are also good ones, but you lump them all together. Don't you see what it's doing? It's driving away potential allies."

"But..." Rain met Tracie's gaze and then turned to Ivy. "But you have to understand that you were with a church that encouraged bigotry and hatred."

"And she left it," Tracie said. "There are good people like Ivy and her family who are standing up and saying we won't let you turn Jesus into someone we don't recognize. When will you do the same? When will you have the courage?"

Rain stared at Tracie. With all her activism, she'd always thought of herself as courageous. Was Tracie telling her she wasn't? "I've advanced a lot of causes. I've marched in many rallies where it got scary. Threats, screaming, things thrown at me, and I've never backed down."

"And when have you stood up to your friends?" Tracie held up her hand when Rain went to speak. "Will you answer one question?"

Rain nodded.

"Have you ever seen something or heard something from our side that made you cringe?" Tracie pointed to her tablet with a look of disgust on her face. "Have you read any hate-filled rants like those directed at Jeannie or me?"

Rain reluctantly nodded.

"Then let me ask a follow-up question. Have

you stood up to them and asked them to stop?"

Rain's gaze dropped to her lap. She could no longer look Tracie or Ivy in the eye.

"It's okay, Rain," Jeannie said, finally speaking. Jeannie always seemed to know just the right time to insert herself into the conversation. "Nobody is trying to shame you. Once you know better, you can do better. And I know your heart. You will do better."

Jeannie's confidence in Rain eased some of the pressure in her chest. "I do want to do better," Rain said in a voice barely over a whisper. "I hate the way things are. I fear for the future for all of us." Her eyes brimmed with tears. "Sometimes, I don't even recognize who we've become. Everyone is fighting with everyone." She motioned toward Tracie. "The attacks are coming from all sides. Hell, sometimes, we're crueler to the people who supposedly share our viewpoints." Rain ran her hand through her hair. "But I don't know what to do, so I keep joining more causes, attending more rallies, thinking maybe something will make a difference, but it keeps getting worse."

"I think there is a solution, and you and Ivy give me hope," Tracie said.

"Us?" Rain narrowed her gaze.

"Yes, you!" Tracie smiled, one of the first of the day, and her face was transformed. "We've been losing good people like Ivy for too long. Good Christian people, who truly want to live Jesus' teachings of love. They're being forced to pick a side. Either come join us who tell them they are ignorant for their faith and hateful for being religious or join Devlin who at least purports to champion Jesus."

Ivy nodded. "We had to choose the lesser of what we considered two evils."

"And we've done the same," Tracie said. "We've fallen down a rabbit hole of absurdity. Any time we speak out, we run the risk of the wrath of self-righteousness, so we keep our mouth shut. And when we do open our mouths, we run the risk of attacks like what's happening to us."

Rain held her breath as she reached out her hand to Ivy. Would she take it? Ivy gazed into Rain's eyes for a beat, and then she grasped Rain's hand and squeezed. Rain released the breath she'd been holding.

"You and Ivy are a lot alike, Rain," Tracie said in a calmer voice. "When faced with a choice, Ivy felt to keep a community, she needed to take two steps to the right. Two steps closer to Devlin. And you, Rain, when faced with a choice, you had to take two steps to the left. Not that you always agreed with it, but it was better than going to the right."

Rain nodded. It was true, sometimes her side went too far, but it was better than people like Devlin.

Tracie brought her hands together. "But instead, what if Ivy took two steps toward you, and you took two steps toward her?"

Rain stiffened. No way would she ever move closer to that side.

Tracie chuckled. "I know it's an uncomfortable suggestion, but hear me out."

"I'm listening," Rain said without conviction.

Tracie spread her hands far apart. "We're so focused on left or right that nobody wants to move, while hate grows on both sides. Maybe it's time to say enough is enough." Tracie turned to Rain. "And don't say their side is more hateful than ours. I'm not here to debate who is more hateful, it's an exercise in futility."

Tracie took a deep breath. "If the good people on both sides took two steps away from the hatred. Took two steps toward each other." Tracie moved her hands closer. "We need to denounce hate and censorship from both sides. Come together." She locked her fingers.

Tracie nodded to the houses on each side of them. "There's red and blue here amongst our neighbors, people who have been there for us when we needed them." She waved her hands between Ivy and Rain. "I see the love growing between the two of you. And I say enough. I'm done with the far right and the far left telling me who my enemy should be."

"If I may interject," Ivy said.

"Certainly." Tracie smiled.

"I hope this makes sense." Ivy gave them a shy smile. "It kinda reminds me of what my papa said is the secret to a good marriage. He told me he never wanted to win an argument with Mama because that would mean she'd have to lose. He'd shake his head and say, *What kind of man would want a victory over his own wife?* But we've become a country where it's win at all costs without any thought of the consequences. And in the end, we all lose."

Rain gazed at Ivy with pride, and her chest filled. Life was strange. Never in a million years would she have predicted she would be sitting next to someone like Ivy, let alone be falling... *Shit.* Rain's pulse raced.

Tracie saved Rain from her thoughts when she clapped her hands. "Exactly. Your papa is a wise man. We need to find a way to compromise. We denounce hate when it comes from the other side, but we sit on our hands and say nothing because we're afraid to call bullshit on our own side. Well, I'm done with that. I'm done with red states versus blue states. I'm done with the politicians and the media telling us we're so far apart. It's time for the adults in the room to take back our country. To sit at the table and find real solutions, instead of trying to force our will on one another." Tracie's voice cracked as she spoke. "Our democratic experiment could crumble if we don't. I didn't fight for this country to have it destroyed. That's why I'm so passionate. Because I still believe we can find our way out of this mess we're in."

Jeannie put her arm around Tracie's shoulders. "And this is why I love this woman so much. The world has beaten her down. She's been attacked from all sides. Yet she still believes. And she will believe until her last breath. And I'll walk beside her every step of the way."

Tracie lowered her face into her palms and wept.

Chapter Forty-two

Rain had been quiet on their drive back to Illinois. They'd made small talk, but Ivy sensed Rain wasn't ready to address what had happened with Tracie.

It must have been hard to see her mentor, the woman she admired most in the world, fall apart. In Ivy's eyes, it was a good thing, but she wasn't ready to tell Rain. It would come out in due time.

"What do you want to do when we get back to my house?" Rain asked. "Or do you want to go home?"

Ivy felt the tension lying just under the surface. "I'd like to stay. That is, if you want me to."

Rain's shoulders relaxed. "I'd like that."

Good. It was a start. They had so much to talk about, but neither seemed to know how to broach it. "It's settled then." Ivy smiled and patted Rain's knee.

Rain dropped her hand on top of Ivy's.

Another good sign, but still things felt off.

"I want to talk about us...but not in the car." Rain glanced at Ivy before she returned her gaze to the road.

"Okay." Ivy's stomach roiled. She wasn't sure how to interpret Rain's words. It could be as simple as not wanting to split her concentration while driving, or it could be that she didn't want to end the relationship while trapped in the car for another hour.

"That was some morning, huh?" Rain said.

Okay. Rain opened the door. Should she walk through it? "I bet it was hard for you to watch." *Damn.* That was probably the wrong thing to say. What happened to letting Rain come to it in her own time? Rain nodded. "I've never seen Tracie like that. I think even Jeannie was surprised."

"Is that why you wanted to leave? Because it made you uncomfortable?"

Rain squeezed Ivy's hand. "I'd be lying if I said it didn't rattle me, but that wasn't it." Rain glanced at Ivy. "I could tell Jeannie was shaken, too. I thought they needed a little time alone. Tracie needed Jeannie, and I think Jeannie needed Tracie just as bad."

"That's sweet. Thoughtful." Ivy's heart opened further to Rain. She knew it was dangerous since she didn't know what would come next, but she couldn't help it.

"After she broke down, she told stories today that I'd never heard," Rain said. "She'd never talked much about her time in the service. When I met her, it was nearly a decade past. I never realized the emotional scars she had from the war or how much pain being kicked out caused her. Tracie has always been confident, bordering on cocky." Rain smiled as she said it. "I never thought about the baggage she carried."

"Don't be so hard on yourself. I don't think any of us can truly understand another person's experience."

"It's not that. We bear the fruits of all those that came before us. The pioneers that blazed the trail, yet I've spent little time studying the history. I finally understand what Tracie has been trying to tell me about my activism all these years."

Ivy waited for Rain to continue, but when she

didn't, Ivy said, "Will you share it with me?"

Rain blinked. "Yeah, sorry, I got lost in my own thoughts. I strutted around like I was something special because I was involved with so many causes. Tracie always rode me, telling me that I needed to focus on a couple things and do them well. I resisted, thinking it would make me lazy if I didn't stand for everything. Do you want to hear something embarrassing?"

"If you want to share," Ivy said.

Deep creases formed on Rain's forehead. "I've jumped on more than one Twitter bandwagon when I didn't even know what was going on. I bet that a lot of the people making comments about Tracie hadn't even read her blog."

"You're probably right. That happens a lot."

Rain sighed. "Most of the issues I support, I only know at a surface level. I run a foundation, and I know too little about most of the organizations we fund."

"But now you know, so you'll do things differently." Ivy smiled and squeezed Rain's leg. "One of my favorite things is to do research. If you wouldn't mind, maybe we can learn some of the issues together."

Rain's eyes held a spark of life when she shifted her gaze to Ivy. "But we won't always be on the same side of the issue."

"I know, but that's not a bad thing."

"It's not?" Rain looked like a little kid who'd just lost her favorite toy.

"Of course, it's not." Ivy crinkled up her nose. "Don't look so sad. We're in this mess because we only flock to people that think like we do, and we demonize those that don't. Social media has made it worse. Algorithms that only put in front of us things that support our viewpoints, but sometimes, our views must be challenged. It allows us to learn, to grow, and to find a better solution to our problems."

"How'd you get to be so smart?" Rain gave her a genuine smile for the first time since they'd started their drive home.

Ivy winked. "I like to read."

≈≈≈≈

Ivy's hair was still damp when she entered the living room and sat on the couch next to Rain. They'd been back for over an hour, but still they hadn't talked about their relationship.

Damn. Ivy smelled good.

"Do we have any more stall tactics? Or are we ready to talk?" Ivy asked.

Rain turned on the couch so she was facing Ivy and smiled. "What happens next?"

"I was wondering the same thing," Ivy said. Rain detected a slight tremble in her voice. The same quiver Rain felt inside her own body.

"Are you okay?" Rain took both of Ivy's hands in hers.

"I'm scared," Ivy whispered.

Rain lifted her eyebrow. "Of me?"

"Of us." Ivy looked away. "We have so many differences."

"We do." Rain nodded. The entire drive, her thoughts had been swirling. Tracie had challenged her to show more courage. Now was her chance. "There's something else I believe I need to learn."

"What?" Ivy's voice was filled with hesitation.

"You said something back at Tracie and Jeannie's."

"I said quite a few things." Ivy smiled. "You're

going to have to narrow it down."

"You said your religion was a big part of who you are."

Ivy nodded. "It is."

"So far, the parts of you I've gotten to know are pretty amazing."

"Okay..." Ivy tilted her head and studied Rain.

"I can't pretend that part of you doesn't exist anymore. I can't keep ignoring it or pushing it away like I have been."

"And? Or were you going to say *but*?"

"No, it's an *and*." Rain squeezed Ivy's hands and smiled. "I'd like to learn more about your religion and what it means to you."

"What?" Ivy's eyes widened.

"You're always asking me questions about A Bridge to the Future and my causes, but I shut down any time you talk about your faith."

Ivy's eyes filled with sadness. "I know."

"It was wrong." Tightness spread across Rain's chest. "And I apologize. It's important to you, extremely important, so I need to listen...to ask questions...to understand."

Ivy's eyes filled with tears. "You'd really do that for me?"

"Yes. And for me. It's time I open my mind, too." Rain held up her hand. "I'm not saying that religion will be for me. It may never be. But by understanding it from your perspective, I might see things differently."

Tears streamed down Ivy's cheeks. "Thank you."

"It might take some time." Rain wanted to wipe the tears from Ivy's face, but she needed to finish her thoughts. "I've got a skewed version of religion from Devlin and people like him. It'll take a while to get past, but I want to try."

"I understand. Unfortunately, it's the loud sensationalists like Devlin that get all the press not the people who are out there trying to do good in the world." Ivy smiled through her tears.

"Besides," Rain smirked, and a twinkle danced in her eye. "I've read the Bible more than you, so you have some catching up to do."

Ivy laughed, and her tears flowed freely.

Rain pulled Ivy in for a hug.

☙.☙☙☙

Ivy wasn't sure how long they'd sat on the couch wrapped in each other's arms. All she knew was her heart was full. Rain wanted to know more about her religion. Surely, that meant they were really going to do this. Whatever this was.

Rain rested her cheek against Ivy's head. It felt so right in Rain's arms. Like home. Ivy burrowed farther against Rain.

Rain chuckled. "As much as I'm enjoying this, we need to finish our conversation."

Ivy groaned. "But I'm comfy."

Rain hugged her tighter. "Me too."

"Another ten minutes?"

"Five."

"Eight." Ivy smiled against Rain's chest.

"Seven. It's my final offer." Ivy could hear the smile in Rain's voice. "I'm setting my timer." Rain twisted, likely pulling her phone from her pocket.

"No!" Ivy said when the alarm sounded. She had nearly fallen asleep in the warmth of Rain's arms.

Rain pulled back as Ivy protested. "How about I make you a deal?"

"What?" Ivy jutted out her bottom lip to note her protest.

"After we talk, I'll pop up some popcorn, and then we can snuggle up again and watch a movie on Netflix."

Good sign. "Do I get to pick the movie?" Ivy grinned.

"I get veto power."

Ivy snorted. "Fine."

Rain's demeanor turned serious. "I know we talked after our kiss, our second kiss, that we would be exclusive."

Uh-oh. Ivy didn't like the sound of where this might be going. Was Sasha back in the picture?

"No!" Rain practically lunged at Ivy when she put her hand on Ivy's knee. "That came out way wrong. I'm not wanting to rescind that."

Ivy let out a sigh of relief. "Then what are you trying to say?"

"I haven't even asked you out on a date yet," Rain blurted out.

Ivy narrowed her eyes. "Huh?"

"A date. I haven't taken you on a proper date."

Ivy laughed. "You pulled me away from your warm chest and scared the shit out of me to ask me out?"

Rain's cheeks colored. "Uh...yeah, I guess. It just didn't seem right. Tracie says I need to court a girl like you."

"She does, does she?" Ivy smirked. "And what kind of girl would that be?"

"A nice one." Rain shook her head. "Ugh, that sounded so stupid. This is not going how I'd imagined it."

Ivy bit her lip to stop herself from laughing. Seeing

Rain so tongue-tied only increased her adorableness. "Let me get this straight. Now that you've asked me to go steady, you think maybe we should start dating?"

Rain slapped her hand against her forehead. "That's how it sounded, isn't it?"

Ivy nodded. "But I thought it was sweet."

Rain's eyes widened. "Just don't tell Tracie. She'll never let me live it down."

"Hmm." Ivy smiled. "Let me pick the movie—no veto power—and I'll keep my mouth shut."

"Ugh. Who knew you had a manipulative side?"

Ivy winked. "Now that's settled. Where and when?"

"Next Saturday." Rain sat up taller. "I'd like to take you into Chicago for dinner and a play."

"Which one?"

"Really? You need to know which one before you say yes?"

"You did just give me rights to pick the movie, so I'll trust you." Ivy winked.

"One more thing." A deep furrow appeared on Rain's forehead.

This couldn't be good. "Why the frown?"

"We're doing this. Dating. Having a relationship."

Ivy nodded. "We've already established that."

"What about your family?" Rain's words came out in a rush.

"What about them?" Ivy narrowed her eyes and studied Rain.

"This." Rain waved her hands between them. "Us. How are they going to take it? Are they going to be okay with it, or are we going to have to...um...hide it?"

Ivy smiled. "They'll be fine with it."

Rain's mouth dropped open. "Just like that? You're sure?"

"Positive."

Rain twisted the bottom of her shirt and seemed to be wrestling to find her words. "I don't know how to say this without it taking us down another rabbit hole. One I think we're starting to come out of."

Oh. Rain's struggle finally made sense. "Are you talking about our religion?"

Rain nodded, but she didn't speak.

"Nothing to worry about."

"But...but...uh...remember I heard some of the sermons at your church."

"My former church." Ivy put her hand on Rain's knee. "I'm telling you, my parents are accepting people. They'll be fine. If there's one thing I know for certain, they L word me unconditionally."

Rain stared for several beats before she finally spoke. "But won't it be a shock to them?"

Ivy nodded. "Sure, it will be. Then Mama will hug me, probably bake some cookies for the occasion, and Papa will make a stupid joke about having another woman around the farm to drive the tractors."

"And Granny?"

"She already knows."

Rain's eyes got huge. "She does?"

"I don't know that for fact, but I'd put money on it." Ivy grinned.

Rain flopped against the back of the couch. "Jesus. I've been having a heart attack over this for nothing?" Rain put her palm against her forehead. "Now I just need to figure out how to tell my parents I'm dating a Christian."

Ivy laughed and fell into Rain's arms.

Chapter Forty-three

"Y ou're serious. That was it?" Rain said into the phone.

"I told you." Ivy's laugh warmed Rain.

"Unbelievable." Rain shook her head. Another stereotype busted by Ivy's family. "And I've been a nervous wreck all day worrying how they'd react, and your mom's baking snickerdoodles to send to me."

Ivy laughed. "Yep. Expect enough to feed your whole office. Oh, there was one other thing."

Rain's palms went cold. *Then the other shoe drops.* She should have known it couldn't be that simple. No way could Ivy's parents be that accepting. "What's that?"

"They want you to come to our big Fourth of July party."

"*What?*"

"Fourth of July. This year, the party will be on the eighth. We always have a big party. Fireworks, bonfire, basketball, and lots of food."

"And they invited me?" Rain's voice likely projected the shock she felt.

"And Tracie and Jeannie."

"Now you're screwing with me."

Ivy chuckled. "Seriously. I talk about them all the time."

"This situation keeps getting weirder and weirder."

"It'll be a lesbian extravaganza at the Nash household."

Rain chuckled. "I guess four lesbians at a party in Mullins Creek would be considered an extravaganza."

"Try six."

"Six?"

"Granny ran into Nadine the other day at Target and invited her and Kari to the party."

Rain laughed. "Extravaganza it is. Let me see if Tracie and Jeannie can come."

"I hope they don't have plans. I know it's only a couple of weeks away."

"Somehow, I don't think they'd miss this for the world." Rain smiled.

"I'm telling you, Papa's trying to build an army of tractor-driving women."

✻ ✻ ✻ ✻

Rain collapsed into her lawn chair. She'd been laughing so hard that her sides hurt. "I cannot believe you just made me do that," she said to Ivy.

Ivy plopped down in the chair next to Rain, laughing even harder than Rain had been. Even in her casual clothes, Ivy was stunning. She wore a yellow tank top that accented the dark tan she'd been getting from mowing lawns and a pair of jean shorts that showed off her shapely legs. Rain tried not to stare since the entire Nash clan was here.

"You suck at driving." Ivy pointed across the yard where Tracie sat behind the wheel of the lawn mower with a determined look on her face and a blindfold covering her eyes. "They're going to kick our butts."

"Valiant effort." Nadine held up her beer and

made a toasting gesture toward Rain.

"Valiant, my ass," Ivy said. "She hit every damned cone, except the first one."

"Ivy June," Mrs. Nash said from the nearby picnic table. "There's no reason for swearing. And give poor Rain a break. I doubt she's ever done it before."

"Thank you, Mrs…um Joan. You are correct, this would be my first time." Definitely her first time. She'd never been on a lawn mower before, let alone doing a blindfolded obstacle course.

"Look at her go," Mr. Nash said. "I think I've found me another tractor driver." He turned to Rain. "No offense, but she drives better."

Ivy laughed and poked Rain in the ribs. She leaned over and whispered, "See, I told you he was recruiting."

The afternoon had been incredible. The Nashes had welcomed her with open arms, as if their daughter had been dating women her entire life. Mrs. Nash had even taken Rain aside and told her how it warmed her heart to see her daughter so happy. Life could be surreal sometimes.

Jeannie's voice filled the air as she yelled instructions to Tracie from the cart attached to the back of the lawn mower.

"I think she's going to beat your time," Mr. Nash called out to Max. "She hasn't hit a cone yet."

Rain nudged Ivy. "Maybe if I had someone giving me better directions, I wouldn't have hit them all."

Ivy laughed. "Maybe if you hadn't been so out of control I could have."

"Or maybe if you weren't laughing so hard, I could have understood what you were yelling," Rain said.

Ivy grinned. "That too."

⚘⚘⚘⚘

With the dying light of the day, Ivy had to squint to see Rain's face clearly. "I think it's about time for a fire," Ivy said.

Rain rose to her feet. "Let me help, Ben."

Papa smiled. "You don't have to. I can call over one of the boys to help."

"Nonsense," Rain said. "Looks like they're in a hot game of basketball."

"They're just playing horse." Ivy glanced over at her brothers. When they were kids, Papa had mounted a basketball hoop on the side of the barn and installed a light, so they could play at all hours. The hoop had been replaced many times over the years from all the use. "They'll be at it until Papa pulls out the fireworks."

Tracie and Nadine stood, too. Ivy couldn't help but smile. Papa had his team.

Once the fire roared to life, Ivy's thoughts drifted off, now that she could better see the faces around her. It warmed her heart. She couldn't remember a time she'd been happier. Sometimes, she thought she'd wake up, and it would all be a dream. They still hadn't solved their *problem,* but she and Rain had gotten much better at not saying the words.

They'd decided not to tell Mama and Papa yet. It had been enough for them to digest that their daughter was dating a woman without making them think she'd completely lost her mind. If they couldn't figure it out, they'd likely let Nadine and Kari in on the secret first since they were spending more time together. They'd almost blown it when they'd switched in the middle of playing tennis. When Rain, a college tennis player, had ended up with Ivy's skills, or lack of, they'd been able to write it off as a joke, but Nadine and Kari had eyed her for hours afterward.

"Were you listening to that?" Papa asked.

"Huh?"

"I knew she wasn't." He smiled. "Rain here just brought up an interesting idea." His eyes held a sparkle she hadn't seen in a while, or maybe it was just the way the firelight shone in his eyes.

"What was that?" Ivy asked and glanced at Rain, who was sitting at the edge of her lawn chair.

"This farm is perfect." She pointed to the barns where the boys played basketball and then at the mower. "It's so much fun. It's like summer camp." Rain was bouncing in her seat now.

Papa nodded along with her. "We could have lots of wholesome activities for the kids. Introduce them to what it's like to live on a farm. To feel that family connection."

Ivy glanced at Tracie, who'd also slid to the edge of her chair. What in the world had gotten them so worked up? "Back up. I'm afraid I've missed something," Ivy said. "What kids are you talking about?"

"Troubled ones," Tracie said. "Like I've been working with through the county."

"And we could help, too," Nadine said. "With the technology. We could wire this whole place."

Papa clapped his hands together. "We've got plenty of space. All those empty barns."

"How hard would it be to get funding from the foundation?" Tracie said to Rain.

Rain stared into the fire for a few beats before

she answered. "The next quarterly meeting is only two weeks away, so it's too late for that. But I think there would be a good shot at the October meeting."

"Whoa." Ivy held up her hands. "Are you talking about starting a nonprofit at the farm?"

"Why not?" Rain said.

"Yeah, why not?" Papa added.

With that, everyone sitting around the fire began to talk at once.

🜲🜲🜲🜲🜲

"I've developed a different type of PTSD with the fireworks," Rain said as she walked hand and hand with Ivy around the barns. They'd decided to take the scenic route back to Granny's house.

"I know, right?" Ivy said. "I just about jumped out of my skin when the first wave of sulfur hit me."

Rain grinned. "I'll never smell fireworks the same way."

"But they were fun. And the ones Tracie and Jeannie brought down from Wisconsin. Wow! The kids are going to be talking about those for a long time. Too bad they had to drive back home tonight."

They walked in silence for a while and enjoyed the sounds of the country. A chorus of crickets filled the night air, and the rustle of corn accompanied them in the background. The moon gave enough light to see the cornstalks swaying in the light breeze. "It's peaceful here," Rain said.

"It is." Ivy moved closer to Rain. "It's our little slice of heaven. Do you really think your plan could work?" Hope filled Ivy's voice.

"I do." They circled the last barn and made their

way back toward Granny's. "If everyone's enthusiasm is any indication."

"And the funding?"

"If the grant is well written, I don't see why not."

"It's probably just wishful thinking." Ivy let out a deep sigh. "Just silly ramblings around the campfire."

Rain shook her head. "I don't think so. Tracie said she'd set up a Zoom call for next week, so we can all talk about it some more."

Ivy chuckled. "Mama and Papa on Zoom, that'll be fun to see."

"He seemed pretty psyched." They passed the big house and made a beeline for Granny's cottage.

"It's a chance to save the farm." Ivy looked up at Rain. "But I don't want him to get his hopes up if there's no chance."

"I don't think it's only about saving the farm. He and your Mama seemed really excited about the prospect."

Ivy smiled. "They do enjoy kids. Why do you think they went and had a second set?"

Rain laughed. "They'd have more kids than they'd know what to do with."

"Do you really think Tracie would move back here to run it?"

"That shocked the shit out of me," Rain admitted. "I don't know what to think, but she sounded sincere. Let's see what daylight brings when everyone isn't under the spell of the evening."

Ivy stopped and squeezed Rain's hand. "Do you think we've stumbled into another curse?"

Rain laughed. "Now you're being melodramatic."

"Yeah, because body switching is so normal."

Rain shrugged. "You have a point."

They arrived at Granny's cottage.

Ivy started to lead Rain inside, but Rain stopped.

"What's the matter?" Ivy asked.

"I need to tell you something before I chicken out."

Ivy turned and met Rain's gaze. There was a hint of fear in Ivy's eyes.

Rain squared her shoulders, faced Ivy, and took both of her hands. "Despite all that's happened, I'm happier than I've ever been in my entire life. And it's because of you." Still holding Ivy's hands, Rain brought them up to her chest and held them there.

"Me too," Ivy said.

Rain closed her eyes and breathed in deeply, enjoying the warmth against her chest. It was almost as if she could feel Ivy pouring into her. *Weird.* After two more cleansing breaths, Rain opened her eyes to make sure they'd not accidentally switched. *Nope.* Rain was still herself. "I need to tell you something," Rain said.

Ivy's hand trembled. "Go ahead."

"I love you," Rain said. An electric pulse ran through her body.

Ivy gasped.

Shit. Now wasn't the time for them to switch. Rain blinked several times. It couldn't be. She'd said the word, but Ivy stood in front of her. Not Ivy as Rain, but Ivy as Ivy.

"What just happened? Did you feel it?" Ivy asked.

"The jolt?"

"Yes."

Rain nodded. "I felt it."

"What was it?" Ivy asked.

"The bigger question is, why are we still in our

bodies?"

Ivy gasped again and touched her own stomach. "No more six-pack abs."

Rain laughed. "Leave it to you. This obsession with my abs is getting out of hand."

Ivy ran her hand over Rain's stomach. "Mmm... still there."

Rain's body trembled at Ivy's touch. "So why are we still in our own bodies?"

"I don't know. Maybe you should say it again, just to make sure and all." Ivy smirked.

"You think that's what I should do, huh?"

Ivy nodded.

Rain put her hand against Ivy's cheek and gazed into her eyes. "I love you, Ivy."

They remained in their bodies.

"I love you, too," Ivy said.

A jolt raced through Rain's body. "Oh, my god, we're still in our own bodies."

Ivy let out a squeal. "We're fixed."

"But how?"

"Love."

"Love?"

"We had to choose. Love or hate." Ivy's smile was enormous.

"And we chose love." Rain's heart raced. She'd told other women that she loved them, but this felt different. This was deeper than anything she'd ever felt before. She loved Ivy, not despite their differences, but because of them.

Rain hadn't realized she was crying until a teardrop rolled onto her lip. She swiped it away. "Now what?"

"Do you really have to ask?" Ivy winked.

What had she missed? She stared into Ivy's mischievous eyes, and then she knew. Rain's gaze darted around Granny's yard. "We can't. Not here."

"I'd suggest we go upstairs," Ivy said with a smirk.

Rain's brow creased. "That's not what I meant."

"I know." Ivy moved closer to Rain.

Before Rain knew it, Ivy was in her arms, and their lips met. As the kiss intensified, Rain stepped back and pointed toward the cottage. "Your grandma is inside. And her bedroom is just down the hall from yours." Rain shook her head. "We can't do this."

Ivy ran her hand across Rain's stomach. "Didn't you hear her say her hip was acting up? The little scam artist."

"Scam artist?"

"Yeah, she was walking around fine all day long, but now she can't manage to get up the stairs to bed. I'm thinking she wanted to give us some privacy."

"Seriously?" Rain's face heated. "And you're okay...um...having...um...making love with your grandma in the house?"

Ivy pushed against Rain, so their pelvises met. "Unless you want to drive me back to your house tonight." Ivy pressed harder against Rain.

Rain moaned, and she took a step back. Her mind was a jumble and her body on fire. "Shit, you're making it hard for me to concentrate."

Ivy licked her lips. "That's what I was hoping for."

Rain ran her hand through her hair. She wondered if her eyes were as unfocused as they felt. "This is all so different. I don't have a frame of reference for this."

Ivy chuckled. "I'm sure you have a lot more experience with this than I do."

"No, I don't." Rain put her hand against her own chest. "I've never told a woman that I loved her before I ever slept with her."

Ivy smiled. "Well, I never slept with anyone before I told them I loved them."

Rain glanced at the house. "Are you sure you're ready for this?"

"More than ready." Ivy leaned against Rain. "Now do you think you can stop talking and put your lips to better use?"

Rain grinned. "My lips have all kinds of plans for you."

Ivy shivered. "Could they start with a kiss?"

"Absolutely."

᪣᪣᪣᪣

Ivy wasn't sure how they'd gotten upstairs to her bedroom. When Rain kissed her, she'd lost all track of time. They could have been kissing for five minutes or five hours. Everything had slowed down and sped up at once.

Rain put her hand against Ivy's cheek and leaned in for another kiss. The kiss grew in urgency as Rain pushed her against the bedroom door and snaked her hand under Ivy's shirt.

Ivy moaned.

"Is this okay?" Rain asked with her hand halfway up Ivy's stomach.

"More than okay, unless you plan on stopping there."

In answer, Rain moved her hand higher until she

found Ivy's bra. Rain didn't make a move to take it off; instead, she ran her fingers over the silky material.

Ivy moaned again. Her entire body felt what Rain was doing to her breast. Ivy wanted to rip her own clothes off and beg Rain to take her, but instead, she closed her eyes and let herself be lost in the moment.

If she didn't know better, she'd believe that Rain had eight hands with the way she was making Ivy's body feel. Rain finally pushed her thumb under Ivy's bra.

When Rain flicked Ivy's nipple with her thumb, Ivy sucked in a deep breath.

Rain's eyes widened, and she stepped back with a look of horror on her face. "I'm sorry, did I hurt you?"

Ivy grabbed Rain by the collar and pulled her back. "We have to get one thing straight. Stop asking me if I'm okay. You're not going to break me. If you do something I don't like, I'll tell you."

Rain stepped closer with a mischievous smile. "Does that mean I get to undress you?"

"Please."

That seemed to be the only encouragement Rain needed. She stepped forward and pressed her body against Ivy's. "I think I better start over."

"Oh, god, you're killing me," Ivy said right before Rain's lips met hers.

Chapter Forty-four

"Hi, sweetie," Ivy said into the phone.

"Where are you?" Rain asked.

Ivy's brow creased. That wasn't the way Rain normally greeted her. It had been over two months ago that they'd first made love, but Rain continued to address her as if it were still brand new and every day was another chance to court Ivy. "Is everything okay?"

"Um, I wondered if I could come out."

"To the farm?"

"Yeah."

"You're always welcome, but you know it's Wednesday, don't you?"

"Shit. I forgot. Church planning night."

"Rain, you're scaring me. What's wrong?"

"I just got a certified letter. I wanted to show it to you in person."

"I can miss a meeting. They can do it without me."

"No. Your meetings are important."

"You're more important."

"Are you sure?" Relief sounded in Rain's voice. "I don't want to be responsible for the Mullins Creek Church not reopening on schedule."

"It's over a month away. Please come."

"Okay. I'm on my way."

❧❧❧❧

Rain paced Ivy's tiny room as Ivy sat on the bed reading.

Ivy scowled as she read, her brows drawing closer together. It was a short letter, so she must be rereading for as long as it was taking her.

Ivy slammed the paper onto the bed. "They can't do this."

"Seems they are."

"Does Tracie know about it?"

Rain shook her head. "Not yet. I called you as soon as I got it."

Ivy leapt from the bed and wrapped her arms around Rain. "I'm so sorry they're doing this."

Rain had been empty inside since she'd opened the letter, but with Ivy in her arms, the emptiness subsided a little. She clung to Ivy and tried to match her breathing to Ivy's. It seemed to be working as her heart rate slowed.

Ivy led Rain to the bed and pulled her down. There wasn't anything sexual to the gesture. It was comforting. Rain lay her head on Ivy's chest, and Ivy gently ran her hand through Rain's hair.

"What are you going to do?" Ivy asked.

"Nothing I can do but go to the meeting and defend myself."

Rain picked up the expensive paper off the bed and turned slightly so her head was still resting on Ivy, but she could also see the letter. The SWAN insignia jumped off the page at her. Slowly, she reread it.

"Can they do that?" Ivy asked.

"You mean kick me off the board?"

"Yes."

Rain shrugged. "I suppose they can. If they determine I've done something to bring negative publicity to the organization."

"Seriously? Negative publicity?" Ivy snorted. "You defended your friend's right to write an opinion piece."

Rain tossed the letter aside. "Apparently, they didn't like Tracie's opinion."

Ivy continued to rub Rain's head. "Tracie is going to blow a gasket."

"I'm not sure I'm gonna tell her."

"What? You have to tell her."

"And say what?" Rain's jaw tightened.

Ivy sighed. "I don't know. But she might have some advice."

"Argh." Rain hugged Ivy tighter. "This sucks."

Ivy picked up the letter. "The meeting is in two weeks. You have a little time to prepare."

Rain lifted her head and kissed Ivy's neck in the spot that always drove her wild.

Ivy moaned. "What are you doing?"

"Preparing." Rain moved her tongue in circles.

"I thought it made you uncomfortable having sex in Granny's house."

"You've cured me." Rain kissed farther up Ivy's neck to the spot right below her ear. "Besides, they're all next door at the meeting."

Ivy's breath caught in her throat. "You're not playing fair." Ivy's voice was husky.

Rain kissed Ivy's neck once more before she lifted her gaze. Any thought of stopping was gone when Rain saw the fire burning in Ivy's amber eyes. "This should clear my head."

"Uh-huh." Ivy drew Rain's face toward hers. "My head needs cleared, too."

Their lips met, and all other thought left Rain's mind.

Chapter Forty-five

The board president indicated for Rain to take a seat at the short table set apart from the regular board table. *Not a good sign.* The table sat at the front of the room and had a lone chair sitting behind it. Rain dropped her briefcase on the table and sat. She took her time opening her briefcase and pulling out the folders she'd brought for the meeting.

The board could wait. It gave her time to get her thoughts in order and slow her racing heart. Once she had her folders, she looked up and made eye contact with the president.

The president cleared his throat. "Rain, do you know why you're here?"

Rain nodded and held up the letter. "It lays it out pretty clearly." Rain glanced at the board members. A few met her gaze, but most busied themselves with the papers in front of them.

The next fifteen minutes, the board president explained the protocol for the meeting, which sounded more like a trial to Rain. Then he reviewed all the information they'd gathered about Tracie, which was more extensive than Rain suspected. He'd ended with questions concerning the nature of Rain's relationship with Tracie. Both of their lives were laid out for the entire board to scrutinize.

"Now that we've established our protocols and have a better sense of Ms. Bennett, I'd like to move on to the reason for this hearing."

Rain bit her lip. *Hearing. Interesting.* Nowhere in the letter had it ever been classified as a hearing.

The president held up several sheets of paper. He nodded to the other board members. "You have copies of these in your packets. Ms. Hargrove, you too should have a set."

"Yes," Rain answered.

"Ms. Hargrove, these are copies of tweets and other comments that appear to come from your social media accounts."

"Yes." Rain wasn't going to say more than she was asked at this point.

"You acknowledge that you wrote them?"

"I do."

Several board members whispered to one another.

"Correct me if I'm wrong, but the posts seem to be in support of Ms. Bennett."

"You're correct. They are in support of her."

More murmurs were heard from around the table.

"Do you understand that the board does not support the bigotry that Ms. Bennett espouses?"

"Could you be more specific?" Rain wasn't going to let them get away with vague accusations.

He leafed through the file in front of him and held up another document. "In your packet is an editorial written by Karin DeWitt in which she deconstructs Ms. Bennett's essays and exposes the harmful nature of her writings."

Rain pretended to leaf through the folder and then frowned. "Um, I don't seem to find Ms. Bennett's original essay in the materials."

"In her blog, Ms. Bennett has shown herself to be

transphobic," he said, apparently deciding to ignore Rain's comment. "We will not have that associated with this organization. We strive to be inclusive. In fact, that's the reason for our existence." The president sat up straighter and jutted out his chin.

Several other board members nodded like bobbleheads.

"We want you to write a formal apology," the president said.

"Apologize for what?" Rain tried to hide her irritation.

"Apologize to anyone you might have offended," the president said and narrowed his eyes.

Rain felt as if she was being stared down by a disapproving librarian. "I cannot do that."

Several board members let out audible gasps.

The president's face reddened. "I'm afraid you're not understanding the gravity of the situation." His voice was loud and filled the room.

"I'm afraid *you* don't understand the gravity," Rain shot back.

"This unwillingness to apologize for your insensitive mistake could lead to your expulsion from this board." He gave Rain a satisfied smile.

"And your willingness to ask me to apologize for the remarks I made is an unfortunate example of censorship. While I know that private organizations are not bound by the rules of freedom of speech in the legal sense, I would hope an organization like SWAN would hold itself to the highest ethical standards."

The president clenched his teeth and pounded his fist on the table. "So you support the transphobia that Ms. Bennett espouses?"

"I want to make it clear." Rain gripped the table.

"I support my trans brothers and sisters. I will defend them against hate in any form."

Several members of the board smiled and seemed to relax.

"I'd like to ask a question," Rain said.

"Go ahead," the president said with a frown.

"How many board members read Ms. Bennett's essay?"

"That is not the point," the president said.

"Oh, I think it is the point." Rain glared. "How can you ask me to renounce Tracie's beliefs when you don't even know what they are?"

"I am confident that the board is well versed on Ms. Bennett's position."

"Really?" Rain narrowed her eyes. "How?" She held up Karin DeWitt's essay and dismissively tossed it onto the table. "This?"

The vice president leaned forward and whispered to the president before she said, "Let me try a different approach. Maybe it would be better to focus on the points in Ms. Bennett's blog post."

"Oh, good, so you've read it?"

The vice president's face fell.

"I didn't think so." Rain crossed her arms over her chest. "Can I see a show of hands of which board members have actually read Tracie's blog, not just Karin DeWitt's or someone else's opinion?"

Before the president could protest, two board members' hands went up.

"You do not call the shots, Ms. Hargrove," the president said in a raised voice.

"Mr. President, with all due respect, I don't feel that I should answer questions when only two board members have read the actual blog."

"For the record, I have also read the blog." The president glared.

"I stand corrected, three members have read it." Rain sighed. "I ask that I be granted the floor."

The president glowered and leaned over to the vice president. They whispered for what felt like ten minutes but was probably no more than a minute. The president straightened in his chair and nodded toward Rain. Hostility radiated from him, but he said, "You may make a statement."

Rain rose from the table on shaky legs. She'd not planned on this, but it was too late to back down now. Tracie's face flashed in her mind, followed by Ivy's. *Courage.* It was time for her to show courage. She walked around the table and stood before the board with nothing between her and them but air.

Rain cleared her throat. "Six months ago, I would likely have apologized and renounced my friend publicly, even though I didn't mean it. Just to keep a seat on this board. But my life has changed since then. There are two women responsible for that change."

As Rain talked, she walked from one side of the boardroom to the other. "Ms. Bennett, Tracie is one. She's been my mentor for over a decade, but I didn't always understand what she was trying to tell me until I met Ivy Nash. Ivy is my girlfriend. The woman I love. Ivy is also a Christian woman that once attended Autumn Harvest Church."

Several members of the board stared at her wide-eyed at the mention of Autumn Harvest.

"Ivy and Tracie have taught me to look at things differently. To look at what's inside someone's heart. And when I did that, I found have more in common with Ivy and her family than I do the despicable people that leveled threats against Tracie and her wife, Jeannie, one of kindest women I've ever known."

Rain turned her back on the group and rummaged through her papers. When she found the pages, she held them up. "I handed out a copy of these before the meeting."

Several board members nodded.

"Let me point out a few." Rain put her finger on one of the entries. "Here is one that threatens death to both Tracie and Jeannie. And here's another. It explains in detail the sexual assault the writer intends to subject Jeannie to."

"I won't read any more, but there are plenty in the packet for you to review." Rain turned and threw down the pages with disgust. "And these people are supposed to be on our side. Part of the LGBTQ+ nation. Well, no thanks. It's time we stand up against people like that. Enough is enough."

Rain walked around the boardroom until she was standing behind one of the board members who'd raised her hand when she'd asked who'd read Tracie's blog. "We need to read, not just read, but discuss opinion pieces like Tracie's. They might make us uncomfortable sometimes, but we still need to do it. Have a dialog. Come up with solutions."

All attention was on Rain as she moved back to the front of the room. "I will no longer blindly support everything *our* side says. I will no longer shout down, dismiss, or laugh at another's opinion." Rain held up a finger. "Unless it is truly based in hate. *But* I will never make that assumption without thorough research."

"Since most have not read Tracie's essay, I would like to read her final statement." Rain cleared her throat before she began to read. "*I do not purport to know the answers, I only hope people much smarter than me open a dialog. Listen to one another and find a way for all people to feel heard, respected, and safe. We must stand with the trans community, but we must also listen to the voices of those with concerns. And not just listen, but answer their concerns without shaming them, shouting them down, and shutting them down."* Rain looked up and gazed around the room at every board member. "This does not sound like the words of someone who is a transphobic monster as Karin DeWitt claims.

"We need to do a better job of determining what bigotry truly looks like. And raising points for the community to discuss is *not* bigotry or hatred. It's what responsible people do when they're trying to better understand an issue."

Rain leaned against the table where her briefcase sat. "It's time we stand up to the bullies. The real bullies. The ones that are leveling disgusting threats and throwing a label on anyone that dares to raise questions. When did we become a community that is so thin skinned that we can't have an honest debate or discuss tough issues? We've become too good at silencing voices. People are afraid to speak up for fear they may be attacked, lose their job, or be kicked off a board."

Rain stood and grabbed her bottle of water. She took two large gulps before she continued. "I need to tell you a little more about my friend Tracie. She is one of the most courageous people I know. She served in the Gulf War, was dishonorably discharged during the Don't Ask, Don't Tell era, and she runs a nonprofit helping at-risk teens. She's devoted her life to the service of her fellow man. And I can tell you with no uncertainty, should a transgendered person be harassed, bullied, or treated unfairly, she'd be the first at their side."

Rain stood and pointed at the board and then at herself. "Shame on us for treating her like a pariah because she had the nerve to ask us to *talk about and solve* some of the issues that have emerged as our community has grown."

Rain's heart was beating out of her chest as she circled the room. "So you can kick me off the board if you'd like and congratulate yourself for ridding yourself of me."

Rain had circled the room and arrived back at the front. She walked behind the table she'd sat at earlier and took another drink. "In the words of Eleanor Roosevelt, *well-behaved women rarely make history.*

"My friend Tracie has never been a well-behaved woman, and I'm tired of being one." Rain's voice rose, but she didn't care that her passion was spilling over. "All these years, I thought I was a rebel because I championed so many causes. I said all the right things. I expressed my indignation at the far-right radicals, but the problem is that I never did the same with the radicals on my side." Rain held up the pages of tweets. "There are horrendous things here. These bullies have flourished because we've enabled them.

"No! I will not be a well-behaved woman. Do what you want with my position on the board." Rain threw the pages into her briefcase and picked up the other files from the desk.

Rain fought against her emotions. "I was honored when I was asked to join this board. I believed that we would tackle the tough issues and the division that lies within our community. Don't get me wrong,

I don't have the answers, but I thought together we could find them. Through tough conversations, maybe we could forge common ground. Instead, I've discovered that open dialog isn't encouraged. In fact, it can lead you to where I stand today." Rain shook her head. "Shutting up voices through fear, threats, and intimidation is wrong. I hope the board will explore why we can't discuss concepts that don't fit into our worldview. Is our position so fragile that we can't listen to a multitude of ideas?

"I've had enough of this inquisition where only three people have read the material we're here to discuss." Rain threw the file folders into her briefcase.

"If this board ever decides to seriously discuss the hard issues facing our community, I would be honored to be a part of it. But I am done being a well-behaved woman." Rain slammed her briefcase shut, picked it up, and walked out the door.

≈≈≈≈≈

"There she is." Ivy grabbed Tracie's arm but stopped herself from leaping to her feet.

Tracie smiled. "Go."

That was all the encouragement Ivy needed. Ivy was out of her chair like a shot. She raced across the bar to Rain.

Rain appeared tired, but a broad smile lit her face when she saw Ivy. Her pace quickened, and she weaved around the other patrons who were enjoying happy hour.

Ivy launched herself into Rain's arms.

Rain laughed and spun her around. "Hell, I might sign up for more inquisitions if I knew this was how I'd be greeted."

Ivy laughed. "I'm just so happy to see you." Ivy leaned back and held Rain at arm's length. "Are you okay?"

"I am now." Rain hugged Ivy again before she nodded toward the table. "I see everyone's here."

"Almost." Ivy smiled. "Kari got stuck in traffic, but she should be here soon. Are you ready to see everyone?"

"As ready as I'll ever be." Rain took Ivy's hand. "But can I ask one favor?"

"Sure. Anything."

"Stay close tonight."

Ivy's eyes narrowed. "Meaning?"

"I'm a little shaky." Rain turned so her back was to the others and held up her trembling hand. "But I'm always okay when you're nearby."

"I'll be right here at your side." To prove it, Ivy moved in closer.

Tracie, Jeannie, and Nadine were on their feet as soon as they walked up. There were hugs all around, but true to her word, Ivy stayed close.

Once the hugs were over, Rain turned to Tracie. "I need a beer."

❧ ❧ ❧ ❧

Ivy studied Rain as Tracie told one of her long-winded stories. Rain picked up her bottle of beer, only her second, and she tilted back her head. After the first beer, Ivy felt Rain relax beside her.

Everyone around the table laughed as Tracie neared the climax of her story. But before she could deliver her line, Rain's cellphone sounded.

Rain glanced down at the screen and showed it to Ivy. *The president of SWAN.* Rain waved at the others and held up her phone. They went quiet.

"Hello," Rain said into the phone. "Uh-huh. Yes. I see. Uh-huh. Okay. Thank you for calling."

Rain set the phone on the table. Ivy grasped Rain's hand while the others leaned in.

"They've invited me to stay and want me to head up a task force."

A loud cheer went up around the table.

Chapter Forty-six

"Come on, sleepyhead," Ivy said, shaking Rain. "I've been up for two hours."

Rain opened one eyelid and groaned. "What time is it?"

"Seven." Ivy pulled back the curtains of their new room. Granny had insisted that they take the large master bedroom on the second floor, claiming that her arthritis wouldn't allow her to keep climbing the stairs. Never mind that she regularly walked two or three miles a day.

Rain rolled onto her back and kicked off the covers. It was a good start. For the first time, she really looked at Ivy. *Wow.* That would wake her up. Ivy had already showered and wore a navy blue suit dress with a white blouse underneath. Rain lifted her head to take in all of Ivy. *Damn.* Her high-heeled shoes accentuated her toned calves.

Ivy must have noticed Rain's reaction because she ran her hand down her skirt. "Is this okay? Or is it too much?" She fidgeted with the hem of her suit coat.

Rain sat up. "Relax. You look amazing."

"Are you sure? Do I look too aggressive?"

Rain thought of commenting on Ivy's light makeup, but she knew it would only make her more self-conscious. Ivy was already a beautiful woman, but today, she was stunning. "You look perfect. I don't know how the grant committee can turn you down."

Ivy gave Rain a half smile and turned toward the mirror. "I don't look too buttoned up—too polished?"

"You could come here, and I could muss you up a little." Rain wriggled her eyebrows.

"Would you stop that?"

"I made you laugh."

"That's not the point." Ivy put on a stern face and pointed at Rain. "You will behave yourself today."

"Where's the fun in that?" Rain rolled to the side of the bed and let her feet dangle.

"What are you going to wear today?" Ivy had moved to her hair and seemed to be straightening one hair at a time.

"Shorts and a T-shirt." Rain bit her lip to keep the smile from her face.

Ivy spun from the mirror. "Rain Anne Hargrove, you will not wear shorts and a T-shirt."

Rain chuckled. "Why not? I'm not allowed in the meeting."

"Still pouting?" Ivy went to Rain and put her hand against her cheek. "You know it has to be this way."

"I know." Rain crossed her arms over her chest not quite ready to give up her pout. "It still sucks."

Ivy kissed the top of Rain's head. "You've done all you could. You've coached us until we could do this in our sleep. You've been wonderful."

Rain snorted. "Tell that to Tracie."

Ivy chuckled. "I thought she was going to throw something at you yesterday."

"Thank god Jeannie was there, or I think she would've." Rain ran her hands through her hair and rubbed her eyes. "I didn't sleep well last night."

"Me neither." Ivy pointed to her face. "I had to

cover the bags under my eyes. Do they look hideous?"

Rain studied Ivy's face. "You look amazing. Nobody could ever tell."

"I think I might vomit." Ivy ran her hand over her stomach.

"Not recommended." Rain smiled. "The funding board doesn't look favorably on grantees who puke on them."

"Do you really think we have a chance?"

"A huge chance. Your project fits the donor criteria to a T."

"I know." Ivy turned away and went back to the mirror.

Rain would be glad when the presentation was over and a decision reached. Either way, they'd find the funds, but it would be so much better if A Bridge to the Future funded the project. "I still think you should have let me use my discretionary powers."

Ivy rolled her eyes. "How many times do I have to tell you that's *not* an option? The project gets funded on its own merits, not by you pulling strings."

Rain knew Ivy was right. For the project to be seen as legitimate, the entire board needed to back it. "You know how hard it's been not to lobby the board?"

"And what did Tracie tell you?"

"That you guys would seek funding elsewhere if I did." Rain glowered. "But I hate not being able to do anything."

Ivy's eyes widened. "You don't think you've done anything?"

"No." Rain rose from the bed and went to the closet. "I'm as useless as tits on a bull."

"Ugh, I wish you'd stop saying that."

"Blame Granny." Rain peeked out of the closet

and gave Ivy a cheesy grin. "She taught it to me. It's certainly not a saying I learned in the city."

"I know where you got it." Ivy put her hands on her hips. "I meant stop saying you're useless. You've prepared us mercilessly."

"I suppose." Rain chuckled and pulled out a pair of khaki pants and a deep green shirt. She'd always thought of it as her lucky shirt. Hopefully, they wouldn't need luck, but she wasn't going to tempt fate.

"Really?" Ivy glared. "Tracie's taken to calling you the drill sergeant, and Papa nearly salutes every time you walk into the room with your briefcase."

"Okay, fine." Rain held her hands up in surrender. "Maybe I've helped a little, but I'd still like to be there."

"You will be in spirit." Ivy took one last look at herself in the mirror. "Have you decided whether you're going to watch?"

Had she? The boardroom was equipped with the technology for Rain to watch it from her office, but could she? Rain suddenly became very interested in picking out her underwear. She'd struggled with the choice all week but was no closer to a decision. On one hand, she'd love to watch Ivy in action. On the other hand, if Ivy struggled, it may be too much for Rain. It would be too tempting to leave her office and slip into the boardroom.

"Are your parents ready?" Rain asked, hoping Ivy wouldn't call her out on her avoidance.

Ivy paused as if deciding and then said, "They were up before me. Mama's changed dresses at least five times already, and I had to tie Papa's tie."

Rain scooped up her clothes. "He doesn't know how to tie a tie?"

Ivy rushed to Rain and took the shirt and pants from her. "Would you please not wrinkle your clothes?" She handed the hanger out to Rain. "Carry them by the hanger, please."

Rain followed Ivy's directions but grumbled the entire time she did. "You never answered my question. He can't tie a tie?"

Ivy smiled. "His hands were shaking so bad that he couldn't get it right."

"He's that nervous?"

"Terrified."

"And your Mama?"

"She's got nerves of steel."

"And you?"

Ivy made a shooing motion. "Go take your shower or we'll be late."

Chapter Forty-seven

Ivy was the first to enter the room.

She kept her head held high as she walked to the presenter's table. Rain gawked at her confident stride. *Damn.* If it were possible, Ivy was even more beautiful on camera.

Jeannie and Tracie followed. Tracie looked dapper in her black shirt and orange and red flamed tie, but Rain would never tell her that.

Ivy paused at the table and appeared to be talking to Tracie. The microphones hadn't been turned on yet, so Rain couldn't make out what they were saying.

Tracie pointed toward the center chair, and Ivy shook her head. Then Tracie turned to Ivy's parents, who stood a few feet away. They looked adorable in their Sunday finest. Who could turn down a proposal from this group?

Ivy's dad pointed at the same chair Tracie had, and once again, Ivy shook her head. He turned to Ivy's mom and said something.

Ivy's mom put her hand on her hip, pointed at Ivy, then at the chair.

Ivy glowered, but she put her briefcase down on the table in front of the contentious chair.

Rain laughed. Leave it to Ivy's mom to get her to do what she wanted. Tracie and Jeannie sat to Ivy's left and her parents to her right. Rain couldn't help but giggle at the symbolism.

The meeting was called to order, and the sound of the gavel dropping caused Rain to jump. *Shit.* Her heart raced. She couldn't believe how nervous she was. She'd done hundreds of presentations in her career, but none had made her feel like this.

In Rain's absence, the president of the board spoke. "As you know, we normally don't have grantees attend a funding meeting. However, due to the size of the grant being requested, we have invited you here."

"Yes, ma'am." Ivy smiled, rose to her feet, and approached the podium.

Rain's heart pounded. Was Ivy nervous? Terrified? If she was, it didn't come across. Ivy's voice was clear and steady as she delivered her opening words. She stood up straight, and her gaze moved around the boardroom as she spoke. Occasionally, she'd refer to her notes, but for the most part, her words came from memory.

Rain's pride swelled. Ivy was a natural and had all the board members' attention. Rain had attended enough funding hearings to know how big of a feat this was. In the age of cellphones, it was hard to keep everyone's interest, but Ivy seemed to be pulling it off.

"In conclusion," Ivy said, "I'd like to summarize the main points. This program will serve mainly youths from high-risk groups. This may include youths living in poverty, youths with gender dysphoria, youths with substance abuse issues, or mental health issues. The only individuals that we are not prepared to serve at this time are those with criminal justice records. Over time, we do want to expand into that arena but feel it's better to grow our expertise and our staff before we do so."

Ivy took a sip of water before continuing. "The

youths may attend for the day, while some may come for a week or longer. We will have a limited number of dorms for these individuals to stay. Once again, we will expand slowly as the need arises.

"A farm is a wonderful place to learn lessons. My parents instilled so many values in me as I worked the farm as a kid. These kids will get the same opportunity. They'll get to tend crops, care for animals, and sit around a table and have a home-cooked meal.

"And most important of all, we will bring in individuals from all walks of life. To work together and play together. In the hopes that they learn they're much more similar than they are different. At The Third Path Agency, we want to show them that there is a path that can bring everyone together."

"Thank you, Ms. Nash," the board president said. "I will open the floor for questions."

Several board members' lights lit, indicating they wanted to speak.

The president called on one. "You have the floor, Alfred."

Alfred cleared his throat before he spoke. "This is a very interesting concept, Ms. Nash, but I have a question about the religious aspect of this project."

Rain groaned. *Here it goes.*

"We'd be happy to answer any questions you may have," Ivy said with a smile.

Alfred looked down at his notes, but Rain suspected he didn't need to. He always came completely prepared. "In doing a little research on you and your family, it was discovered that you used to attend Autumn Harvest Church."

Ivy nodded. "That is correct, but we no longer attend."

"If it's not too personal, may I ask why?"

"Certainly." Ivy smiled. "I can only speak for myself, but Mama and Papa are here should you want them to address the issue. I'm embarrassed by my association with that church."

"How so?" Alfred seemed to be surprised by Ivy's answer.

"The church does not practice Jesus's teaching. In fact, quite the opposite. When our old church closed, we scrambled to find a new church. We didn't do our due diligence. Instead, we were lured in by the buzz and the number of people joining it."

"How long ago did you leave the church?"

"About five months ago."

"Have you joined another church?"

"Kind of," Ivy said. A few people snickered at the answer, and Ivy smiled. "I know that sounds like a strange answer. Let me explain. Once we left the church, my parents began fielding calls from others who weren't happy with Autumn Harvest. Right now, we have over two hundred names on that list, and it seems to be growing every day. We've been working on restoring our old church. We plan on holding the first service the first week of November. Our old pastor's daughter will be leading the congregation."

"And what denomination will it be?"

"Nondenominational."

"Will it be a requirement for the participants in The Third Path Agency to attend?"

"Heavens no. It will be an option for anyone that wants to go, but we will never make it a requirement."

Alfred steepled his fingers and nodded. He appeared to be deep in thought, but Rain suspected he was doing it for dramatic effect. "You are aware, Ms.

Nash, that some of the greatest hatred brought down on humankind was a result of religion, aren't you?"

"Yes, sir." Ivy looked down for a few seconds before she met his gaze. She put her hand against her chest. "It pains me that is the reality of organized religion, and it's one of the reasons for this project. I've learned so much over the past few months."

Ivy turned to Tracie and smiled before she continued. "And I must tell you, at times, it was uncomfortable. It was heartbreaking to see that a religion that has brought me so much solace has brought others so much pain, so much grief. You see, it brought me to a crossroads. I thought I had to choose one road or another, but I discovered I could make my own path, and hopefully, others will come along with us. That's the purpose of this project."

"Can you elaborate on the paths you're referring to?" he asked.

"Certainly." Ivy moved behind Tracie and put her hand on Tracie's shoulder. "This wise woman helped me understand. A cry went up from the Christian community, and it came mostly from the evangelicals who had the ear of the media and politicians. They told us if we didn't follow them, we would be deserting Jesus, so we took two steps, or probably more, to the right. It didn't feel good at the time, but we were convinced the alternative was worse."

"And what alternative was that?"

"If we stepped to the left, we would be joining people who wanted to curtail our ability to practice our religion. We were faced with the lesser of two evils."

"Ms. Nash, I'm an atheist. Would I be welcome in your program?"

"Absolutely." Ivy put her hand against her chest. "Everyone must choose their own beliefs, and we need to respect those beliefs." Ivy put her hand on the podium. "Unless it instills hate against any other group, which unfortunately many churches like Autumn Harvest do. But there are many more churches that crave a more loving and accepting environment. Those are the people we're trying to reach, to get them to join us on the third path."

"The third path?"

"Yes, the one where everyone approaches each other with love and the desire to understand, instead of with hatred and self-righteousness." Ivy smiled and then tilted her head slightly, so it appeared she was looking into the camera.

Rain suspected it was a message to her.

Epilogue

Rain shouted as Benjamin Nash, dressed in a tuxedo, held the big scissors over his head like a prize fighter who'd just won the championship belt. In some ways, they had won the championship, as he cut through the ribbon to officially open The Third Path Agency.

The past six months had required a lot of hard work, but it had been the best time of Rain's life. She hadn't been to the gym in months because she got her workout helping the construction crews ready the place for business. They worked every day but Sunday. Ivy's family still insisted it was a day of rest, even though they sometimes sneaked out in the evenings to lend a hand.

Rain had gone to church with the Nashes on a few occasions, but she had yet to decide whether she would do it on a more regular basis. Surprisingly, they didn't seem to care and loved Rain just the same.

Tracie and Jeannie had moved back to Illinois and found a house in Mullins Creek, so Tracie could be the first executive director of the newly established organization. Ivy had enrolled in college, so she would be ready to take over once Tracie retired. Nadine and Kari had donated their time and expertise to set up the technology on the farm. The high-tech equipment was such a juxtaposition to the remodeled barns that were fashioned to look like an old-time farm. Nadine's mother had passed, and they had decided to stay in town and had opened their own tech consulting firm.

News crews from not just around the state, but around the country had poured in to cover the story. Rain's parents' connections hadn't hurt on that front, but the media had clamored at the story of how a small conservative farm town had come together with one of the most progressive foundations in the state.

Rain and Ivy's story had likely helped. Rain had been astonished when Ivy agreed to talk to the media about their unlikely relationship. She and Ivy had discussed it at length before they made their decision. Ivy knew it would bring more attention to the cause, even if it meant outing herself.

The overwhelming response had been positive, with the exceptions of Devlin, Mr. Haskins, and a few of the townspeople who'd decided to stick with Autumn Harvest. Nearly ninety percent of Autumn Harvest's congregants who resided in Mullins Creek had returned to Mullins Creek Church when it reopened.

Tracie grabbed Rain's arm. "Hurry up, you need to get in place."

"But they just cut the ribbon," Rain complained.

"Which means you've got about fifteen minutes. Ivy put me in charge of you, and I won't let her down."

Rain snorted. "Tell me again why I chose you."

Tracie ruffled Rain's hair. "Because I'm your best friend."

"Sheesh. The hair. Don't mess it up."

"Then come along peacefully."

Rain followed Tracie to the tiny outbuilding next to the big barn, where the festivities would take place. Rain smiled at the large lettering on the front of the barn. The Samuel B. Crawford Center, named after Benjamin's fallen war buddy.

Rain nodded at the barn. "Thanks again for stopping Ivy and me from embarrassing her papa."

"I knew he'd take it hard." Tracie smiled. "Only someone who's been in battle can quite understand it."

"I've never seen a grown man break down like that."

"That's because you never served." Tracie clapped her hand on Rain's shoulder. "I can tell you, though. He was touched by it."

Rain put her hand on her chest. "I think we all were."

They slipped inside the outbuilding. What a bang for the first official event at The Third Path Farm. Rain peeked over her shoulder as she followed Tracie. The guests were pouring into the barn. She didn't realize she knew this many people until she saw them all gathered at once.

Camera people took footage as everyone milled around. Rain thought she'd slipped the camerawoman assigned to her, but she'd been wrong. The woman sprinted across the dusty road with her camera on her shoulder. The green light was on, which probably meant she was filming Rain as she stared out at the gathering.

Great. She probably had a dumb look on her face. Rain smiled and waved, hoping to give her some better shots to work with.

Once they'd ducked inside the small building, Tracie turned to Rain. She brushed something off Rain's shoulder before she straightened Rain's bow tie. "Are you ready for this?"

"As ready as I'll ever be." Rain grinned. That wasn't true, but she didn't want to act too eager, or

Tracie would tease her for years. Rain had never been more ready for anything in her life. It had been over a year ago that she'd first met Ivy.

Who knew a conservative Christian and an agnostic progressive could find love in such an unlikely place? Rain snickered.

"What are you laughing about?" Tracie asked.

"I bet not many people can say they found their true love while fighting over a *Jesus sucks* sign."

Tracie laughed. "I'd guess none."

The camerawoman hadn't been filming, but her ears perked up. "What was that?"

Rain waved her off. "Nothing. Nothing." That was one story they'd never tell. Besides, no one would ever believe them. It would be a story they took to their graves.

Jeannie peeked her head into the outbuilding. "They're ready for you."

They followed Jeannie and entered the barn from the back.

Rain leaned over toward Tracie. "You've got it, right?"

Tracie patted her pocket. "Right here."

❧❧❧❧

Rain stood next to Tracie in the front of the barn as the others filed in and filled the space around them. Rain smiled and greeted them as they took their places.

Pastor Bidwell, the new pastor at Mullins Creek Church, touched Rain's sleeve and said, "Are you ready to start?"

Rain's heart raced, but she nodded.

"Okay," Pastor Bidwell said and pointed to the

left.

The crowd hushed as the familiar music filled the barn. All the guests turned to look down the aisle as the barn door slid open.

Rain gasped as Ivy entered with her arm looped through her father's. Rain had never seen a more beautiful woman. Her simple yet elegant white gown trailed behind her as they slowly made their way up the aisle.

Despite the hundreds of people in attendance, Ivy was the only person Rain saw. Rain clenched her teeth, willing herself not to cry. She looked to Tracie for support and was shocked to see tears freely rolling down Tracie's cheeks.

She'd have to give Tracie shit for it later, but now all she wanted to do was watch her bride make her way up the aisle.

⁕⁕⁕⁕⁕

The ceremony had been like a fairy tale. No matter how hard Ivy tried not to cry, she'd not been successful. Seeing their family and friends surrounding Rain as she entered had been too much, and she hadn't stopped crying since.

When Pastor Bidwell pronounced them married, Ivy had broken into sobs and clung to Rain. Through tears, Rain laughed and cried as she spun her around. A roar went up from the crowd as they kissed.

Dreams really did come true, as long as you let fate take you where it will, Ivy thought as she took Rain's hand to exit the barn. They took their time as they greeted guests along the aisle.

Ivy didn't think her smile could get any bigger

without cracking her cheeks. As they approached the back row, Ivy stopped dead in her tracks.

Rain halted when Ivy pulled on her hand. "What's wrong?"

Ivy couldn't speak as she stared at the woman with the gray hair and matching gray eyes.

Rain looked to where Ivy was staring and gasped.

The old woman took two steps toward them and put a hand on both of their arms. She smiled and said, "You chose love?"

"Yes." Ivy held up their clasped hands.

"You have learned the lesson." The old woman smiled and turned to leave but turned back. "Love always wins."

Before they could say more, the woman slipped from the barn.

"Come on." Rain pulled Ivy forward. "We have to ask her how she did it."

Ivy hurried with Rain toward the door.

When they emerged into the cool evening, Ivy glanced around. Violet sat in a lawn chair just outside the door. "Which way did that old woman go?" Ivy asked.

Violet narrowed her eyes. "Have you been drinking? I've been sitting here since the service ended, and I haven't seen any old lady except for Granny."

Rain and Ivy stared at each other.

Rain shrugged. "It doesn't matter. We've learned the lesson."

Ivy fell into Rain's arms, and their lips met.

About The Author

Rita Potter has spent most of her life trying to figure out what makes people tick. To that end, she holds a Bachelor's degree in Social Work and an MA in Sociology. Being an eternal optimist, she maintains that the human spirit is remarkably resilient. Her writing reflects this belief.

Rita's stories are eclectic but typically put her characters in challenging circumstances. She feels that when they reach their happily ever after, they will have earned it. Despite the heavier subject matter, Rita's humorous banter and authentic dialogue reflect her hopeful nature.

In her spare time, she enjoys the outdoors. She is especially drawn to the water, which is ironic since she lives in the middle of a cornfield. Her first love has always been reading. It is this passion that spurred her writing career. She rides a Harley Davidson and has an unnatural obsession with fantasy football. More than anything, she detests small talk but can ramble on for hours given a topic that interests her.

She lives in a small town in Illinois with her wife, Terra, and their cat, Chumley, who actually runs the household.

Rita is a member of American Mensa and the Golden Crown Literary Society. She is currently a graduate of the GCLS Writing Academy 2021. Sign up for Rita's free newsletter at:

www.ritapotter.com

IF YOU LIKED THIS BOOK...

Reviews help an author get discovered and if you have enjoyed this book, please do the author the honor of posting a review on Goodreads, Amazon, Barnes & Noble or anywhere you purchased the book. Or perhaps share a posting on your social media sites and help us spread the word.

Check out Rita's other books

Broken not Shattered - ISBN - 978-1-952270-22-2

Even when it seems hopeless, there can always be a better tomorrow.

Jill Bishop has one goal in life – to survive. Jill is trapped in an abusive marriage, while raising two young girls. Her husband has isolated her from the world and filled her days with fear. The last thing on her mind is love, but she sure could use a friend.

Alex McCoy is enjoying a comfortable life, with great friends and a prosperous business. She has given up on love, after picking the wrong woman one too many times. Little does she know, a simple act of kindness might change her life forever.

When Alex lends a helping hand to Jill at the local grocery store, they are surprised by their immediate connection and an unlikely friendship develops. As their friendship deepens, so too do their fears.

In order to protect herself and the girls, Jill can't let her husband know about her friendship with Alex, and Alex can't discover what goes on behind closed doors. What would Alex do if she finds out the truth? At the same time, Alex must fight her attraction and be the friend she suspects Jill needs. Besides, Alex knows what every lesbian knows – don't fall for a straight woman, especially one that's married…but will her heart listen?

Upheaval: Book One - As We Know It - ISBN - 978-1-952270-38-3

It is time for Dillon Mitchell to start living again.

Since the death of her wife three years ago, Dillon had buried herself in her work. When an invitation arrives for Tiffany Daniels' exclusive birthday party, her best friend persuades her to join them for the weekend.

It's not the celebration that draws her but the location. The party is being held at the Whitaker Estate, one of the hottest tickets on the West Coast. The Estate once belonged to an eccentric survivalist, whose family converted it into a trendy destination while preserving some of its original history.

Surrounded by a roomful of successful lesbians, Dillon finds herself drawn to Skylar Lange, the mysterious and elusive bartender. Before the two can finish their first dance, a scream shatters the evening. When the party goers emerge from the underground bunker, they discover something terrible has happened at the Estate.

The group races to try to discover the cause of this upheaval, and whether it's isolated to the Estate. Has the world, as we know it, changed forever?

Survival: Book Two - As We Know It - ISBN - 978-1-952270-47-5

Forty-eight hours after the Upheaval, reality is beginning to set in at the Whitaker Estate. The world, As We Know It, has ended.

Dillon Mitchell and her friends are left to survive, after discovering most of the population, at least in the United

States, has mysteriously died.

While they struggle to come to terms with their devastating losses, they are faced with the challenge of creating a new society, which is threatened by the divergent factions that may tear the community apart from the inside.

Even if the group can unite, external forces are gathering that could destroy their fragile existence.

Meanwhile, Dillon's budding relationship with the elusive Skylar Lange faces obstacles, when Skylar's hidden past is revealed.

Thundering Pines – ISBN – 978-1-952270-58-1

Returning to her hometown was the last thing Brianna Goodwin wanted to do. She and her mom had left Flower Hills under a cloud of secrecy and shame when she was ten years old. Her life is different now. She has a high-powered career, a beautiful girlfriend, and a trendy life in Chicago.

Upon her estranged father's death, she reluctantly agrees to attend the reading of his will. It should be simple—settle his estate and return to her life in the city—but nothing has ever been simple when it comes to Donald Goodwin.

Dani Thorton, the down-to-earth manager of Thundering Pines, is confused when she's asked to attend the reading of the will of her longtime employer. She fears that her simple, although secluded life will be interrupted by the stylish daughter who breezes into town.

When a bombshell is revealed at the meeting, two women seemingly so different are thrust together. Maybe they'll discover they have more in common than they think.

Betrayal: Book Three - As We Know It - ISBN - 978-1-952270-69-7

Betrayal is the exciting conclusion to the As We Know It series.

The survivors at Whitaker Estate are still reeling from the vicious attack on their community, which left three of their friends dead.

When the mysterious newcomer Alaina Renato reveals there is a traitor in their midst, it threatens to tear the community apart. Is there truly a traitor, or is Alaina playing them all?

Dillon Mitchell and the other Commission members realize their group might not survive another attack, especially if there is someone working against them from the inside. Despite the potential risk, they vote to attend a summit that will bring together other survivors from around the country.

When the groups converge on Las Vegas, the festive atmosphere soon turns somber upon the discovery of an ominous threat. But is the danger coming from within, or is there someone else lurking in the city?
Before it's too late, they must race against time to determine where the betrayal is coming from.

Whitewater Awakening - ISBN - 978-1-952270-74-1

Can two lost people find themselves, and possibly each other, halfway around the world?

After a tragic accident, Quinn Coolidge leaves everything behind, hoping to find solace in a secluded life in the Ozarks. Her solitude is disrupted when her best friend unexpectedly shows up with a proposition she may not be able to resist.

Faced with a series of failed relationships, Aspen Kennedy is left wondering why she can't find true love. With each new partner, she immerses herself in their interests, hoping to find the connection she's been missing. That should make her the perfect girlfriend, shouldn't it?

Come along with Quinn and Aspen as they travel to Africa to take on one of the most grueling whitewater rafting courses in the world. With the amazing Victoria Falls as their backdrop, the pair will have to look deep inside to discover what holds them back. Will the churning waters of the Zambezi River defeat them, or will it lead them to a whitewater awakening?

Out of the Ashes - ISBN

When unusual seismic activity is detected on Mount St. Helens, volcanologist Nova "Cano" Kane, along with a team from the United States Geological Survey, is sent to investigate. The year is 1980, and there hasn't been a large-scale eruption on the mountain in over one hundred years.

Dr. Allison "Allie" Albright is a prominent professor at the University of Washington where the seismic activity is being tracked. As more scientists pour into Seattle, she braces for the possible return of Cano.

Neither Allie nor Cano has fully recovered from their breakup four years earlier. Both live with the pain and regret of how their relationship ended. Maybe it's best to leave it in the past and focus on the job at hand.

They must battle the limits of predictive science, the shortsightedness of bureaucracy, and the bias of the media, while fighting their complicated feelings for each other. As Mount St. Helens continues to churn, so too does their attraction.
Which will erupt first—the volcano or their feelings for each other?